MW01396892

# A GAME OF HEART'S DESIRE

# A Game of Heart's Desire

## Episode I:
### Before the Games

LILINOE K. RUSSELL

Copyright © 2024 by Kealohanani LLC.

All rights reserved. This book or any portion thereof may not be reproduced or used in any manner whatsoever without the express written permission of the publisher except for the use of brief quotations in a book review.

Publishing Services provided by Paper Raven Books LLC
Printed in the United States of America
First Printing, 2024

ISBN 979-8-9907790-1-3

*To all the readers who have watched The Bachelorette series, fallen in love with more than one contestant, and were seriously disappointed that the bachelorette couldn't choose more than one.*

# CONTENTS

Preface .................................................................. i
Prologue ............................................................... 1
Chapter 1: The Late Night Show ............................ 15
Chapter 2: A Son's Choice ..................................... 26
Chapter 3: A Pack in Crisis ................................... 32
Chapter 4: Stalker Syndrome ................................ 36
Chapter 5: Leaving Love To Fate .......................... 39
Chapter 6: Bullying The Bully .............................. 44
Chapter 7: Interview Day ..................................... 49
Chapter 8: When Siblings Fight ............................ 56
Chapter 9: Full Circle ........................................... 63
Chapter 10: Running Blind ................................... 68
Chapter 11: Making Friends ................................. 78
Chapter 12: Quartz Lake ...................................... 88
Chapter 13: A Gift From A Little Friend .............. 94
Chapter 14: The Funeral ...................................... 98
Chapter 15: Divine Intervention ......................... 108
Chapter 16: Mothers Know Best ......................... 114
Chapter 17: Making a Good Impression .............. 117
Chapter 18: Back Where I Started ...................... 123
Chapter 19: Guard Detail .................................... 136
Chapter 20: The Head Guard .............................. 146
Chapter 21: Falling into Routine ......................... 153

Chapter 22: Sodie's Secret ............................................. 168
Chapter 23: Nine Lives ................................................. 178
Chapter 24: Shadows and Light ............................. 180
Chapter 25: Welcome Home .................................... 200
Chapter 26: My Family .............................................. 213
Chapter 27: Running Away ...................................... 229
Chapter 28: Anders's Past ........................................ 243
Chapter 29: Acclimating ........................................... 260
Chapter 30: A Not So Sweet Homecoming ............ 278
Chapter 31: One Set of Tracks ................................ 289
Chapter 32: Hard Truths ........................................... 292
Chapter 33: Without a Trace ................................... 294
Chapter 34: So Many Changes ................................ 298
Chapter 35: Submissive ............................................ 310
Chapter 36: Staying The Course ............................. 316
Chapter 37: Allegations ............................................ 323
Chapter 38: Murderous Alpha ................................. 335
Chapter 39: We Shouldn't ........................................ 341
Chapter 40: It Doesn't Change Anything ............. 346
Chapter 41: Not Here ................................................ 352
Chapter 42: Death Card ............................................ 356
Chapter 43: Is That Supposed to Be Cool? ........... 370
Chapter 44: I Was A Fool .......................................... 375
Chapter 45: Misunderstanding ................................ 381
Chapter 46: Chaos and Questions .......................... 391
Chapter 47: Unfinished Business ............................ 404
Chapter 48: I'm Going to Kill Her .......................... 410
Chapter 49: No Turning Back .................................. 412

Chapter 50: So Many Emotions ............................ 419
Chapter 51: Tired of Hiding ................................. 429
Chapter 52: The Afterburn .................................. 439
Chapter 53: I'm Not Giving Up ............................ 451
Chapter 54: I Hate You  ........................................ 455
Chapter 55: It Had to Be Done ............................ 463
Chapter 56: Awakening The Alpha Queen ............ 466
Acknowledgements ................................................ 479
About the Author ................................................... 481

# PLAYLIST

*Unbreakable* – Fireflight
*Get Me Out (Orchestral Version)* – No Resolve
*My Arms* – Ledger
*Broken (feat. Amy Lee)* – Seether
*Villain* – Rain Paris
*Best Part of Me* – Jeremy Renner
*Easy On Me* – No Resolve
*Awake and Alive* – Skillet
*Come to This* – Natalie Taylor
*I Found You* – Andy Grammer
*Let Me Love You (feat. Lacey Strum)* – Love and Death
*Heavy (feat. Rain Paris)* – Fame on Fire
*What Have You Done* – Within Temptation & Keith Caputo
*Titanium* – Charice
*I Was Made for Loving You (feat. Ed Sheeran)* – Tori Kelly
*No Air* – Caleb and Kelsey
*Unstoppable (The Voice)* – Brynn Cartelli
*Badass Woman* – Meghan Trainor
*I See Red* – Everybody Loves and Outlaw
*Fall In Line (feat. Demi Lovato)* – Christina Aguilera
*Worth the Fight* – No Resolve
*I Hate Everything About You* – Halocene and Violet Orlandi
*Bring Me to Life* - Evanescence

# TRIGGER WARNINGS

This is a "why choose" paranormal shifter romance with some dark aspects to it that includes triggers such as murder, gore, graphic language, graphic sexual situations, child assault and rape (not depicted), toxic relations between the main characters, child abuse and neglect, suicidal thoughts and ideations, human trafficking, drugs and alcohol use. There will be cheating. Future books in the series may also include kinks such as bondage, blindfold sex, breath play, agoraphilia, and BDSM. Because this is a "why choose" romance, there will be multiple partners (sometimes all at once).

Please proceed with caution.

LILINOE K. RUSSELL

# PREFACE

Every story has a beginning. Every culture and every species has a story to tell of how they came to be. These stories have become the foundation for who we are, why we look the way we do, why we behave and act as we do.
But as these stories have been told from generation to generation they have changed, and their truth became altered—even worse, forgotten.
Before corruption and greed came to the Luna Solar realm, the white wolf shifter species once existed. A rare species, unlike other shifter species known worldwide, it is said that the white wolves were never actual animals or humans but magical beings from the Fae world.
These intellectual beings possessed magic.
Those who migrated to the new realm believed they could harness the white wolf's powers if they had total control over the lands, as it was rumored that the powers of the land resided within its earth and waters. Soon, a band of shifters called the Resistance declared war.
The great war happened.

Genocide occurred.
There were no white wolf shifters left,
and magic ceased to exist.
Time passed. New generations were born. Some remembered and carried on while others lived in total ignorance.
All hope is not lost. One day, when a new generation is born, they will harness the magic of their originals. Together they will bring back the traditions that were once forgotten, reunite our realm, and bring peace.
Then, and only then, will the white wolves return home, and the white wolf queen will reign again.

# Prologue

### May 05, 2014

Through the haze of blood, sweat, and tears, I see him standing there, looking down at me as I am punched, kicked, and held down against my will.

"Stay down, you worthless bitch!" one of my tormentors growls right before he kicks me in the face.

Despite the wave of nausea and the darkness creeping in, I spit out the blood filling my mouth and push myself back up into a standing position.

I will not give in. I will not submit. Not today. Not ever.

A blow to the back of my head careens me back down onto my hands and knees.

"Submit!" a familiar voice shouts. I angle my head to glare up at Kat, who used to be my best friend when we were younger. I push down the bitter sting of betrayal tightening my throat. When she catches me staring at her, she narrows her eyes and curls her upper lip in a sneer. Bending forward, she pulls her arm back, slamming her fist into my cheek.

"So pathetic. Can't believe we're related!" my brother Bart sneers at me before sending another kick into my side.

More laughs, more snickers, more shouts of "pathetic!"—"weak!"—"ugly!"—"submit!"

A forceful boot in my ribs knocks me onto my side. I continue to fight the darkness that wants to take over. I don't know how much more of these hits my body can take, but I refuse to give in. I roll back onto my hands and knees and push myself back up into a standing position.

Wavering for a few seconds, I shake my head, hoping to clear my vision and fight off the darkness that wants to shut down my body. I open my eyes, lift my chin, and angrily stare at the Young Alpha standing off to the side, watching, waiting for me to submit, but I won't.

With another punch to my face, a crack sounds in my head, and blood gushes from my nose. I fight the wave of nausea and threatening dizziness. Wavering on my feet, I tighten my body and widen my stance. Arms wrap around my body.

"Aww, she thinks she's better than us," one of my tormentors softly laughs and rubs his nose against my cheek. "Maybe she needs a different kind of lesson." His hands roam up to my breast, then back down over my abdomen.

Another male tormentor steps forward and runs his finger along my other cheek. "I bet you I can get you to submit as I ram my dick into your tight pussy," he whispers into my ear.

I lift my chin, refusing to move, refusing to cower.

"When we're done with you, you'll submit and beg for more."

I start to feel hands tear at my school's uniform, lifting my skirt, pulling down my bra, cupping my breast, and grabbing my ass. My lips begin to tremble, and I feel the tears start to stream down my face. I continue to hold up my chin, and I glare at the fucking future Alpha asshole still standing there, watching.

"We're going to make you the pack whore because that is all you will ever be worth." A chorus of laughter ensues around me.

"Yeah, the ugly pack whore!" Kat barks out.

"Enough!" A sharp, loud command issued by the Young Alpha freezes the group in place. The air suddenly fills with an impenetrable silence. "I've had enough of this shit show!" the Young Alpha barks out as he turns to leave. His little group of followers lets me go as they all scamper to follow him.

"There's always tomorrow." One of them snickers.

"Or the next day," another one chimes in.

"And the next," my brother snarls as he looks down at me.

Kat throws a knife at my feet. She tosses over her shoulder as she turns to leave. "Just do us all a favor and get it over with."

I stand there, refusing to show any weakness or let them know that they are so close to winning. I stand my ground for as long as my body will allow. The threatening darkness, nausea, and dizziness slowly take over as their backs face me in retreat. The ground begins to tilt. Unable to fight it any longer, my body slumps onto the ground as the world slips away.

I don't know how long I was out. It could have been seconds, minutes, maybe an hour. As I blink open my eyes, I realize that the sky darkened slightly, and it is now almost evening. Shit, I'm supposed to meet Ms. Fields for my music lesson!

I slowly sit up, and a wave of nausea and dizziness hits me. I close my eyes and take a deep breath, willing the sensation to pass. I open my eyes again, slowly turning my head to look for my discarded backpack that was torn off me just before the attack. I see it several feet from me near a tree. As I push myself onto my knees, I look down at myself. Blood splattered down my front. My blouse is torn wide open. My skirt is up around my waist.

I push my skirt down with shaky hands and gather the front of my blouse as I get to my feet. Staggering forward, I reach for my backpack, taking out my jacket. Slowly, painfully, I pull it on, taking into account the open cuts and bruises. Sharp pain slices through me as I lift my arm, squeezing my eyes shut. I finish putting my jacket on, zip up the front, and pull the hood over my head. Kicking at the dirt as I make my way to Ms. Fields's house, I find the knife Kat threw at me earlier. Wincing as I bend down, I pick it up and tuck it into the waistband of my skirt.

Slowly, I make my way across the cracked and chipped walkway leading to Ms. Field's tiny cottage. I hear the familiar creak of the screen door.

"Oh my god, Grit!" Ms. Fields cries out, covering her mouth with her hand as she sees me approaching her front door. I flinch at the sound of my name. I hate my name. Tears start to well in her eyes. She whispers, "What have they done to you?" She motions for me to enter her home and closes the door as I step into her tiny living room. "Come sit."

She gestures to the bench in front of her piano and disappears into the hallway just off the main entrance. She has a warm washcloth and some towels when she returns. She starts to clean my face.

"I'm going to speak to the principal and the Alpha's first assistant. This needs to stop! They pick on you every single day."

Gently, I grab her hand and shake my head slowly. "No," I croak. "If you go to the principal or the first assistant, you can lose your job. I won't allow you to do that. The school needs you. The students need you." Well, the good ones, anyway.

The Young Alpha issued an order at the beginning of the school year. Any faculty who interfere with my "lessons"—more like punishments—will be subject to termination of their position with the school and possibly even punishment by their own peers. They could face the same torment that I am facing now.

Ms. Fields is the school's music teacher and one of my favorites. She was always kind to me from a very young age. I met her when I was seven. She caught me in the school's auditorium tinkering with the piano while I was hiding from my brother and his asshole friends. She didn't question why I was in there. She didn't scold me. She just sat next to me and started teaching me how to play the piano. I have been seeing her almost every day after school since then. These music lessons provided me with an escape from a not-so-great life that I have been given. They were also my protection.

Slowly shaking my head, I look up at Ms. Fields and study her momentarily. Her long chestnut brown hair is up in a messy bun. Instead of wearing her usual school-issued teacher's blazer, she's wearing an oversized sweater and black yoga pants. She's not very tall. In fact, she's probably one of the smallest members of the pack. Because of her small stature, she could be mistaken for one of the high school students. She has an angelic face, soft features, and a tiny nose. I love her big, light brown eyes with a blue ring around them.

I tell her again, "No, I'll be fine." She eyes me, and a look of sadness fills her eyes.

Holding my hand in both of hers, she looks down. "I can't continue to stay on the sides and watch them attack you. This bullying has gotten worse." Her gaze shifts back up to me. "It's bad enough that you endure abuse even in your own home. I have to do something."

I lean slightly forward and whisper, "I'll be fine. I promise."

She squeezes her eyes shut, and a single tear escapes, sliding down her left cheek.

Removing my hand from her grasp, I reach behind me for my backpack. I pull out a slim wooden box. The moment I saw this box, I thought of Ms. Fields. I snared hundreds of rabbits and sold their pelts to make enough money to buy this box. It's handmade by one of our very own pack members. He carved an intricate design of lavender and daisies into it. It's the perfect gift; daisies are Ms. Field's favorite flowers, and lavender is mine.

I hand the box to her. "I want to give you a gift to thank you for the music lessons and for taking care of me."

"A gift for me? Grit, you shouldn't spend your hard-earned money on me. I know what you had to do to get the money for it." She hands the box back to me. I hold up my hands and push it back toward her, refusing to take it back.

"You never let me pay for my music lessons, and you're always feeding me, cleaning me up when I'm a mess." I sigh as I gesture to myself. "You sew my uniforms back together. Sometimes, you even manage to get me new ones. I saw this, and I thought of you. I wanted to give you something, to thank you." I watch her hand as it glides over the cover of the box. Before she can lift the lid, I cover her hand with mine. I tell her with a shaky voice, "I survived every day of this hell because of you. If something were to happen to you because of me, I couldn't live with myself." I look up at her. "Please, let it be and take my gift." Leaning forward, I kiss her forehead and give her a gentle hug.

I feel her shoulders shake as she cries, squeezing me gently in her embrace. "I don't understand why this is happening to you," she sniffs.

I pull back from her embrace and shrug. "Pack tradition. Only the strong survive." I press my hands on my thighs and push myself up to stand. Wincing, I pull on my backpack and head for the door.

"Wait, don't go home. Stay here. Let me get you cleaned

up and feed you dinner."

I shake my head. "I should go. The monster is with his friends, and my parents are out of the territory for some kind of business meeting. If I get home now, I can set myself up and avoid him when he gets home."

Ms. Fields takes a step forward. "Stay here. Please, stay with me. I can petition for you to live with me. I can tell the Betas that I'll take their," she makes air quotes, "burden off their hands. Let me make this right."

If only it could be that easy. They won't let me go. To let me go would be admitting that they did something wrong, and that would make them look bad. Their image and power in this pack are all they care about. No, they will never let me go. They would let their own son, my brother, torment me, beat me, and perhaps one day even kill me before they ever admit they have done anything wrong.

"Grit, please. I know someone who can help. If I get a message to him…"

Vehemently shaking my head, I cut her off. "No! If you get caught, they'll execute you!" Swallowing, I lower my voice to whisper, "They will kill you just like the others who tried to help me. Please, please, you've already done so much for me."

"Grit, they're going to kill you." More tears stream down her face as she silently pleads with me to stay, but I can't put her life in danger. I lean up on my tiptoes, kiss her cheek, give her a hug, and then head for the door.

She follows me, holding the screen door open with one hand and the box I gave her with the other. At the end of the walkway leading to her tiny cottage, I turn to look at her one last time and wave goodbye.

My heart feels like it is going to leap out of my chest, my lungs feel like they're going to explode, and the muscles in my legs burn. A cacophony of sound fills the air behind me: growling, jaws snapping, laughter, and whoops of joy. Fuck. Fuck! They're getting closer! In the not-very-far distance, a piercing howl breaks through the harsh, discordant sounds behind me, sending shivers of fear up my spine. Another howl emanates through the territory, then another.

It's a signaling system my brother and his friends made up. It's a red flag, a warning that they're coming for me. This time, they're going to make sure I don't survive. I know it. I can feel it. I need to get out of here, off this territory, and find sanctuary. My mind races with panicked thoughts. Would they believe me? Help me? He was supposed to be here. To meet me, help me. But he never showed. I'll have to do it on my own. I internally pray to the gods and to the moon goddess that somehow I make it.

My steps falter, and I fall to my hands and knees. The beating earlier took a lot out of me. Gasping for air, I push myself up. I'm almost there, almost to the territory line. Hope, hope fills me, and a renewed sense of energy bursts through me. I'm running toward the boundary with everything I have left in me because my life depends on it.

I tear through the brush, jumping over tree roots. I hear the crashing of the brush and the pounding of paws and feet behind me. Fuck! They're closer. I'm practically sprinting now. Then it hits me. Why the fuck am I running? Without slowing down, I look around for a low-hanging branch that I can reach. If I can climb up a tree, I'll be able to jump from tree to tree. There, up ahead, I see one. Despite my body's protesting aches and pains, I push myself to run harder, faster.

As I reach the hanging branch, I leap into the air with all of my might. Catching the branch with both hands, I hoist myself up. Just as my upper body makes it over the branch, a snarling wolf catches my leg with his teeth. I hang on tightly to the branch as he jerks my body down. Desperately I try to shake off the wolf, ignoring the pain shooting up my leg from the canines digging into my flesh. Whoever he is, this wolf is relentless, shaking his head and growling. His teeth sink deeper into my leg. With my other leg, I try to kick his head while still hanging onto the branch desperately.

Another wolf comes, jumping up and raking its sharp claws down my back. I scream in agony, and my grip on the branch loosens. Together, they bring me down, tearing at me with claws and teeth. Whimpers escape my lips; I try to hold my cries in by pressing my lips together. With each tear of my flesh, I just want to scream or, better yet, die, but I won't give them that satisfaction.

Twisting, turning, kicking, punching, trying so hard to get out from under them. I kick out with my other leg, catching one of the wolves in the jaw. As it lets out a whimper of pain, I pull my leg back from its grip, scrambling back to my stomach, hastily digging my feet and elbows into the ground to crawl away. I'm too slow. The other wolf pounces on top of me, pinning me down with its weight. I hear a chuckle coming from somewhere in the dark, along with a low growl emanating from one of the wolves.

Bart slowly walks forward. "Aww, poor little brat, you honestly thought you were going to outrun us? Where the hell do you think you're running off to, huh?" Crouching down before me, he grabs a handful of hair.

I let out a grunt as his nails turn into claws and dig into my scalp.

"Even if you cross the territory line, no one is going to save you." He leans down near my ear. "This is pack business, and everyone knows that the other packs do not interfere with pack business, stupid bitch!" He shoves my face back down into the dirt.

"Skunk, where the fuck is the rope!" he shouts as one of the wolves with a white stripe along its back emerges through the brush, holding a rope in his mouth. "I thought you chickened out on me. Glad to know you still have your balls." Bart snickers as he grabs my head.

The wolf... er... Skunk lets out a low growl before he huffs and moves to stand by another wolf with blood staining its muzzle, my blood. Bart's vise-like grip yanks my head back. I try to fight despite the large animal sitting on my back. It's futile because he wins, slipping the rope over my head and around my neck. I study his face, looking for any signs of love or compassion, but all I see is hate and rage. My parents never did love me. There was no coddling, no hugs, or kisses. No kind words. Instead, I endured curses and slurs, slaps and punches, and Bart delighted in torturing me too.

His eyes are full of cruelty and excitement. No love for his little sister exists there.

"Why?" I whisper.

His face reddens, and a corner of his lip turns up in a sneer. "Why? Because your very existence makes us sick. For generations, my family has done everything to wipe out your kind, and yet you still exist. Now I have to clean up their mess and get rid of you for them! Those ungrateful bastards!"

What the hell is he talking about? My kind? He's my brother for fuck's sake. I mean, sure, he has brown hair and brown eyes like both of my parents, and I have blond hair and blue eyes. I'm sure it's a throwback from some recessive trait generations back. I don't get a chance to think about his stupid words anymore.

"But we're going to have some fun first." He tears his cruel sneer away from my face and nods at someone.

Kat slowly saunters over with a smug grin on her face. She's wielding a knife in her hand, waving it back and forth between her fingers as if she's showing off a prize.

"This is going to be so much fun! I've been wanting to do this for ages!" She kneels in front of my face and leans down so she can whisper into my ear. "Did you really believe him when he said he was going to meet you tonight? When he promised that he was going to help you, save you?" She snorts when I don't answer her and huffs. "It was all an act, Grit." I stare at her knee, refusing to let her get to me. She barks out a harsh laugh, leaning back to rest on her heels. "He told us, you know." My eyes move up to her face. "How he convinced you, how he made you believe that you were his true mate." Raucous laughter erupts from all the Bart groupies and bounces off the trees. She pretends to pout. "Guess you wish you submitted now, don't you? Grit." Her pout turns into a cruel smile.

I don't want to believe her, but he isn't here. He never came.

"Shut the fuck up and do it!" Bart shouts out. She cocks her head to the side as if studying me; the knife in her hand reaches straight toward my face.

As the knife slices into my scalp, I let out a scream. Blood seeps into my eyes. Pain wracks my body, and when I just can't take any more pain, darkness takes over.

I lie there on the forest ground in a semiconscious heap. Bart is standing over me, blood dripping from his hand. It isn't enough, wolves shredding me to pieces. He has to beat me too. All of that just isn't enough for these sick bastards.

I feel a tug. My heart freezes in my chest when I realize the rope is still around my neck! I grab for it—I'm too late! I'm being dragged backward. I feel it tighten, cutting off my air. I struggle to claw at my neck, trying to get my fingers under the noose, choking, sobbing, kicking my legs as my body is dragged through the dirt. My upper body lifts into the air. No, no, no, I feel my feet leave the ground. I reach for the rope behind me to pull myself up. I can't breathe.

Dots threaten my vision. The rush of roaring blood sounds in my ears joined by a high-pitched ringing noise. My lungs are about to burst from lack of oxygen. I reach for the knife in my waistband. It's there! But my fingers are numb and soaked in blood. My hands tremble.

Don't give up—don't give up! I yell at myself in my mind as I try to saw through the rope. The knife slips from my grasp. My arms fall to my sides. My body stills, and my erratic heartbeat slows to a stutter. It's over. I have no fight left in me. The beating of my heart stops. I. Submit. To. Death.

# Chapter 1
## THE LATE NIGHT SHOW

### JESSICA

#### March 24, 2025: Present Day

With trembling hands, I fidget with the skirt of my dress and pull down my sleeves. My heart is beating hard and fast against my chest. I can feel the beads of sweat starting to form over my upper lip. I peak through the thick heavy drapes anticipating my introduction on *The Late Night Show with Sammy Cane.*

I watch her give her opening. I could have stayed in the dressing room and watched on the monitor, but I am so nervous that I came out here instead. She is a pretty woman with dark blond hair, warm brown eyes, and a beauty mark just above the right corner of her mouth. She was once a famous pop singer. She has a fun, energetic way about her and has the audience laughing and clapping.

As Sammy Cane finishes her opening, I force myself to look around the studio. At the heart of the stage sits a loveseat for the guest strategically placed next to an armchair for the host and a rounded coffee table where a coffee mug of water or tea patiently sits waiting for me. A small band sits off to the side of the stage opposite me. My eyes shift upward to the open ceiling with large bright canned lights fixed to the beams; I can already feel the warmth of the blinding lights. Behind the filming crew and stagehands milling about quietly sit five rows of seats for the live audience. A tiny flicker of panic stirs in my gut, quickening my already rapidly beating heart when I notice that every seat in the studio is taken. Quickly, I scan the audience looking for a familiar face. My shoulders drop in relief when I see my mother sitting next to Sixes in the third row directly in front of where I will be sitting for the interview.

"I am so excited to introduce you to our special guest tonight. She is a singer/songwriter, the CEO of WP Corporation, and now the main star of our favorite reality TV show, *A Game of Heart's Desire: The Alpha Games.* Please welcome Alpha Princess Jessica Langhlan!"

The curtains part, and the audience cheers as I make my way onto the stage. Still trembling with nervousness, I force a smile onto my face, hoping it doesn't look scary or forced. I do a little twirl to show off my dress.

I promised my friend Akiyo that I would showcase her latest design. I'm wearing a long, fitted, high-split dress, off the shoulder with long sleeves, in a green-and-gold gauzy Asian print with high strappy heels that I can barely walk in.

Internally, I'm praying that I don't trip. Slow and steady, I tell myself as I feel my ankle wobble on these ridiculously high heels. Finally, I reach the hostess. Relief fills my chest as I make it without tripping, thank goodness. Sammy welcomes me with a big hug. My nervousness melts away.

"Thank you, Alpha Princess Jessica, for joining us today. We are so excited to have you! It is such an honor to be in your presence!" She motions to me to sit on the loveseat.

I wave my hand in front of me as I take my seat. "What are you talking about? You're Sammy Cane, the first contestant to win *So You Think You Can Sing* in the very first season. The first and only music artist to have multiple number-one hits stay on the top ten pop music charts for months. Not to mention the first female artist to own her own record label just one year after entering the industry. You paved the way for many young artists with a dream within the Northern A territories and worldwide." She blushes at my own fangirling and drops her head. I continue. "I have been a huge fan for years. It's an honor to be in the presence of the Pop Queen," I tell her, pressing my still-shaky hands over my chest. The audience starts to cheer. I raise my arms, pumping them up and down, encouraging the audience to applaud louder.

Her face reddens with my praise, and she waves her hand to quiet down the audience. "If I'm the Pop Queen, then you are the Queen of Rock!" The audience erupts with clapping and more cheering. She turns to the audience and continues, "Did you know that a couple of the top hits that I sang when I first started, 'Unstoppable Woman' and 'Armor,' were written and composed by the artist formerly known as 'G'?" she asks the audience. She thumbs her hand toward me.

"Yes, everyone, if you haven't heard about it yet, the Alpha Princess Jessica Langhlan recently revealed that she is the mysterious artist 'G,' the rock star famously known for hiding her features behind a mask."

I start to laugh. "When did I become the 'artist formerly known as 'G?'" I hear gasps and murmurs in the audience.

Sammy shrugs. "When the world found out who you really are, did you think that everyone would still call you 'G?'"

I shrug. "Oh… I didn't think about it. I didn't exactly plan to, you know, come out behind the mask the way I did." I didn't even speak to my manager since the whole thing happened. I just let my lawyer and PR rep take care of it.

"How have you been? It has been a long time since I have seen you," I ask Sammy, changing the subject.

She smiles. "I am great! Busy, between working and raising my little family, but I can't complain. My two little girls are growing up way too fast." The screen behind us shows her two little ones, one of them missing her two front teeth. The audience awws in response to the picture.

"They are too precious!" I coo.

Sammy's head jerked toward the end of the stage, where a man wearing headphones with a mouthpiece starts making hand motions.

She turns her attention back to me. "Speaking of busy, underneath the mask and the title. I don't think anyone realizes how smart, talented, and hardworking you really are." My mouth instantly dries up at her insinuation. I casually reach for the cup filled with water and take a sip.

I clear my throat before replacing the cup on the table.

"How do you mean?"

She slips her hand between the armrest and the cushion of her chair and pulls out index cards with the show's logo printed on the back. "Well, for starters, at age fourteen, you challenged the LS territories aptitude test and acquired a high school diploma. At sixteen you earned a bachelor's degree in business, and at nineteen, you finished your MBA overseas." She leans over the arm of her chair closer toward me. "Do you know what I was doing at sixteen? I was sneaking out of my house and into karaoke bars and open mic nights."

I let out a breathy laugh. "And just look at where that had gotten you today." I motion to our surroundings. Which gets me an eye roll in return.

"If you only knew the half of it." She gives me a mischievous smile. I can't help but chuckle.

"Anyways, we can talk about that some other time in private, over lots and lots of cocktails." We giggle together before she switches gears again and looks back down at the index cards. "You have practically built an empire of a multitude of businesses from hotels, restaurants, clubs. Some of our sources have reported that you have silent partnerships with wineries, whiskey distilleries, and other small businesses around the world."

I can feel the heat in my cheeks build as she continues to list all my business accomplishments. "And on top of all of that, you recently became the CEO of a worldwide business consulting company."

Shaking my head, I try to peer through the blinding lights, seeking out my mother and assistant. "I think you're giving me way too much credit than I deserve. I have business partners, board members, hardworking management teams and staff that helped me to grow a successful business or businesses. I also have a beyond amazing assistant who helps keep me in line. I didn't do it alone."

She waves the cards in front of her as if there's a sudden bad smell. "Oh please! I for one know exactly how much work goes into putting together a business. It's not easy, let me tell you. I'm just thankful that I had gone through all of the ups and downs of becoming a business owner before I had kids. Most people don't realize how much heart and soul you pour into a business. The sleepless nights. The tears. It's like selling your soul to the devil!"

"No, really, I—"

She leans forward and places a hand on my knee. "You are amazing. It's okay to let the world see it. All the sources we inquired with had nothing but wonderful things to say about you and your work ethic. Even those within the music industry have said the same, and that includes me. My personal experience working with you was by far one of my most favorite memories."

I give her a bashful smile and incline my head. "Thank you."

She gives my knee a friendly squeeze before she moves on to the next topic, the one I am actually here for.

"You're here tonight mainly to promote the premiere of the show *A Game of Heart's Desire: The Alpha Games*."

I let out an audible breath and nod.

Before I can respond, she leans further in, frowning, and says, "I don't get it."

I shrug. "What is there not to get?"

"Well, because you're you. For crying out loud. There have to be miles of men lining up who want to be with you. Why do you need to be on this show?"

A man from the audience suddenly yells, "I'm single! Mate me!"

I give a breathy laugh. Then I look down at my hands, twisting them onto themselves. I've been asked this question a million times. It never gets easier to answer.

"I think you pointed out the obvious. I have spent a little over a decade trying to discover myself and make a career." I shake my head, embarrassed that I need to admit this out loud. "After a few mistakes, I convinced myself that I don't need a mate, that my career or careers and family is all that I need. But as it turns out, there are rules, laws, you have to adhere to when becoming a female Alpha. With that also come personal sacrifices, not just to keep my role but to do what is suitable for my pack."

Still frowning, she says, "I get that, but again, why the show?" I don't have an answer, at least not one I can honestly give. I'm trying to keep to the script or the words I should say according to my PR guy, but it just seems so, I don't know, fake.

Shaking my head, I take a deep breath and tell my scripted confession. "Everyone thinks my life is all glamorous and romantic, traveling all over the world, meeting new people all the time. The truth is I haven't made many attempts to make a connection with anyone. Even though many of my friends are males, it's not like I could make a phone call and say, 'Hey, friend, are you still single? Great! How about you and I hook up and get mated before my twenty-fifth birthday?'" I jest.

That last part was not in the script. My PR guy is going to have an aneurysm. Sammy gives me a sad smile.

Swallowing, I continue. "Look, I know it's not the ideal way to find your mate. Trust me, I remember a time when I sat with friends watching the show, and I couldn't help but think, what's wrong with them that they can't find a mate the normal way? I used to make rude comments and make fun of the female contestants," I say with a snort. "I guess karma has a funny way of giving it right back to me because here I am, promoting the show." I end with a shrug.

A look of disappointment sits on Sammy's face. "Well, I hope you find your true mate." She looks at me thoughtfully, reaches over, and takes my hand. "I always thought you were special. You write and compose music with so much love and emotion. You deserve to have a meaningful relationship in your life."

Smiling sadly, I look back down at our hands. That is kind of her to say, but love, including a meaningful relationship, isn't in the cards for me. "Thank you. That means a lot to me, especially coming from you."

The same man with the headphones motions to Sammy again.

"Well, it's that time everyone!" The audience goes wild with jeers and cheers, loud clapping and whistling. "Let's play a game!"

My eyes widen. I was warned about this, but I honestly thought we took up so much time already that it wouldn't come to this. I glance over at the corner and see my PR guy's face. He's shaking his head in a warning. There's a part of me that really wants to piss off my PR guy for making rude comments and annoying remarks throughout the week.

This morning, when he drank my coffee on purpose and then refused to stop to get me another one. Well, let's just say he's not my favorite person.

I narrow my eyes at him and paste on my *fuck you, Gary* smile.

Turning my attention back to Sammy, I rub my hands together and with a firm nod, I tell her, "Let's do this."

Finally, it is all over. I make my way to my mother and assistant Sixes, who moved from their seats among the audience to join our PR guy Gary, and Anders my head guard, backstage.

"Nice job. Cute act, by the way, acting all meek and innocent," Gary sneers at me in a hushed tone to avoid drawing attention.

I lean closer to him, and in just as low of a voice, I tell him, "I'm in this mess because of your great idea in the first place. Besides, this was also your idea to act like a bubbling idiot to throw people off." With a wide fake smile, he looks around, making sure there are no onlookers.

"No, you wouldn't have needed to pretend to be a bubbling idiot if you would have just chosen a mate in the first place, Princess." I roll my eyes at him, and he stalks off, letting my mother know he will meet us back at my place to discuss the plans with the production team.

My mother gives me a gentle smile and reaches for my hand. Before she can say anything, someone from behind me clears their throat. We all turn to see one of the stagehands or cameramen. Anders takes a closer step toward me, and I put up a hand to stop him. I can tell this man isn't a threat. He looks a little nervous.

"Uh, excuse me, Princess. I'm sorry to bother you, and I know you probably want to get going… Uh… you see there's, uh… a little boy sitting over there." He thumbs in the direction of the audience's seats. "He's asking if he can meet you. He… uh… He says he's a huge fan of yours." The poor guy is sweating as if I am going to bite his head off.

I give a slight chuckle to ease some of his tension and nervousness. "A little boy?" I ask him.

His shoulders relax. "Yeah, cute kid, he made his nanny bring him here today. We don't normally let children in, so I was just as surprised to see him sitting in the audience seats. He really wants to meet you."

I crane my neck to see if I can spot him. There he is, a tiny little guy, maybe not more than five years of age, with jet-black hair, sitting next to a young, ash blond-haired female.

Anders leans in to whisper in my ear, "I don't think that's a good idea. It could be a setup." I watch the two. The little boy is talking animatedly to his nanny, and she is intent on the conversation. They don't seem like much of a threat. I look around them, and they're alone.

"It's just a little boy and his nanny. If you're so worried, come with me, or…" I look at the man who came to make the request, "will it be okay if you bring the boy and his nanny backstage?"

"It won't be a problem. I can get them now if you like."

I look over at Anders. "Will that work better for you?"

His face is stern, and he doesn't answer me right away,

probably calculating in his brain what the odds would be if the little boy came to us instead. He finally nods, and the man leaves to retrieve the pair.

# Chapter 2

## A SON'S CHOICE

### CONTESTANT #16

Reaching over, I gently remove the TV remote from my son's hand. I'm sitting in my king-sized bed next to my son, and we're watching *The Tonight Show* featuring the Alpha Princess Jessica Langhlan. He's propped up against the headboard with a couple of pillows against his back in the same way mine are. His jet black hair is smoothed down to perfection, he's wearing a button-down, deep blue, pinstriped pajama set instead of his usual cartoon character sets. I'm a little amused that he had gotten dressed up like this to watch a show on TV, as if he was trying to make a good impression.

It's close to the end of the show. Someone from the audience yells, "Sing a song!"

"Yeah, one of your songs!" and a few more shout out the

same request.

"Sing?" the Alpha Princess asks, slightly surprised at the request.

The host suggests with his hands that she should go for it and says, "Sure, everyone's excited now that they know who the masked singer 'G' is. Go for it."

The Alpha Princess makes her way to the band and whispers something to them. As the band starts to play the intro to the song, she closes her eyes and starts to sing. I'm instantly enraptured by her beauty, her voice, and when the lyrics of the song hit me, a deep ache envelops my heart. The camera shows the audience, capturing them swaying to the music, and the host has a wide goofy grin across his face as he watches on. As the camera focuses on the Alpha Princess, it catches a single tear falling from the corner of her left eye.

Clearing my throat, I push down the emotions building and chance a glance over in my son's direction. He's mesmerized by the beautiful woman singing, even though he doesn't quite understand the meaning behind the beautiful melody. When the commercial starts, signaling that the show is over, I click the remote, shutting it off.

He looks at me and says, "She's beautiful, Daddy."

I lean forward and kiss his head. "She really is, son."

He smiles. "Inside and out?"

"I guess you would have to be to write songs like that and sing with so much emotion that everyone around you feels precisely what you feel when you sing."

He nods, looking a little smug at my answer. He surprises me when he says, "I met her."

I immediately drop my smile and frown at him. "What

do you mean you met her?"

"Panny took me to watch her funny story. Panny's friend let us go behind the curtains to meet her."

"Penny," I say to correct him. He's five years old, and sometimes I forget how young he is because he talks like he's an old man. My fault, I'm sure. I speak to him like he's an adult.

"Penny," he says, correcting himself. "I told her, Dad."

Confused with his reply, I asked, "You told her what?"

He let out a long breath as if I am too stupid not to understand what he is telling me. "I told the Alpha Princess that if she meets you, she will know that she's your true mate." Not this again. Ever since he had seen her on the news, that's all he has been talking about. "She's the one, Dad! She's your true mate. I know it!" He crosses his arms and pouts.

I lean towards him and tickle him. "Is she now?"

He starts to squeal and giggle. "Yes! Yes!" he shouts out.

I pull him down and cover him with the comforter. "You know what I think?" I tell him as I gently hit him over the head with the pillow. "I think it's time for you to go to bed. It is way past your bedtime."

He groans and gives me a slight pout. "No! No negotiating. You agreed. We shook on the deal. I let you stay up past your bedtime to watch *The Tonight Show*. You would go to sleep as soon as it was over."

He scrunches up his tiny nose. "Ugghhhh, fine."

I lean down, kissing him on his cheek. "Good night, son. I love you."

"I love you too, Dad." He puts his tiny arms around my neck and hugs me. Then he whispers, "She's the one, Dad. I can feel it. I felt it when I met her."

I pull back and search his pale blue eyes. "Son, I just don't think it will work. It's complicated. It's an adult thing. Don't ask any more questions, alright? Go to sleep."

"You have to fight for her. She's the one, Dad, please."

I shake my head. "Go to sleep. We can talk about this when it is not so late." He makes a disgruntled noise and slides under the covers, turning his back to me. Still, I don't want to have this conversation, especially with my five-year-old son, who shouldn't even understand what true mates are to begin with. Note to self: talk to my mother about limiting her rom-coms and whatever dramatic romance movies she watches in front of my son.

I make my way to the kitchen. My nanny is removing the dishes from the dishwasher. "What the hell do you think you are doing taking my son to a late-night show hosting the Alpha Princess?" I'm loud, practically shouting at her. She almost drops the dish in her hand. I scared her... Good, honestly, what the fuck was she thinking?

"I'm sorry, Alpha. Your parents bought the tickets. I assumed you knew about it," she replies, looking down at her hand, trembling now.

"My parents bought the tickets?" She nods. Is that who put this whole stupid notion of the Alpha Princess being my true mate in his head? What the fuck are they thinking? I still want to ream the poor girl even further, but the truth is this wasn't her fault. I'll deal with my parents later. I'm still pissed about the whole thing.

My voice hasn't softened. I point my finger at her. "The next time my parents buy tickets to anything or tell you to take him anywhere, you clear it with me first. I don't care if you think I already know about it. He is my son! Is that clear?"

"Yes, Alpha, this won't happen again." Her eyes are still cast down; shit, her face is red. She looks like she's ready to cry.

I turn to leave to go to my office, and in her tiny voice, my nanny says, "She's nothing like how I thought she would be. She was sweet, down to earth. She was good to Jackson, gave him attention, and made him feel... important. Like the honor was hers meeting him for the first time." Fuck, fuck, fuck! Not her too. I don't turn around to face her. "They bonded... I think Jackson is right." She rushes out in a single breath.

With my back still facing her, I answer her with a lethal edge in my voice, "I won't discuss this shit with my employees. Is this clear? We are not friends. If you want to remain an employee, I suggest you stay out of my personal affairs, including my conversations with my son."

"Y-Yes, Alpha, my apologies for overstepping." Good, now that is clear, I storm off to my office.

I need to talk to my parents. I know that they treat all their employees like family, especially the pack. I don't mind what they do, but I wouldn't say I like it. It sometimes gives the employees and pack members the impression that they can talk to us like we are friends. Give us personal advice; mind our fucking business, betray us. Like they have the right to. I'm a private person. I like to keep my life and my identity confidential. I don't want to be friends with everyone who works for me, including our pack. I'm their boss, their

Alpha, and it shouldn't have blurred lines. It's safer that way.

I sit heavily down in my office chair and lean forward, placing my elbows on my desk and my face in my hands. Growling my frustration into my hands. I flip open my laptop and take a deep breath. I pull up my itinerary for the next three days. What the fuck am I thinking? Why am I doing this? After that little rant in my head, I'm a walking, talking, fucking contradiction. This isn't who I am. I'm going against everything I believe in. I'm going against everything that I naturally am. I'm taking an extended vacation from work. I can't remember when I last went on a vacation. I'm leaving my father back in charge of the firm and the pack.

I turn my head and see the picture of my mate and me, taken on the day of our mating ceremony. We were laughing at something, probably some joke she made. Our mating wasn't based on love. Well, romantic love anyway. It was an arranged mating, but I couldn't have been any luckier to end up with my best friend in the whole world. The day she died, I would have lost myself entirely if it wasn't for my son. I would have reverted to how I used to be—an uncaring, heartless bastard. I look down at the picture now in my hands. Emily never wanted me to give up on my hopes for reuniting with my one true love. She always believed that I still had a chance. "I fucking hope you're right, Em. I hope you're right because if not, I will be making an ass of myself in front of millions of people."

# Chapter 3

## A PACK IN CRISIS

### CONTESTANT #19

I look down at my hand with a tumbler filled with whiskey, neat. I haven't touched it. This is my second glass. The first glass I had filled with ice, and the ice melted, watering down the whiskey, so I threw it out. Determined to get some kind of peace or something to help quiet my rampant mind, I made another drink, this time without ice, and I still haven't touched it. I'm sitting on my family's home balcony facing Ruby Falls. At any other time, the sound of the falls would be welcoming and calming. It used to be a sound that would put me to sleep, but not tonight. So much shit is running through my head.

"There you are, sweetheart." I turn my head to face my mother. She has dark circles under her eyes. Her eyelids are swollen, probably from crying. A stab of guilt hits me in the gut. I did that. I haven't seen my mother for years. When I finally come home, I break her heart.

"Hey, Mom." She runs her hand along the back of my head and rests it on the nape of my neck. I turn my attention back to the scenery in front of me.

Clutching my glass tighter in my hand, I tell her, "I'm sorry for staying away for so long. Maybe if I had come home sooner, none of this shit would have happened."

She clucks her tongue, "Stop doing that to yourself. Things have been bad for a long time. I'm glad you left when you did."

I keep running through everything that has happened recently in my head, over and over. It wasn't supposed to happen the way it did. Nothing ever turns out the way it should. Not when it comes to her.

Now I need to fix everything that Dad and that asshole Beta fucking destroyed. How the fuck did Dad let this happen? I used to look up to him. He was everything I believed in until he wasn't.

"Our pack is in a state of crisis," I snarl. She's silent, running her thumb back and forth at the base of my hairline. "I need to fix what they did to our pack. It has to start with this union." I squeeze the tumbler in my hand tighter. I can feel the glass starting to crack. I throw it over the balcony. I'm angry and frustrated, and I wish that I could beat the shit out of something. No, I want to beat the shit out of the Beta that my father trusted so much and his son. I take my shaking hand and rub it over my face. Then I look up at her. "She already rejected the betrothal contract. If she doesn't choose me in this stupid game..."

She shakes her head. "I'm so sorry, sweetheart. I wish I could have been stronger. I wish I had done something to intervene in all of this…"

I take her hand from the back of my neck and kiss it. "No, I… should have done something. Instead, I just stood there and watched them destroy her." The truth is I was a coward and didn't really try. I squeeze my eyes shut as if I could squeeze out the memories of what I should have and didn't do.

My mother sighs and bends down in front of me so that now we're at eye level. She grabs my face in both of her hands. "Look at me. You're a good boy. You remind me of your father, the young man I fell in love with."

I scoff. "No offense, but you're his true mate. You would love him and follow him, even if he was the devil reincarnated."

She tsks. "I'll let you in on a little secret, my son. Just because a woman finds her true mate doesn't mean we don't have free will. We can still make our own choices. We keep that to ourselves to let the males think they are in charge and have control over us."

She chucks my chin before she continues, and I give her a tight-lipped smile. I'm almost thirty years old. She still does these little pats and touches like I'm still a child.

"Like I was saying, you remind me so much of your father when he was young before the Betas corrupted him. You have a good heart, just like him. He cared a lot about this pack. He and his father built all of this just for them. And you, despite everything going on, have added to it for your…

pack... Don't sell yourself short. You have come a long way since that time. You were just a boy. There wasn't much you could have done."

I shake my head. "I could have done plenty... I didn't have the balls to do it. I was trying to please Dad, even though I knew it didn't feel right in my heart."

My mother grabs my face again. "Stop! You can't undo the past. All you can do is move forward, live in the present, and learn from past mistakes. It's all any of us can do right now." I try to pull away from her, but she holds firm. "Now listen to me. Frederick can take care of things while you're gone, and business operations will run as normal. The Alpha King was kind enough to send some guards to help until things settle, and you still have me." She quirks an eyebrow awaiting my challenge. She continues, "Sweetheart, I know you want to do what's right for the pack, but listen, the most important thing is you do this because it's right for you. You'll win her back. Just let her see the real you and show her what's in here." She taps her hand over my heart as I place my much larger hand over hers.

Easier said than done. Because the real question is—will she choose me? Especially after she discovers who I truly am and the part I played in her life.

# CHAPTER 4

## STALKER SYNDROME

### CONTESTANT #20

I turn off the TV just before the Alpha Princess starts to sing. My phone rings, but I don't answer it. I'm too angry to speak to anyone right now. How can she do this to me? How can she even entertain the idea of being with another man? A man that is not me. I have been patient. I have given her space and time. I walk over to the cabinet in my room and open the double doors revealing pictures of my beautiful princess. I pick up a bundle of her hair tied together in a knot, bring it up to my nose, and inhale the lingering scent of lavender and honey. It instantly hardens my cock.

My phone rings again, and I place my precious one's strands of hair back in its place, and I run my hands over broken pieces of a golden mask that she once wore when she performed as 'G.'

"Soon, baby girl. I will have you soon, and once you're mine, I will punish you for running away from me." I run my thumb over a picture of her crossing the street in the city. I followed her for years, collecting her belongings, hair ties, panties, and earrings. I strategically placed hidden cameras in her home. I watched her every movement, down to watching her take showers, masturbate, fucking other men. I gingerly close the doors to my cabinet and lock the door.

My phone rings again. "What the fuck do you want!" I yell into the phone.

"You know I can't keep calling you. I have time limits."

"Not my fucking problem!" I shout.

"Stop being a baby. This is important! Get your head back in the game!"

I lean against the wall. "What the fuck do you think I've been doing?" I ground out into the phone. Her voice annoys me. The way she speaks annoys me. Everything about her annoys me.

She hisses into the phone, "Everything is in order; all you have to do is win the bitch's heart, get her to mate you, and then kill the fucking bitch!" I end the call and punch the wall, picturing her face.

These last couple weeks have been hell dealing with my family, and I am not in the mood to listen to their shit. I may not be as conniving as my sister, but I don't need to be. I have charm, wit, and I'm intelligent. She's the one in prison for life, and at thirty, she will be there for a very long time. As shifters, we can live until we are 200 years old. She was a miserable piece of shit anyway. She deserves to be in jail;

hell, she deserves the death penalty. I can do this. I can win over the Alpha Princess, make her my mate, and convince her to turn over her business, pack, territory, and everything else she owns to me.

But I don't want to kill her so soon. I didn't waste years of my time following her, loving her from afar, wanting her. Fuck them. I'm going to do this my way, maybe after we have a couple of pups. Hmmm, that's a great idea, and when she has the last one, maybe by then, I will tire of her. I can blame her death on the birthing process. No one will suspect it was me. I ball my hands into fists at my side. The truth is I don't think I want her dead.

She is everything I have ever wanted in a mate. She is intelligent, tough, sexy as hell, and she fucks like an animal in bed. Precisely the kind of woman I am attracted to. I hate weak women who cry and whine all the time. Like my stupid sister. Women who can't take a good cock irritate me. But the Alpha Princess, I can't imagine that I will have a problem with her; in fact, I think she will put up a good fight. Thinking of her in my bed, fighting me, digging her nails into my skin as I force her to take my big cock, makes me hard. Fuckkkk... I want her. I want to pound into her and hear her moans and screams. I want to look into her eyes and see her anger, her hatred for me. Then I want to see that anger and hatred turn into pleasure as she realizes how good the pain can feel for both of us. I want to feel that silky-soft pussy suck my cock as she comes. I groan as I push down on my hardened cock with my palm. I'm so fucking turned on right now just thinking about her. Soon enough, I tell myself, I won't need to take care of myself to the fantasy of the Alpha Princess riding my cock because she will be mine.

# Chapter 5

## Leaving Love to Fate

### CONTESTANT #24

A knock on the door takes me out of my rapt thoughts. I clear my throat, "Come in," I call out and close my laptop.

"Hey, I just wanted to check in and let you know that everything is in place."

I regard my friend, rubbing my index finger under my lip.

"I want her guarded at all times, especially at night. She has a habit of getting into shit when she thinks the rest of the world is sleeping."

He gives me a slight smirk and a shrug of his shoulders. "We've already got it covered, and besides, she has the guards that watch over her." I shake my head. I almost laugh at my friend's remark. She is so damn stubborn, too stubborn for her own good. She thinks just because she trained with the guards that she is invincible. She has gotten into more trouble than anyone I have ever met in my entire life.

"Not good enough. I want eyes on her at all times." He lets out a breath, and I can tell he's preparing to give me a speech or talk me out of my decision, but I already made up my mind. My future is set for me, and there is nothing that is going to change it.

"You don't have to go through with it. I think you still have a chance. You just need to fight for her and prove that she will always be your girl." I look down at my desk and start to rub my shoulder.

"It's too late," I say in a barely audible whisper. "She made her choice, and I have made mine. I'm to be mated tomorrow."

He narrows his eyes at me. "Why are you going through with this? My brother and I have been by your side for years. In all that time, all you ever talked about was how you're doing all of this for her." He gestures to the room, my home. "Now that you have a chance to fight for her, you hide behind political bullshit and tuck your tail between your legs and run. Never took you for a pathetic coward and a liar."

I curl my hands into fists, but I stay seated in my chair, slamming my fist down on my desk. "Fuck you! She has made her choice!" I shout.

He glares at me. "Listen, you miserable piece of shit! I'm sick and tired of watching you go through the motions of your life like a zombie. Don't wake up lying next to a girl you don't want. Get your girl. It's not too late!"

I stand from my seat. I am so close to losing my shit, but

I don't want to hurt my friend, so I keep my feet rooted in their position. I have already lost too much. I can't afford to lose any more friends. There aren't many, and he is one of the few I trust with my life.

He shakes his head, "You're a coward. You claim to love her, yet here you are, being led by the balls." Sarcasm drips heavily into his words.

I clench my jaw, and through gritted teeth, I growl out, "She made her choice!"

"You keep saying that, but did she? You know what? I'm done. I'm not coming back when it's over. I'm not going to hang around and continue to watch you live a miserable life. I'm going to do what you should be doing. I'm going to choose her." Before I can set myself in motion to smash his fucking face with my fist, he shows me the finger and heads out the door.

I pick up the chair I was sitting on and hurl it at the door, splintering it and shattering it to pieces. In my raging fit, I continue to push the contents of my desk onto the floor. I kick and punch at the wall behind me. I turn to destroy my desk. Glass shatters around me; smoke fills the air. I fall to my knees and bring my bloodied, trembling hands to my chest. I am breathing hard, fighting for control before I do something worse that I might regret later. My vision starts to cloud with unshed tears, and I roar with rage and sorrow. I hang my head and let the tears drip off my chin.

A woman's laughter fills the room's silence. "What are you doing?" she says with a slightly raspy and breathy voice.

I start to look around the destroyed room. Jessica? "Stop what you're doing and come here." Her sweet, infectious laugh echoes across the room again.

"I'm capturing the moment, so I can remember this forever," I hear myself saying.

"Whatever happened to just good old-fashioned memories?" she retorts. I sift around the floor's contents and find her voice coming from my laptop. It must have opened when it crashed to the floor; the screen is cracked, but I can still see the video playing. I sink onto the floor. I lean my back against my broken desk and place the laptop on my lap.

We're two young kids who snuck off to make out. I'm caressing her cheek with my free hand and kissing her, holding my phone above us, doing exactly what I told her I wanted to do. I smile as I see myself side-eyeing my phone, ensuring the camera is still on us. I return to giving her my full attention, kissing her. The kiss is long, not sloppy or desperate, but full of passion, love, and desire. I finally pull back with a big goofy grin, run my nose along hers, and tilt her chin slightly so the camera catches sight of her beautiful face.

She turns back, making a fake attempt to bite my fingers. "You don't need to remember me with videos," she says, pouting. I lean forward to nibble at her bottom lip, cutting her off, pulling her bottom lip with me as I pull back again. I give her a playful growl. "I don't plan on going anywhere unless it's with you," she whispers against my lips, placing her tiny hands on either side of my face. "I love you," she tells me, kissing my lips.

"Mine," I growl.

"Forever," she says as she pulls back and starts to kiss me along my jawline. I drop the phone as I reach for her. I remember wanting to envelop her in both of my arms, feel her body pressed against mine. The last thing captured is a squeal, and we laugh before the video ends. I toggle back until I reach that part when I turned her face to the camera and pause it. My heart sinks, bile rises to my throat, hot, burning tears sting my eyes, and I'm torn between wanting to punch another hole in the wall or throw up.

I want to smash my computer into a thousand pieces and destroy every reminder I have of her, but I can't bring myself to do it. Instead, I sit there staring at her face frozen on the cracked screen.

This can't be how our story ends. He's right. I can't let her go without a fight, without her knowing the truth. I torture myself further by clicking open the file I was staring at before my friend walked in. I upload the file, fill it out, and attach it to an email.

I'm going to leave it up to fate. If I hear back from them before my mating ceremony tomorrow, I will fight to win my girl back. If I don't, that's my answer, and I let her go for good this time.

# CHAPTER 6

## BULLYING THE BULLY

### CONTESTANT #25

My PR guy is staring at me as I read through the contract. I look it over one more time, and without hesitation, I sign the bottom of it. I slide the papers across the table towards him; he shakes his head and sighs as he leans forward to collect them.

"You could do so much better," he mumbles.

I narrow my eyes at him, daring him to continue.

He pinches his lips together. "Look, all I'm saying is that this girl isn't worth your reputation or your time. I know some models, or, if you want a good girl, I have some friends."

I slam my palm on the table, "I don't want anyone else! If you so much as sneer at her name again, I will ruin your career so fast, you'll be living off the streets."

He holds up his hands. "Alright, alright! My apologies for stepping out of line. I just think you can do so much better. You deserve better. Especially after all the shit you've been through." I look down at the wood grain of the conference room table that has been in my family for generations.

"What I deserve is a chance to tell her the truth. A chance to start over. No more secrets, no more lies. A real chance at what was supposed to be ours." Running my hand through my hair, I face away from him.

Frustrated with me, he rubs a spot on his forehead between his brows. "She's going to be the death of you."

Slowly, I turn my head back to face him. "That's a chance I'm willing to take. Now make it fucking happen. Get me in the lineup or you will be out of a job."

He grimaces. "Getting you in won't be a problem. What might be the problem is the Alpha Princess. I can get your foot in the door, but I can't guarantee you'll make it past the first round of eliminations."

I eye him, taking in his dulling brown hair, and the wrinkles in his business suit. He's been traveling all over the Northern A and the LS escorting Jessica as they promote the game. I should feel sorry for him that I forced him out here to meet with me, but I don't.

"Just get me in. I'll take care of the rest." I motion for him to leave.

He shuffles the papers into a neat pile before placing them in his briefcase. "She must have one hell of a magic pussy."

Rage rolls up my spine before he can finish what he's about to say. I unleash my magic, wrapping it around his throat, slamming him down on the ground, picking him back up, and throwing him against the wall. I hold his body suspended against the wall.

Slowly, I stalk toward him, my magic tightening around his throat. His eyes practically bulge from his eye sockets, his face turning a sickly shade of purple. I lean closer. "If I didn't need you to get me into the game, you would be fucking dead right now."

He croaks. I release my magic, letting him crash to the floor in a heap. He's gasping for air, crawling towards his briefcase. He picks it up by the handle and pulls himself up to stand. His trembling hand reaches for the doorknob. Folding my arms across my chest, I glare at him.

"Gary," he turns his reddened face in my direction, "consider this your last warning. One more degrading word out of your mouth—I don't care if you're talking to yourself, to anyone, or to her. If I hear anything!"

He vehemently shakes his head. "You won't. I will treat her with nothing but respect from here on out." I grind my teeth, not trusting his given word. I don't fucking trust anyone. I stare him down, looking for any clue that he's placating me just to escape my ire.

"You're replaceable, Gary. Everyone is replaceable. Except for her."

He nods. "I understand, sir."

"Good, now get the fuck out of my sight." Without another word, he's out the door. I turn back toward the conference room and clean up my mess.

Heavy footsteps enter the conference room just as I am finishing up. "Hey, was that Gary I just passed heading out?"

I grunt to my cousin in response. He pulls out a chair and sits at the table across from me.

"Okay, was that not a good meeting?" He lifts his legs and rests them on the table and tilts his chair back. I grimace. He smirks.

"It was fine. I just don't understand why my parents keep him around."

He shrugs. "He's an ass, but he is good at his job. Trust me. I went through a few of them. Gary's the one who sent over the current one I have, and I have to say I'm impressed. He highly recommended her, so I have to say he knows what he's doing."

I absentmindedly nod, not really giving a shit about how good he is. He has been mean to her and insulting her to her face and behind her back for years. I'm sick of it. I don't even know why he took her on and why she agreed to work with him.

He snaps his fingers in my direction. "Did you hear what I just said?"

I look up at him. "No, not a damn word."

He rolls his eyes. "Well, if you would pay attention, I just said you didn't need to go to Gary in the first place. I told you I had your back." He places a folded piece of paper on the table.

I pick it up and look down at it. There's an address and some room numbers scrawled on it. I glance up at my cousin, frowning, then look back down at the address. It's the address to the hotel that I own. I raise a brow at him. He has a smug look on his face.

"What the hell am I supposed to do with this?"

"Pack your bags and head into the city. That is where you will be meeting the production team's manager for your interview." I jump over the table and knock him off his chair in a bear hug. He laughs as he slaps my back. "Told you I had your back."

I squeeze his shoulder. "Thanks, man. This means a lot to me." He slaps my back one more time before pushing me off him.

"Well, get going. Your interview is in three hours." I look down at the watch on my wrist, noting the time. "Oh, and make it count because filming literally starts in two days."

# Chapter 7

## INTERVIEW DAY

### JESSICA

#### March 31, 2025: Present Day

"Good morning, Alpha Princess. I trust you slept well?" I'm standing in my bedroom in front of my large glass windows, looking over my pack's houses. Daylight has just broken through, painting the sky in beautiful shades of yellow and orange. I haven't slept. There are too many thoughts in my head, making me feel like I'm on a hamster wheel running for my life but going nowhere fast. I feel like I don't have control over my own life, and tomorrow, tomorrow is when I meet the men. Alpha males that I have never met, men that I know nothing about.

The production team insisted that it needed to remain a secret. They need to capture on camera my genuine reactions.

The only one who really knows the identity of these men is my parents. They personally handpicked every one of them, based on whom they felt would be the best match for me.

I sigh, thinking back to the day my father and I fought about this whole situation. I cringe thinking about it. Did I make the wrong choice? Should I have just chosen? I've been telling myself that I don't want or need a mate. I'm an independent woman. I don't need a mate for protection, financially, or emotionally, and I'm not weak. I have worked so hard to pave the way for myself...

"Alpha Princess?" I turn to face Carmen, the production manager, I think that's what her title is, anyway. She's the woman behind the scenes that delegates, navigates, and basically tells me how to live my life for the duration of the show.

I give her a small smile. "Good morning, Carmen. Sorry, I was lost in my thoughts." I sigh, "I didn't sleep—in fact, I don't think I left this very spot since I returned home last evening."

She moves closer to me and awkwardly pats my shoulder. "Well, let's get you to hair and makeup. Then we will get started. We have the entire day to film your interview, take pictures, and showcase you with your parents. Whatever we cannot get through today, if that should happen, we will have tomorrow early morning till about noon to do any catching up. Then we will prepare you for your introduction with the men." I nod and smile, biting my tongue as I follow her out of my suite and to the hair and makeup room.

Two hours later, and with my mother's approval, Carmen gushes, "Aww, Alpha Princess, you look so beautiful!"

"Like I always said, it really does take a team to make me look this good." I deadpan. Carmen doesn't respond to my dry humor. Tough crowd.

Ignoring me, she claps her hands together, "Perfect, now sit here, and we'll get started on that interview. When you speak, look directly at the camera and I will sit here and ask you follow-up questions as we go along. This is Christian, our main cameraman. He will be with you most of the time, catching your every move on film."

Christian looks up from his setup and gives me a warm smile.

I wrinkle my nose at him. "I hope there are limitations, especially when it comes to following me to my bedroom and using the bathroom. I kind of draw the line there."

He chuckles, "Ditto." At least he gets my humor. I look him over quickly; he's not a large guy, slim, just at six feet tall. He has reddish-brown, shaggy hair. As he's looking into the camera, a stray strand falls into his eyes. He has a straight nose, brown eyes, and thick dark lashes. I frown. I could swear I have seen him before.

"Have I met you before?" I ask him.

"Nah, I have one of those faces. I probably remind you of a brother, or next-door neighbor, some guy you ran into at a bar, a random guy you went to school with and never talked to."

I laugh. "Those were some very specific examples."

He shrugs.

"Since you're stuck with me for the next six weeks, please call me Jessica. It's too much calling me Alpha Princess all the time. That goes for you too, Carmen." She doesn't look up from her clipboard. Alrighty then, she is the most focused person I think I have ever met.

"Okay, Jessica, now here is how I want to approach this. Of all the interviews you did promoting the show, my favorite was the *Late-Night Show with Sammy Cane*. I understand you went off-script, but I liked it. You gave the viewers a glimpse of who you are and what they may have a chance to see during the show. You showed them that you're funny, sassy, different, vulnerable, and someone they can relate to or want to be friends with."

I look at Christian. "Are you recording this?" I ask him.

He frowns. "Why do you ask?"

"Oh, I just want my PR guy, Gary, to hear this, so when I tell him he can shove it, I can do it with a big confident smile."

"Jessica, please focus," Carmen says, still looking down at her clipboard. Does this woman ever laugh at jokes? Besides, if you know my PR guy, you would understand where I was coming from. I roll my eyes and scrunch up my face at Christian; he shakes his head and laughs.

"Let's get started. Start with introducing yourself, then tell us how you came to be on this show. Look at the camera when you're speaking. Oh, and if it helps, just remember that the gentlemen will be going through the same type of interview as well." Why would that make me feel better?

I flick my eyes upward before I look back at Carmen.

She isn't paying attention to me. I catch the sight of myself on a set of monitors Carmen is sitting in front of. The start of anxiety starts to creep into me, and my breath catches. The realization that this is really happening hits me. I've been going through the motions of promoting the show, but it didn't feel real until now. I take another breath, trying to calm myself. I can do this. I have to do this…

"Jessica?" Christian questions. "Just look at me when you talk, like we're good friends and we're just hanging out swapping stories."

I nod. "Sorry, I, uh… I think it just sunk in that this is real. I don't usually like being the center of attention, especially when I feel so… exposed. Which is odd, right? Because of what I do for a living. I spend a good deal of my life hiding out in the open, if that makes any sense." I know I'm rambling, but I need to get it out of my system.

"What does that mean? Always hiding out in the open?" Carmen asks. I look over to Christian, and I start to answer her question.

"Have you ever played peekaboo with a little child? After playing with them for a while, you start to realize that, for some reason, that child thinks you can't see them when they have their eyes covered with their tiny little hands. They know you are there, but because they can't see you, they think you can't see them. That's how I hide out in the open. As a music artist, I wear a mask and color my hair, so no one recognizes me. My fans and music manager just chalk it up to being a little eccentric." I give a small laugh and smile at Christian. "Because I think no one can see me, when I am up on that stage, playing music, singing, I feel free. I'm sharing who I really am with thousands of strangers, sharing stories of anger, heartbreak, moving on, and losing loved ones. I get to close my eyes and do something I'm passionate about and love. When I am at work, I wear business clothing and glasses, another mask. I'm a no-nonsense girl, and I can be a force to reckon with. But I love that part of my life too. In my business, it isn't just about making money, it's about helping others to build careers and businesses of their own. Then there's my part with the guards. I've always felt a little more comfortable in that setting. Again, it's all about protecting others, but even then, I have to hide a part of myself just to fit in… Are you familiar with that superhero, uh… Superman? During the day, he pretends to be a nerdy guy with glasses. He's sweet, clumsy, and nervous. Then at night or when there is some kind of disaster, he transforms into Superman with superpowers. His role is to protect those around him and defeat the bad guys. He either hides behind a pair of glasses, or he hides behind his insignia. Did anyone ever stop to ask him what his life would be like if he didn't have to hide? Would he even know? Anyways, I'm still trying to figure out who I am without the different masks. So, sitting here with no mask, no work to hide behind, talking about myself, it's an unnerving experience."

"You're doing fine," Carmen says from her seated position near the monitors. "How about we skip the introduction part for now, and we go right into how you ended up here on the show?"

I let out a breathy laugh, "Oh gosh, that is a loaded question. Uh…Where do I begin?" I look down at my hands, trying to collect my thoughts and find an appropriate answer.

"Just be honest, Jessica. This is the whole point of the

interview. Viewers want to know the real you."

I nod, clear my throat, and look back up at the camera. "Did you ever have one of those dreams where someone flips the channel, and you're in a different one, and it keeps going on and on from one dream to the next like someone has control of a switch? Two weeks ago, to the day, that's kind of how my day started, except I didn't have control over the remote, and I kept finding myself in one situation after another."

"Tell us more about that day," Carmen encourages.

"I could do that. Not sure how much time you have," I say with a laugh.

"Give it a go. We can take breaks in between, and I can guide you along with follow-up questions if need be."

I look between Carmen and Christian. "Okay... The only way to explain how that day went means I have to fill in some details of my life over the past ten years. It might get a little confusing, but if you pay real close attention, it will all make sense eventually, I hope."

# Chapter 8

## WHEN SIBLINGS FIGHT

### JESSICA

#### March 14, 2025: 5 a.m.

"So, this is what it comes down to, huh? After all these years, you three are going to gang up on me?" I say to my brothers—the twins Justin and Jeremy, and Luke—who are slowly circling me. I decided to come down to the basement of our family's mansion, where it had been converted into a gym/training area for an early morning workout. My brothers decided to ambush me here. I take a stance as if I am getting ready for a fight.

"Just tell us where you're hiding it and we'll let you go," Justin says with a sly grin on his face.

"Yeah, no harm, no foul. We get what we want, and you're free to go." I roll my eyes at Jeremy.

I turn to Luke. "And you? What part do you have in this?"

He shrugs. "You know me, anything for a good fight, and I always have my brothers' backs." I cringe inwardly at the sting of his remark. Luke and I have a love-hate relationship; I'm adopted, and he tends to remind me of that with snarky innuendos every chance he gets.

Over the years, I have just come to accept what we are, a complicated train wreck of love and hate, friends, sometimes enemies. So complicated that it sometimes drives pain deep into my heart.

"Just tell us what we want to know, Jessica," Justin says, cutting into my thoughts.

"I am not telling you anything. Besides, I can take the three of you on, so bring it." I motion with my hand for them to attack. Through my peripheral vision, I see Luke's smile widen. Alright, tough guy, I will take you down first and shove your smug smile up your…

Justin dives for me, and Jeremy crouches down in an attempt to sweep my legs out from under me. I jump and turn just in time. Luke comes at me just as I land. Striking out, I block him, grab him by the wrist, and turn sideways, kicking him in the chest and sending him a few feet back.

Jeremy comes at me quickly, but I don't attempt to get out of his line of attack. Instead, I take a few steps toward him. Just as Justin is sneaking up behind me, I surprise both of them as I jump into a spread-eagle, kicking both of them in the chest.

Luke's footsteps coming in toward me hot, I drop to my knees as he is almost on me, and I hit him in the stomach. I rock back on my heels and jab him in the knee, causing him to fall. Rolling into a crouch, I jump to my feet, swiveling around in time as Justin has recovered from my kick. I strike; he blocks. Justin is fast, but I'm faster. I keep striking, and he keeps blocking. Jeremy is on me again. I drop down to take out his legs from under him, but he jumps out before my leg can connect with his.

Tumbling out and away from the twins, I see it! Springing to my feet, I run toward the broom against the wall.

Luke jumps into my path. "No cheating." He tsks.

"Oh, like three-on-one isn't cheating," I sneer at him.

He smiles at me, showing off his dimples, that fucker. I narrow my eyes at him and rush toward him. Gaining momentum, I jump up and twist my body, clearing over his head, landing behind him, my back to his back. I slam my elbow into his kidney. He grunts as his foot thumps the ground stepping forward. I take advantage by landing a back kick to his rear.

I'm impressed with myself that I made that jump. Luke stands at six foot three or more by now. He's broad-shouldered and muscular. His arm reach alone could have pulled me down. Hearing his oomph when I kick him in the ass gives me even more satisfaction that I got him. Feeling a little triumphant, I don't bother to look back. I step into action to get that broom.

I don't get very far. Luke grabs my arm, pulling me around to his front, and holds me up against him. He smiles down at me, again with those ridiculous dimples!

"That was impressive, but I think I got you, just where I want you." Smiling back, I stand on my tiptoes, leaning in to whisper. His eyes widen in surprise as I get nearer.

"I'm immune to the Luke Langhlan charm, so, I think… I got you."

Before he can respond and before the twins get any closer, I jump up, wrap my legs around his waist, and throw myself back. Twisting my body as we fall, I plan to wrench myself out of the hold. Luke surprises me by gripping me tighter and twisting at the same time in the opposite direction. I initially land on him; he takes the impact fully from our fall.

In this position being on top is not a bad thing. I leverage my elbows to disengage his arms, push off his chest, and use my legs to backflip off him, grabbing the broom just in time to hit Jeremy. I strike him in the chest first, then his arms and abdomen. Each strike comes in swift motions; he can't block them in time. At the same time, I'm also blocking Justin's strikes from behind me. I hit both of them so rapidly, it stuns them. In a final swipe of the broom handle, I take Justin's legs out from under him. Wasting no time, Jeremy goes down seconds after.

Stepping out from between them, in case they try to grab my legs, I spin the handle of the broom, smiling jubilantly down at them both. Groaning and clutching at body parts, they make no further movement to get back at me. Pumping my fist in the air with a whoop, I jump up and down, pumping the broom up and down with my other hand.

To my shocking surprise, the broom jerks out of my hand. Luke grabs it midair, tosses it across the room, and dives right for me, pinning me to the ground. Damnit, I took my eyes off the other enemy. Shit!

He yells out to the twins, "Quickly, find whatever it is

you need to find while I have her." I squirm, buck, and try to kick my legs. He maneuvers himself, pinning both of my arms down and holding my legs down with his own. I hear the twins running out of the room, laughing triumphantly.

"Nooo, don't, that isn't for you!" I shout. I narrow my eyes at Luke. "You idiot! I made those brownies for the Whitemore pack."

He laughs. "I hope you made a lot. Those two will probably get through two pans by themselves."

"Ugh, get off me!" I demand, but I know it's pointless since he's twice my size. I don't give up, though. In my pathetic effort, I'm still squirming, bucking, and grumbling.

Luke looks down at me, his expression turning serious. "Can we talk?"

"No, I don't want to talk to you, traitor! I have to stop the twins!" I spit at him. He leans his face down as if he is going to kiss me. My eyes widen. What the hell is he doing? I turn my head.

He whispers in my ear. "Stop doing that. You're turning me on, and I really need to talk to you." What the hell did he just say? He pushes his hips into me, and I can feel his hardening cock. Freezing in place, I keep my head turned, refusing to face him.

"If I let you up, will you stay and talk to me?" he asks.

I nod my head, but I don't intend to stay.

"Jessica," he growls, "this is important to me, please."

I turn my head slowly to look at him. Oh man, with those emerald green eyes, blond hair, and dimples, I can see why women have such a hard time resisting him. Still, there's something about the look on his face that shows he's sincere.

"I can't," I say so softly, it's almost a whisper.

"You can't or you won't?" he asks, searching my eyes as if he can see the answer. He looks like he's torn, and it makes me feel funny, a little regretful and guilty... almost. "When will you be back?" he asks, still looking at me intently.

"I'm not. I plan to head straight to the city after I am done at the Whitemores'. I promised Akiyo I would help her with her show."

He groans. "Jessica, you just got home the night before." Some hair had fallen into my face. He gently tucks it behind my ear. "It's been a long time since you and I have spoken. There are some things I need to say to you. For starters, I owe you an apology." I frown. Where is this coming from and why?

I shake my head. "Luke, I really need to get going. I don't want to be late."

He sighs, "Jessica, you make it so hard to talk. Look... I don't want to fight. I want to make things right between you and me. I want..." He shakes his head. "I want to talk, but I need you to listen first. Can we please meet after the show?"

I shake my head. "I'm not trying to be difficult—I just have obligations, and I promised Akiyo I would stay for the afterparty."

He's still looking down at me intently. His jaw is clenched like he's trying to hold back something, and he closes his eyes as if he's trying to make a decision or calm himself down. I'm not sure which one it is.

"Tomorrow then?" Before I can hesitate or make any more excuses, he leans down and whispers into my ear, "Please, Jess, this is important to me."

He looks so sad suddenly, so I nod and softly say, "Tomorrow." He looks relieved and gives me a small smile. He moves back and helps me get to my feet. Hurriedly, I make my way to the training room door. I need to find the twins before they demolish all the brownies I made.

I'm almost to the door, when I hear Luke. "Jess, I'm sorry if what I said hurt you."

I toss him a glance over my shoulder—what the hell? What is going on with him today? Frowning, I reply, "What are you talking about?"

He hangs his head. "It hurt you when I said that I always have the twins' back." I shake my head, dismissing him before he continues, "You may not think I do, but I will always have your back too."

I'm not sure how to respond to his apology. I want to say something, but it's not nice. I'm still deeply hurt by him, and I don't know if I can ever get over all the things said and done. I take a deep breath. Without any hesitation, I am out the door and looking for the twins.

# CHAPTER 9

## FULL CIRCLE

### JESSICA

March 14, 2025: 7:15 a.m.

The twins got into my brownies, but they were nice this time and left enough behind to take to the Whitemore pack gathering. With brownies in hand, I make my way down to the car waiting for me.

Anders, our family's head guard, is stoically standing next to the car, dressed in his formal guard attire. The deep hunter green of his attire makes his pure-white hair and pale blue eyes stand out. His white hair is such a contrast to his features. He has a young face that I swear would put him in his late forties or early fifties at least. Rumor has it that he's in his eighties. Which I guess could make sense since he has so much experience in his line of work. He has had training worldwide, especially in the Asian territory, in weaponry, hand-to-hand combat, martial arts, and then some. I overheard my parents saying that he was once in the Russian military as a spy. Rumors are rumors until proven otherwise, but from what I witnessed firsthand, I know he's an experienced fighter/guard. Which is what really matters.

I frown at Anders, unsure why he's here. Not that I don't want him to go with me; it's just that I'm sure he has something better to do than escort me to the Whitemore territory. Odyssey, my friend and fellow guard, stands next to Anders. He's also wearing his formal guard attire. Maybe Anders isn't coming with me after all. The driver's door opens, and Ean pops out also dressed in his guard formal uniform.

I shoot Odyssey a questioning look; he keeps his face neutral, not giving anything away. Turning my attention back to Anders, I ask, "Where's Xavier? Is he okay?"

Anders grimaces before he answers, "Xavier is fine. I gave him the day off. I knew you would object to a car escort so the three of us will escort you in the same car to the Whitemore territory."

Am I that difficult to deal with, that he feels he needs to have two top guards including himself to escort me? Odyssey gives me a cheeky grin. Oh he must love this, primarily because he knows I won't argue with Anders. I roll my eyes at Odyssey and hand him the smaller package I'm carrying.

His eyebrows shoot up in surprise, "What's this?" he asks.

"I made those for Xavier to thank him for being stuck with me all day and night. I guess you and Ean will have to share."

He looks a little hesitant before he peers into the bag, and then he frowns. "Are these your famous brownies?" I nod.

"Shit, I have to share with Ean? He'll eat them all before I even get a chance," Odyssey grumbles.

I laugh in response, "Well, I guess it's a good thing he's driving then."

Anders makes a disgruntled sound, shooting me an irritated look, and opens the back passenger door. I take that as my cue to hurry up and get into the car. Without further delay, I slide in. Anders follows in after me. I look over at Anders; the privacy glass is up so we can talk in private.

"Thank you," I tell him, "I hope this isn't too much trouble. I'm sure you have more important things to do than escort me today."

With another grimace, he starts to speak. "I am here for two reasons. One is business, and the other is personal." Personal? I have never really known Anders to do anything personal. He has always been dedicated to his head guard position.

He continues to speak. "I haven't spoken to you for some time, and I wanted an opportunity to, umm…" he clears his throat, "discuss some things." I'm still looking at him. He's not facing me now, so unlike him—he usually likes to keep eye contact. He's also perspiring, even though it's not warm in the car. The air conditioning is on full speed, probably courtesy of Ean, who likes to run it extremely cold because he's always hot.

Anders clears his throat. Did he say something? He's still gazing out the window, and he's still not looking at me.

He lets out a breath, rakes his fingers through his hair, and finally faces me.

"I would like to discuss my personal reasons first before we get into business matters if that will be okay with you?"

I try to keep the look of surprise on my face. Nonchalantly, I respond, "Sure, whichever you feel comfortable with."

Again, another grimace. "I don't particularly like discussing my personal business with anyone, so with that said, it's important to me. I would like to talk first." Important to him? Wait, isn't that what Luke said earlier this morning? He had something important to talk to me about. What is going on with this day?

"Anders, if it makes you uncomfortable, you don't have to talk about your personal business. We can cover business, and you can slide it in somehow when you are ready. It's a two-hour-long drive."

He shakes his head, and he finally makes eye contact. "I'm worried about you. I just wanted to see how you're doing with the passing of Alpha Agnus. You two were quite close, and well, I know you don't handle these things quite well."

I look down at my hands which are on my lap. "Thank you for your consideration, but I'm fine. I was with her the night before it happened." I looked up at Anders, who is watching me intently. "I'm fine, really. I know she was old. It's all a part of that circle of life. She left this world peacefully, she didn't suffer, and she wasn't murdered. I'm not going to run away if that's what you're worried about."

Anders reaches over and places his large hands over mine. I find the warmth of his hand comforting, and I welcome it.

"Speaking of the circle of life," I tell him, "we both have come full circle in this as well." He cocks his head, showing me he is unsure of what I am referring to. I give him a small smile. "Ten years ago, you and I were in a similar car, just like this one, except instead of going to Whitemore territory, we were driving away from it. Driving towards what turned out to be the beginning of my new life."

Anders squeezes my hand. He lifts it, and kisses it with fatherly affection.

# Chapter 10

## Running Blind

### JESSICA

#### May 17, 2014: 9 p.m.

I wake up with a start and bolt straight up in my bed. My vision is hazy, and I can't make out where I am. It smells funny, almost clean, so clean it's sterile. A loud beeping noise pierces my brain, creating a sharp pain in my ears and in my temples. I pull up my hands to cover my ears, but I'm attached to something. I have what feels like tubes and lines attached to my body. I'm scared. My brain is screaming at me that I need to run, I need to get away, I need to be safe.

    I start pulling at everything. I feel liquid starting to pour out from some of the tubes; it doesn't smell like blood, so I keep pulling, removing everything I can find by feel. I can't see clearly. It scares me even more. I'm determined to get away. I need to protect myself. One last tube is attached to the center of my throat, and it's being held in place with a cloth strap. Feeling around my neck, I undo the strap and pull out the device embedded in my throat. I start coughing and choking, and a slimy substance starts to pour out from the gaping hole.

    I want to cry. Who did this to me, and why? Without wasting any time, I slide out of bed. I can hear someone coming. The loud beeping and high shrill piercing noises get louder. It must have alerted someone. I slip into the hall quickly. It's dark, and I can't see anything, but I am not sure I could to begin with. I rely on my instincts and other senses, backing up against the wall, trying to hide in the shadows, and I slide away from the oncoming sounds of footsteps. The footsteps sound hurried like they're running toward an emergency. I find a door against my back, so I open it and slip in. I feel around, and I find a shelf that feels like cloth. I smell laundry detergent. I close my eyes and take a deep breath. Suddenly, I see the room in my mind. The shelves are lined with some kind of clothing, and I realize I feel the cool air against my backside. I'm partially covered. Quickly, I grab a pair of pants and slip them on. They're large on me, so I tie the drawstring at my waist and roll the hem of the pant legs up so I don't trip over them. I tear off the gown that's only covering my front, and I feel another tube attached to my stomach. There's a sticky fluid dripping from the tube. Without hesitation, I rip the tube out from my stomach and instantly feel pain and a burning sensation. It passes quickly. Tossing the tube to the floor along with the long gown I was wearing, I grab a shirt and pull it on. I need to get out of here.

Before I slip back out the door, I hear voices, loud commanding voices. "Find her! She has to be around here somewhere. She's hurt. She couldn't have gone very far!" I hear footsteps in the hall, so I shrink back behind one of the shelves and crouch down.

I can hear myself breathing through the hole in my throat. It's a horrible sound of air rushing in and out mixed with fluid, sort of like a low rattling sound. Gross. I fumble through the items on the shelving, feeling for something close enough to resemble a piece of cloth or napkins on the shelf, and I wipe at the slimy, slick… drool? Eww… I wipe at it again, and I place my hand over the hole to quiet the noises I make when I breathe. Fuck, who did this to me and why? I don't have much time to think it over. I hear the passing of footsteps going down the hall. I tuck the cloth into the waist of my pants and make my way back to the door, slipping back out into the hallway.

I don't know where I am, but I can clearly see the layout of the building in my head. I know exactly where the exit is, so quietly, sticking to the shadows, still holding my hand over the hole in my throat, I make my way toward the exit. On my way over, I walk into a chair. The chair makes a scraping noise. Holding my breath, I stay very still, listening for anyone coming toward the noise. It's quiet, so I start to move forward, trying to avoid the chair in my path, when my bare foot touches something on the floor. I nudge it with my foot again. I must have knocked it off the chair. I am not sure why, but I pick it up, and I can feel that it's a hooded sweatshirt. I put it on immediately. It's huge on me, but I don't care. It's perfect. As I pull up the hood to cover my face, a distinct fragrance assaults my senses. It's a mixture of dirt, grass, and sunshine, paired with a clean-smelling cologne. I can smell subtle hints of bergamot, melon, and cucumber. This may sound a little weird, but the essence of the scent reminds me of a strong male.

For what it's worth, it's comforting, and I instantly feel calmer, stronger. I chuckle to myself. It's like when a superhero puts on their cape. Confidence takes over, and I feel more assured that I can get out of here and to safety.

As stealthily as possible, I make my way out of the building. Once outside, I plaster myself against the wall of the building. My eyes are still closed. Did I not open my eyes this entire time? In my mind I can see my surroundings, which is odd, right? I mentally shake myself; I don't have time to think about it. In my head, I see that there's a road leading to a gate. I just need to get to that gate. Then I can run and follow that road to wherever it may lead. I can't just run out onto the driveway before the building. Someone will definitely find me and haul me back into the lab of doom.

With my free hand, I pull the hood down further to cover my face. Breathing in the scent of the owner of this shirt, instantly, I feel the tension in my muscles ebb away. What the hell is wrong with me? I need to get out of here. He may be one of the men holding me hostage here and doing all of these science experiments on me. Yeah, I know I have a very wild imagination, not sure where it's coming from, though. I'll think about it more later when I find a place to hide and feel safe again.

I start sliding against the wall and round a corner closest

to the road I need to get on. Crunching on gravel comes from the direction I need to head to. Without giving it any thought, I run toward the sound, and I can see the outline of a tall, broad man. He's large on top, so his base stance is a bit wide. I push myself to run harder, and before he can see what's coming, I dive between his legs, using the pull of the slide to get back to my feet and keep running toward the road. Another man comes from the right side running toward me, so I deviate from my path, and I push myself to run faster toward him. He bends low, holding his stance as I get closer as if he's going to grab me.

Using the momentum of the run, I jump up, using my left foot to push off his shoulder, and grab a low-lying tree branch above his head, hurling myself up onto it. I start to grab at the other branch above me to climb higher. Slowly, I inch my way across the branch toward a roof of a building, and I leap forward.

I fall short. "Catch her!" I hear someone shout out as I miss the roof. I shoot out my arm, catching the edge just in time. I grip the roof with my other hand, and I start to swing back and forth. As my body swings closer to the wall, I push against it with both feet, and I flip myself onto the roof. I land with a hard thud on my back. Bringing my legs toward my stomach, I push off with hands on either side of my head, and I land back on my feet. Running along the roof, I start to look for the gate in my mind. I'm closer.

I look off to the side of the building, and the two men I outsmarted and got away from are now running alongside me. I hear shouts from different men. "Block the gate!"

"Lock the gate!"

"Don't hurt her!"

"If she falls, catch her!"

I come to an abrupt stop at the end of the roof, and I almost fall forward. Waving my arms, I bring myself back. I look around and decide I need to get down, so I jump onto the closest man. I catch him off guard, falling to the ground together. Pushing off his back, I land on my feet and run toward the gate.

"Get her!" I hear. "Watch her—she's a tricky one!" There are three men in front of me. One starts to run toward me. He's expecting me to jump up, so he keeps his body upright. How does he know, and how do I know what he is expecting? I fake an attempt to go left, and when I see his body move to the left, I twist and head for the right. Jumping up, I kick one man in the chest. He wasn't expecting that, and neither was I. It was an instinct. As he bends forward to clutch his chest, I plant my other foot on his shoulder, and I grab onto the iron gate. It's locked with chains, so I climb up the gate, swing my leg over, and let go. Landing on my feet, I spare no time to look at my surroundings and run. The vision of my surroundings in my head are gone, but I keep running. Anywhere is better than here, right?

Pushing my legs, ignoring the pain to my feet as I run over tiny pieces of gravel and sticks, I keep moving forward. The squeaking sound of the iron gate startles me, urging me to move faster. Thudding footsteps are following behind me. From the sound of it, there are many of them now. The footfalls are heavier, louder like a stampede of horses coming after me. That could only mean one thing—they shifted. Fear tingles up my spine, and I try to push my legs harder, faster.

If they catch me, they will tear me apart. I hear growling, shouts, and curses in my head. How the hell are they in my head?

My body screams with pain, my lungs burn, but I refuse to give up. Shouting sounds in my head. *"Get around her!"*

*"Cut her off!"*

*"Catch her from the right!"* I veer to my left.

*"How the fuck is she so fast!"*

*"Shut the fuck up and get her!"*

*"We are all going to have our asses if something happens to her!"* Growls and snarls penetrate through my mind, and I sense their determination.

I squeeze my eyes shut. I have no idea what is in front of me. I feel tall grass brushing against my body. Focusing on the voices in my head, I do the opposite of everything that they attempt to do. The harder I focus on their voices, a vision of a wide-open space opens up in my mind. Hope fills my chest.

Until I trip over something on the ground. Falling forward, I quickly scramble to my feet and keep running. That little trip cost me. I can feel the wolves after me, getting closer. How do I know they're wolves? I shake my head with my thought; I just know that I need to get away. They're going to hurt me, maybe kill me.

Fatigue threatens to sink into my muscles, and I'm not sure how much longer I can keep this up. My feet burn, and I can only imagine they are bleeding at this point.

*"Cut her off from the left–don't let her get any further away!"* I take that moment to run straight ahead, and then as I hear them get closer, I head to the right. They're getting closer.

My heart pounds harder from equal parts exertion and fear.

My feet hit dirt, then gravel, and before I can focus on that vision of my surroundings, I hit a wall. A literal wall. On impact, I fall backwards and land on my back. Shit, a sickening cold feeling creeps up my spine. I'm so fucked. I scramble to my feet, trying hard to hold back the threatening panic. I put my arms out to feel what is in front of me.

An image pops into my head, an image of a house covered by overgrown weeds and vines. Gliding my hand along the wall, I make my way around it. I sense the wolves getting closer. I try to get around it faster, I trip and fall over bushes and whatever else in my path. I find a window covered in boards. I grip a board and try to pry it off with my fingers, but it doesn't budge.

I try again, using my leg as an anchor against the wall to give me more strength. After a few tries, the board gives, a loud crack echoes in the night air, and yet again, I fall backward, landing on my ass with a hard thud.

"*Find her–she has to be here!*" I scramble back up to my feet, grip the windowsill, and squeeze between the opening I created. Falling into a room with a loud crash, I quickly drag my body back, hiding in the room's shadow.

I can hear the gurgled, raspy sounds of my breath. I find the cloth on the waist of my pants. I'm surprised it's still here. I wipe up the disgusting body fluid coming down my neck and cover the hole. Slowly, I crawl my way to the door. Stopping to listen for the men and wolves chasing after me, all I can hear is the rapid beating of my heart.

I open the door slowly, praying it won't make a noise, and head down the hall. I still can't see anything. I'm not sure if I am going in the right direction. It just feels right. In my mind, I see a kitchen up ahead. It doesn't take long to find myself in it. My tongue is sticking to the roof of my mouth. I'm so thirsty and desperately need to drink some water. Feeling my way around, something cool brushes my fingertips followed by the tangy smell of metal. Slowly, I pat around and realize it's a sink and feel for the faucet. Sickly wet air escapes the hole in my throat as I sigh with instant gratification. I wash my face, and I start to drink the cool water.

Immediately, I start choking. Water spews from the hole in my throat. I slide down the cabinet to the floor, trying to catch my breath between coughing fits. Finally, after what feels like forever, I'm able to take a deep breath. I right myself and stand back up at the sink, trying to clean myself up as best as I can. My mouth is still dry, so instead of drinking the water, I rinse my mouth out.

The haunting sound of wolves howling forces me to crouch back down. I cover my head with my hands as the growling and panicked shouts ring through my head. They're all shouting simultaneously, and it's hard to decipher what is being said. I crab-crawl back away from the sink in case they decide to look through the kitchen window. My back hits a solid wall, and I slide my hands up to inspect it. When I realize it's a door, I quickly pull it open, just enough to slide my body inside, and gently close it behind me. I can feel the darkness on my skin. The smell of cardboard boxes and the metallic scent of aluminum cans fill the stale air.

I cringe when I realize I'm in a pantry, a dead end. They're going to find me. When they do, I'm dead. I'm so dead. I slide back away from the door into a corner, pulling my hood further down my forehead as if it could hide me or make me invisible. I no longer hear the overwhelming shouting and growling in my head. With my ears, I hear muffled talking. I can't make out what is being said. But I know they're coming for me. I don't know how long it will be before then. Shifting quietly, I wrap my arms around my knees and rest my forehead on my arms. I stay there for a long time, waiting for someone to find me, waiting to be caught.

# Chapter 11

## MAKING FRIENDS

### JESSICA

May 18, 2014: 8 a.m.

The wolves are chasing me. I hear their jaws snapping, the low growls emanating from their chests. I look down at my arms. They're bleeding from deep, long wounds along my inner forearms. Pain infiltrates every fiber of my being. My lungs are burning, and my heart feels like it will explode in my chest, but I must keep running. I can't let them catch me. They will kill me. I feel the tug of something stiff around my neck. I'm falling backward. A rope, I have a rope around my neck, and I am being dragged backward. I claw at my neck to get my fingers under the rope. I can't breathe. I throw myself forward, hitting my head… on a shelf?

I feel around me, definitely a shelf. It takes me a moment

to recall where I am. I must have fallen asleep while waiting for my capturers to find me. I'm no longer in a curled-up sitting position and have a blanket over me. Rubbing my forehead, I slide down and sit up, avoiding hitting my head again.

I reach up and feel around my neck. There is no rope. I pull up the sleeves of my hoodie; there are no gaping wounds, and there is no blood. I don't smell blood on me either. The rough texture of my arm tells me that there were wounds there. I'm a little confused; then I remember the hole in my throat and feel for it. Yep, it's still there. The front of my sweatshirt is wet, gross... I feel around and find the cloth, and I wipe my neck and cover the hole with my hand. It's disgusting.

I bring myself up to my feet—where did the blanket come from? I look around, and it dawns on me that I can't see. Everything is a blur of shadows and light. If I can't see, how did I get here? How did I run last night? How did I get away from those men chasing after me?

I feel panic start to rise from my chest. I can hear my heartbeat speeding up. I press harder against the hole in my throat, trying to quiet the sound of my rapid breathing. I smell him, the owner of this sweatshirt. I grab the front of it and bring it to my nose. I instantly calm down. His scent makes me feel safe. I drop the fabric between my fingers and feel a blush take over. Gods, I'm a mess. I'm swooning over a guy I never met. Shit, he could be one of the men trying to hurt me. I rub my face with my free hand.

Then I hear a voice. *"Well, are you going to come out, or are you going to stand in there all day, talking to yourself?"*

I stiffen. *First of all, I am not talking to myself. I'm thinking. Secondly, the door is closed. How do they know I'm standing?* Tentatively, I take a few steps forward. Stretching out my arm, I feel for the door and push it open. Light fills the kitchen. It's daytime. I'm not sure what part of the day it is.

"*Well, aren't you a smartass?*" the voice says, breaking through my thoughts. I try to look around to see where the voice is coming from and who it is coming from. I can't see, remember? Shit, but I don't hear the voice either. That doesn't make sense. I rub my face and laugh to myself. I know what this is, I'm actually dead. Or am I still dreaming? This has to be a dream—a literal nightmare—because I have a gaping hole in my throat, and my bodily fluids are draining down my neck. In my head, I picture myself gagging, and I inwardly cringe as I hear myself breathe again.

I hear a chuckle. Correction, I hear the chuckle inside my head. "*You're not dead, and you are definitely not dreaming. Now come closer so I can look at you. My eyes are not what they used to be.*"

I hesitate and turn my head, trying to see if I can recognize a shape or an outline. I can see a little more through my left eye if I turn my head to the right.

In front of me, several feet away, I see a long table with several chairs and someone sitting at the end. The outline of the person's shoulder shows it's slightly hunched forward. A strange light surrounds the outline in an almost ethereal way, and fluffy hair sits on their head. The surrounding glow makes it look like a halo.

Tentatively, I step forward. "*Well, hurry it up. I am not getting any younger.*" The voice is in my head again. Am I deaf too?

A laugh. *"Not deaf, dear, but maybe a little daft."* Daft? I now recognize the voice to belong to a woman, maybe a slightly older woman. I was just called daft, as in stupid. Keeping my head to the right, I quicken my steps to approach the person sitting in the chair at the table.

*"No, daft as in silly, wiseass."* I keep moving forward, a little perplexed with what is going on. How is this happening? I must have miscalculated my steps because before I know it, I collide with a person. Shit! What the hell? I try to speak, but air gushes out from the hole in my throat. Before I can move my head back into place so that I can see, hands grab my chin, and with a firm grip, my head is being moved from side to side.

"What you must have been through to get here," the woman says. "Now, take a deep breath and visualize your surroundings with your mind, as you have done before."

Visualize my surroundings with my mind?

"Be quick about it. There isn't much time." I don't know how I "visualized" my surroundings in the first place. Why is this woman so convinced that I can?

"Because you can. Now, stop overthinking and do it." Do what? Huh, maybe I escaped from a nuthouse. Or I escaped into a nuthouse. Or maybe I… Something hits my arm, then another hit to my other arm. Whack, a hit to my leg comes next. Irritated, I take a deep breath, and the room comes into sight with a little old lady in front of me holding a cane. Her arm is extended out to the side, and she is attempting to hit me again. This time, I grab the cane from her hand before it hits me in the other leg.

"About damn time. Now sit and have some tea." Frowning at the old woman, I move to sit in the chair she's pointing at. She returns to her seat and scoots the chair a little forward. She's not much taller than I am, has all-white curly hair, and is wearing a tracksuit in an aquamarine color. I place her cane near her, so she can reach it when she is ready to stand back up. As an afterthought, I move the cane to the other side of me in case she decides to use it again to hit me.

*"You don't miss much, now do you?"* she laughs. Miss much? She doesn't answer me physically anyway because her mouth doesn't move, and her voice reaches inside my head as she sips her tea. *"Not only are you a wiseass, but you're also quite observant, and you catch on to things quickly. When... you don't overthink so much."* Still frowning, I look down at the cup of tea sitting in front of me. I can't drink that. I think back to my choking episode when I tried to drink water from the faucet last night.

*"Try again. You might be a little surprised."* How is she inside my head? I obviously can't talk with this stupid hole in my throat, and yet she's holding a conversation with me inside my head. I rub my forehead. I must be a ghost or maybe a zombie. I'm a walking dead carcass. That would make more sense. Hole in my throat, I can't see. I start patting myself down to feel my body, and I feel a pinch on my thigh. Ouch! Seriously! I start to rub my thigh.

*"Not a zombie, after all."* Another laugh comes from the old lady in my head. *"And... I am not inside of your head; you're inside of mine. Drink your tea."* Still rubbing at my thigh, that hurt, I grumble to myself. Grimacing down at the cup of tea again, gingerly picking it up as if it's full of poison, I raise an

eyebrow. This isn't going to be pretty. As I bring the teacup to my lips, I think, *Can't say I didn't warn you.*

I take a small sip. Expectantly, I wait for the choking and coughing to start, but nothing happens. I pull the cloth I had earlier from my sweatshirt pocket and wipe at the hole. No warm liquid is pouring out. The hole is still there. I can hear myself breathing. I place the cloth back into my pocket, and I feel the hole with my hand. It's still there, although it's not as big as it felt like it was earlier. I wipe my hand down my pants leg and pick up the teacup, taking another sip. No coughing, no choking.

"*I don't like that you refer to me as an old lady.*" I glance over at her. *Sorry, I didn't think you could hear my thoughts.*

"*My name is Agnus, or you can call me Aggie. You're on my territory.*" I'm on her territory. I have to think about that for a minute, trying to remember exactly how I got here. I don't even know where I am or where I came from. I try to think harder. I don't know where I'm from. I can't pull up memories from my life before waking up as some kind of science experiment. My hands start to tremble, so I set the teacup down in front of me. Agnus reaches over and touches my hand. "Do you at least know your name?" Staring down at my teacup, I try really hard to think about it, but nothing comes up. I don't know who I am.

"Finish your tea. It might come back to you." She pats my hand.

Finishing my tea, I'm surprised that no choking episodes or tea is dripping from the hole. Physically, it's impossible. So was running away from a large pack of wolves last night. I think I'm blind. I set the cup back down. So many questions whirl around in my head.

Agnus grabs my teacup, peers into it, and slowly moves it around. *"Interesting,"* I turn my head to look at her, my vision blurring and refocusing like a camera. Her brows furrow like she's trying to solve a puzzle. She stares intently into the teacup, humming to herself, jotting down notes in a notebook next to her. What is she doing?

*"I'm reading your tea leaves,"* she answers me. Still studying my teacup, she doesn't say anything for a long time, just jots down notes. Then she places her pen down and closes her notebook. Reaching over, she grabs my hand, giving it a reassuring squeeze.

"All will be well, my dear. Now, the bathroom is down the hall. Wash up, and we will take a walk when you're all done." She looks down at my feet, "No shoes? You ran all the way here with no shoes?"

I shrug in response and head down the hall.

*"In the room, three doors down from the bathroom, is my Marisol's room. She might have a pair she left behind in the closet. Have a look before you come out. Then meet me on the porch."* After fumbling and bumbling my way through cleaning myself up, I realize how much we take the gift of vision for granted.

I then head to the bedroom Agnus pointed out. I close my eyes, allowing the vision of the room to enter my mind. It's a little girl's room, although it looks a little unused. I walk over to the windows, which are boarded up. I can see the missing board I had pulled out earlier. In the closet, a line of shoes caked with dust sit on a shelf. A worn pair of Converse tennis shoes catch my eye. I grab them, dust them off, and try them on. They fit perfectly. Smiling, I wiggle my toes and then head out the door and onto the porch to meet Agnus.

"Alpha Agnus, is everything okay?" An elderly man with salt-and-pepper hair, tall and lanky, approaches the front porch.

"Yes, everything is fine, Miller. I am just taking my friend on a walk around the territory."

"Your friend, Alpha?" he replies.

"Are you questioning who my friends are?" She places her hands on her hips. One side of my mouth ticks up in a smirk. At that moment she appears intimidating, and the man actually winces in response.

"Uh, no, Alpha, it's just, uh." He clears his throat. "You, uh, don't like people, uh, or have very many friends."

She laughs at him and pats his arm. "Yes, yes, well, I like this little one. Which says a lot, doesn't it." She looks over at me and winks.

Miller holds out his hand and introduces himself. "I'm Miller, Alpha Agnus's right-hand man." I wipe my hands on my pant leg and shake it.

I try to say something, but a breathy squeak is all that manages to come out of my mouth.

Agnus pats my arm, and she tells Miller, "She's a little shy. Why don't you come with us and give her a tour of the place?" Embarrassed at myself and the state I'm in, I dip my head and try to cover the gaping hole in my throat. I pull my hand back; he grips my hand tightly in his. His eyes narrow as he scrutinizes me, suspicion clear on his face. I don't blame him. I'm a child that basically showed up out of nowhere.

"Does your friend have a name?"

"Of course she does, Miller," Agnus tsks.

"It's Jessica." She says it so fast and with ease like it's true.

His eyes widen at first, but he recovers quickly, masking his features. He looks me over one last time before releasing my hand. He nods his head and says, "Very nice to meet you, Jessica."

I give him a tight-lipped smile and nod back. He offers Agnus a hand to help her down from the porch.

"Your little friend Jessica wouldn't have been responsible for all that racket last night, would she?"

Agnus stops in her tracks. "Why, Miller, are you being rude to my guest?"

"Uh, no, Alpha, it's just... Well... I... I'm just looking out for you, Alpha, and the pack of course." She swats his arm.

"Just shut your ass and take us on that tour!"

I cover my mouth and try to hide my giggle behind my hand. Miller gives me a side-eyed glance. She's a feisty old woman; then again, I guess you would need to be as an Alpha. Huh, I wonder why she never introduced herself as Alpha when she told me her name.

Both Miller and Alpha Agnus show me their little pack community—their homes, the small school, even the tea plantation. Whitemore pack is known for its white tea. According to Alpha Agnus, the secret is their water source. It is believed that the Quartz Lake's water in the back of the plantation has healing properties. The water is siphoned from the lake and used as a water supply to the plantation as well as the pack's water use.

At the end of the tour, they show me the Quartz Lake. Alpha Agnus points to the other side of the lake and says, "Beyond the lake is the seventh territory. Are you familiar with the history of the seventh territory?"

I nod my head. As she stares out across the lake, there is something about the look on her face that makes me feel sad, wistful even.

Without facing me, she says, "Good, it's important that you learn where you came from. It's important to learn the struggles and the sacrifices the generations before you made so that you can have the life that you live in now and in the future."

She's speaking so low, that it's almost impossible to hear. But I hear her, and I know deep in my heart that she isn't just talking about history in general. She is speaking of something completely near and dear to her heart. I move forward so I can see her face a little more, and I catch the slight shine of unshed tears. She blinks a few times as if pulling herself out of a memory.

"You should sit and rest over by the lake. Maybe even take your shoes off and dip your feet. When you're ready, return to the house and you can work on making my lunch."

I almost nod my head in agreement; then I pause, cocking my head in her direction. What makes her think I know how to cook is beyond me, but I shrug and stare back out at the lake.

"You better figure it out. I missed breakfast this morning."

I shake my head, and a wheezy, fluid-filled laugh escapes from the hole in my throat.

# Chapter 12

## QUARTZ LAKE

### JESSICA
May 18, 2014: 11 a.m.

Removing my shoes, I sit near the lake's edge, dipping my feet in the cool water. Peering out over the other side of the lake, I start to think about the seventh territory. It's a large area of unused land. It is so vast that it is said to be one of the most extensive territories compared to even the six significant territories of the Luna Solar realm, which has become known as the LS territory. The seventh territory was once known as the habitat of the white wolf shifter species. The history books state that the great war took place almost 200 years ago; the war started because of greed over land and power.

So many innocent shifters died, and, in the end, it

resulted in the extinction of the white wolf shifter species. No one has gained control over the seventh territory since the war. Over the years, so many Alphas have tried to lay claim to this territory, but the land has been protected by the Alpha King. Under a royal decree, the seventh territory will remain vacant until the rightful owner returns. It is said that only the Alpha King knows the valid owner of this land. It is a name that has been passed from Alpha King to Alpha King. Because of this secret and the greed of others, there is a rumor that a small group of shifters known as the Resistance plan to start another war and take over the monarchy and the seventh territory.

It's a rumor, but nowadays, you can never tell. Greed is a potent evil.

As I ponder over the recollection of this memory. I frown at the clear water before me. How is it that I can remember all of that, and yet I can't remember my life before I woke up yesterday in that strange place with all of those weird tubes stuck in my body? I rub my eyes with the heel of my palms. Resting my elbows on my knees. I feel exhausted, confused, and scared. What will happen to me now? I can't remember my age or where I came from. I don't even know my real name, especially my last name. Will I end up in an orphanage if no one claims me? Do I want to be claimed? I think about the gaping hole in my throat, and I listen to the harsh wet sound of my breathing.

The more I kept thinking about my predicament, the more questions pop up into my head. What have I done to deserve this? Am I a bad person? Did I do something wrong? The thoughts are endless; the questions I have are numerous.

I feel so alone, helpless, lost even. As the overwhelming sensations start to build in my chest and the threat of tears builds behind my eyes, I hear a soft rustle coming from across the lake. I drop my hands from my face and peer out over the lake.

Gasping in shock, my hand instinctively flying up to my throat, my body freezes. Directly across from me, sitting on the opposite side of the lake's edge, is a white wolf.

I don't move, afraid to scare her away. I'm not sure why I think it's a female, but something in my gut tells me it's a she. I cock my head to the side, analyzing the beautiful being. The wolf does the same. I turned my head to the right, making sure I'm seeing this clearly with my own eyes and that it's not some weird made-up vision in my head. My vision blurs, blinking and readjusting until it comes into focus. The wolf is right there, head turned in the same direction as mine. I lift my hand to rub at my face; the wolf lifts her paw. She mimics my every move.

I close my eyes, convincing myself that I'm hallucinating. Without moving my head, I open my eyes and glance down into the lake's clear water. Seeing the reflection of my hooded face, I glance over to see the white wolf's reflection there as well. A ripple in the smooth water distorts the reflection of the wolf. As it settles, the wolf is no longer alone.

I lean slightly forward to take a better look. In the reflection of the water, on either side of her, stand four other wolves. On her left sits a golden-haired wolf, fur as bright and warm-looking as the sun, emerald green eyes staring back at me. He reminds me of an empty field of lush grass bathing in the warmth of the golden sun. He makes me feel happy and safe. Eyes caress me, almost like a touch on my skin.

A chestnut brown-haired wolf with deep amber eyes that glow almost orange sits next to him. As he stares back at me, his eyes change from amber to purple, to red, then black before returning to their original, amber color. I could have sworn that his fur changed colors like his eyes, reminding me of a chameleon. It's almost as if there's an invisible barrier standing between he and I. Despite the barrier, his eyes convey a fierce protectiveness.

To the right of the white wolf, who is still mimicking my every move, sits a copper-haired wolf, fur glowing like flames in the sun. His intense steely grey eyes hold contact with my own. A calming feeling settles over me, and this intense urge to want to run my fingers through his fur hits me. I am filled with the insane notion that he would burn the world down just for me.

Movement from the black wolf catches my eye. Shifting my attention over to him. I study him. His fur is so black it's almost blue, and his dark blue eyes are intense. He exudes a menacing, dangerous energy around him, and an intense seriousness that supersedes the other wolves. I run my eyes down the front of his body, landing on the shadows beneath his paws. In my peripheral vision, the wolf moves his head, the shadow lagging behind in movement just a fragment of a second. I glance back up at the wolf's head. I could swear as his head moves back to face me, a blur of an image of a second head catches up behind, similar to what I had seen in his shadow. I look back into his eyes, and I'm shocked to see a lighter blue color in its place. Even his energy has changed to a much lighter one, not as dominatingly menacing or dangerous, but still just as intense. Almost as if he has two souls trapped in one body. I should feel scared of him, but I'm not. His stare bores into me; a feeling of confidence and self-assuredness fills my soul.

I look back over the reflection of all five wolves. The feelings of love, security, and strength flow between all of them. It forms a protective bond around them. I glance up away from the reflection. I want to see their physical forms sitting at the edge of the lake, but there is nothing there except for empty space and the view of the seventh territory. I drop my gaze back down to the lake, and the reflection of the wolves is no longer there.

Lost in astonishment, I stopped paying attention to my surroundings. I freeze. A low growl rumbles against my ear, and hot moist air brushes along my cheek. A horrible stench of rotten meat reaches my nose. Another low growl, and hot air whispers against my skin.

Not sure why I do it, slowly, I turn my head to look, and all I see are teeth. Moving as slowly as possible, I pull back, so I can move or roll out of the vicinity of a very angry-looking wolf's face. It's not any of the wolves I had seen in the reflection of the lake just a few minutes ago. It's a strange and ugly-looking wolf with two colors, half dull brown and half gray, a deep jagged scar along his muzzle.

Before I can pull away completely, the wolf growls and lurches forward to attack. I raise my arms up to protect myself, falling backward into the lake. I stand up, sputtering in waist-high water, looking frantically around for the bicolored wolf. There is nothing there. I wipe water from my face, rub my eyes, still sputtering, half choking, choking from the water that had gotten into my lungs through the hole in my throat, I look around again. There are no wolves anywhere in sight. I squeeze my eyes shut, wipe my face again, and exhale. I scold myself for daydreaming, forcing myself to get out of the water before I drown. I take another look around me before I move. In the distance, just before the trees beyond the lake, I catch a glimpse of a white wolf running toward the trees into the seventh territory. Wiping my eyes again, making sure that I'm not dreaming this time, although my eyes are not the greatest, this time I am sure of what I saw.

# Chapter 13

## A GIFT FROM A LITTLE FRIEND

### JESSICA

#### March 31, 2025: Present Day

Carmen raises her hand holding a pen, stopping me from continuing. "Was that a vision?" she asks.

"I'm not sure what that was exactly," I say with a slight laugh. "I was practically blind at the time, still recovering from injuries. It could have been a hallucination or, like I said, a daydream," I say with a shrug.

"Hmm..." Carmen says, tapping her pen on the clipboard on her lap. "I've done a lot of interviews in my career, and sometimes when someone wakes up from a near-death experience, they claim to have seen the other side or dreamed of angels or loved ones that passed. But I have never come across anyone who has had awakened visions. This will be the first one for me."

I laugh. "Is that a thing?"

She shrugs and starts making notes on her clipboard.

No one has ever described what I had seen that day as an awakened vision before. Then again, I've not told anyone about that experience except Alpha Agnus. "I told Alpha Agnus about what I had seen, sometime later. She thought it had to do with the Quartz Lake, giving me a peek of what's to come. I honestly forgot about it until just now."

"So, what made you think about it?" Christian asks from behind the camera.

"It's silly actually." I dip my chin, and I can feel a blush begin on my cheeks.

"You would be surprised what's considered silly in our line of business," Carmen says without looking up from her notetaking.

I reach into my pocket, and I take out a folded paper. I open it and stare down at a drawing that my new little friend had given to me that day of my interview with Sammy Cane. He drew five wolves sitting near a lake.

Unlike my vision, where the wolves sat behind the lake, his drawing places them in front of the lake, a messy glob of blue behind them. He draws every wolf in the exact order I had seen them. Bright yellow for the golden wolf with green eyes. The chestnut brown wolf with two different-colored eyes, different-colored legs, and a circle around him. The red wolf looks like he is on fire, and even the black wolf has two heads. The white wolf with sky-blue eyes sits between the four wolves in his interpretation. She is much larger than the other wolves. On the corner of the paper, he even has the ugly-looking wolf with a scar on its muzzle, half gray, half brown, snarling.

I lift up the paper and show it to them. Christian zooms in on the drawing. "I made a new little friend last week, and before he left with his nanny, he gave me this. His nanny said he's been drawing wolves since he could hold a crayon. But she's never seen him draw a group of them with so much detail before."

Christian motions with his hand, and I lean forward and hand the paper to him. "Amazing detail for a little kid. How old is he?" His eyes skim over the drawing.

"Maybe five, judging from his size."

Carmen hums as she looks over Christian's shoulder at the picture. "Did you get his name, by any chance?"

"Yeah, his name is Jackson, cute kid, smart, kind of reminded me of an old man based on his mannerisms and the way he spoke."

Carmen hums again and taps her finger on the arm of the chair. "What's this?" She points to something in the upper corner.

Christian shrugs. "If I had to guess, it looks like two angels, one with black hair and one with white." He looks up at me and smiles. "The one with the white hair looks like she's carrying a candy cane."

"Obviously, the one with the cane is your Alpha Agnus, but who could the one be with the dark hair?" Carmen asks while eyeing the drawing.

I frown. I've stared at that picture so many times; I never saw angels in the drawing. Christian turns the paper around, facing it to me. Sure enough, in the upper corner are two figures with wings. It's so small. That had to be the reason why I missed it.

Christian hands me back the picture, and I look at it one more time. "Emily, she died a few years ago." I trace a finger over the tiny angels. "She was my best friend and just as important to me as Alpha Angus."

I blink back the tears threatening to spill and clear my throat. "I guess this could only mean one of two things. I either made up the whole story in my head after seeing this, or it's confirmation that what I saw really happened."

Christian winks at me. "My instincts tell me it's the latter."

I nod as I carefully fold the paper and place it back into my pocket.

Carmen eases back into her chair, clasping her hands together and resting them in her lap. "Okay, so let's take it back to what happened two weeks ago, the reason for you being here."

# Chapter 14

## THE FUNERAL

### JESSICA

March 14, 2025: 9:05 a.m.

"You've grown quiet. What are you thinking about?" Anders asks, pulling me out of my thoughts of when I first met Alpha Agnus.

I let out a sigh. "I was just thinking about the first time I met Alpha Agnus." I shake my head. "I was so upset with her when you showed up to pick me up. I felt like she ratted me out."

He let out a laugh. "We chased you all the way from the clinic that night. You definitely gave those guards a run for their money, including me." He chuckles and smiles at me. "After running around for a bit, searching for you, I finally decided to knock on her door to let her know we were looking for you, but she was already on the porch. Said that she dreamed about you and wanted to get to know you a little more, to come back tomorrow evening after dinner. I tried to protest, but she wouldn't have it. I wouldn't back down either so I told her I would return under the Alpha King's orders. She basically flipped me off and slammed the door in my face."

I laugh, "Sounds like something she would do."

He shakes his head. "I'm not sure why, but that entire day turned into shit, and we couldn't come to get you until that time anyway. When I returned, she told me that your name was Jessica and that I needed to raise you with the guards, that I was to bring you back regularly so she could spend time with you. She said that the two of you had become friends and she liked your company." He raises his eyebrows, "I thought she was losing her mind. Then she said something like, 'Don't repeat the same choices of others. History doesn't have to be something that we only learn from history books, but something we also need to learn from those closest to us.' With that said, I brought you back to the clinic as I was ordered to do and had a long discussion with the Alpha King about what we were going to do with you."

I frown. "What did she mean by that?" I ask him.

He lets out a long breath. "I didn't know at first, but then I realized what she was talking about… much later." He falls silent again and turns his head to look back out the window.

I have no idea where to turn the conversation, or if I even should. Why is he acting so odd today? So, I clear my throat, gaining Anders's attention. "She always played by her own rules—I mean her own funeral is by invitation only."

I shrug.

He smiled. "I know. I was invited. I think I would have been insulted if my own grandmother didn't invite me to her funeral."

My head whips up to look at him fully now. "Grandmother?"

He hangs his head down and nods.

Anders doesn't have time to explain any further. We are pulling into the Whitemore territory. My head is still whirling with confusion and, well, plain curiosity. Getting out of the car, Anders instructs both Ean and Odyssey to stand guard at the hall's main entrance.

Miller greets both of us. "I think we're ready to get started. You are the last of the invitees to arrive."

I smile sheepishly. Miller smiles at me knowingly. I hand the packages with the brownies over to Miller. "As requested."

He opens the package and smiles. "Oh yes, this was her favorite, mine as well." He reaches forward and touches my shoulder. "I remember the first time you made these. It was the first time we all met you."

I nod a little wistfully. "It became a tradition that I made these for dinner every time I came here after that."

Nodding solemnly in agreement, he hoarsely whispers, "A great tradition, one I will always treasure."

Sissy comes up next to Miller. "Jessica." She hugs me, grabs both of my hands, and gently squeezes. "Come. Alpha Agnus requested that both you and Anders sit up front opposite Marisol, Morgan, and Peter."

I look at Anders, and he just nods. It would make sense that Anders sit in the front, now that I know Alpha Agnus was his grandmother, but me, I'm just a friend. Ander gives me one of his warning looks, so I don't say anything and allow Sissy to guide us to the front. I walk over to Marisol to give my condolences.

She warmly gives me a hug. "Thank you." Not sure of what I should say next, I reach down and gently squeeze her hand.

Morgan and Peter both come up on either side of me. Peter pats my back, and Morgan gives my arm a squeeze.

"Our Aggie loved you so much," Peter says.

"I loved her too. She was like a grandmother to me. I have a lot to thank her for. She was a large part of my life. I am who I am partly because of her influence. I hope you all know how much she loved all of you. She talked about you all so much. If I didn't know any better, I would have never known you were her stepchildren. She always thought of you as if you were her own."

Marisol dabs away the tears that started. With a hoarse voice, she says, "I always thought of her as if she were my own mother too." Peter and Morgan just nod in agreement. I don't miss the tears forming in Peter's eyes. Peter, the youngest of the three, spent the most time with Alpha Agnus growing up.

Miller approaches and whispers, "Shall we get started?" Marisol nods, and I take it as my cue to take my seat next to Anders.

The funeral procession is exactly as Alpha Agnus planned—short and to the point.

When the funeral ends, Miller clears his throat. "She requested that all five of you be present for the reading of her will."

He looked at everyone, and we all nod one by one. Of the three stepchildren, no one says anything about Anders being present. Do they know? We follow Miller back to Alpha Agnus's home and take a seat in her office. Miller takes a seat behind Aggie's office desk, clears his throat again as he lifts the documents up to read them aloud.

"As the direct female descendant of Alpha Agnus Whitemore, Princes Jessica Langhlan will succeed me as Alpha of the Whitemore pack, and as the Alpha, she will be heading Whitemore and Parker Corporation as CEO."

I feel the blood drain from my face and a tightening in my throat. I start to shake my head in protest before I can get any words out. Miller holds up his hand indicating he isn't finished reading.

"I am reading verbatim from Alpha Agnus's will." He takes a deep breath. "Jessica, I can see you starting to protest after that information. Don't overthink this. Despite your feelings that you are not competent, capable, or worthy, you are the next Alpha. I have read your tea leaves many times over the years. I have spent time with you, and I have in my own way prepared you for this role. This is your divine path. Miller will provide you with the appropriate documents for the plantation business, including my notebook. Morgan and Peter will provide you with all of the accounts and legal paperwork of the corporation. Take a deep breath, Jessica. Everything will work out in the end."

Miller hands over the worn notebook to me and scans over the paper before he continues. He looks over at Anders.

"Well, uh...there are a couple more things you need to know." Anders, standing directly behind me, places a warm hand on my shoulder and squeezes. Miller swallows. "I think that you are aware that the Whitemore plantation borders the entrance of the seventh territory. What you are not aware of is that Alpha Agnus is the title owner of the seventh territory. She has been protected for many years through the royal decree that her mother before her had set up with the Alpha King at that time. Now that Alpha Agnus has passed, the royal decree does not protect you as her successor."

Miller holds eye contact with me, letting the information sink in; then he continues.

"Not only are you the Alpha of Whitemore pack and CEO of her company, but you are also the landowner and ruler of the seventh territory, also known as Quartz territory. Because of the LS laws in regard to female Alphas, you must be mated before your twenty-fifth birthday in order to keep your position as Alpha of the seventh territory."

I stare blankly at Miller. I'm trying to process everything in my brain.

Miller takes in a deep breath and looks at me again. "In other words, to keep the pack and the territory protected and to prevent a direct challenge for your position, it is required that you are to be mated before your next birthday." The room remains silent. My birthday is in less than eight weeks.

I squeeze my eyes shut; my hands are starting to shake. I can feel the fucking panic begin to take over, rising from my chest. Tears are starting to well up behind my eyelids. I can't do this. I don't care what she thinks—I wasn't prepared for this role. And mated! I have to be mated! I can't...

Anders's warm hand still on my shoulder tightens again in a gentle squeeze. "Jessica, breathe." Taking in a shuddering deep breath, I open my eyes and look up at Anders. I start to shake my head. I look over to Morgan, Peter, and Marisol. "Why me? This isn't right—I think she made a mistake," I whisper.

"She's been preparing you to take on this role as Alpha and CEO of the corporation since you met her," Marisol says with an earnest smile.

Miller, who is sitting at Alpha Agnus's desk, nods his head in agreement. He didn't even like me when we first met. Why is he agreeing to this?

"I'm sure you have many questions. We are here for you, and we will help you, but Alpha Agnus has foreseen that you wouldn't need much of our help as you settle into your role and become mated."

There are more encouraging statements from both Peter and Morgan, but they fall on deaf ears because of all the whirling and chaotic crap running around in my head. There is one burning question flipping over and over in my mind, and I need an answer now. Looking up at Anders, I ask, "What does she mean I'm a direct descendant?"

"You haven't told her?" Miller snaps.

He clenches his jaw; then he looks away, avoiding all eye contact with me. "You're the last surviving female of our family bloodline. According to our pack traditions, the Alpha status is handed down from female to female."

Our family bloodline. Our family... Aggie is Anders's grandmother... How?

"That means... You and I..."

He finally looks at me, eyes shining with sorrow. "You're my daughter. I—"

Waving away any immediate answer, I stand and storm out of the study. I need some air. My heart is pounding so hard I can hear it in my ears. My hands are trembling, and my head is so fucked up right now I can barely keep any thoughts straight. All this time. All this time! Both Anders and Alpha Agnus knew who I was to them, and they never said a damn thing. I feel hurt, betrayed, angry and confused all at the same time. I pace near the edge of Quartz Lake.

How the hell did they keep this a secret? If I ever thought my life was in danger before, this, all of this, puts my life as well as the life of the pack now in my charge at so much risk.

Loud thunderclaps overhead echoing over the territory, reflecting my anger. The sky darkens, casting a sinister shadow over the lake's cool façade.

My hands are clutched into fists. I bring one hand up to wipe at the tears streaming down my face. To my surprise, I'm holding Alpha Agnus's notebook, the very same notebook I have seen her write in from our first meeting after she looked into my empty teacup. I don't even remember taking it from Miller.

I frown down at the notebook in my hand. Her tea readings were always accurate. I have seen her predictions come true myself. But as many times as she had read my tea leaves, I often wondered why she never told me about my path, my future true mate, or anything really. I never pushed because, sometimes, I felt like I didn't really want to know or need to know. Over time with all the stupid shit that happened in my life, I convinced myself that I didn't need tea leaves to tell me my divine path or who my true mate would be because I made my own path.

If she couldn't tell me what I needed to know when she was alive, then to hell with it. I toss the notebook into the lake. I stand there and watch it sink slowly down into the lake's bottomless end. Angry tears stream down my face. No, I don't need tea leaf readings or visions dreamed up by a woman who is no longer here to answer my questions. And I definitely do not need to nor want to read about the lies and secrets kept from me all these years.

I reach into my pocket, to pull out a tissue I had stuffed in there earlier. My phone falls out, landing on my foot. I pick it up, wiping dirt off the face of it against my dress. When I flip it over to inspect it, Emily's contact information lights up on display. The phone rings. "This is Emily—you know what to do."

My heart breaks, shattering into a million pieces. I clutch the phone to my chest, and I cover my mouth with my hand as I let out a sob. Emily… she was my ride or die, my person; she knew when to give it to me, to take me out of my head. She never held back what she thought, and I loved that so much about her. I didn't deserve her. I was a horrible friend, always caught up in my own shit. Despite how shitty of a friend I was, she was always there for me. In times like this, she would have been the first person I would have called.

I'm such a selfish bitch. Here I am, wishing she was here to talk to when it's my fault that she's not here anymore. Guilt, regret, and the anger and loneliness I was already feeling work their way harder into my chest. She is the very reason why I can't be an Alpha. My best friend in the whole world died at the hands of monsters, and I couldn't protect her. I couldn't stop it from happening. Still clutching my phone to my chest, I fall to my knees and scream. Lightning streaks the sky, and thunder booms, my scream getting lost in the sound.

My mind is spinning out of control. How am I supposed to protect a pack? How am I supposed to protect a territory that was part of the reason for war and greed, the cause of the deaths of so many innocent shifters? How many more people need to die because of me? I can't do this. I can't do this. I'm not strong enough. I feel myself start to fall apart. I can't bring it back together.

Then I hear it—a voice. My phone falls from my hands. It startles me because it feels as if someone slapped it out of my hand. I reach down to pick it up. I must have accidentally dialed someone.

"Jessica? Jess… is everything okay?"

# Chapter 15

## DIVINE INTERVENTION

### LUKE

#### March 14, 2025: 11:45 a.m.

I knock on my father's doorframe of his study. When he acknowledges me, I walk in. "Jessica is literally on her way to talk to you. She's quite upset. I think she'll need to talk with Mom too." I take a seat on one of the chairs in front of his grand desk.

"The funeral must be over then. I can't believe I wasn't invited to Alpha Agnus's funeral. It's not usual tradition for the Alpha King to not be present at one of the Alpha's funerals. I would have liked to be there for the pack as well as Jessica."

I rub the back of my neck. "It's not the reason why she's upset—I mean, it's part of it." I let out a sigh. "Alpha Agnus has named Jessica as her successor, and in doing so the truth has come out that Anders is her biological father."

My father frowns. "Let me guess. Anders hadn't told her before the reading of the will."

"Doesn't sound like it."

Through gritted teeth, he sneers, "Shit! We talked about this!" He grabs his phone, rapidly typing out a text.

"Did you ever wonder how of all places she ended up with us? She literally ended up in Anders's backyard. Ran blind and broken into Alpha Agnus's home?"

Without missing a beat, or looking up from his phone, he answers, "Divine intervention."

I let out a huff, and under my breath, I mutter, "Divine intervention."

His eyes lift to mine. "Or fate, whatever you want to call it. She ended up where she needed to be. I believe in that, at least."

I grimace. "Fate, fate sure has a fucked-up sense of humor."

He gives me a half-smile. "I take it you haven't talked to her yet?"

I shake my head. "No, and I have a feeling it will be even longer before I get a chance to."

Before my father can say anything else, the twins come crashing through the door.

"Where's Jess?" Jeremy asks. "I could have sworn she'd be here by now. She's so loud."

"Loud?" I ask.

Justin shrugs. "She's freaking out. It's like her thoughts are shouting in our heads."

Jeremy straightens his posture a little more, and a look of surprise crosses his features. "Holy shit, she's the Whitemore pack's successor?" He turns his head to look at Justin. "What the fuck? Anders..."

My mother walks in then and slaps Jeremy in the back of his head. "Can't you wait until Jessica gets home so that she can tell us herself?"

Jeremy grumbles, "Did you have to hit me so hard?"

I laugh; this is our family. It's like a circus, especially with the twins around.

Jessica walks into the study. "Great, you're all here!"

I turn to look at her. She looks like she's out of breath. Her clear blue eyes, lighter than the clearest blue sky, look bloodshot from crying. Her pale blond hair hangs down to her waist, looking a little disheveled. I could have sworn her hair was a darker blond this morning. She has baggy gray sweatpants on, a sports bra, and she is currently pulling on a flannel shirt. As I'm looking her over, I catch sight of her taut abs and her full breasts.

My dick twitches, and I long to take her into my arms and fucking kiss her. I want to hold her and reassure her that she can do this and I will be here for her in any way that she will let me.

She leaves the flannel unbuttoned and reaches up to pull out her long hair. Maybe it's a good thing my brothers, Jessica, and I do not share a mind-link. I shift in my seat, adjusting my position without actually adjusting my dick. Fuck, this isn't the time.

I rub my thumb over my forehead, trying to hide my reaction. Still looking at her, since I can't seem to look away, I finally recognize that the clothes are mine—well, aside from her sports bra. It's the clothing from my stash that I keep out in the barn in case I need a change of clothing when I come back from a shift.

Wait a minute. When I shift…I sit up straighter in my chair. "You shifted?" That sounds more like an accusation than a question. The commotion stops, and everyone freezes. She looks at me for the first time since she entered the room, and I can't miss the flash of annoyance that crosses her face.

"Of course I did. It was the only way to get here in minutes instead of in a couple of hours."

My father looks up from his phone. "Jessica, you know that…"

She brings up her hand, "I know, I know. I was careful. No one saw me."

He places his phone down on his desk, then announces, "Anders is on his way."

Jessica rolls her eyes. "I don't want to talk to him right now."

Justin comes up to her side and places an arm around her shoulders "Can't say that I blame you, but he just might have a reasonable explanation for this."

A twinge of jealousy shoots up my spine. I wanted to be the one to comfort her, to place my arms around her.

Jessica turns her head to look at my father, and I can see the hurt and unshed tears in her eyes. She opens her mouth to say something; then she closes it again, cocks her head, and turns toward the door just as Joe, our butler, appears.

"I'm sorry for the interruption, sir, but we have unexpected visitors," he says, addressing my father.

Jessica's eyes widen, and she turns back to my father, "It's the second territory Alpha and his Beta." Fuck, she even has a connection with our staff. What the hell? A growl threatens to let loose. I run my hand through my hair, trying to hide my jealousy.

My father stands up from his seated position behind his desk. "Dammit, I told them in the last email they sent me that we would meet with him when we were available!"

"Sir, the Alpha and his Beta refuse to be turned away and are insisting that they speak to you posthaste." Joe's face remains expressionless as he awaits further instruction.

My mother steps closer to Jessica. "Joe, bring them into the drawing room." She cups Jessica's face in her hands. "We'll go upstairs and get you changed into something more appropriate for a meeting."

She shakes her head. "He doesn't want to meet with me. He wants a meeting with the Alpha King to override my decision to refuse aid. Beta DuPont refuses to accept my role among the guards. He isn't going to stop until he and his son have their way."

"That's just bullshit!" Jeremy snaps. "You're a royal. You were given the role to oversee guard business by our father and Anders. Whatever you decide, he doesn't get to rebuke that. You ultimately have the final say."

She looks at me then, and I can see the turmoil of emotions in her eyes. She's still all over the place. I don't need to hear her thoughts to know that she's conflicted right now. I'm a little happy that she's looking to me for guidance and a little sad that she's only doing it because she's feeling stuck.

Softly, I tell her, "Go get changed. Dad and I can buy

some time before you join us."

She shakes her head and looks down at her tiny bare feet. "I can't do this right now. It's too much all at once."

I stand up from my chair and take the few steps between us to stand in front of her. I lift her chin with my finger. I look into her beautiful clear blue eyes. "You can do this. I've seen you tear lesser men apart in meetings and on the field on a good day. I would hate to see what you can do to an asshole on the receiving end of a bad day."

Her eyes search mine. My heart aches that she must search my eyes for sincerity. Can't she see how much I adore her? I smile, showing off my dimples. She lets out a slow breath, casts her eyes back down, and nods.

My mother starts to usher her out the door. The three of us follow them out.

"Hold on, you three." My father says, "Let them wait. In the meantime, Jeremy and Justin, go round up the leads and a couple of guards. I hope Anders reaches here in time."

Justin and Jeremy nod and take their leave without question. On the other hand, I look at my father with a questioning look.

He shakes his head. "I don't have a good feeling about this. Jessica is on edge, and those assholes are up to something."

# Chapter 16

## Mothers Know Best

### JESSICA

March 14, 2025: 12:20 p.m.

My mother helps me pull together an outfit, a long sleeve button-up pale blue blouse with a collar and black pull-on crop pants. I pair the clothing with my favorite pair of chucks instead of the black flats she placed near the bed. I smile at her as she shakes her head. It's an unspoken compromise. As much as I would prefer to stay in the clothing I had on, I can't face the Alpha of the second territory looking like a teenager who just got out of bed. It's quiet between the two of us. I see the change in expression on my mother's face as she contemplates what to say.

I take a seat at my vanity table and start to apply a little makeup. My mother comes up behind me and starts to brush my tangled hair. It's been a while since I had it cut or styled. My pale blond hair hangs down to my waist. I tend to keep it in a bun or a ponytail to tame it; otherwise, it's all over the place, and I'm not one to style it other than color it to hide the paleness of the blonde. Lately, I've been coloring it a darker blond, sometimes brown. It had been dyed just a few days ago, but when I shift, it turns my hair back to its original color. I don't have time to color my hair right now, so I just have to make do with it.

I rarely let anyone see my natural hair color because the paleness of my hair sticks out like a sore thumb, especially against my slightly tan skin. Most women, including men with fair hair, also have fair skin. For some reason, I have a warm complexion. I tan easily when out in the sun. The darker I get, the more my hair seems to glow in comparison. Many women pay top dollar at the spray tan booths for skin color like mine. What a waste of time and money. I wish that my skin tone was a little fairer. It's easier to hide scars when your skin is fair. I place my foundation brush back down on my vanity, and I reach over to my jewelry box to fish out a choker to place over the scar on my throat. The one I had been wearing earlier—my favorite—is now with Ean. I handed it to him when I decided to shift and run instead of ride in the car with Anders for another two hours.

I let out a sigh and catch my mother's green eyes watching me in the mirror. She finally breaks the silence between us. "I'm sorry that your father and I didn't tell you about Anders and Alpha Agnus. Together, we decided that we would let Anders tell you when he felt the time was right."

I look down at my jewelry box. "I just don't understand

why he would wait, and even then, he couldn't tell me when we were alone in the car on the way to the funeral."

She pursed her lips and nodded. "I understand why you would be upset, but I can also understand why he would have a hard time. It's not an easy position for either of you."

I try to shake my head, but she has my hair in a vise grip as she puts it up in a French twist. "He should have told me...."

My mother snaps her eyes to mine in the mirror, causing me to stop in the middle of what I am going to say. "What difference would it have made if he told you today or ten years ago? Would this knowledge change your relationship with your father and me, with the twins? Would it have changed your relationship with Alpha Agnus?"

She didn't mention Luke; it's not a secret to anyone that we have an uncomfortable relationship. Focusing back on her question, I frown. If I had known sooner that Anders was my biological father, would it have changed anything? Would it have changed me? Would it have changed the relationships I had developed over the years?

# Chapter 17

## MAKING A GOOD IMPRESSION

### JESSICA

May 18, 2014: 5:30 p.m.: Whitemore Plantation

I'm almost done with the final touches for dinner when Miller walks in. He doesn't knock but just walks in through the kitchen door. I hear his footsteps, and I recognized his smell.

He looked at me and smiles. "Smells delicious, I can't wait to try it." I smile back and nod. I make a place for him at the table as I did for lunch. He walks to the living area where Agnus has been. She's up; I peeked in on her a few times. She had been reading while sitting in a recliner with a crocheted blanket over her lap.

I hear Agnus talking loudly. "Miller, help me out of this death trap. I've been sitting in this chair for hours, and I can't seem to get myself out of it." I frown; she didn't tell me that she wanted to get out of the recliner. I stop what I have been doing and quietly head toward the living area. Miller is attempting to pull Agnus out of the chair, holding onto both of her hands and placing a foot on the footrest of the recliner, trying to push it in at the same time. He almost gets the footrest back into the chair when it springs up, throwing Agnus back into the chair, pulling Miller forward into her. I clap my hand over my mouth to hold back a laugh, and a squeak of air rushes out from the hole in my throat. They don't notice me; Agnus is too busy trying to push Miller off her, and Miller is trying to get off of her at the same time.

Agnus starts swearing. "Miller, you are a fucking idiot. Get off of me and get me out of this damn chair."

His face is flustered. He scrambles back onto his feet and leans forward to push the footrest in with his hand at the same time as Agnus leans forward to scoot up, headbutting Miller in the process. Shocked, Miller falls onto his butt. Agnus starts to growl and swear under her breath. Using her legs, she tries to push the footrest down, but it won't budge because Miller's knee is under it. I place my other hand over the hole in my throat, hiding the squeaky rush of air coming out of it. I can't help it; I'm cracking up at the comical sight in front of me. Agnus grabs her cane and hits Miller in the chest, trying to push him back all the while she keeps trying to push the footrest down with her legs.

"Fucking smartass. Get over here and help me out of this chair." Wiping my hands on my pants and then wiping my eyes from the tears that started to form, I move toward them with a wide grin on my face. When Miller is finally able to move his legs, I push the lever down on the side of the recliner, and the footrest retreats into the pocket of the chair.

Agnus hits me in the shoulder with her cane as she scoots forward. "Smartass." She sneers.

Miller, red in the face, reaches forward to grab Agnus's hand, but she slaps him away and stands up on her own. Still grinning, I go back to the kitchen, wash my hands, and continue with what I had been doing before the whole chair fiasco.

---

Dinner turns out to be an unplanned gathering. I'm glad that I made more than enough food to feed everyone who stops by. It also helped that each visitor brings something to add to the meal. I'm pretty sure the pack members who arrive, especially Peter who came all the way from the city, are here to check up on me.

Throughout the meal, everyone's skepticism and hesitancy toward me lessens. I especially win them over with my brownies, topped with freshly made whipped cream and fresh strawberries. As some of the guests start to take their leave, I receive compliments and hugs. Miller, Peter, and Agnus decided to adjourn to her study for after-dinner drinks.

At this point, my body is screaming at me in pain. My vision is going in and out. I am determined to finish everything I start to the end. I need to prove that I could be an integral part of this pack. Even though I can't be 100 percent sure since I couldn't remember, I'm pretty sure where

I came from, no one would miss me. I really hope that Aggie, or rather Alpha Agnus, will keep me. I want to belong to her pack.

Gathering the dishes up from the dining room table, there is a knock on the front door. No one is around to answer it, so I make my way to the door. The second knock is a little more persistent, so I open it. A man with all-white hair and a young face that doesn't quite match stands at the door entrance.

He smiles and says, "Are you ready, little one? It's time I take you back to where you came from." I stiffen in response, back to that place where they had all the tubes inside me. Oh hell no! I turn and run back to the kitchen door.

Alpha Agnus stands right in front of it; she grabs my chin and says, "No running. I asked that they return to collect you." Upset and disappointed, I yank my chin out of her grasp and turn away from her. I feel so betrayed. I thought she liked me, and I thought I did well enough for her to want to keep me here.

She places her hand on my shoulder, turns me to face her, and hands me back my hoodie. "It's not the time for you to stay. You're a little early." Not really understanding what she means, I grab my hoodie and put it on. Feeling defeated, I head for the front door. Two cars are waiting for me. In front of the passenger doors of the first car are two big men. I slowly approach them and stand there, pulling the hood of my sweatshirt over my head.

"No funny business," this tall giant of a man says. "We got you figured out. This time you won't escape." He gestures to the car in the back, and four equally big men get out of the car. I shrug, trying to give the impression that I am not intimidated. The slightly shorter one, and I mean slightly as in five inches shorter compared to the other man who spoke first, steps forward. I stagger back, just a little unsure of what he would do.

He reaches out a hand and introduces himself. "My name is Chris. I'm the third lead guard. This guy is Elias; he's the second lead." Hesitantly, I take his hand and shake it. Guards? Shit! I am in so much trouble. I squeeze my eyes shut at the thought of how much trouble I am in. I hear shuffling in the gravel. When I open my eyes, the bigger man, Elias, steps closer and bends forward so that he is at eye level with me.

"You're not in trouble, little one." He moves his head to the side, gesturing to the four others standing in front of the car in the back. "Those men are guards, but they are not important." One of the four men snorts. I try to let out a huff; instead, a huff of air and a whistling noise come out of my throat. Chris makes another step forward, and I take another step back.

"How did you survive the day out here?" I shake my head and shrug. The movement creates a spinning sensation; my body sways slightly, and a large hand clamps over my shoulder.

"It's okay, little one; we just want to take you back to the clinic, so the doctor can look you over and take care of you. You're safe here with us." Not sure if I can believe his words or his intentions, I try to take another step back; instead, my knees buckle, but before my body can hit the ground, I am caught in large arms. My vision has gone blurry again, and my body is screaming with pain. I have no more fight in me. I let whoever caught me take me to the car and deposit me in the back seat. My body is done, and I can't push past the fatigue and weakness I had been fighting earlier to prove my place here in the Whitemore pack. For nothing, I worked so hard for nothing. I let the tears fall, accepting my defeat.

Large hands touch my face and wipe away the tears. "Don't cry, little one. My name is Anders. I'm the head guard. You're not in trouble. I'm taking you home." I turn my head all the way to the right so I can see the man who possessed the gravelly voice sitting next to me. It is the white-haired man. I grip the seat with my left hand as anxiety starts to rip through me, and the car pulls away from Alpha Agnus's home. Home? I don't know where home is. How can he ensure that I will be safe? Look at me.

My mind started to whirl with all these horrible thoughts and visions of what home will be like once I return. My heart starts to race; I can hear my harsh raspy breathing through the hole in my throat. I want to jump out of the car. Anders places a gentle hand on my knee, and another hand gently places itself over my left hand; I'm shocked I didn't hear someone get into the car and sit next to me. I turn my head, but all I see is a blurry shadow and an outline of a man. I face back to the front of the car and frown. The large hand over my own gently strokes the back of my hand with his thumb.

He leans over close to my ear and whispers, "I got you." My panic starts to ebb away. I lean my head back against the car seat, close my eyes, and allow the soothing feel of the hand caressing mine to lull me to sleep.

# Chapter 18

## BACK WHERE I STARTED

### JESSICA

#### May 19, 2014: Emerald Pack Clinic

A glint of a knife shining from the light of the moon comes straight for my face. A high-pitched manic laugh echoes around me. The knife slices into my cheek, my eyelid, my scalp. Screaming with every slice, until my throat feels raw, the knife aims straight for my eye. I pull my arms up, crossing over my face to protect myself. *"Stop! Please stop!"* Breathing harshly, I open my eyes and look around at my surroundings. My vision is back to a blur of shadows and light. I sit up slowly this time, recognizing the smell of the sterile room. I am back in the room I escaped just the other day. Back to where it all began.

I stop to think about how I got here. I remembered

the man named Anders coming to Alpha Agnus's house to collect me. I must have fallen asleep in the car. Still trying to take in my surroundings, I remember the man named Chris telling me that they had wanted to get me back to the clinic where the doctor could take care of me. But I also remember Anders telling me he was taking me home. Is this the clinic? I can feel my heart racing and the echoes of my harsh wet breathing bouncing around the room. I close my eyes, trying to calm myself down. I feel a warm hand holding my right hand and another hand gently rub my back.

"Shhhhh, you're safe, sweetheart. No one will hurt you." It's a soft, soothing tone, a female voice. When I turn my head, I can't see what she looks like. There's a hint of mint accompanied by a delicate flowery scent of jasmine and vanilla. She continues to rub my back. I pat down my body. I have a tube back in my stomach, another line in my arm. I am back in that weird dress thing that only covers my front. I reach for my throat; there is no tube there this time, but the hole is still present. The woman makes a shushing noise and continues to rub my back, gently squeezing my right hand.

"The tube in your stomach is feeding you. The line in your arm keeps you hydrated. It's to help you, not hurt you." She makes another shushing noise and continues to rub my back, helping to calm me down.

"I'm so sorry I wasn't here when you woke up the other day. You must have been so scared. Between myself and my boys, we have been at your side since you were brought in. But my oldest son had to leave the other day for school. We all reluctantly left your side, not thinking that you would wake up. You've been in a coma-like state for almost two weeks."

More shushing as she continues to rub my back. I let my shoulders drop, and the tension in my body starts to relent.

"I'm here now, and I am not going to let anything bad happen to you, little one." I nod and squeeze her hand to let her know that I am okay now. With gentle hands, she gently guides me back down on the bed.

"My name is Shakti. I know—it's a bit of a strange name, especially for someone born and raised here in the LS. I can tell you how I was named if you like?" I nod my head, encouraging her to continue. "My father was a businessman who met many people overseas. One day, he met a beautiful shifter princess, a daughter of an Alpha King, in India on one of his travels. He met her only once. She was a little girl, not more than four or five years old, but he couldn't get over just how beautiful she was for a child. When he had met his true mate, and they finally had a daughter after having four boys, he was adamant on naming his daughter Shakti because he felt his daughter was the most beautiful girl he had ever seen, and his daughter would forever be his princess. I wish he were still alive today. I think you would have liked him." I reach out to find her hand and give it a gentle squeeze.

I smile at her story and imagine how beautiful she is. I just wish I could see what this woman who stayed by my side and comforted me looks like. But even with turning my head as much to the right as I had yesterday, I can't see anything.

It makes me worry that I've lost my vision completely. Without a voice and no vision, how am I going to survive? What kind of life could I possibly lead? Feeling sorry for myself, I'm just about to cry again. What a mess. No one wants a weak person in their pack. A crybaby is weak.

A commotion right outside my door takes my attention away from my self-pity moment. I try tuning in to what is happening outside but can't hear anything. Inside of my head, I hear two male voices grumbling with each other, but I can't understand what they are saying exactly. The words are too fast, much faster when compared to when someone is speaking out loud. The door of my room bangs open. I have to really focus to grasp what they are saying.

*"Ohh, great job, dumbass! You nearly woke the dead."* Let's just call this one "voice one" and the other one "voice two." The funny thing about these voices, as I pay closer attention, is that they sound exactly the same in my mind. It is the intonation and the personality behind the words used that helps me to differentiate the two.

*"Shut up! You're the one who had to shove past me as I opened it,"* Voice Two snarks back.

Shakti moves away from my side. "Just what the hell are you doing? I told you two to stay outside in the waiting area until she had woken up and the doctor looked at her." Her tone isn't harsh, but it is firm. Ah, this must be two of the boys she mentioned earlier.

*"I told you we should wait,"* Voice One says. I can picture an elbow hitting some faceless person in the chest in my head.

*"Pshhh, like I'd listen to you anyhow. She needs us. You heard her thoughts just as I clearly did,"* Voice Two responds, and again another vision of a jab with an elbow forms in my head.

I frown. How are they doing this? It's almost like when Alpha Agnus's voice had been in my head and she told me to use my mind to visualize my surroundings.

*"You met Alpha Agnus?"* Voice One asks.

"Well, are you two going to explain yourselves?"

"Sorry, Mom, but... we, uh...Ouch, what the hell was that for?" This time Voice One is speaking out loud. I can physically hear him this time.

*"Shut up! Maybe the little one doesn't want anyone to know,"* Voice Two hisses in my head. I'm getting confused and overwhelmed as the banter keeps going on and on between the two of them at lightning speed.

"Sorry, Mom, it's just that...." Voice One stops mid-sentence. In my head he wants to know if it's okay to tell her my secret. I hesitate at first, worried that she won't like me anymore, especially if she thinks I'm weird.

*"She's our mother. You can trust her, just like you can trust us."* Trust. For some reason as I roll that word around in my head, it feels like such a foreign concept to me. Even though my instincts tell me that I probably could trust them, I'm not sure it's safe. A slow-growing sense of fear starts to grow deep in my chest.

*"You can trust us. Our mother knows that we can communicate to each other in our minds. If you ever meet our big brother, you'll learn that he's special too. It will be fine."* I still feel a hesitation pulling at my heart. But I kind of want her to know. I guess, if something were to happen or they kick me out on the streets, it's better to find out now, rather than later. I nod.

"Oh, for fuck's sake, we can communicate with her the same way we communicate with each other," Voice Two rushes out.

"Jeremy! Language! How many times do I have to remind you?" Shakti scolds, not really reacting to what he just said. I mean, I would have freaked out or maybe reacted differently.

"Nah, my mom's cool. I'm Justin, by the way." Voice One says it out loud, so his mother can hear him too. "The abrupt one is Jeremy. I love how you picked up on the differences in your head." A slew of images of someone getting a beatdown flash in my mind. I'm assuming those are coming from Voice Two or Jeremy.

"Mom, she can't see or talk. It was getting to her. We just want to let her know that she's not alone and we could help." Justin is cordial when he speaks, or maybe that's just the way he talks to his mom.

"She's scared and sad." Jeremy says it softly this time. An image of a tiny person sitting in a hospital bed filter in, followed by another one of a tiny-looking being attached to tubes, thin, frail, face hollow and sunken in akin to a skeleton. A woman is dressed in a smock and matching colored pants, busy working over that same being, rearranging lines and repositioning the body. Is that me? He's showing me what I look like. Wow, I look like death is lingering closely. With the flashes of images, an emotion is attached to each one: worry, fear, concern, sadness. They are concerned about me. They don't even know me, and they are worried about me.

"The doctor should be here shortly. He went to one of the pack members' homes to help with the birthing. I usually go in, but I wanted to be here when you woke up. I didn't want you to feel abandoned again or scared." She's addressing me instead of one of her boys.

I think it's strange, not sure why, but it feels weird being addressed over her own flesh and blood. I mean, I only just met her, and I really do feel like she cares about me in the short time.

"*She does. We all do.*" One of the boy's voices enters my head again.

"Mom, she's wondering why you care about her," Jeremy says to his mother.

A hand grips my own. I catch the scent of her floral perfume. "Because for some reason, the moon goddess brought you to us. I'm going to take care of you as if you were one of my own."

I have no words, no thoughts that can express the feeling that starts to bloom in my chest. I don't know why, but there's a lingering feeling that makes me think that I have never had this kind of care before. I feel two hands touch my feet, recognizing that they belong to the boys that came crashing into my room.

"Well, hello, little one, you're awake." It's a man's voice that I haven't heard yet. "I'm Dr. York. We haven't officially met." I see a blurry shadowed figure standing off to the side, but I'm not sure if he is doing anything else.

"She can't see, Dr. York, and with the hole from the tracheotomy, she can't speak yet." Shakti says, addressing Dr. York. A whiff of blood permeates the air around him; that's concerning. Why does he smell like blood? I began to shift in my bed, the threat of anxiety starting to well up in my throat.

"Uh, Dr. York, why do you smell like blood?" one of the boys asks the doctor.

He chuckles. "Occupational hazard. I got bitten. I could have sworn I cleaned up before entering the room."

"I can, uh, still smell the blood," Jeremy says to him. He

seems to be the most vocal of the two so far. Justin seems to be the one mainly addressing me in my head.

I hear water running, then the friction sound of soft paper against plastic.

"*He washed his hands. You're fine,*" Justin tells me through our connection. I nod to him in response.

"If you boys don't mind. I'll have you leave the room while I examine this little one." Footsteps shuffle with the rattling sound of plastic and metal skimming across the floor. Anxiety tightens in my throat. I really don't want to be left alone in the room with him. I feel something squeeze my foot, and I start to bring it toward me.

"*Relax, Mom will be here, and both she and the doctor will explain to you out loud what the doctor is doing. You're perfectly safe. Jeremy and I will be outside, listening in.*"

The tightening sensation starts to loosen, but it doesn't completely go away. I hear their footsteps leave the room, and the door gently closes.

"*We're right outside,*" Justin reassures me.

"You've made a connection with the boys already. I see. That's good. You need support. It will help you to heal."

I nod my head, and I hear footsteps moving around.

"I'm just moving to the foot of your bed, sweetie. I'm right here." Shakti says and gently places her hand on my foot, letting me know exactly where she is. I can feel the doctor's presence at the side of my bed now.

"I'm going to start examining you now. My hands are a little cold. I just washed them."

I nod again, letting him know I'm ready.

"So, Anders informs me that your name is Jessica. I

assumed that your name possibly started with a G. Maybe it stands for an initial of your last name," he says.

"Dr. York, where did you find that information? I wasn't aware," Shakti says.

"Oh, I wasn't completely sure, so I didn't mention it. It was a letter found written on the tag of one of the articles of clothing she came in with. It was barely legible," he says in a brushed-off manner.

"G" as in the letter "G." For some reason, it feels familiar. Feels almost right; it also feels like I hated it.

A laugh sounds in my head. *"Little G, I like it. I think I'm going to call you that instead of Jessica."*

I roll my eyes as if the person in my head can see me.

"I'm sorry. Is everything okay?" the doctor asks. Startled by his sudden question, I quickly nod. *Great, I almost got into trouble. Thanks a lot, dude.* This time another sound of laughter from both of them rings in my head.

The exam lasts for a few minutes. The doctor asks closed-ended questions so I can either answer by nodding or shaking my head. I have to concentrate on what the doctor asks me because the boys' thoughts sometimes overwhelm my head, and I can't filter them out.

At the end of the exam, Shakti and Dr. York discuss the different surgeries I will need. A surgery to repair the hole in my throat. Laser eye surgery to fix my vision. Orthodontic surgery for my teeth. I try to pay attention to everything the doctor says, but some of the words he uses, I don't quite understand. Shakti seems to have everything under control. She asks questions and agrees or disagrees with some of the suggestions the doctor makes. It feels like I'm her child sitting in the bed and not some stranger who just showed up out of nowhere. I am afraid to have any hope that I can stay with her, especially after the disappointment I experienced last night.

Four weeks have passed, and the surgeries haven't gone as well as everyone hoped. I am severely anemic from losing so much blood. The doctor mentions my body is malnourished, so healing also took longer than it would have for any standard shifter, including one who hasn't transitioned yet. Although the hole in my throat has been repaired, the initial incision damaged some of my vocal cords, and scar tissue developed, preventing me from creating sound. A specialist came to see if they could improve some of the damage. Otherwise, I won't ever be able to talk again. The laser eye surgery didn't go as planned either. The damage was so bad that I needed to have repeat surgeries and a special lens implant inserted into my eyes, just to be able to see. Even after the surgeries, my vision is not 100 percent, and I need to wear glasses.

Surgery after surgery, setback after setback, I start to fall into a mild depression, but the boys, or rather the twins Jeremy and Justin, don't give up on me. Not sure why two sixteen-year-old, nearly six feet tall, blond-haired, green-eyed twins want anything to do with me. Still, they visit every day usually after school. Sometimes even stay the night. If they didn't have school, they won't leave me alone. Always acting as my interpreter and making me laugh at their stories about school and their pranks.

Before I could see, I pictured Shakti to be a beautiful woman. As it turns out, she is, tall, at least five feet nine, slender. She has big green eyes just like her boys and long blond hair. She too never leaves my side unless someone is with me.

Anders stops by daily to check on me and talk to Dr. York. Even Chris and Elias stop by to see how I am doing. The never-ending visits do help with my internal battle of depression and despair. But it creeps in when I am left alone, especially at night when those around sleep.

The nightmares continue to haunt me, so much so I give up on sleep altogether. To make things worse, I finally have the courage to look at my reflection, really look at myself. Standing in front of the bathroom mirror, I turn my head to inspect the left side of my face. I examine the scars; a long, puckered, angry, red, jagged line trails down from the corner of my left eye down to my chin, and another one starts at the corner of my mouth, sweeping up to my ear. The whites of my eyes are a blood red, making the paleness of my blue eyes stand out even more. They remind me of vampire eyes or how I picture them in my head anyway. My lashes have begun to grow back in short little stubs, my right eyelid has a pink scar, and the center of my lashes has not grown back in. Not sure if they ever will, especially with that scar.

Turning my head back and forth slowly, I examine the rest of my face. The too-big glasses hide most of my face and become more of the focus than the scars. I rub my recently shaved head. Shakti tried her best to salvage what was left of my hair. In the end, I asked if she could just shave it all off. In so doing, it makes the angry pink and red bald spots on my scalp stand out. I lift my chin to examine the freshly healing surgical scar forming over the base of my neck where the hole in my throat had been. A faded pink line circles around my neck just above it. I slowly trace it with my fingertip. This one looks like it is fading, and I hope it does. It's a little harder to hide.

Sighing, I undo the ties at my neck and back and remove the clinic gown, looking down at my chest. Dr. York seems to think that I am about the age of ten or twelve. Cupping my breasts, I am about a full B cup if I were to use an actual bra instead of a sports bra. I don't think a ten-year-old would have boobs, but who knows? I run my fingertips down my arms along with the linear pink-and-white scars, stopping where horizontal scars are weaving together with the linear ones, making it look like a tic-tac-toe pattern on my right wrist. I turn so I can see my back in the mirror. The worst of the wounds are there.

Long jagged markings run down my back to the back of my right calf. There are also a few on the back of the left one. It almost looks like I have been mutilated and sewn back together. I turn forward and look down at my thighs; there is only one faded pink scar on each side, rectangular-shaped and about an inch long. There are no scars on my chest and stomach. I still have the tube in my stomach, not just because of the surgeries on my vocal cords, but because of another issue, my teeth.

I look back up to the mirror, staring at my face and trying to pretend to smile, to see my teeth. My teeth have been broken in half, some down to the gums, and some of my bottom teeth twist and jut out crooked. The orthodontic specialist came in and tried to salvage my teeth as much as he could, removing the ones he just couldn't save. He placed braces to fix the ones still present, using spacers in place of the missing ones. Shakti promised that implants would be used once everything else was fixed. I'm not an idiot. Implants cost money, and good ones that stay in place when you shift cost more than a fancy condo in the city.

I know it's silly and probably vain of me to feel upset about what I look like. I know that I should be dead. I don't know how old I am, but I would eventually like to meet a boy someone I could one day fall in love with, but who would want to kiss me with fucked-up, ugly, missing teeth? Who would want to touch me or look at me with all of the scars on my body? How many times would I have to explain myself every time someone asks about the scars?

I look worse than a street junkie or a boxer, like someone threw me in a meat grinder, pulled me out, and sewed me back together. Opening my mouth, examining my teeth again, I smile one more time just to see what I look like. I take another last look at all the wounds and scars. When I can't stand what I am seeing any longer, I remove my too-big glasses, slide down to the floor, and silently sob.

# Chapter 19

## GUARD DETAIL

### JESSICA

#### June 25, 2014: 9 a.m.: Emerald Pack Clinic

The twins got into trouble at school and are grounded. Their punishment includes their visits to me. Shakti has some business that requires her to leave the territory but promises she will be in constant communication with Dr. York and will have someone stay with me, so I am not left alone. She will be back as soon as she is able. Since last night, I have not seen anyone other than Dr. York and my nurse Mimi.

A sharp knock at the door makes me jump. Four large men enter my clinic room.

"Anders sent us." A deep baritone voice comes from one of them. I adjust my glasses on the bridge of my nose to get a better look at all of them. The tallest one with wide shoulders and black hair is the one speaking. He looks like Elias with dark brown eyes, so dark they're almost black, a square jaw, a strong brow, and a broad nose. He has muscular arms, a skinny waist, and stands with legs slightly apart. Otherwise, I think he would probably tip over.

"I'm Ean," he says with a smile. I scrunch my face as I study him; then it hits me. He is the one whose legs I slid between back when I ran from the clinic. I look around at all of them again. These are the four guards I escaped, but I could swear I had seen five of them. Two I outran and three by the gate. My eyes widen. Were they the four men by the car when Anders came to pick me up? Ean lets out a bark of a laugh. "Oh, you remember us now, do you?" I give him a tight-lipped smile and nod my head.

"What's wrong, little one? Cat got your tongue?" a blond-haired guard says. He almost looks like the twins. Tall, green eyes that sparkle with mischief, but he isn't as broad-shouldered as the twins, and his blond hair is a couple of shades darker. He is leaner, with long muscular arms. I notice that his right forearm is slightly bigger than his left, causing the veins to pop out more on one side. Looking back at the blondie's face, I raise an eyebrow and point to my throat, which still has a dressing over it from the most recent surgery. He raises both hands as if surrendering and shrugs.

"Oh, right, sorry about that." He stretches out his right arm in a gesture to shake my hand. "I'm Charlie. You jumped me, by the way, from the roof." They all start to laugh.

Keeping my lips shut tight, I smile and blush slightly as I gingerly place my small hand in his much larger one. I hold up two fingers of my other hand. I actually got a jump on him when I used him to jump up onto the branch.

Another tear of laughter starts again. "All right, all right, you got a jump on me twice," he mumbles as he quickly brings my hand up to his mouth and kisses the back of my hand.

I can feel the heat in my cheeks burn. As fast as possible, I draw my hand back, creating more snickers and laughter from the other guards. Ignoring Charlie, I face the other guard standing next to Ean.

"I'm Sodie," he says, giving me a slight wave, "I was by the gate. You kicked me in the chest." He says that with a smile, but he rubs the center of his chest as he speaks.

I hang my head a little as a way of apologizing. Ean claps him over the back and chuckles some more.

Sodie is nearly as tall as Charlie and as broad as Ean, but he doesn't have that heavy-on-the-top look. His hair is a dark reddish-brown, and his dark brown eyes are slightly lighter compared to Ean's. Before I can finish looking him over, a voice speaks up from the back of the room.

"I'm Liam," the last guard says, giving me a two-finger salute. He is the shortest of the group, but all that means is that he is just a few inches shorter but still within a six-foot range. He has deep copper-colored hair, closely shaved at the sides, longer on top, lying on his forehead just above his matching-colored brows and golden skin. His long dark lashes surround steel gray eyes, making them more intense as he scrutinizes me right back. Light freckles dance across his nose and cheeks, and he wears a diamond stud in his left earlobe. He's leaning back against the wall with one leg propped up behind him. His muscular arms are folded over his chest, carved muscular biceps pushing out against the sleeves of his t-shirt. I catch a glimpse of chiseled abs beneath a slightly raised hem of his shirt. I scan down the rest of his body and notice his sweatpants stretch over his muscular thighs.

He looks irritated, almost like he wishes he were anywhere but here. He is different-looking compared to the rest of the guards, but still very handsome. He makes me blush a little as he continues to look me over.

Quickly I look back to Ean, who starts to speak again. "The other one you escaped from is Shadow. He's not here. I'm sure you will meet him soon." He bends at the waist so we're eye level. "I hear you've been cooped up in this room. Want to take a walk around?"

Leaving the room sounds amazing. I nod my head enthusiastically.

"I checked with the doc, and he felt it would be good for you."

I look around the room, then down at myself, grateful I'm wearing baggy sweatpants and an oversized t-shirt. I had been complaining to myself that I was getting pretty tired of my behind hanging out for everyone to see in that clinic gown. Shakti brought some clothes for me to wear. Without a second thought, I shoot out of bed and grab my shoes from under the hospital bed, the hoodie I still had from the first night I woken up, and a baseball hat Jeremy gave me to cover my bald head. Scrambling to get everything on, I move to the door.

"Slow down, little one. Where's the fire?" Ean asks.

I grin at him. I so need a change of scenery.

"Jeeze, you're fast. Are you sure this is a good idea?" Sodie asks, looking at Ean with a concerned expression.

"Nah, she won't go anywhere. We're friends now," Charlie says, putting an arm around my shoulder. Shaking my head, I slip out of Charlie's arm and push Ean out the door.

Ean barks out a laugh. "All right, little one. Don't get pushy." I don't know if I have ever been more excited to take a walk in my life, but I am right now in this moment. I continue to push Ean out the door, and barks of laughter follow me from the rest of the guards—well, except for one of them, Liam.

I shoot a quick glance at him over my shoulder. He still looks irritated as all hell. I wonder if this is some kind of punishment being here or if I crushed his ego when I ran from them. I shrug at the thought. Maybe he just sucks at being a guard, and it pisses him off that an untrained little kid like me got the best of him. I think on that for a bit as I follow Ean down the corridor.

"I'm glad you brought a sweater. The weather has been a bit unpredictable lately. It's either gloomy as hell with small peeks of sunshine or storming, especially at night. Never did see the weather quite like this before," Ean says as he leads me out of the building. Sounds fitting, like my mood. As we step outside, the weather is clear skies and sunny, perfect for a walk.

"Well, I'll be damned. It was gloomy just a few minutes ago, and I swear it was going to rain," Sodie says, frowning as he looks up at the sky.

"See, that's what I'm talking about," Ean grumbles.

We start our tour at a statue of three wolves in front of the clinic. The clinic is at the heart of the Emerald territory, combining both the Emerald Pack and the Guards. At the beginning of their time here in the LS territory, the guards were known as the Black Obsidian wolf pack, which came from a long line of warriors from the original Northern A territory before it had been divided. When the small group of Black Obsidian wolves arrived here in the LS territory, the White Wolf Alpha granted the Alpha a territory of his own next to the Emerald Pack territory. In appreciation for allowing the Black Obsidian Pack to stay in the LS territory and giving them a piece of land on which to build upon and prosper, the Black Obsidian Alpha swore their allegiance to the white wolf Alpha and had offered their services as protector to the white wolves. During the last great war, many of the guards had died lending aid to the white wolves.

In the end, it was the war that caused the extinction of the white wolves. When the Emerald Pack Alpha had been named King of the LS territory, the Black Obsidian Alpha had sworn their allegiance to the Emerald Pack Alpha, now known as the Alpha King of the LS territory. Because there were so few Black Obsidian wolves left, they had merged their pack with the Emerald Pack, and the Black Obsidian Alpha had resigned himself to head guard. The Alpha King and the Head Guard worked to rebuild the guards between both packs. Over time with still so few guards available between both packs, it was decided to allow recruits to join from other packs. Because both territories were merged, the Black Obsidian Territory became the training grounds for the recruits and home to some of the guards. The statue represents the original White Wolf Alpha, the Black Obsidian Alpha, and the first Emerald Pack's Alpha King.

Ean smirks at the end of his history lesson and adds, "My family carries the original Black Obsidian bloodline. We have for generations either been in the guard or had a hand in leading it in some compacity."

"Thank you, kind sir, for the brief history lesson. For a moment there, I thought I was back in orientation," Liam mocks.

"Watch it. You're still a recruit, and I am your commanding officer," Ean sneers.

With a smirk, Liam shakes his head in response and continues to walk alongside Sodie, shoving his hands in his pockets.

Charlie bumps my shoulder with his and says, "Don't worry, little one, you'll get used to the overabundance of testosterone around here." He winks at me and smiles before turning his attention back to Ean.

I blush a little, not used to that kind of attention. Seriously, has he seen me? I have, and I look equivalent to a twelve-year-old boy who's been through a meat grinder.

"Don't you have an off switch?" Liam grumbles from behind us. Charlie just laughs and throws his arm around my shoulders.

It leaves me feeling a little uncomfortable, so I grab his arm and place it back to his side, patting his muscular arm in an attempt to tell him to leave it there. It brings on another bout of laughter from the group, including Liam. I can't help but silently chuckle too.

"Guess you found someone immune to your charm," Ean barks out in between a laugh. I just shrug in response.

To say that the training grounds are impressive is an understatement. Money is not spared when it comes to equipment, training weapons, and weightlifting equipment. The dorms are like walking into a hotel. They have everything from a miniature movie theater with couches to a rec center with a pool table, dartboard, ping pong table, and a poker table. Their cafeteria is an all-out buffet fitted with round dining tables covered in white linen, silverware, and crystal glasses. They have a spa and an indoor heated swimming pool.

I know that I have never seen anything like it, but this, this is everything I could have imagined. The only thing missing is the guards' academic area. I thought I would find myself in an extensive library filled to the gills with books and many classrooms filled with teachers, a lab room filled with dead animal specimens, beakers, and chemicals used for science experiments, a music room, or something close to it. None of that is present. There is only one classroom and one teacher, and after everything else I've seen, I can't help but feel a little disappointed.

At the end of the tour, I find myself standing in front of an obstacle course. It is vast and long; it has everything from quintuple steps, a rope swing, a barrel role, something Ean called a jumping spider wall, a jump hang, spinning logs, a curtain slider, and a swing circle. I can't even recall the endless names Ean keeps blurting out. He says that no one makes it through the obstacle course on the first try, and even then, only one person has ever made it through within sixteen minutes.

I stare at it long and hard, imagining myself going through the obstacle course. I bet I could do it, or I would at least like to give it a try.

Nudging my shoulder, Charlie is smiling down at me. "What's going on in that head of yours, little one?"

I shrug.

Sodie comes up next to me. "I bet this little one would give any of the recruits a run for their money." I beam at this idea.

Liam interjects, "Nah, it's a little more than jumping up into trees, roofs, and climbing up a gate."

I slightly cock my head toward Liam and return the look of annoyance on his face. I hope that is a strong enough nonverbal statement to shut him the hell up. He surprises me, though, and actually smiles at me.

Ean claps me on the back, jerking me forward. "I would put my money on this little one. She's definitely got grit."

I flinch at that word "grit." It makes me want to grind my teeth and pull out hair that I don't have. Surprised at myself over that knee-jerk reaction, I shake it off and elbow Ean in the stomach. I gesture my head toward the obstacle course, asking in my nonverbal way if he would let me give it a try.

Ean shakes his head. "Oh hell no, little one. I was given specific instructions to keep you occupied and safe, which means there is no way in hell that I'm going to let you run this obstacle course." I pout. All he does is snort. "Come on. I told Anders I would bring you by his office."

I fold my arms over my chest and shake my head. Ean narrows his eyes and leans forward. Without saying a word, he grabs me by the waist and hefts me over his shoulder, knocking my hat and glasses off. He doesn't stop; he just keeps walking. I pound his back with my tiny fists and try to kick my legs. The roar of laughter follows us to our next destination.

# Chapter 20

## THE HEAD GUARD

### JESSICA

June 25, 2014: 11:16 a.m.

Ean literally pushes me through the door of Anders's office. My too-big glasses sit askew on my face after Ean harshly placed them back on. I push them up the bridge of my nose with my index finger and adjust my hat so that the brim faces forward instead of the haphazard way he plopped it on my head.

    Anders just watches me without saying a word. I study the stern look on his face, the rigid way he holds his posture, the way his arms rest on his desk stiffly. I have never been to Anders's office before, and our brief interactions in my room at the clinic are not formal visits, but we are now in his domain. Curiosity gets the better of me, and I start to look around the room. The walls are adorned with shelves that contain leather-bound books. Forgetting myself at the sight, I walk toward the shelves, running my fingers along the spines of the books, reading the titles as I pass them by.

Over the past couple of weeks, studying with Justin and Jeremy, I discovered that history is one of my favorite subjects. I especially love reading. Reading has been my solace since my vision returned, especially at night. Anders's office is like a little mini library, something I hoped to have seen on our tour earlier. I would love to get my hands on some of these books. He has everything from sonnets, and classic novels, to history books from all over the world, including historical books on the art of war and weapons. This is like a candy store, so much better than walking into any clothing or makeup store.

On the far wall before Anders's desk, there is a five-tier shelf full of books of various sizes and shapes. The spines of these books are worn, cracked, and peeling from overuse and opening and closing probably several times over. I just stare at the numerous volumes. I pull out a small, slender leather book and carefully open it. On the very first page, scrawled in neat cursive, is a name. On the second page, there is a date and a handwritten entry. These books are not printed books but handwritten journals.

Staring down at the journal in my hand, I smile. I can feel my heartbeat starting to pick up with excitement. It is like finding treasure. I want to know who wrote these. There are so many of them. Were all these journals written by one person? I have this strong urge that I need to start with the very first book. Would Anders let me read these?

Anders stands up from his desk and strides towards me. "So, you like to read, huh?" He gently takes the book in my hand and places it back in the space where I had pulled it from. Before I can protest, he reaches up, takes the first book on the top shelf, and hands it to me. "These are journals from the original Obsidian Pack Alpha, or who we now refer to as the original head guard. Of course, while most shifters can live over 150 years, many of the head guards, due to war, have not lived as long. These journals are passed down from head guard to head guard. They contain a series of events that you will never read in history texts and accounts of their personal lives."

I wonder if Anders keeps his own journals, and where would he keep them?

Anders lets out a laugh. "I do keep my own journals, but I keep those in a secret place. Only my replacement will have access to them once I pass or leave my position, as it is tradition. Many traditional Alphas keep the same tradition. It's a way for the former Alphas to leave their legacy behind and to help guide the future Alphas in their current role. It was once thought of as a way for the future Alphas to understand the foundation of how the pack has come to be and a means to prevent the current Alpha from repeating mistakes made in the past."

Anders stops speaking, and for a brief moment, some kind of emotion crosses his features, but he quickly masks it and gives me a small smile.

"History lessons are designed to teach future generations how to analyze and solve problems in the present and understand the past leaders and the cultures. It's supposed to strengthen our critical thinking skills so that we don't make the same mistakes. Today, with social media, technology, and, well, just the basic understanding of history being manipulated, we have forgotten who we are and where we came from. As shifters, we have forgotten how to rely on our basic animal survival instincts." He pauses and looks up at the shelf full of journals, then back at me. "As the head guard, I try to teach the recruits the importance of who we are, what we truly are protecting, and what we represent. That is why the history of all things pertaining to the LS territory is the most important thing the recruits learn."

I look down at the journal and then back up at Anders. This sense that I could learn so much not just from these journals but also from Anders fills my heart. I move to hand the journal back to Anders. I don't want to ruin it, and I have no idea where I will end up. Maybe one day I can return, and he will let me read these precious artifacts of our history. We can sit and have meaningful conversations about the past.

Anders finally takes the journal from my hand after studying me for a moment. He places the journal back in its place. "It will be here when you are ready to read them, although I would prefer it doesn't leave my office."

I look up at Anders, unsure how to interpret his words. I don't want to have false hope, so I look back down at the floor and nod.

He places his hand on my shoulder. "All this talk about journals and history gives me an idea." He releases my shoulder and turns back toward his desk. Once behind it, he pulls out a drawer and takes something out. Curious, I take a few steps to stand before his desk. He hands me a leather-bound book. On the book's cover is an emblem imprinted into the leather, filled with gold overlay. A dark green emerald sits in the center of the emblem, and diamonds embellish each corner of the triangle. I run my hands over it. I love the way it feels beneath my fingers. I open the cover to reveal a blank page. It's a journal.

I arch my eyebrows in question. What is this?

He clears his throat. "I know that you can't remember anything prior to waking up in the clinic, but I think this might help. Journal writing isn't just about documenting events. It's about reflection. You could write about your experiences, things that you discover about yourself, maybe even your nightmares."

I finger the journal and run my hands over the emblem again. This looks expensive. I can't accept this. I shake my head and hand the journal back to him. He doesn't take it.

"The emblem on the cover is the guard's crest designed by the first head guard. The emerald represents the Emerald Pack; the white diamonds represent the white wolf species. I think this was meant for you, little one."

Hanging my head down, I try to fight the tears threatening to spill over. I start to fidget with the journal in my hands. I'm not sure why Anders is so invested in my wellbeing. When the doctor determines that I am to be discharged from the clinic, I will most likely end up in an orphanage. With my memory gone, I cannot aid Anders in investigating my attack. Since I'm not from this territory or belong to the Emerald Pack, there really is no reason to investigate what happened to me unless someone reports a missing child to the guards.

Anders looks up at me and narrows his eyes. "You are definitely not going to an orphanage, and since you're still recovering, according to Dr. York, you will be here for a while." He lets out a short, breathy laugh. "You're quite observant, aren't you?"

I scoff. I don't have a choice. My vision sucks, I have no voice, and my only option is to listen and take note of my surroundings. I never know when someone will attack or betray me. So, I need to be prepared. One can never be too sure, and I am not going to make the mistake of assuming I will stay with a pack when I am not asked to again. The memory of Alpha Agnus returning me to the guards still stings.

"On second thought, you're not as observant as I thought you were," Anders says, taking me out of my little self-pity rant. I narrow my gaze. Before I can think any more thoughts, my eyes widen as I realize that Anders is talking to me as if I were speaking aloud. I cock my head to the side and furrow my brows. How is he doing this?

He chuckles. "It's not me; it's what you're doing. You have a neat little talent there. I have not come across many shifters who can mind-link outside of their animal form, including very powerful Alphas."

I shake my head in response. Alphas? I am no Alpha, and how does a mind-link actually work? Did I do it on purpose, or does it just happen? Like the twins, they can communicate only with each other through their link.

"You think too much. It makes me wonder, when you find your voice again, if you will talk nonstop like you do in your head."

I scoff again. *Can you blame me if the only conversations I can carry is in my own head?*

He shakes his head. "Alpha Agnus warned me you were a bit of a wiseass."

# CHAPTER 21

## FALLING INTO ROUTINE

### JESSICA

June 30, 2014: 6:45 a.m.

The guards and I fall into a comfortable routine. Ean comes in the morning and takes me for a walk around the training facility. Then I meet Anders in his office, where I sit with Anders for a couple of hours. If something comes up and needs his attention, I curl up in one of his chairs and read the journals of the original head guard. I take his other books back to my room and pore over them every night.

Charlie comes by to walk me back to my room. He brings his guitar and sings for me the first night. I am mesmerized by how he moves his fingers over the strings and fingers the keys. I am intrigued by the coordination it takes to strum, change notes, and sing simultaneously. The music makes the pain in my body subside. My heart doesn't ache, my nerve endings aren't jumpy, and I feel safe. When I close my eyes, it is as if I am whole again, alive, not broken, scarred, and stuck in a clinic room. After a few songs, I ask Charlie through hand motions to teach me how to play. Giving me his flirty smile, he obliges, and he has been teaching me how to play the guitar every day since then.

Sodie comes by in the evenings. He teaches me how to play poker, trumps, and blackjack. He promises that once I get better, he will start to teach me how to gamble. I think about playing cards with the twins and testing my ability to beat them at some of these games.

Liam has the night shift. He comes in with that same pinched expression. He sits in the corner of the room at an angle where he can see both my bed and the door. He sits there all night reading, never once looking up to check on me or speak to me. He never gets up to use the bathroom, take a walk, or move just to take a break. Sometimes when I'm sure he is not going to look up, I study him over the pages of my own book. When contemplating something he has read, he rubs his lower lip or plays with the diamond stud in his left ear. He lets out a long breath and runs his long fingers through his hair when he gets frustrated. Occasionally, he has a slight twitch to the corner of the right side of his mouth as if he is trying to prevent himself from smiling.

I can't help but wonder if he silently studies me too like the way I study him. I can feel the heat of a blush rise from my chest up to my cheeks so I bury my face in the book that I am reading so he can't see. If he even notices me at all.

I'm not sure if it's because of all the silence at night;

I can't help but miss the twins. Usually, by now, they're falling asleep over their textbooks or already asleep snoring. Although I appreciate the quiet, especially when they're in my mind whenever they're around, I miss the chaos. I miss them.

A dull ache throbs in the middle of my back as I sit in my clinic bed. I place the book down, and I try to stretch and twist. The discomfort doesn't get worse; it doesn't move. I try to think if I have pain anywhere else, but it's so hard to tell. My body hurts all the time. This ache persists in the center of my back, and it's new. Ignoring the pain because it's tolerable, I go back to reading my book. It's probably a new pain that I'll experience for the rest of my life.

I lean back on my bed and stare out the window. The sky is gray, and a light drizzle has started.

"Hey, you feeling okay?" Liam asks from his corner. He hasn't left yet. I forgot he was still sitting in the corner. I do a quick internal check in my head. Yep, all the everyday aches and pains are still present. Especially in the middle of my back. I start to think about that dull ache for a little bit; it's not worse, just still there. I shrug it off, pushing myself up to sit at the edge of the bed, and nod.

When I glance over at Liam, he's looking at me, running his index finger below his lower lip. I feel the heat creep into my cheeks, so I turn my head and continue to stare out the window.

"You ready to start your day with all this awesomeness?" Right on schedule, Ean shows, taking me out of my moment, and I welcome the distraction.

I glance over first at Liam, who is still frowning and

watching me; then I look over at Ean walking into the room and give him a small smile.

"Alright then, you know the routine. Breakfast first, then we can get you out of here." Ean places a cup of my meal replacement in front of me. The sight of it makes me want to puke; in fact, I don't think I even finished my other one from last night. I turn to look at the cup sitting on my nightstand. It's empty. Huh? I don't remember finishing it. I turn my head to look over at the corner of the room. Liam has already left. Did he drink it?

Turning my attention back to my "breakfast," a sharp shooting pain rips right through me, forcing me to lean forward. I squeeze my eyes shut. I open them slowly as the pain fades back to a dull ache.

"Everything okay there?" Ean asks with a look of concern on his face. I nod, pick up my shake, and down it as fast as possible. A change of scenery will help with my mood and whatever is going on with my body.

We don't take our usual path this time. Ean talks, oblivious to his surroundings. I'm not listening to him this time.

My stomach hurts, and nausea keeps threatening to take hold. I probably drank my shake too fast, so I keep brushing it off. Using my surroundings as a distraction, I catch a glimpse of Liam coming out of a building. He has a book in one hand, and he just casually strides out onto the grassy area, probably heading toward the dorms. A group of three guys come out of the building after him, walking a bit faster as if they're trying to catch up.

One of them shouts, "Hey, Fitzpatrick, I'm not done

talking to you!" Liam keeps his casual pace and continues to walk, not even glancing back to acknowledge the guy shouting out at him. The other two pick up their pace.

One of them knocks the book out of his hand and sneers, "You think you're better than the rest of us, just because you got the VIP assignment." A guy with curling tan-colored hair mocks Liam from behind. Liam stops walking, still not acknowledging them, walks over to where his book landed, and picks it up.

I grab Ean by the shirt to stop him. I point over at Liam.

He shakes his head. "This is the way things are; if you're going to be a guard, you need to learn how to stand up for yourself." Facing the situation, Ean crosses his arms over his chest and watches. I turn too, mimicking Ean's stance, and fold my arms over my middle.

All three of the guys now surround Liam. The guy that had shouted at Liam first has dark brown hair. He is slightly bigger than Liam. I can't see his face. The silent one wears a hat. His build is similar to Ean's, but he isn't anywhere as tall.

"You know what I think. I think you got a thing for her. I hear she looks like a little boy," the guy with the dark brown hair taunts.

Liam doesn't respond. He just pushes past the guys in an attempt to walk away. The guy with the hat grabs Liam by the shoulder and forces him to turn back around.

"I bet it must bring back some great memories, doesn't it?" The dark-brown-haired guy steps in closer to Liam and gets in his face. The curly-haired guy whacks the book out of Liam's hand again. "Maybe, I should pay her a visit and show her what a real man can do."

Liam yanks his shoulder out of Hat Guy's grip, pushes past them.

"Come on, fight me! I know you want to!" Liam picks up his book and keeps walking away. They won't leave him alone. Two guys grab him from behind, hold his arms down, and turn him to face their leader.

As the guy pulls back his arm to hit Liam, I tug on Ean's arm. *Stop them. Stop them please!* Thunderclaps and dark clouds start to roll in. *Ean! Stop them!!It's three against one. This isn't right!* I try to motion with my hands to relay what I want to say to Ean, but my efforts are futile. If he isn't going to stop them, I will. Pushing away from him, I successfully take three steps before Ean grabs me by the hoodie and drags me backward.

"It's okay, little one, watch." Thunder claps again, and I can feel my heart racing. When I turn back to the fight, Liam has somehow managed to get out of the hold the guys had him in. I watch in frustration as all three guys punch, hit, and grab Liam. As I start to follow the fight, Liam is blocking each kick, each punch, striking back. Liam manages to floor one of the attackers and land two punches to his face; another one jumps him from behind. Liam rolls out of the way just before he lands on him. Liam jumps up, striking him with a kick in the face. He turns and grabs the one that started this whole thing by the throat and mercilessly hits him over and over.

Blood starts to spill, and an image flashes in my mind. I'm no longer watching Liam hit his opponent. I see myself receiving blows to the face. I watch in slow motion as a fist hits me and a man—no, a teenager with brown hair not much younger than these guys—yells, "I fucking hate you!"

*Stop!* I scream in my head as lightning strikes through the sky. Liam stops mid-hit, looks up at me, and I stare back. *Please stop!*

He looks down at the guy in his grips, leans forward, and with a snarled expression, he grounds out, "If you go near her, I will rip your fucking head off!"

I watch as he releases his grip, and the guy falls to the ground. He strides over to his book lying open on the ground, picks it up, and walks away. I look out in front of me and see all three attackers in a bloody heap lying on the ground. My stomach curls, and nausea takes over. I push away from Ean, scurrying over to the nearest bush I can find, and lose all of my stomach contents.

Ean comes up from behind me and pats my back. "Whoa there, little one, I think I should get you back to the clinic, too much excitement for the morning." Still dry heaving, I shake my head. Another streak of lightning flashes in the sky followed by a clap of thunder.

---

Anders isn't happy with me. He wears a pinched expression and stares straight ahead. Even though he is busy and needs to follow up on the incident with Liam, he still walks me back to the clinic.

Anders finally glances over at me and asks, "What was it about the fight that made you sick?"

I replay the whole fight in my head, the flashback I saw, the look on Liam's face as he hit the other recruit.

Anders stops walking abruptly and turns to look at me directly. "Do that again." Confused by what he is asking me to do, I shrug my shoulders. "It was like watching a movie. Replay that whole incident in your mind again, especially when you have that flashback of that person hitting you. I want you to hold that memory."

It's no use; I never see faces. If a face is in my line of vision, it's too blurry or covered by shadows.

He leans down, resting his hands on his knees, so he is at eye level with me. "Just give it a go. Plus, I want to see and hear what you saw." I do what Anders asks me to do. When he is satisfied, we return to my room, where he leaves me so he can attend to the recruits, promising that someone will be here shortly.

Charlie shows up sometime after lunch. He shows me a notebook with thin scrawled handwriting. He says that I inspired him to write a song. I look over his scrawled penmanship and read the lyrics. With a tight-lipped smile, I nod at him and point to his guitar.

With his sinfully charming smile, he obliges my request and plays some chords, but it just doesn't fit. Charlie wants it to be a slow song. It just doesn't feel right. The lyrics feel better as a faster song. Something more upbeat, something that matches his personality and his style. Together, we change the music chords, move the lyrics around until it finally all comes together.

Charlie reaches over and chucks my chin. "You got some real talent, little one. It makes me wonder if you ever played before." I lift my left hand and wiggle my fingers. No calluses. He reaches out, grabs my hand, and rubs his thumb over my fingertips. "No calluses," he says, looking back up with a serious expression. "I hope you get your voice back. It would be nice if you and I could sing a duet together."

I let out a huff and push my glasses back up, wrinkling my nose simultaneously.

He raises his brow and smirks. "Don't give me that look. Call it intuition. I think you were musically inclined before." He shrugs. "You know everything and could probably sing too."

I playfully roll my eyes at him.

"I'm serious. I think we could make a great duet. Look at what we did in a few hours."

I just shrug in response.

"I guess in time we'll find out." He winks, and just like that, he's back to his flirty, joking ways and starts to pack up. "I can't wait to show the guys what we put together," he says, clapping his hands together. "I will see you tomorrow and let you know how it went." He leans over and gives me a big hug. "Get some rest, little one." He kisses my cheek.

Liam walks in just as Charlie pulls away. Liam, wearing his regular pinched expression, lifts his chin in Charlie's direction, and takes up his standard post.

Charlie looks amused as he watches Liam. He grabs his guitar and notebook and heads out. Liam is earlier than his usual time. I'm assuming Sodie will be staying with me tonight.

Sighing, I gather my things and head to the bathroom. When I emerge, I put my little bag full of toiletries that Shakti had given to me in my nightstand drawer. On my bedside table is a little medicine cup full of vitamins and supplements and a tall glass filled with the meal replacement shakes that I am supposed to drink.

"The nurse just stopped by. She said she will be back with your injections in a few minutes."

I nod without turning to look at Liam. I move to grab a beanie sitting on my nightstand, and I notice a notepad and pen sitting next to it. I pick up the beanie and pull it on my head without disturbing the tablet.

"Charlie returned not long after you went into the bathroom and brought a notepad. He said in case inspiration hits you and you want to write more song lyrics."

Smiling more to myself than at Liam, I pick up the notepad and pen. Liam rarely talks; this is the most he's spoken to me since I met him. I like the sound of Liam's voice and that slight accent, wow. If he would talk more, I wouldn't mind listening to him. There is something soothing about it, sexy even. I blush slightly and distract myself by quickly scribbling a question on the paper. Walking up to Liam, I hold it up in front of him.

Slowly, he looks up at the paper, then at me, then back to the paper. "No, you're stuck with me until morning." I show him an okay sign and walk back to my bed. I suddenly feel a little self-conscious. I'm not used to having Liam here so early.

Nervously, I glance over at Liam sitting in the corner of the room when Mimi returns with the injections. I freeze when she asked to look over the wounds on my back, and the surgical incision on my throat. I had forgotten about the dressing changes. I'm used to having Sodie around at this time. With his expressed interest in the medical field, he tends to help Mimi. It never bothered me for some reason when he was in the room for my regular check-in.

Mimi hands her wound care kit to Liam and chides me when she realizes that I haven't taken my meds yet. A heat of embarrassment floods my cheeks when I realize that I will have to change back into that gown that exposes my backside.

Dr. York comes in shortly after Mimi leaves for his usual check-in and asks his routine questions of the day. I probably should tell him about the new pain in my mid-back and the stomach discomfort. I don't want to do any more tests and scans and another treatment plan added to the laundry list that I already have. I'm sure, if I take a two-hour nap, I will be fine. I've been pushing myself, like Dr. York just lectured me about.

With another cross over my heart, I promise to try to get some sleep tonight with another promise that I will finish my shake. I really can't wait to get this stupid tube out of my stomach. Maybe this is what's causing some of the discomfort. If it's still there tomorrow, I'll bring it up then. After Dr. York leaves, I pick up the glass and start to drink the horrible thing.

Staring down at the pale-yellow concoction and frowning, I only manage to get a third of it down. I already feel full.

"You have some of it on your upper lip." Jumping slightly at the sound of Liam's voice, I look over to him, pointing at his lip. Embarrassed, I swipe at my lip with my fingers. He chuckles, stands up, grabs a paper napkin from the dispenser on the wall near the sink, and hands it to me.

Grabbing the chair Dr. York had been sitting in earlier,

he moves it closer and sits in it. Seriously, is he going to sit there in front of me while I drink this crappy-ass drink? But he doesn't move, nor does he look up from his book. Looking down at my hands, I don't know what the hell to do with myself. Sodie usually just talks to me. Even if he can't hear my thoughts, he talks to me about whatever comes up. Looking around the room as if I haven't done that a million times already, my mind wanders back to the fight Liam was in earlier.

Did he learn how to fight like that in the program? Gods and to think I was going to try and stop the fight myself because Ean wouldn't do a damn thing. That would have been humiliating, like I could ever protect someone like Liam. I didn't exactly do a good job of protecting myself, obviously.

I wonder if I will be able to stay here? If Anders would let them teach me how to fight like Liam. Maybe if whoever did this to me found me again, I would be able to fight them off, or at least be able to protect myself.

Without making it extremely obvious, I chance a peek at Liam, only to find him looking at me. Oh shit, why is he looking at me? Looking for something to do, I pick up my shake and make an attempt to finish it. Making sure I wipe my face with the napkin, before Liam points out another shake mustache, I set the glass back down and scoot back on to my bed, facing away from him to feign interest in my book.

"I was worried that I scared you off. After you watched that fight." He says it softly, concern lacing his voice.

I frown down at my book. I might have felt overwhelmed

at first, mostly concerned about him. I was so frustrated with Ean for not stepping in. I pull myself up from my semi-reclined position and swivel around to face him. Dropping my gaze to my lap, I shake my head.

"I heard you went straight to Anders after, and you communicated what you had witnessed to him." Still looking down, I nod. A soft laugh escapes him. It's a nice sound, and it makes me blush a little. "I also heard you tried to stop the fight, and Ean had to drag you back by your hoodie."

I want to bury my face in this mattress and suffocate myself with the blankets right now. Gods, I know it was stupid, but hearing it out of his mouth makes me feel like a complete idiot. I just want to curl up and die right now.

His large hand rests on my knee. "Thank you for having my back. I don't come across that very often. It meant a lot to me that you would even try, especially knowing what you've been through."

Nodding my head briskly, I continue to stare down at his hand on my knee. His thumb gently brushes the fabric of my pants a few times before he removes it. An uncomfortable silence passes between us; I shift back, facing away from him, and lean against the mattress in a reclined position. I take a sidelong glance at him one last time before picking up the book I had been reading.

"You should get some sleep," he says without looking up from his book.

I look up at the clock on my wall. It's barely eight o'clock. Why is he telling me to go to bed now? I snap a narrowed eye look his way, making sure it's clearly written on my face that I don't intend to fall asleep right now.

He sighs, gets up from his chair, turns on the lamp near my bed, and turns off the overhead light.

Returning to my bedside, he holds out his hand. "Book." He makes a gimme motion. I shake my head. He makes the motion again. Pouting, I give in and hand him the book. He places it next to his on the table. Hmm, he's reading *The Art of War*. I read that book two nights ago. "Glasses." I cross my arms over my chest and wrinkle my nose.

He lets out a breathy laugh. "Glasses."

I roll my eyes, remove my lenses, and hand them over.

He reaches down and presses the button that lowers the head of my bed, grabs his book, and sits back down. Lying flat on my back is uncomfortable, but I try to stay that way for a bit, because I don't want to turn my back to him or even face him. Why is he sitting there? I can feel my face heating up again. I liked it better when he isn't so close. I squirm a little, trying to get a little more comfortable, but I can't take it. Giving up my resistance to lie on my side, I finally turn over to face him. I try to look anywhere but directly at him.

"Most people close their eyes when they sleep," he mumbles without lifting his gaze.

I let out a slow breath and close my eyes. Suddenly, a sharp pain tears through the center of my body. I pull my knees up into my chest, but this time the pain doesn't dissipate. I squeeze my eyes tighter, and I try to will the pain away, but that doesn't seem to work either.

I feel a warm hand on my shoulder. Before I can open my eyes to look up, a wave of nausea hits me. Pushing myself up into a sitting position, everything starts to spin. I can feel myself falling forward or sideways; I can't really tell which direction my body is leaning toward.

As the dizziness starts to recede, I slowly open one eye to look at Liam who is standing right in front of me holding me upright. Another sharp pain rips through me again, more intense than it had been the first time, forcing me to lean forward. Resting my head on Liam's chest, I try to catch my breath, but the pain is unbearable. Nausea hits me again, and my stomach starts to curl. I try to push Liam back, but it is too late.

I cover my face, embarrassed with what just happened, but another rush of pain and nausea starts all over again. It feels like someone is stabbing me right through the middle of my back into my stomach. I can't think of anything else. I can barely catch my breath from the pain.

A warm hand rubs my back. "Breathe, just breathe. I got you. The doc or the nurse should be here any minute now."

My head is spinning, and the sound of rushing water sounds in my ears. I hear muffled voices, but I can't make out what they are saying. Then there is nothing but silence and darkness.

# CHAPTER 22

## SODIE'S SECRET

### LIAM

#### June 30, 2014: 8:25 p.m.

Where the hell is the doctor and the nurse? I pressed the emergency button what feels like an eternity ago. She's in pain. I should probably rush out and call for help, but I don't want to leave her alone. She doesn't make a sound, but I can see the pain written all over her face. Her pain is so intense I can almost feel it myself. She tries to push me away, but I refuse to move in case she falls over.

    She pukes all over me; I know it makes her embarrassed, but I don't care. Her safety is what matters the most. Shit, why didn't she tell the doctor what happened this morning? I sat in the corner of the room and watched her downplay all the answers to the doctor's questions. I didn't want to interfere or call her out. At the same time, she didn't really lie. He didn't ask her if anything new started today or last night. I knew something was wrong, and I didn't do anything about it.

I look down at my vomit-stained shirt and pants. Instead of a sickly yellow color to match the supplement she drank just a short time ago, this looks like bright red blood mixed with dark coffee grounds. I start to rub her back, murmuring something to her to keep her calm. I don't even know what I'm saying. I'm trying to hold on to my own control as anxiety threatens to take over. My heart is hammering so hard against my chest. I'm trying to control my breathing, to keep it together. Fuck, I need to do something. If the doctor doesn't get in here soon, I'm going to pick her up and carry her to him. Just as I finish that thought, Sodie walks in.

"Get the doctor and the nurse!" I bark at him. He backs up and rushes out the door. I hear his quick footfalls disappear down the hall and his shouts for help. He rushes back through the door. Before I can say anything to him, Jessica slumps over in my arms.

"Where the fuck are they?" I growl.

Sodie looks me up and down. "She's vomiting blood."

Anxiety squeezes around my heart, as her body goes lax, her lips turning white. "I'm fucking carrying her to them."

Before I can gather her further into my arms to carry her out, Sodie's arm strikes out, grabbing my shirt. "Wait, let me try something."

"We don't have time!" I grind out, ready to punch him if he tries to stop me again. Her breathing becomes shallow. I can hear her heart rate slowing down to a dangerously slow rhythm.

He looks at me with wide eyes. "Trust me, please." He

climbs into the hospital bed, reaches between the two of us, and places his hand over her abdomen and his other hand over her back. A bright white light emanates from his hands.

"What are you doing?" I ask him, but he doesn't answer me. Finally, the sound of footsteps grows louder from the hall. The doctor and nurse rush into the room, and they stand there in stunned silence for a brief moment. The doctor takes in the sight of my clothing and the puddle on the floor.

Turning to the nurse, he tells her to call for backup staff and to prep the small operating room in the clinic. Sodie looks scared, but he continues to hold his position. Jessica starts to stir. Her breathing slowly returns to normal, her heart rate picks back up, and color returns to her ashen-colored lips. The doctor rushes forward, and the light coming from Sodie's hands starts to fade. He removes his hands and backs up to make room for the doctor, but I don't move from my position. What the hell did Sodie do?

"Liam, I need to get in closer to take a look at her."

I hesitate for a moment, still holding on to her. I shuffle to the side to make some room. The doctor looks at Sodie warily. Then he gives Jessica his full attention.

Anders rushes into the room along with the nurse. The doctor looks up from his position and announces, "I need to take her into surgery right now." Jessica hasn't opened her eyes or regained consciousness. I don't want to let her go. "This is life or death. We need to go now," he says to Anders.

It has been two days and three nights of fucking hell. Jessica has some random spontaneous internal bleeding, the cause of which the doctor can't determine. She's lost so much blood her organs are starting to fail. The doctor started a blood transfusion, and she had a horrible reaction to it. He couldn't tell if it was a bad batch of donor blood or if she built an immunity to what was given to her before.

When the medical team stabilized her, everyone was asked to get tested to see who would be a match. The only one who came close to being a match was one of the recruits named Darwin. He was able to donate blood to her. Still, even with the blood transfusions, her body wouldn't heal. The wounds she sustained from her initial injuries broke open, and she developed an infection. It was one thing after another. I kept overhearing the medical team say over and over how they had never seen anything like it before.

So many things are happening to her tiny body again. She was doing so well; it's like she has taken one giant leap backward. She's back on a breathing machine, but this time, they have a tube down her throat. Heart monitors are back on, IV bags hanging from a pole. No one can figure it out. I think the only thing that keeps her alive is that at every chance, Sodie uses his healing magic on her. Even he can't understand why it isn't enough.

I'm sitting at her bedside holding her hand, just like I had that night we brought her home from the Whitemore plantation, internally praying for some kind of miracle. Is it too much to ask for another one? She already survived the first time. I hear yelling and arguing coming from the hall. I kiss the back of her hand, before getting out of my chair to check on what the hell is going on.

"No!" Jeremy shouts.

"I'm sorry, boys. I think we reached the point where we have done all that we could. Without the machines..." Shakti's voice breaks.

The doctor steps forward, placing a hand on Shakti's shoulder, and gently squeezes. Anders turns around, swiping both hands through his hair. Ean has fat tears falling down his face. This is bad. This is fucking bad if Ean is crying. I don't even want to look at Charlie or Chris. I might lose my shit if I do. Elias's head is tilted back, facing the ceiling.

"You can't. Mom, please," Justin whispers. Shakti breaks down into tears, turning her face into the doctor's shoulder.

Jeremy's face is an angry shade of red; he's breathing hard, hands balled into fist at his side. "Are you going to call Luke? Are you going to tell him that all his efforts were for nothing because we gave up on her!"

I can't listen to this. No, she's not dying! I feel like someone stabbed me in the fucking chest. Heat radiates off my body. My chest starts to heave. My vision turns red, and I'm on the brink of losing control. But I don't fucking care. I'll burn this whole fucking place down if she dies.

A giant hand wraps around my throat, and my body crashes against a wall. I roar out in anger, striking out. My fist hits something solid, but it doesn't budge. The hand around my throat squeezes harder, cutting off my air supply.

"Get it together!" a harsh, low voice whispers in my ear. "We have enemies here. I'm not going to lose you too!" My rage blinding me, I grab at whatever my hands can get a hold of.

The hand loosens from my throat, and I'm pulled into a strong bear hold. I let go of whatever I'm gripping in my hands and wrap my arms around a large body gripping onto the back of his shirt. "She can't!" I mean to scream, but my words come out in a sob. "She can't die." As soon as I let myself fall apart, I recognize the person holding on to me. Ean.

Sodie is the last one to find out. Chris is the one who broke the news to him. He falls apart just as badly as the twins and I did, if not worse. We hang our heads, silently crying, as we witness one more person who cared about this tiny little girl fall apart. It's amazing how much of an impact she has made on all of us in such a short amount of time.

When Sodie calms down, we follow the doctor into the room. We solemnly watch as the nurse, with shaky hands and tears streaming down her face, removes the IV lines, turns off the machine that had been breathing for Jessica, and removes the tube down her throat. However, the doctor stops her from turning off the heart monitor.

Nathan, Shakti's mate, wraps his arms around her, gently kissing the top of her head as she cries into his chest. He reaches over, placing his hand on Justin's shoulder; Justin reaches over and places his hand on Jeremy's.

It's been sixteen hours. There have been no changes in Jessica's vital signs. The rhythmic beep of her heart bounces around the clinic room. Nathan convinces everyone in the room to take a breather. Sodie and I volunteer to stay and notify them if any changes occur. Earlier, we pulled Jessica's bed to the middle and placed chairs around it so everyone could take turns and sit around her. Sodie is sitting across from me. He looks like crap, and I can only imagine that I must look just as bad as he does.

Emily strides into the room, her long black hair tied up in a high ponytail, arms crossed over her chest, lips pursed, looking like she's ready to tackle anything that's about to get in her way. Her dark eyes, nearly as black as Elias's, roam over Jessica's body. Her eyes widen in shock, before they soften and begin to shine with unshed tears.

"Why didn't anyone call me sooner? I had to hear about what happened from Luke who's in another country. My own brothers are here every day, and I didn't even get a phone call or a text. You look like shit by the way. Do you need a break? I can sit here, with her, and text you if something happens." She takes a deep breath and I squeeze my eyes shut. I don't have it in me to take part in Emily's ramblings, but the irritation brewing inside of me isn't her doing. I open my eyes to meet her questioning gaze and let out a long breath.

"You hadn't met her, and you were at summer school in the city."

"That's not fair. I wanted to meet her as soon as I heard she was here, but every time I asked, I was told it wasn't a good time. I drove here as fast as I could without getting another speeding ticket." My heart softens. Knowing her, she must have dropped everything as soon as she heard from Luke to be here.

"I'm sure your dad appreciated it."

She nods, then plops herself down in a chair next to Sodie. "Yeah, except this is the one time I think he would have been a little more forgiving," she says on a sigh. I give her a halfhearted smirk.

Sodie hasn't looked up or acknowledged Emily since she walked in. He just sits there, eyes vacantly staring down at Jessica.

Emily gently nudges his arm with her shoulder. "I'm Emily by the way." Sodie slowly rotates his head to look at her. He tilts his chin up in acknowledgement.

"I'm Sodie, one of the recruits."

"I assumed you were a recruit. It's nice to meet you. I heard you're one of the highest-ranking recruits aside from this guy." She points her thumb at me. "The leads are quite impressed with your work ethic and perseverance. They have high hopes for you as a guard. That's why you were assigned to VIP detail." I don't know what it is that Emily said, but his face pinches as if he is in pain, his eyes glass over. His eyes shifts over to me.

Without saying it out loud, I know that he's silently asking if he can trust her. I nod my head. He places his hands over her abdomen and her heart, infusing her body with his healing magic. Emily gasps in surprise, but she remains silent. As the minutes go by and nothing happens, our hope starts to dwindle.

With a heavy sigh, Sodie drops back into his chair. Despair grows heavy in the room.

Emily reaches out and places her hand on Jessica's leg. "I read somewhere that magic healers have the ability to pull energy from other magic wielders around them to strengthen their magic. I'm not a magic wielder, but some generations back, there's a rumor that we carry white wolf shifter blood. Maybe if you pull from my energy and tap into Liam's energy, we could help."

Sodie scoffs. "You read that somewhere, like from one of those damn romance novels girls like to read."

Emily glares at him. "If you must know, I read it from a journal of my great-grandfather, who happens to be the son of the original head guard, asshole. And for the record, I don't read romance novels."

Sodie's eyes widen in surprise before he shifts them back to me. Right, he had no idea that Emily is Elias's daughter.

"Just do it, numb nuts, before everyone returns," Emily growls, then leans over the bed, placing a hand on my shoulder. Without saying a word, I lean forward and place my hand over Jessica's heart. With a tilt of my head, I silently nudge him on. Sodie places his hand over mine and his other one on Jessica's torso. Together, we give Jessica everything we have.

When Shakti and Chris's mate Tater return to the room, we are exhausted, but there is still no change. Seeing the weariness deep in our bones, Shakti forces the three of us out of the room.

"You three need a break. We'll take over and call if… anything happens." Shakti's voice breaks. Tater rubs her arm in support, turning her head at the same time to wipe at the moisture around her eyes. Tater, like Emily, hasn't met Jessica officially, and yet she's already mourning over her.

My gut twists as the look of sorrow increases on both of their faces. Both Chris and Elias's family have been coming and going in support of Shakti and the twins. It shows what a tight-knit family they are, why solidarity and unity are instilled among the guards.

Hanging our heads, we nod. Sodie is the first one to stand. I give Jessica's hand a final squeeze and reluctantly head for the door.

# CHAPTER 23

## NINE LIVES

### JESSICA

#### March 31, 2025: Present Day

Carmen is staring at me with wide eyes. "How the hell are you alive?"

I shrug. "I ask myself that same question all the time. At this point in my life, I should have died twice."

She shakes her head in disbelief. "On top of the trauma you already suffered, you survived some kind of random internal bleeding, anaphylaxis, sepsis, organ failure. I mean, the list goes on. How?"

I let out a breathy laugh, "Dr. York can't figure it out either. He called in specialists, and they couldn't understand it themselves. No one really knows how it happened in the first place. I mean, there were theories." I lift my hands, shrugging.

She frowns. "So just like that, you got better and woke up."

"Not exactly. After I was taken off life support, I didn't die, like the medical team and specialist had predicted. I started to breathe on my own spontaneously, and my heart rate remained slow but steady. After about... oh, I don't know, twenty-four hours maybe... Sorry, this is all secondhand information. My timeline could be off. My vital signs started to improve, and I slowly started healing. I understood that there was only one donor I could receive blood from without having a reaction, so they gave that a try, monitoring closely for any signs of rejection. When there were none, they moved forward with that and slowly incorporated other treatments. It was very limited because my body just started to heal on its own, like a normal nontransitioned shifter being should have. It took almost a week or so before I woke up."

Carmen purses her lips, wearing a look of incredulity. "Did you experience other medical emergencies?"

"Yeah, near-death experiences seem to be my forte." Licking my lips, I look around the room before continuing. "My brothers and I have a standing joke, you know, since, I'm adopted and without any recollection of where I came from. They used to tease me and say that I was part feline."

"Feline?"

Christian and I bark out a laugh at Carmen's reaction to my inside joke. Clearly, she doesn't get it.

"You know, cats have nine lives. I think I'm down to my last one."

# CHAPTER 24

## SHADOWS AND LIGHT

### SHADOW

#### July 25, 2014: 10 a.m.

Anders lets out a harsh breath and places a single fist in front of his mouth. He looks stressed, like the weight of the world is on his shoulders.

"If you tell me what's going on, I can offer some advice." Not sure how great my advice will be, but if it's guard-related or legal counseling, that I can do.

He shakes his head. "A lot has been going on since you last checked in. I didn't want to involve you since there wasn't much you could do, and I wanted you to focus on school."

"I see. Obviously, you're having some kind of internal war going on, because normally, you look more put together."

He scoffs. "I take it that's an idiom for you look like shit," he deadpans.

I stare blankly back.

He sucks in a breath and puts back on that mask I'm accustomed to seeing him wear. The "head guard" mask.

"Actually, there is something that I wanted to run by you. A few weeks ago, there was another incident between Marcus, Dustin, and Boris."

"Let me guess, Liam was their target?"

Anders grunts in answer. I'm not surprised to hear about this. From the moment Marcus Greystone stepped foot on training grounds, he has been gunning for Liam. I've tried everything I could to prevent Greystone and his two cousins from the Northern A territory from becoming a part of the recruit program.

"Let me guess, Alpha Greystone got involved?" He most likely pulled a political card, which is how his son and his two nephews from his Luna's side were able to get in.

"You know he did. He coddles that punk even when he does something wrong. I also suspect that they're here for other reasons. We've been keeping a close eye on those three and giving out very little guard information, which is a disadvantage to the rest of the remaining recruits."

"Sounds like you have everything taken care of." He pauses and simply shakes his head. The guard program has been under threat before. He and the other two leads have this under control. Unfortunately, with Alpha Greystone involved, this isn't a legal issue. This is more of a political problem, and once politics become involved, things are not always black and white. But Anders knows this already. He doesn't need my advice on this situation. I wait for him to continue.

"Marcus verbally threatened Jessica in a sexual manner. It could have just been a barb or a taunt. With Liam's history with the Greystones, he responded to his threat physically. My concern is that in retaliation, Marcus will make good on his threat."

"Jessica?"

"She's our VIP... case... for lack of a better way to describe her status." Before I can inquire further, Chris and Elias walk into the office.

"Shadow, been a while, how are you doing?" Chris asks as I stand from my sitting position and dip my chin. Chris does the same in return and sits on the edge of Anders's desk. He comes across as friendly and a little charming, but don't let that fool you. He is one hell of a guard and one hell of an interrogator. I've seen him rip apart shifters who thought they were tough and make them cry.

"Doing well, thank you for asking," I reply. Took me years to be able to respond to a simple question in less of a formal way. I dip my head to Elias, right before he takes the seat opposite my own. Taking that as my cue, I return to my seat.

"I hear you just wrapped up your bachelor's degree, heading into law school?"

"I'm finishing up my last year in law school."

Chris frowns. "I thought you were Charlie's age?"

"I am. I finished my bachelor's early. Got a head start on law school." The corner of my lips twitch as I force myself to smile.

Chris nods as if in approval. "Oh yes, now I remember, must have heard the information wrong." Chris claps his hands together. "So, we are all here. What do you have for us, Shadow?"

"It took me a while to gain permission to enter Territory Two under the guise of a recruiting officer looking for potential recruits. Fortunately for me, Alpha Rhineheart's PA was the one who responded to my last and most recent email. Unfortunately, too much time has passed, and my attempts at an investigation came up a little short."

Anders steeples his hands in front of him and places his fingertips to his lips, "Well, let's see what you came up with."

Reaching down, I pick up the items I had brought in with me and place them in front of Anders on his desk. "There is no missing child reported throughout the entire territory. I didn't even come across a fresh grave or a headstone in their pack's cemetery. I hacked into the school's database, and there is no female child listed with a first or last name with 'G' in it."

Anders starts to frown. Then he asks, "The school uniform, was it a match?"

"Yes, all the students were wearing the same standard uniform as the ones you had given me." He doesn't respond so I continue. "I did meet with one of the teachers—I believe she was a music teacher. She was the only one willing to speak with me, not that I had gotten much information from her. This is purely speculation, but there was something terribly off about the entire pack, especially at the school. If I had to guess, it was as if everyone was... well, mourning mixed with a sense of fear. Except for a bunch of punk-ass teenagers who could use a lesson in manners, especially the punk who leads that group."

"Let me guess—the Alpha's boy?" Elias asks.

"I didn't get the sense he was an Alpha, just some punk with a mouth. He only caught my attention because he had a fairly new scar on his left cheek."

"Like he was in a fight?" Anders asks as he looks down at the two bags I placed on his desk. One was the uniform he supplied me with from the girl they call "little one." "What's this?" he asks, holding up a backpack.

"After coming up empty-handed, I decided to take a walk through the forest, see if I could find anything on my way back to the territory border where she was found. I found it under some bushes, in the forest."

Anders starts to go through the backpack and passes items to Chris, who starts flipping through a notebook.

"After finding the backpack, I came across a shredded hooded jacket. It's in the bag with the uniform. Oddly enough, the tag is still intact with the letter G written on it. I found some markings on a tree not far from where the jacket had been. About several hundred yards further, I found the tree she was hung from." Anders looks to both Chris and Elias.

"What grade do you think this textbook belongs to?" He reaches over and tosses it to me. A slip of paper falls out, except it isn't a piece of paper. It's a photograph of a girl with a heart-shaped face and platinum blond hair that is tied up in a ponytail falling over the front of her shoulder. The photo cuts off before you can see the ends of her hair. Her striking dark eyebrows contrast with the paleness of her hair and long thick dark lashes. Beautiful full lips turn up into a smile, showing perfectly straight white teeth. Her smile doesn't reach her eyes, those beautiful, clear, ice blue eyes with a dark ring around them.

I'm mesmerized by the striking beauty of that young girl. My heart rate speeds up, and I squirm in my seat. My body's reaction is making me uncomfortable. Huh, it's not like me to respond this way to anyone, let alone a picture of a young girl. The deep rumble of a distinct voice tries to push forward in my mind. I push it back down. Not now. Don't do this now.

Elias bends to pick up the picture, looks at it closely, and hands it over to Chris. Chris inspects the photo, and a sad smile crosses his lips. He reads the words on the bottom of the picture. "Ruby Falls High School, class of 2015." He flips the photo over, but there is no inscription on the back. Class of 2015, that means that girl will graduate next year. Even though she is beautiful, she looks a bit young to graduate so soon.

He hands the photo over to Anders and watches him intently. Without looking away, he asks, "Did you see a girl at the school who looks like this?"

"If I had seen a girl who looked like that, she would have stood out." All the pack members, including their children, have the same characteristics—chestnut brown hair and brown eyes. Like most packs, you can tell who belongs. They all share the same coloring. Nowadays, it's a little harder to tell as packs have intermingled due to leaving their territory for school or business, but the Ruby Falls Pack are a very traditional pack. They keep to themselves, and it is rare for anyone to leave the territory.

A firm knock on the door interrupts us. Ean ushers in a tiny boy wearing a baseball cap, glasses that take up most of his face, a large t-shirt, gym shorts that fall just below his knees, and an old pair of chucks. Suddenly, a deep emotional ache fills my chest. My vision tunnels. All I can see is the little boy as a burst of white light and lightning knocks me back into my chair and steals my breath away.

His aura takes over the entire room, shedding the darkness and shadows that engulf me, realigning my soul. The light is calling to me. I want to leap out of my chair and embrace it. Embrace him. I grip the armrest, keeping myself rooted firmly in my chair. Mentally, I shake off the strangeness of this feeling that has formed deep in my chest, but this ache is so much deeper than anything I have ever recalled feeling before, and the light has curled not just around my heart but deep into my soul.

"What did I tell you about your hat?" Anders asks gently.

What the fuck just happened to me? I stare down at the floor, trying to analyze what just happened. Did I just imprint on a boy? My head whips toward Ean, who hovers over the boy protectively. He nods at me in greeting, and he looks back down at the boy with a goofy grin. Confusion starts to cloud the rational part of my brain. I watch as the boy removes his hat. Ean reaches down to the top of the boy's head and ruffles up already-disheveled hair poking out at all sorts of angles. White-blond hair.

The boy gives Ean an annoyed look, then moves toward Chris, hugging him. "Hello, little one, did you enjoy your walk this morning?" Little one? Little one... Hold on, is this...

Elias's voice booms in the office. "Why does he always get the first hug? What am I? Invisible?"

He or rather she nods up at Chris, releases him, then moves over toward Elias, who stands, making her look even tinier. She hugs him.

"Did you get some sleep last night?"

She nods. Elias gently touches her face, tipping it up to inspect it like a doting father. I see the scarring on her left cheek. Satisfied with whatever he was looking for, he drops his hand. "Good, glad the boys are looking out for you."

Elias says it with so much tenderness, something around my heart squeezes. What is that? I reach up to feel my chest. Maybe it's something I recently ate. It can't be that. I only eat the exact same foods every day, at the same time of the day. I never stray from my biological schedule.

Guiding her by the shoulders, he turns her toward me. "Little one, this is Shadow. He's one of our best guards or was our best guard. He lost his title since you outran him too."

Ean scoffs from his side of the room. "Best guard? What the hell am I? I'm the one busting my ass training the newbies, while this one goes off to a fancy college."

"I don't see you doing any training now. Besides, I'll earn my title back eventually," I counter back, lifting an eyebrow at Ean in a challenge. He's been training his whole life to become a guard. Then I show up, and things just fall naturally to me without trying. It frustrates him to no end. I think it frustrates him even more that I don't respond to his jabs or the competitiveness that means so much more to him.

His brows rise in surprise; then he frowns as he looks me over. I realize my facial expression is not one of my practiced ones. I don't banter with anyone. I frown. What did she do to me? I catch movement from the little one as she timidly steps closer to me and holds out her hand in a gesture to shake my hand. She really is so tiny, proportioned correctly from what I can see despite the large clothing.

Elias was just about to stop her. Normally, I don't shake hands or hug. I don't like being touched. Yet as I reach out and take her dainty hand into mine, a burst of white light and a tingle of electricity snake up my arm and embed themselves into my chest. I study her face, her breathing. She doesn't have the same response as I'm having now. I frown, bending slightly to get a good look at her. Nothing. How can this be?

"Can you remove your glasses?" I ask. She jerks back just a little, as if what I am asking is like a slap in the face. "I hadn't taken a good look at you when we first met, retreating back and all that." I smile at her, a genuine smile. I don't want to intimidate her or scare her away from me. Reluctantly, she pulls her hand back and reaches up to remove those ridiculously large glasses.

It's her, the girl in the picture. Same heart-shaped face, dark contrasting eyebrows. She no longer has thick, long, dark eyelashes. All that's left are short little stubs. I can see the scars much clearer on the left side of her face, like someone took a knife and deliberately cut into her flawless skin. My gaze travels back down to her full lips that I feel compelled to want to bite and suck. *Fuck*, I mentally groan. What the hell is wrong with me? I'm not a child molester. I clench my jaw, and I tear my eyes away from her lips to look down at her neck. A white puckering scar sits in the hollow of her throat. The hand holding her glasses has white scars that run along her arms and across her wrist. On her other arm, more scars glare up at me from otherwise flawless skin. *What the hell did they do to you?*

Anger starts to spread through my entire being. I want to kill the fucker who hurt her. I swallow down the emotions that start to flare up in my chest. I clear my throat.

"You look good. Of course, I am referring to what I read in the report since I don't really have anything to compare it to. I trust you are doing well?"

I wince. I sound like an asshole. I feel eyes on me. Everyone in the room is scrutinizing me. She gives me a tight-lipped smile and a nod. Does she not talk? She hasn't said a word since she walked into the office. She turns away from me to face Anders.

"Yes, I received your application. We can talk about it after I'm done with this meeting," Anders says to her. I look around the room. Was I so lost in my thoughts that I didn't hear her speak?

Chris laughs, "Little one, girls are not allowed in the guard."

She turns to look at Elias. "Don't look at me. I don't make the rules, little one, you know that." She stares at Elias just a little longer, then at Chris, and back to Anders.

Anders holds up a hand. "Jessica, I promise we can talk about this later today. No more arguments." She lets out an irritated sigh, and Anders looks her over and gives her a smile. "You have my word; we can discuss this."

She nods, heads over to Elias, gives him a hug, hugs Chris, then rounds over to Anders behind his desk and gives him a hug and a peck on his cheek.

He blushes. "'Bout time, I was starting to feel a little left out." She pats his shoulder and heads out the door, taking her light with her. She doesn't even look back at me or say goodbye. I can't help but feel a little—what? Miffed that she dismissed me so easily. Especially when I'm barely holding it together.

"Did I miss something?" I ask. "I could have sworn I didn't hear a word come out of her mouth."

Anders clears his throat. "My apologies, Shadow. I should have explained while she was here. She doesn't speak because the tracheostomy caused some complications. This past week she's been able to voice small sounds and short phrases but nothing substantial. She's also used to being unable to speak so she doesn't. Initially, when she was brought back from Whitemore plantation, she bonded with the Langhlan twins and me and was able to communicate through a mind-link. Recently she has started to mind-link with both Chris and Elias. She doesn't know how she's doing it, and when asked, she can't seem to do it willingly. Her mind-link is also one-sided. We can hear her, but she cannot hear us."

"Mind-link?" I ask. "Mind-link usually works only when one is in wolf or animal form and with members of the same pack. Only a true Alpha can communicate with pack members in human form through a mind-link. Even then, that's rare. Obviously, she's a magic dweller. I could see her magic surrounding her, it practically took up the whole room."

Anders frowns. "I'm sure there's more to this, but without knowing her origins..."

I stare at Anders, looking to confirm the truth. As clear as day, I see it.

"I'm sorry, Anders, what is your relationship with the girl?" Chris smiles, and Elias chuckles.

"You see it too, don't you?" Chris asks.

"What is it you see?" Anders asks with a stern grimace.

I give him a crooked smile. "You mean other than you both share similar characteristics? Such as the eyes, nose, and, if her hair were any lighter, it could be almost white?" It comes off as a question, but it's more like a statement. He stares at me, so I continue, "She has magic. Strong magic, stronger than anyone I have ever come across, including yours."

Anders leans back into his chair and wipes his hand over his face. "This can't be," he whispers.

"Where's the paternity test?" Elias asks him. "The results should have been here by now. It's been a few weeks."

Anders reaches forward and pulls an envelope from his desk's top drawer. "I didn't have a chance to open it."

"Or maybe you were trying to convince yourself that you didn't need to," Elias jabs.

Anders hands the envelope to Chris, who gives it to Elias.

"Why would you request a paternity test?" I ask Anders.

"She needed a blood transfusion when she first arrived. The doctor asked if everyone could get tested for a more direct match."

"Anders was the only one who came close to being a match." Chris chimes in, "The only reason the doctor asked Anders is because he was pretty desperate."

"Then a few weeks ago, Jessica had a reaction to the blood transfusions Anders had given to the doctor to keep on hand just in case." Elias then adds, "One of the specialists he brought in asked if Anders was a direct blood relative." Elias shrugs. "Of course he denied it."

Anders looks away. "I don't have a daughter. I would know," he mumbles to himself.

"That you know of," Chris says. "Look, you can be in denial all you want, but you know deep down inside that it's a possibility. Otherwise, you wouldn't have agreed to the paternity test."

I watch as Anders drops his head and looks down at his desk. He's looking at the photograph in front of him. A crimson flush creeps up from beneath his collar.

"Aside from the hair and eyes, she looks like her mother." He says it so softly it's barely a whisper.

"It's 99.9 percent a match," Elias tells Anders at the same time. Elias hands me the test results. I think Anders already knew, even before the blood typing. I think he didn't want to admit it to himself. Especially given the way she was found.

His shoulders tense, jaw clenches, and the flush turns to an angrier red. He slams his fist down on the desk.

"Dammit, I can't believe she would do this!" He looks over at Elias and Chris. "Was this some kind of retaliation against me?" he shouts, and the two men stare at him, unblinking. "When I find her, I am going to fucking end her!" He's breathing hard, and the temperature in the room drops dangerously low.

Chris hops off the edge of the desk where he perched himself and faces Anders. "Wait! You don't know the whole story; you're jumping to conclusions. At this point, we still don't know what really happened or how it happened."

"What really happened?!" Anders shouts. "You saw what

she looked like when she was brought to the clinics—you heard what the doctor said! Years of abuse, malnourishment. She was tortured, her back was filleted, they cut off her hair, her lashes, and they tried to mar her face. She was beaten, strung up, and hanging from a tree, barely alive! Multiple surgeries! Failed surgeries and even after all of that, she still nearly died just a few weeks ago!"

Standing, I hold up my hands in front of me, trying to get Anders's attention before ice shards start to fly. "Look, Chris has a point. We don't know what really happened. We can't go flying into a territory and start killing people without any proof of who actually did it. All we—I mean, you… All you can do is focus on right now. That's what we… you can do for the girl right now." Why the hell do I keep saying we? This isn't about me right now. This is about Anders and the girl, and as much as I am on board with killing the fuckers who hurt her, we need to keep our heads. I mean his head. Shit.

Anders is still breathing hard; he's glaring at me, "We can figure out the rest later," I tell him. He's standing now, leaning over with both hands planted on his desk. Frost forms around his hands, and his harsh breaths come out in clouds. I look to Chris and Elias. Worried looks cross both of their faces. I have never seen Anders like this. Still leaning forward, he tries to regain his composure by closing his eyes and taking in slow several deep breaths. The room temperature starts to return to normal.

"I am going to kill the asshole responsible for hurting my daughter, and not one of you better stand in my way." He says the words with a deathly calm.

"I'll be right there by your side, my friend," Elias says

with a sneer.

Chris nods and starts to speak again. "No child deserves what happened to her. We need to be logical about all of this and come up with a plan. A plan to take care of her right now and keep her safe."

Once calm, Anders slumps back down in his chair and swipes a hand over his face. His hand lingers just over his mouth. "What the fuck am I going to do? I can't have a daughter. I just can't. Every female of my bloodline carries a curse." He sighs and starts to rub his temples. "Pretty fucking obvious—the curse is already affecting her."

Chris starts to pace, then says, "Technically, it's not a curse. It's a bunch of greedy bastards that think they can gain something by hurting others. Just so happens the females in your bloodline are their main target."

Anders is still rubbing his temples. "I'm gonna have to take her to Ryuku. I don't have a choice." A pained expression crosses his face, and he starts talking again, mostly to himself. "She'll never forgive me. If I take her away from here and dump her in the school in the Asian territories, the same way my boys were dumped, the way I was dumped, away from the bonds she has already developed here." He closes his eyes and shakes his head.

Chris shakes his head too. "Save that as a last resort. You saw the way Ean is with her and Charlie, not to mention the twins. Don't forget about us. We have all formed some kind of bond with her as well. And Shakti, if she hears about this..."

Anders hesitates. "If I am being completely honest with myself, I want her here, but who the hell am I to raise a daughter? I have only ever raised boys—well, here anyway."

Selfishly, I want her to stay too. If I can find a way to keep her here, I can look after her in my own way. Then everything clicks. "Why can't you do it all?" I ask.

"What?" three voices pipe up at the same time. When I look around the room, three pairs of eyes are staring at me like I have grown an extra head.

I give them a shrug, playing it off like it's not a big deal. "You said that Shakti has formed a bond with the girl. She's a woman. I'm sure there is some womanly instinct there that can help you to raise a girl. So why don't you have an honest conversation with The Alpha King and the Luna Queen and ask them to adopt her? That way you can still be a part of her life and involved with pertinent decisions that affect her."

Chris snaps his fingers. "Like hiding her out in the open. No one will question the Alpha King about an adoption."

I see Elias's head slowly nod as he contemplates all of this.

"No one outside of us and the Alpha King and Luna Queen need to know of her true origins. As far as anyone knows, she's just a girl who was found in distress, rescued, and taken in. From what I overhead in a one-sided conversation, the girl wants to be in the guard, so let her. That way you can train her yourself, keep an eye on her, and still be very much involved in her life. She won't be far from home. She can still be with Shakti. The Langhlan twins will be in the next group of recruits, so she will still be around them as well as all of you, including Charlie and Ean since they work full time with the recruits and their training. Then once her magic comes in fully or after she finishes the recruit program, whichever comes first, send her to the Asian territory."

Anders eyes me wearily. "Jessica… Her name is Jessica. What makes you think I can allow a girl into the recruit program?"

I give a short laugh. "That little thing that walked through your office door just moments ago looked like a little boy to me."

Elias shrugged, and Chris smiled. "That just might work actually," Chris said.

"Will it?" Anders snaps. "What the hell are you going to tell your daughters when they find out? Some of them wanted to be in the guard, and we flat-out said no. How many other girls have we flat-out said no to? Remember the protest we put up with when one of the girls we rejected's mother turned out to be a journalist?"

Elias shrugs again. "Fuck it. If anyone finds out she's a girl, we can always just say it was a pilot program."

I shake my head. "Actually, you don't need to do any of that or lie. The Guard bylaws state that the recruits are to be male. However, there is a section in there that states that all royal heirs need to participate in the guard program. Since Nathan is the Alpha King and Shakti is the Luna Queen, that makes Jessica a princess. Even though she is adopted, it does not change her given title. Under the royal clause, it does not specify male or female. Even if you were sued or had a huge protest, that clause alone protects the guards."

Anders drops his hands from his face and looks over at both men.

Elias starts to laugh. "That is why you are the best guard we ever had."

"And a soon-to-be badass guard lawyer," Chris chimes in.

I can see the wheels turning in Anders's mind. He lets out a long breath. "I need to talk to Nathan and Shakti first, make sure that this is what they want. I can't force them to take on my responsibility."

"Do you honestly think it's going to be a problem? I wouldn't put it past Shakti. She already had a plan in place once Little One was going to be discharged from the clinic. Faith hasn't asked me once to take her in, and you know how she is. She kicked me out of my own home when I first told Eugene that I wasn't going to take his boy in. Did Tater say anything to you?" Elias looks at Chris, who stops pacing.

"Actually, she hasn't." Chris snorts, facing Anders with a goofy grin on his face. "You need to have that conversation with Shakti. I think it's already a done deal. Little One isn't going anywhere."

Elias chuckles, "You may want to take him," jerking his head in my direction. "Chris and I can hold up shop here."

Anders lets out a heavy sigh. "Before you all leave, I have one more thing I need to bring up. We need to discuss Sodie's placement with the guards."

I lean forward. "What's going on with Sodie?"

"It's nothing bad. He's asked to stay on as an active guard. He wanted to be personally assigned to Jessica until we knew what we were going to do with her as far as placement. I initially had no problems with it. However, given the circumstance, I think it will be best for Sodie to go to Ryuku for more training."

I frown. Not everyone who has magic needs to go to Ryuku. "Did his magic become stronger or change?" I ask.

Chris looks at me and cocks his head. "You sensed his magic?"

"Yes. I wasn't very concerned about him revealing himself. Most light manipulators often don't bring attention to themselves and can stay under the radar. Unless I am wrong."

"I think there is more to him than maybe he even realizes, or he's just really good at concealing it. Either way, he saved Jessica's life, and as a thank-you, I want to help him in return."

"How did he save Jessica exactly?"

"He's a healer. Had he not been there when he was, she wouldn't be here right now, giving us hell to let her into the recruit program." They all nod in response.

Chris's face brightens. "He mentioned in his interview that he had an interest in the medical field. Now I know why. I agree. Let's give him every opportunity to make it happen."

Elias nods in agreement.

"I was going to bring this up later, but since we're here, I may have a potential candidate in mind that I want to discuss with you. I came across this candidate accidentally when I was in Territory Two. He was a little elusive, but I can't blame him. He doesn't exactly belong to a very forgiving territory particularly when it comes to magic. He kind of reminded me of Liam—a little broken, untrusting, bit of a loner. He is past the recruiting guard age. I'm thinking I would like to send him there."

"So what it is that he can do?" Chris asks.

"He has the ability to manipulate water, which is how I found him, messing with the water element near the falls."

Chris shrugs. "Okay, so what's the big deal? We've come

across a few shifters in the past that can do that."

"Have you ever met someone who can manipulate the water element, shield kinetic energy, and neutralize magic?"

Elias's eyebrows shoot up, and he leans forward. "A shield? You found a shield? That's like finding a needle in a haystack."

"It gets better. There's something else he can do. I've seen it in his aura, but he hasn't tapped into it yet."

"You're saying you found a triple threat?" Elias asks incredulously.

I smile at him knowingly. "Imagine having someone like him as a guard."

Chris whistles, and Anders nods in agreement. "Okay, if you trust him and the kid is on board, I'll get everything ready. I can send you the details that you can pass on to your recruit. I really wanted to send Liam along with Sodie, but this is the second time he has declined."

"Is there a reason why he has declined?" I ask Anders.

He frowns and shakes his head.

Elias answers instead, "He won't say. I really wish I could break down some of that barrier he has constructed so tightly around himself."

# Chapter 25

## WELCOME HOME

### JESSICA

July 25, 2014: 1:30 p.m.

Dr. York is sitting in front of me, legs crossed, my medical chart on his lap. His posture is relaxed, face void of creases especially between his brows. When he finally looks up from my chart, a soft smile touches his lips. "Everything is looking good. Your hair has grown at least three inches. Even your eyelashes are coming back in. All of your wounds have closed. Labs are almost back to normal levels. I have to say that I am pleased with how well you've been healing over the past few weeks. I have to admit you gave us all quite a scare. I'm happy things turned in your favor."

"Me too," I rasp out. His smile widens.

"Voice is slowly coming back too. Which reminds me—

I've put in a request for speech therapy. As soon as I hear back from them, we can get that started."

Nodding my head in understanding, I watch as Dr. York finishes jotting down a note in his scrawly messy handwriting.

Without looking up, Dr. York starts to speak. "Do you know what all of this means?"

A sense of dread creeps up the back of my neck. If I know what all this means? Is he referring to my labs? No, he looks too happy to be referring to my labs.

"You no longer need constant medical supervision. The rest of the treatments can be done outside of the clinic."

Yep, that's exactly what I was afraid he was going to say. My hope that I would be here long enough to get into the guard recruit program has crashed and burned. Shakti hasn't mentioned anything about taking me in. I guess that means orphanage here I come.

My lip is starting to tremble, so I pull it in and put on a brave face. I can't cry. This is supposed to be good news, great news even. But it makes me so sad, knowing I won't be here anymore. I refuse to cry in front of Dr. York. I'm not his problem, and I'm not going to make him feel guilty or sorry for me. I give him a small smile and nod, trying my best to look happy and appreciative for everything he has done for me.

He pats my knee before he stands. "I'll tell Anders the good news." As soon as he's gone, I reach for the journal under my pillow and pour my disappointed feelings out onto the blank pages.

It's been more than a few hours since I had last seen Anders, and other than Ean, I hadn't seen the rest of the guards all day. Maybe Anders told them not to come now that I'm being discharged. Sighing, I continue to look out the window. Dark clouds have taken over, and large raindrops slide down the glass pane. I stopped crying about an hour ago. It looks like the weather has decided to continue to cry for me.

"Everything okay, Jessica?" Facing Anders, I nod, and give him a sad smile.

Anders clears the threshold and sits at the foot of my bed. When I look past his shoulder, I see that strange man I met earlier, Shadow, is standing in the doorway.

Wait, is this the same guy? He looks different somehow. I look him over from top to bottom. He's removed his suit jacket and tie. Some of his buttons are undone, exposing his throat. Slowly, my eyes return to his face. He has the blackest hair I had ever seen; it's so black it's almost blue even. He wears his hair short on the sides, a little long on the top. He has a widow's peak. The front of his hair curls into a slight wave before it sits on his forehead just above his dark brows. Thick dark lashes surround dark blue eyes, or they were dark. Maybe it's the lighting because they look lighter right now. The corner of his lip twitches, like he finds my analyzing him amusing.

That's what it is; he looks amused. When I first walked into Anders's office, he looked like a robot or like a life-sized cardboard cutout of himself. He was stiff and void almost. Now he has animation, and his face reflects, I don't know, life.

"I'm sorry that I took so long. My meeting took a bit longer than I had originally planned."

*I understand.*

"Thank you." He reaches down and picks up the book I had in front of me. I had planned on reading it when I was done with my journal writing. I guess I won't be finishing it; I'll need to return it before I go.

"Weapons of martial arts. Hmmm, this wouldn't by any chance have anything to do with you wanting to be in the guard?"

I look down at my hands. *"It was in your office. Thought I would give it a good read, maybe familiarize myself with some of the weapons, in hopes that I would get in."* I wrinkle my nose at him. Anders smiles and shows Shadow the book I was reading.

"Will it be alright if we table our discussion regarding the guard recruit program? There are some things I would like to discuss first."

Well, that's a polite way of saying no. My heart sinks, and the sadness I was feeling earlier increases. The rain taps harder against the windowpane.

"I didn't say no, just yet. There are some things I need to think about, and I need to discuss this with Chris and Elias." A small sliver of hope flickers in my chest. With just my eyes, I look up at Anders as he continues, "Shadow is our recruiting officer, I have given him your application. He will look it over, and depending on what we collectively decide, he will be in touch."

It's not a definitive answer, but it does give me something to look forward to, or at least a small possibility that they're not writing me off completely.

Anders chuckles. "Don't think too much about it. I

haven't made up my mind yet, but it's a start. We can talk about it more a little later."

I lean forward, wrapping my arms around Anders in the biggest hug I can manage. "Thank you," I rasp out, this time using my voice.

I jump off my bed and bound over to Shadow to give him a hug too. As I wrap my thin, skinny arms around him, something starts to tug at my heart. His body tenses, and I hear a quick intake of breath. Am I hurting him? Maybe he doesn't like being touched, and I just hugged him.

Oh shit. I start to release my hold around him when I feel his arms awkwardly come around me. The tension I felt earlier softens. I take a chance and peer up, expecting to look up at his chin. Instead, striking blue eyes are looking down at me. A clashing of light and dark alternate back and forth before settling on a lighter shade of blue.

He stares blankly at me for a few more seconds before his eyes shift to Anders behind me, and he frowns.

"It stopped raining," he states, shocked. Taking that as my cue to stop hanging on to the strange man, I drop my arms and turn to look over at the window. It did stop raining, and the sun is out in all its warm glory.

Anders turns his head toward the window. "So it seems," he whispers almost to himself.

Shadow starts to look around me, then asks, "Does it always feel like the weather matches your feelings?"

I shrug, looking to Anders to interpret for me. *Not that I've noticed.*

Anders shakes his head. "Jessica, why don't you mind-link with Shadow, so you can tell him yourself?"

*I don't know how to.*

"You've done it with Chris and Elias. Why don't you just—I don't know, humor me—give it a try?" I look down at my hands, which I have clasped in front of me, and I start playing with my fingers. I'm not sure how to do it willingly. With Chris and Elias, it just happened. The same way it just happened with Anders and the twins.

I angle myself slightly to look back at Shadow. I look straight at his forehead, pretending for an instant that I can get past this invisible shield or barrier that lies between his skull and brain. I start to feel ridiculous the longer I stare at his head. Dropping my gaze to his face, I expect a look of annoyance. His features are soft, and a slight smile touches his lips. At least when he smiles now, it doesn't look like he's constipated or holding back a fart.

He lets out a hearty laugh, and my eyes widen to the size of silver dollars. "That's too bad. To think this entire time, I thought my smile looked genuine."

"*Nope, definitely looked like it was constipation.*" I press my lips together to prevent myself from smiling too big.

"I'll keep that in mind. Thanks for the tip."

"*Yeah, sure, any time.*" I can feel heat rising in my cheeks. Yeah, I don't think I like the idea of him hearing my thoughts. It feels too much like an invasion on my privacy. Regaining my composure, I clear my throat. "*So in answer to your earlier question, no, I haven't noticed if my moods correlate with the weather.*"

Shadow's features change from amused to solemn. "Maybe something you should start paying attention to." His eyes shift from my face to Anders. "Well, I really should be going. I'll keep in touch to let you know when I will be by again."

Anders nods farewell.

Shadow looks at me one more time before he turns to leave. "I'm looking forward to our next meeting. I'm interested to see what else pops up in that head of yours." I stand there by the door and watch his retreating back, still trying to make sense of him. He's peculiar; that's for sure. As I continue to watch him stride down the hall, I can't help but notice how tall he is—at least six-two, with wide shoulders that taper down to a narrow waist. Wow, that's a very nice ass. His girlfriend is a very lucky girl. I shake my head as if I need to clear it and turn to head back into my room.

Anders's narrow gaze is on me. "Please don't tell me that you look at all the guards like that." I feel the heat rise from my chest to my cheeks, and I look down at my hands. Oops, I forgot that he could still hear my thoughts. I wrinkle my nose and give him a grimace.

"Oops? Do not make me take you to our dungeon and lock you up until you're 100," he grits out.

I cock my head to the side. *We have a dungeon? Did I miss that part of the tour?*

"Stop being a wiseass."

Anders's phone rings. "I need to answer this. You'll be discharged within an hour. I'll be back to collect you." He lifts the phone to his ear and walks out of the room. Whatever it was that he needed to talk to me about changed when he had got that phone call. I guess he lost the nerve to tell me that I'm going to an orphanage.

Mimi comes in with an injection and a medicine cup

full of supplements. I thought I was done with those. I haven't gotten any since I had woken up from that whole ordeal I went through. Shakti isn't here to question it, and the twins can't interpret for me. My voice is still too weak to get more than a word or two out. So, I just go with it and let her give them to me.

When Mimi leaves after administering my last dose of medicine, I pack up my belongings. I don't really have much. Everything fits into the two shopping bags Shakti had come with one day filled with things she thought I would need during my stay. I'm left alone with my thoughts. So, I clean my room, making it look presentable as if no one is here. I just need to keep myself busy. I don't want to cry.

I hope while I am cleaning my room that the guards stop by. When Shakti and the twins returned to visit me daily, the guards kept to their routine. I started to think of them as friends, family even. Especially Liam, I thought we had gotten closer. He even read to me at night, so I would fall asleep. I guess it was all in my imagination.

As time creeps slowly by, my heart starts to ache. The twins haven't come by, and neither have Shakti. It hurt that they didn't say goodbye. It starts to rain harder.

It feels like forever by the time Anders shows up again. He takes my two bags and looks me over. "Do you have everything?" I nod. I change from my baggy T-shirt and shorts to jeans and a shirt. I pull my hoodie on, the one I found that first night I had woken up. Anders heads out of the room and starts to walk down the hall. I stall behind him, turning to look at my room one last time.

This is the only place I can remember feeling like home,

and now I'm leaving without knowing where I'm going or where I will end up. My chest starts to hurt, and my throat feels like it is closing up. I start to tug at the neckline of my hoodie. It feels like I can't breathe. Tears start to fall, fogging up my glasses. My whole world is changing again, and I don't know what to do.

A warm arm comes around my shoulder, and a large hand cradles my head, bringing it to a warm chest. As I take a deep breath, a fresh clean smell with a hint of campfire smoke permeates my senses. I squeeze my eyes closed in relief and cry into his chest. Liam.

"Shhh, I got you. Breathe." I wrap my arms around his waist, and I cry harder. I feel his other hand rubbing my back in a circular pattern. Slowly, my throat starts to open up again, and I feel like I can breathe. I feel safe. Another hand starts to rub my back, and all the lingering panic melts away.

Liam kisses my temple, and I pull back to look over at the other person beside me. It is Sodie. More tears start. I was starting to think that they weren't coming at all. I lean in to hug Sodie, removing my glasses to bury my face in his chest.

"Don't cry, little one. You're going to like your new home. I promise," Sodie says.

I just nod my head against his chest. I pull back, looking up at Sodie's face, and give him a small smile. I reach for Liam again, and I give his arm a squeeze.

"Come on," Liam says, holding my tiny hand in his much bigger one. "Anders looks like he's ready to murder us. We're the reason why he's late."

I wipe my face with the sleeve of my hoodie and sniff as I try to smile. Sodie chuckles behind me as Liam leads me to the front.

Replacing my glasses, I see that Anders is standing next to a car. He opens the back passenger door and motions with his head to get in. I look over at Liam and Sodie. My heart sinks that Ean and Charlie didn't come to say goodbye too. Anders is still standing by the door waiting for me to get inside, but I want to take one last look around before I do.

"I really do hope you're not contemplating running," Anders says. Snorting, I shake my head. If I did, wouldn't he know? I take a small step closer to the car, then stop. "If it makes you feel better, these two are coming along." I look over my shoulder and see Sodie moving to the front of the car, and Liam is rounding the back to get in from the other side.

I take a deep breath and get in. Anders follows as I scoot over. My hands are gripping the seat. Once everyone is in, the car pulls away. I look behind, watching the clinic disappear as the car continues to drive to our destination. Anders places his hand on my knee, and Liam pulls my hand from the seat, holding it gently as he rubs the back of it with his thumb.

The drive is literally five minutes before the car turns into a long driveway with tall iron gates. As we get closer, I can see a roundabout with a fountain sitting just in front of a large mansion. My heart starts to pound, and I can feel all the blood draining from my face. Is this the territory's children's home? I knew it; I knew they were going to take me to an orphanage.

The tears start to well up. I feel like I am going to throw up.

Anders squeezes my knee. "Jessica, this is not an orphanage. Relax. This is going to be your new home." The car comes to a stop. Liam squeezes my hand gently, bringing me back out of the beginnings of a panicked state.

He leans in, whispering in my ear, "Breathe. No one is going to hurt you. We won't leave until you're settled."

I look to Anders; he gives me a slight smile. "I promise that you will be pleasantly surprised." I slide out of the car and follow Anders to the front door. He knocks. I try to hide a little behind Anders. A man with thinning black hair, bushy eyebrows, dark eyes, and a thick black mustache answers the door. He nods at Anders and moves to the side, holding the door open to let us in.

Anders reaches behind to usher me through the door. "Joe, this is Jessica. Jessica, Joe works here. He is also a trained guard. If you ever feel unsafe or need help, you can trust Joe."

Joe lifts up his right hand and shows me the back of his hand where he is sporting a large ring. The ring has the guard crest, and it holds an emerald and a diamond in its center. I stretch out my hand to shake Joe's hand, and he happily takes it, bowing. There's something about Joe that instantly resonates with me.

*Very nice to meet you, Joe. I wish you could hear me say it because I think I already like you.* Joe pulls back his hand slowly, eyes widened, looking over to Anders.

Joe leans forward so that we are at eye level. "It is very nice to meet you, Jessica, and I think I like you already too."

He stands back up, and I give him a small smile. "Here, let me take those." He gestures to both Liam and Sodie to hand over my shopping bags. "I'll have these taken up to your room, but first, let me show you where everyone is anxiously waiting for you."

He ushers us in so he can close the front door and leads us further into the large mansion. I start to look around. We pass a grand staircase that leads to a second floor; we pass smaller rooms that I try to peek into. Then it hits me—I'm going to work here. I wonder if I'll be part of the cleaning staff or the kitchen staff. Joe abruptly stops in front of me, and I almost walk into him. He turns and looks at Anders.

Anders chuckles. "You're not here to work as a servant or as the kitchen staff. Stop dragging your feet, and you'll find out exactly why you're here." He pushes me gently forward as Joe turns and continues to lead the way. I look back over my shoulder to see that Liam and Sodie are following close behind.

Joe leads us to the entrance of a room, and I hear the twins' voices in my head. They're here! Justin and Jeremy are here!

"Surprise!" a group of people shout. I grab my throat and take a step back. Anders places his hands on both of my shoulders and leads me forward. Ean, Elias, Charlie, and Chris are standing in the room along with some other unfamiliar faces. A large banner hangs on the back wall that says, "Welcome home, Jessica!"

Shakti approaches me with a smile on her face and gives me a big hug. "Welcome to your new home and family, sweetheart."

211

I look around the room at all the faces staring back at me and I want to turn around and run. It is all so overwhelming. I don't deserve any of this. Weird and stupid to feel this way when everyone has been so nice to me. I feel guilty that I am not showing them any appreciation and that I have nothing to give back. Fear starts to take over, another panic attack threatening. I am going to be punished soon, for making a fool out of myself and making them look bad.

I start to tremble. I need to hide. I think about the rooms we passed on the way to this room. Would they mind if I slipped into one of them?

# CHAPTER 26

## MY FAMILY

### JESSICA

July 25, 2014: 5:30 p.m.

Two hard bodies crash into me, Justin and Jeremy.

*"Why does she think she's in trouble?"* Jeremy asks in my head.

*"You're not in trouble, and you don't need to hide."* Justin reassures me, *"You're our sister now. Everyone here is your family."*

Jeremy is looking at me for reassurance that I won't run.

"Come meet everyone. We're all excited that you're here!" Justin is smiling down at me. I hesitate at first; then I look to Anders, who nods in approval. I face back to the twins and nod. I'm still shaking and feel like I need to run and hide, but with my two... Wait, they said... Sister? I frown, but before I can think any more on what they had just told me, I'm facing Elias.

"Little one, I want to introduce you to my family. You already know my oldest, Ean." I nod. "This is my beautiful mate, Faith." He has his arms around this tall, beautiful woman with long dark hair and kind dark eyes. Her face is round and feminine.

She quickly pulls me into a hug. "I'm so happy to see that you're doing well." She gives me another gentle squeeze before she pulls back. "You have already met Liam. He is the newest member of our little family. We took him in a few years ago and unofficially adopted him." I turn my head to look for Liam who is now standing next to Ean. He actually smiles at me. "This is Elijah, our youngest." Elijah is not nearly as tall as Ean, but he has the same dark hair and dark eyes. His features are a little softer, not as broad as Elias's and Ean's. I look between Faith and Elijah; he takes after his mother. He doesn't move, just looks down at me, so I give him a little wave. He jerks his chin up.

"Why do I get introduced last? You even introduced Liam before me. It's because I'm a girl, isn't it?" This tall, beautiful girl, with long dark hair just like her mother's, steps out from behind Elias. "I'm Emily. I'm not the youngest—I'm actually older than Elijah by like two years. I wanted to come and visit when I first heard that you were here, but Ean wouldn't let me. It's not like I would have bothered you. I go to the private school in the city, and I'm only home on the weekends." She grabs me and gives me a big crushing hug. "Oh, wow, we need to work on getting you some better clothes." I grimace and look back at the twins. "Don't worry. Between Sixes and I, we'll have you looking so good, the boys will have to lock you up. Do you talk? No, not much, that's okay. Elijah doesn't talk much either, and everyone knows that I can talk enough for every..."

Ean clamps a hand over Emily's mouth. "He doesn't talk because you don't let him. Jeez, calm down. You're going to... Ouch! Did you just bite me?" Everyone in the room laughs, and I clamp my hand over my own mouth to cover my raspy wheeze.

Emily winks and leans in to whisper, "You and I are going to be the best of friends." She gives me another hug. Just as she releases me, I'm being pulled over to stand in front of Chris.

"My turn," he says with a smile. "Little one, this is my beautiful mate Tater." Chris's mate is not as tall as Faith or Emily, but she is just as beautiful with dark blond hair, big hazel green eyes, a sharp nose, and an oval face.

She gives me a hug. "I'm also the head of the household staff. If you need anything you can usually find me in the kitchen." I smile and nod. "This is my daughter Sixes. She also works here, and I have personally assigned her to you. If you need absolutely anything, don't hesitate to let us know." I nod again.

Sixes gives me a hug. "Yes, Emily is right. We're going to have to do something about your style. Not to worry. You're in good hands." She gives me a big smile.

I frown at her, looking down at my baggy outfit. This is as good as it gets.

"Give it a rest, you two. She's not a doll," Charlie says from behind Sixes. Charlie smiles at me and gives me a wink. "She looks perfectly fine, just the way she is."

Chris clears his throat and gives Charlie a sideways look. "You've already met Charlie. Tater and I have four more girls. Two of them are away at school, and the other two had some things to take care of, but you'll be seeing them around." I smile and nod. I guess I'm going to be doing a lot of that since my words are so limited. "This old man is my father Duck. He's also the main ranch hand and takes care of the dairy." I look up at a tall elderly man with dull gray hair and kind green eyes. His face has a deep tan and is slightly leathery from working out in the sun, and his smile reaches up to his eyes. I can already tell I'm going to like him.

"Hello, little one, it is a pleasure to finally meet you." He reaches out to shake my hand. His hand is large, weathered, and callused. I turn them over so I can look at them better and rub my hand over his fingers.

"I hear you're learning how to play the guitar?" I nod enthusiastically. "If Charlie gets too busy to work with you, I don't mind stepping in. Some of the dairy hands and I put together what we call a garage band. We would love to have you come around and maybe one day join us." I give him a big hug. Chuckling, he pats my back.

"Dad, maybe you can take her out to visit the ladies when she gets settled," Chris says. *Ladies?*

I look to the twins, and they start to laugh. "He means the cows, Jessica," Jeremy explains. I blush. *Please tell him I would love that,* Justin interprets for me.

Scanning the room, I find Shakti standing next to a tall man who is at least six foot five. My eyebrows raise. He looks exactly like Chris. Are they twins?

Justin chuckles. "You've already met our mother. This

is our dad. No, he and Chris are not twins—they're cousins. Duck and our grandfather were twin brothers." I look around the room, and I don't see another elderly man anywhere.

*"Where's your grandfather?"* I ask Justin through our link.

*"He passed away before we were born."*

*"Oh, I'm sorry. I didn't mean to ask."*

*"It's okay. We would have told you eventually. You're family now."* Jeremy says. I look back to the man that could be Chris's twin. He's wearing dark jeans and a button-up, long-sleeved, tan plaid shirt. I'm not sure why I didn't notice him immediately. His energy is so huge, powerful, very... My eyes widen and I take a step back. My mind starts to whirl.

I'm in the biggest house in the territory. The two lead guards are family... I take another step back... The twins said sister. I'm their sister... No, no, no... He's the Alpha King. I look at Shakti... She's the Lunar Queen.

Anders rests a warm hand on my shoulder. "It's okay. You're not in trouble," he whispers in my ear.

I shake my head. *"I don't deserve this. What if I'm a bad person? What if what happened to me is because I did something wrong? What if... What if whoever did this comes after me and hurts the Alpha King and his family? I can't stay here."* My glasses start to fog, and the tears spill from my eyes. Anders turns me so I face him. Chris and Elias stand on either side of him. *"I can't put the Alpha King and the Lunar Queen's family in a position that can hurt them."* I remove my glasses and start to sob.

"Jessica, look at me." I wipe my face. "Do you think that I would bring you here if I had any doubt that you would put their lives at risk?"

I sniff. *"You don't know me–I don't know me! What If I did something that caused me to be in this position? Even if I didn't do anything, what if whoever did this to me comes after me again and puts this family's lives in danger? We don't know anything!"*

Anders leans forward so that he is now eye level with me. "I will never let anything happen to you or the royal family. It's my job to protect them, and that includes you."

I rub my nose with the back of my hand and shake my head. *"I don't deserve this. I don't deserve to be here."*

"Why do you feel like you don't deserve to be here?" Chris asks, rubbing my back.

*"I just feel like I don't."* It's a feeling I have deep in my bones.

"Little one, you're a young girl. You didn't deserve what happened to you," Elias says. His hand is on my other shoulder.

"Everyone deserves a second chance," says a deep voice from behind me. The Alpha King places his large hand on my back. "We want you to be a part of our family, of our pack. Look around you. Everyone here wants to get to know you and wants to give you a life that you deserve." I feel a slight squeeze around my heart, and I turn my attention back to Anders.

"I will never let anything bad happen to you ever again. You are mine to protect, Jessica. You are here because we want you here. I want you here." Anders says with so much sincerity, it makes me want to cry even more.

"As much as I appreciate your concern for me and my family, it is also my job to protect them as well as you. Besides, there is one other person here who feels this is where you belong. If she had anything to say about it, she would have been the one to convince me otherwise." The Alpha King gently turns me to face the back of the room. Sitting in a chair, holding her cane, is Alpha Agnus.

"Well, it's about damn time I got some attention. I was beginning to think I made the two-hour drive up here just to be ignored." She huffs, and everyone in the room starts to chuckle. "Jessica, this is where you belong. I know for a fact you're not a bad person and what you've been through is not because of something you did. You were just in the wrong place with the wrong people. You need everyone in this room, and whether they realize it or not, they need you."

The Alpha King chuckles. "You better listen to her... She's a little scary." He whispers, "Even I'm afraid of her."

"Now are you going to humor me and give me a hug, or are you going to just stand there and continue to cry over what-ifs?" I wipe my face, clean my glasses, and replace them on my face, and I walk over to Alpha Agnus to give her a big hug.

"Now there's my girl." When I pull back, Miller stands next to her chair, and I move to give him a hug too.

He pats my back and tells me, "You're looking well. I see they are taking great care of you."

"Well, do we get to eat, or is everyone just going to stand around and watch this poor girl take it all in?"

"You heard her, everyone. Let's eat," the Alpha King announces to the room.

The room erupts with laughter and talking as everyone starts to gather around the buffet set up along one wall.

Shakti wraps her arms around my shoulders from behind. "Thank you for joining our family. I knew you were mine from the moment I met you." She kisses the top of my head. The Alpha King is talking to Chris and Anders while they stand in line to fill their plates. When he catches me watching him, he winks and carries on with his conversation.

I grab Justin's arm. *"Can you tell him I'm sorry for making such a fuss? I'm sorry if I embarrassed him,"* I say to Justin through our link. He repeats what I said to his father. It surprises me when he approaches me and leans down so that he is at eye level with me.

"I'm not embarrassed at all. You're entitled to how you feel. In fact, it is our fault for putting this on you. We should have approached this with a little more caution, talked to you, explored how you feel. We were excited and jumped in without feeling it out. We're the ones who owe you an apology. I promise we won't make this mistake again." He holds up his little finger.

Justin explains, *"It's a pinky promise. It's something we do in this family. Along with voting. I'll tell you all about that later."*

Holding up my little finger just like the way he does, he wraps his large one with mine. My heart fills with something strange. It makes me feel safe and cared for. I look around the room as I drop my hand from his. I have a family now.

From a distance, I watch as the Alpha King wraps his arms around Shakti's waist. He leads her to where everyone else is sitting with their food, places a plate in front of her, and kisses her head before he leaves her. He stands back in line. No one serves him or stops what they're doing to let him go first. He stands there talking to everyone as if he is not royal. He claps Anders on the back and talks to him as if they're old friends. I watch as Shakti talks to Tater, Sixes,

Faith and Emily. It's so casual—no airs, no hierarchy.

Justin and Jeremy are talking to Liam and Sodie like they always did when they were in my clinic room. It doesn't change now that they are in their own home. I like it; it feels right.

"Jessica." Alpha Agnus crooks a crooked finger at me. "I expect a visit from you at least once every other month."

"*I thought you were done with me.*"

She scoffs, "Don't be a smartass. Just because I knew this is where you belong for now doesn't mean I abandoned you. Besides, I need you to come back to make me those brownies. Miller had everyone make me brownies since you left, and it wasn't the same."

I cover my mouth and laugh. "*You did not make everyone make you brownies?*"

She raises an eyebrow and whacks me with her cane.

"Miller, how many brownies have we gone through?"

He grimaces. "I lost count. Please come back, Jessica. She's driving everyone crazy."

I make another raspy laugh and shake my head. "*They're just brownies. I don't know what's so special about them.*"

She frowns. "Just tell me you'll return and make them again. Give Miller a list of what you need. I'll make sure we have everything in stock."

I shrug. "*Here I thought you wanted me to visit because you wanted my company.*" I roll my eyes.

"Don't be a wiseass!" she growls. I wrinkle my nose, then give her a tender smile.

Behind Alpha Agnus, I catch sight of a piano sitting in the corner of the room. I hesitate at first, then decide I want to look at it closely. It is a baby grand piano, shiny black as if someone polished it regularly. With the pad of my index finger, I touch it, then feel guilty for leaving fingerprints, so I go back and wipe it down with the hem of my hoodie. I slide over onto the bench, and I lift the cover, revealing the piano keys. A music book is left on the sheet music holder. I thumb through the sheets, and some of the music titles look familiar.

"*Play something.*" Alpha Agnus's voice enters my head.

"*Like what?*"

"*Just close your eyes and play something. It will come.*" Doing as I am told, I place my fingers over the keys. They begin to move. In my head I see colors taking shape in a kaleidoscope. Behind closed eyelids, I see a yellow white light radiate from my heart into my fingers. It isn't just a few notes of sound. I make music; I play a song.

It is slow and haunting at first; then it turns light. It matches the way I had felt just a few minutes ago—sad, worried, an underlying fear that rested in my gut, to relief, then acceptance. Now even though I am unsure of how things will turn out, it will be okay—I will be okay. I play the last few notes, ending the song.

I open my eyes to look down at the keys and my fingers. I turn my hands over again and again, checking to make sure it was my hands. I can't believe I played. I don't know where that even came from. Then I realize the room has grown quiet. I look up. Everyone has stopped what they are doing to stare at me.

Oh god, am I in trouble? Why do I keep screwing this up! I look around again, waiting to get yelled at or slapped. Instead, when my eyes fall on Shakti, she has her hand over her mouth, and tears are streaking down her face. She slowly approaches me, and I wince, waiting for my punishment.

"That was beautiful!" she exclaims as she places her hands over her heart. "Can you play another one?" I don't even know how I knew that one in the first place. I hesitate, and she adds, "It's okay—give it a try. It's okay if you play the same one. It was beautiful."

I don't want to disappoint her. Swallowing, I take a deep breath, close my eyes, place my hands over the keys, and another song flows through me. When I play the last notes, I leave my hands in place, and I slowly open my eyes, to see not just Shakti standing there but Anders and the Alpha King. My parents, my family.

The party lasts for a couple more hours before everyone starts to slowly leave. Alpha Agnus is the first one, complaining that her old bones need to endure a two-hour drive back to her territory. She makes arrangements with Shakti and Anders for my next visit to her territory; then she is gone. When it is time for Emily to leave, she promises that she will be back to hang out often.

Ean grunts at Emily. "You're going to wish I kept her away longer. Trust me." I shake my head at Ean. I like Emily. She talks a lot, so much so that the twins don't need to interpret for me at all, but she also had charisma and charm.

I watch her make Liam laugh. He's different around her, more social, and for the first time since I've met him, I see a playful side to him as he teases Emily and banters with Ean and Charlie. When the boys gang up on Elijah, Emily jumps in and basically hands them their asses. I just met her, but, in my heart, I know she's right. I can already feel a bond between the two of us forming.

Slowly, the others began to leave as well. Before he leaves, Anders approaches me. "You'll be okay. I won't be very far, and I'll be seeing you regularly. Besides, I haven't forgotten about our tabled discussion. We'll talk more about that later. For now, get acquainted with your new home and family." He pulls me into a quick hug. "Liam will check the perimeter. When he's satisfied everything is in order, he'll return to the training facility. Don't run... Promise?"

*"I won't go anywhere."* I cross my heart.

"Good," he says, squeezing me one last time before he turns to leave. Sodie hugs me next. He is the only one here tonight that doesn't have family. I want him to know that I think of him as my family. When he pulls back, I point to his chest and then point to mine.

He smiles. "Are you adopting me?" I squeeze his hand and nod. "Good, I already think of you as my family too. I'll be seeing you." He touches my chin, then turns to leave.

Liam stands off to the side. He doesn't move at first. Frowning, he scans the area. He gently grabs my arm and leans in to whisper into my ear, "When you find your room, flick the light on three times so I know you're okay and settled in for the rest of the night. There is no rush. Take your time." Before I know it, he disappears into the night.

Returning to the foyer, my new family is waiting for me. "Ready to see your new room?" Shakti asks.

"Tomorrow, we can give you the grand tour. You're free to go wherever you please and you can play the piano whenever you like. This is your home now. I want you to think of it as your own," the Alpha King adds.

"You can call him by his name," Jeremy says to me. "You don't have to keep referring to him as the Alpha King." He snickers, and I elbow him in the ribs.

I glance over at the Alpha King. When we reach the top, he turns to me. "It's okay to call me Nathan. In time when you are comfortable, you can call us Mom and Dad if you want to." I look down at my toes, unsure how to respond to his kindness. He puts his hand on my shoulder and make a gesture to follow Shakti.

Shakti points out the guest rooms as we make our way along the hallway. She notes the twins' bedroom near the end of the hall and Luke's room on the opposite side. Then Shakti opens double doors to a room at the very end of the hall.

"This used to be the boys' playroom, but they've outgrown it and spend most of their time in their own rooms. I thought you might like it. It has better lighting and more space." I peek into the room behind her. There are large floor-to-ceiling windows facing the rest of the territory, a hearth with a sitting area in front of it, and on the opposite side, there's a desk and a short panel of floor-to-ceiling bookshelves. She walks further into the room, and I follow her. There's a huge canopy bed with lavender bedding and gauze curtains. The furniture is white with an antiqued look. The desk and shelves match the décor.

"I wasn't sure what color scheme you would like, I thought pink was too girly and blue too boyish so I chose purple. If you don't like anything, we can always change it." I spin in a slow circle, and I shake my head. I love everything about the room. It's perfect. I slowly walk to the sitting area and notice the centerpiece on the coffee table. It's a rectangular-shaped planter with succulents and sprigs of lavender. The small couch is a sage green with a matching chair. Above the hearth is a large flatscreen TV. I look back down at the planter, and I smile. I don't know why, but something tells me that I love lavender, and that purple has always been my favorite color. The green is a perfect combination.

"She loves it," Justin says out loud, and I nod to confirm what Justin has said.

"You nailed it, Mom. Apparently, she loves lavender," Jeremy says, as he picks up another pot with sprigs of lavender in it. "Is lavender a flower or a bush?" Everyone starts to laugh at him. "What? I'm serious."

Shakti shows me a door that enters into the private bathroom. It's huge with a walk-in shower, a clawfoot bathtub, a water closet, and a double vanity. Why would I need two sinks?

Justin laughs, "It's just the way the bathroom layout is."

"I noticed you liked the Lavender and Honey soap collection I got for you, so I stuck to that. We can get you something else if you like."

At the very entrance of the en-suite, where we passed double doors before entering the full bathroom, she pulls it open. It's a full walk-in closet. It has some clothing in it, but not enough to fill it.

"I have picked up some clothing for you, but I thought we could go into town and you can pick out your own clothing. There are some cute little boutiques there that I think you might like. If not, we can order something online."

She walks out of the closet and stands in front of the

glass French doors. She pulls them open and steps out onto a balcony. There is a little wrought-iron table with two chairs and a lounger.

"You can sit out here and have breakfast or study if you get too cooped up indoors." When she enters the room again, she hits a button on the side. It draws in heavy drapes. "The curtains block out the light if you decide you want to sleep in during the day or just feel the need for privacy." She hits another button, and the drapes open back up. There's a vanity on the wall opposite of the bed; then she walks to the bookshelves. "Anders told me you like to read. He gave me a list of books he thought you might like to get your little library collection started. The boys have an extra laptop and an iPod that they don't use, but I can get you your own."

I shake my head; this is more than enough. If I didn't know any better, I'd think I'm still in a coma and this is all a dream. This can't be real. Just when that nagging feeling that I don't deserve any of this starts to fill my head, Jeremy puts his arm over my shoulder. Then he pinches me.

*Ass*! I slap him in the chest.

He grunts at first, then laughs as he rubs his chest. "Did that feel like you're in a coma?" he taunts.

"Jeremy! That wasn't nice!"

Nathan starts to laugh. "Shakti, leave them alone. It's what siblings do. Besides, I think she can handle it."

The twins stretch out on my bed and turn on the TV. Shakti and Nathan sit down at my sitting area and check in with me before they leave me for the night. This is more than I could ever hope for. I am perfectly content with everything that they have done for me. Eventually, they wrangle the twins out of my room to give me some peace and let me get settled in.

When everyone is out of my room, I remember what Liam asked me to do. It has been a long time since he left. I run out onto my balcony and look around, but little good that does because I can't see a thing. I listen to see if I can pick up on anything, but I hear nothing. He may have left already, but I do what he asked anyway. I walk to the entrance, and I flip the light switch three times.

# Chapter 27

## RUNNING AWAY

### JESSICA

July 25, 2014: 11:45 p.m.

I know I promised I wouldn't run away. But does it count if I run back to the place where it all started? I turn on the light of what was once my room in the clinic. The entire room has been emptied. It looks like I have never been there. The bed has no sheets, but I climb onto it anyway and sit in the middle. I'm not sure why, but being here just makes me feel better. This feels like something I deserve more than the luxury of my new home. I just sit there in silence, lost in my thoughts.

A knock at the door startles me. When I look up, Liam is standing in the doorway leaning against the frame with his arms crossed over his chest. The sight of him makes my breath catch.

He gives me a crooked smile. "I followed you back here." I avert my eyes and look down at my hands. He probably thinks I'm an idiot. "How about we take a walk?" I hesitate. I would prefer staying here. "No one's in the clinic, so I don't think it's good for you to stay here alone."

Sliding off the bed, I follow him out of the room. We walk in silence as we leave the clinic. I don't know where he's taking me, but I trust him. I wish I could talk to him. I wish he could hear my thoughts. I wonder... maybe he could. I have done it with Shadow, but I don't really know how I did it... I lift my hand and reach out to Liam, and I gently touch the back of his arm.

He stops walking and looks sideways at me. "I can already hear your thoughts."

Frowning, I pull my hand back. *How?*

He shrugs. "Not sure. It happened that night you were running from the clinic. At first, I thought I was imagining it. Then, when we returned to pick you up the next night, your thoughts, your voice was in my head. I knew you weren't feeling well and were trying to fight it. I could feel your panic starting... Then I stood guard outside of your door every night after you returned, and I could still hear your thoughts in my head."

*"Why can't I hear your thoughts?"*

"I'm not sure. It could be because I'm built different. The twins are happy and secure with their lives. I had a different way of being raised. I tend to shut people out. I spent my entire life erecting a wall, probably to protect myself."

I frown. *"What happened to you?"*

He stops walking. When I look up, we are standing in front of the obstacle course. He motions his head for me to follow him. He takes me around, and he motions for me to climb up this wall. I hesitate at first, unsure why he wants to go up there.

"You'll see."

I take a few steps back. With a running start, I jump up, grabbing on to a peg, and I start to climb. I smile to myself. This... this is what I need—to feel something... to feel... alive. Liam climbs up after me. I'm almost at the top of the wall when I glance down at Liam.

My foot slips out from under me. I can't find my footing. My heart flutters with panic. I'm too high up; a fall could result in breaking my neck or cracking my head open. Either way, I would definitely end up dead. I reach up to grab hold of another peg, but I miss it.

"Hang on. I'm coming to get you," Liam calls up.

I will my racing heart to slow down. Then I start to feel it. Air, no... wind starts to surround me. As my grip falters, I let go, falling backward. I open my arms and allow the wind to take me. I stop falling. The wind pushes me back up to the top of the wall. I correct my position to a stand, and I gently place my feet on the perch. Slowly, I turn to look for Liam. When I look down, he's almost to the top. I reach down to offer him a hand, but he doesn't take it. I narrow my eyes at him... I wonder... I picture air around him pushing him up. In the next instant he's pushed up with a gust of air, landing on the perch in a heap.

My eyes widen. I didn't mean to do that. I start to laugh, covering my mouth.

He dusts himself off. "Ho...how?" is all that he manages to get out. He grabs me and pulls me to him. "Shit," he breathes out, his warm breath caressing my cheek. "How long have you known you could do that?"

I shake my head. *I didn't.*

He pulls back, looking down on me. "The lightning... the rain... That's all you. You're doing that," he says.

I'm not sure. I replay the conversation with Shadow before I was discharged. I hadn't really noticed before. He starts to shake his head. He grabs my hand and crosses over to the other side and sits, letting his long legs dangle over the edge. I follow suit and sit next to him.

Then he starts to laugh. "You were checking Shadow out?" Huh? How did we get from *I didn't fall to my death because the wind carried me up to the perch* to *I was checking Shadow out?* "I saw it in your conversation. You were replaying it in your mind."

I was not; I was merely making an observation. I cringe. It's the second time I had gotten caught doing that.

"Sure, like you weren't checking Charlie out that first time we came to your room," he deadpans.

I was not checking him out. If I was checking anyone out, it was... I clear my throat. I need to think of something else. He's looking down; then he starts to rub his lip. I wish I knew what he was thinking.

Sitting there in silence, I relish the feel of the night. The sky is clear, and I can see the stars. I glance over at Liam. He's still rubbing his thumb along the back of my hand. He said he could hear my thoughts that night they came to pick me up from Whitemore plantation. Hear the panic in my head. The panic started in the car. I close my eyes, enjoying the feel of his thumb brushing against my skin. He was in the car with me that night. It was him, the man who calmed my fears.

"There are two places I like to go when I need to think," he finally says. "Here and a place near the edge of the territory, near the cliff. You can see all of the seventh territory from there. I can show you the next time. It's much prettier during the day." He goes silent again, but it doesn't last very long.

"When I learned that you couldn't remember your past, or what happened to you, I envied that. The ability to forget all the bad and horrible things that happened, the ability to be able to start over with a clean slate. But after watching you, hearing your thoughts, seeing how you react to things. Not fully understanding why you feel the way that you do. The nightmares that haunt you. I started to realize that it's actually more like a curse instead of a blessing. You can't work through your feelings if you don't know why they are there in the first place. If I had to guess, you were made to feel inferior to them, made to feel like you had to earn everything including feelings. If you showed any signs of weakness, you were probably punished for that too. I know because that was how I was raised, and I may not have the scars on the outside, because all my scars are here." He taps his temple.

Unshed tears fill my eyes; I squeeze his hand. He gets me, even though I don't really get myself.

*"How did you come to live with Elias and his family?"*

"I ran away from home. Anywhere was better than that hellhole. Then I met an old man, when I was living on the streets. He took me in, gave me shelter, food, a warm place to sleep at night. He educated me, taught me how to redirect my anger, and taught me how to fight. He became my best friend, the only person I could trust. Right before he died, Elias Blackguard showed up. Then after Eugene passed, Elias returned and brought me here." He sighs, releasing what sounds like the weight of the world.

"When I first came to stay with Elias and his family, it took a while for me to open up. Even though I had made one good friend, it was still hard for me to believe that there were other good people in this world. I've been with them going on three years, and I still haven't been able to let them in completely. I'm telling you this because these are good people. You can trust them. They already love you like your family. They will accept you as you are, maybe even love you harder because you are different."

He releases my hand and holds it palm facing up. A ball of fire forms. When he closes his hand, it extinguishes the flames.

"Between my shitty ass-attitude and all the baggage I came with and the magic I wield, they never once pushed me away. They still love me and protect me. They will do the same for you. So will I."

I have so many questions. Liam patiently answers them as he continues to hold my hand. When he is probably talked out and tired of answering my questions, Liam decides it is time to take me back, but I don't want to go back to the mansion. I'm not ready yet. We agree he will take me to see Anders.

We climb down the other side of the wall using the ropes.

Liam reaches the bottom first. When I am close enough to the ground, he picks me off the wall. As he is setting me down, I can feel the heat radiating off his body. I can feel his warm breath on my face. His lips are close enough, that if I lean in just a fraction closer, I will be able to feel them pressed against mine. Then I remember that I have braces and missing teeth, that there are scars on my face, and that I am wearing glasses so big that they nearly take up my entire face. I squeeze my eyes shut, and I turn my head, embarrassed that I had those thoughts to begin with. Any man who looks like Liam would never find someone like me attractive.

As soon as my feet touch the ground, I quickly turn, pulling the hood of my sweatshirt up and over my head and shoving my hands into my pocket. I quietly follow Liam to Anders's office, trying to divert my thoughts from wanting to kiss him.

We reached Anders's office. Once inside, Anders looks me over. "Why don't you get comfortable and find something to read? Liam, may I speak to you outside?"

I don't want Liam to get into trouble. Quickly, I step in front of Anders. "*Wait! I ran away from the mansion back to the clinic. We just talked. He helped me to understand whatever this is that I am going through. He didn't do anything wrong.*"

Anders smiles. "He's not in trouble, and neither are you. I just want to speak to him, that's all." He holds up a hand. "I'm worried that I've been selfishly keeping Liam on the night shift, and I want to ensure that he can keep up with the final parts of training." He raises his eyebrows.

I release a breath. "*Okay, he's a good person. He deserves to be here. I don't want anything to jeopardize his position here because of me.*"

"That won't happen." Reluctantly, I step aside to let Anders follow Liam out the door.

Not that I didn't trust Anders, but I want to make sure he really isn't going to reprimand Liam for taking care of me tonight. I press my ear up against the door. Their voices are a low murmur, and I can barely make out what is being said. I close my eyes and concentrate on their surroundings. Just like that, both of their voices infiltrate into my mind.

"Did you see any sign of Dustin, Marcus, or Boris when you went back to the mansion?" Anders's familiar, gravelly voice resounds in my mind.

"No, but I found a few of their tracks. It was definitely Marcus and Dustin's. Boris is too smart and sneaky for him to leave any traces behind."

"It's a good thing you followed your instincts and went back. I'm not too sure on the exact time frame, but Sodie and Darwin had seen Boris lingering near the clinic."

"Yeah, I got the text from Sodie, so I took her somewhere safe and made sure we weren't followed."

"Good, thank you. I got it from here. Why don't you get some rest?"

"Sir, Marcus is after her because of me. I'm sorry for my part in this mess."

"No one is blaming you for anything, son. These assholes were raised to be criminals."

"Sir, if they hurt her, I can't promise you that I won't—"

"If either one of them touches a hair on her head, you have my full fucking permission to end them, no questions asked!"

"Yes, sir." I hear the shuffling of feet. In a panic I push away from the door, grab a book, and sit on one of the chairs. I'll have to think about what I overhead some other time. So Anders can't know that I was eavesdropping.

When he returns, he doesn't ask me why I ran back to the clinic, or why I didn't return. "Are you warm enough? Do you want some water?" We fall into our comfortable modes—him working, me reading. When the light of dawn starts to break, Anders stands from his seat and stretches. "Let's take a walk."

I pull my hood on and follow Anders. We walk in silence. He doesn't say where we are going or what we are going to do. When he stops, I look around and notice a group of men running toward us. I pull my hood down further to cover my face and lower my head after I adjust my glasses. As the group starts to get closer, I hear shouting and glance sideways, noticing Anders standing there with arms folded as he watches the group. Charlie and Ean are in the front. Ean shouts another command as they cross in front of us. They look to us, raising a hand in salute. I keep my head down, watching only with my eyes.

Charlie gives me a big smile and a wink after he passes Anders. I try not to smile as I hear Anders groan. The rest of the men follow, saluting Anders and facing back to the front as they pass, except for three of them. I can feel their eyes on me. I lower my eyes, as if I could make myself invisible. I only glance back up to catch the back end of the group, which is Liam and Sodie. Sodie smiles at me before he faces the front. Liam, on the other hand, doesn't look my way at all. I start to feel weird and worried if Liam regrets telling me about his past and showing me his secret. I try not to think about it since Anders can hear my thoughts.

I glance at Anders as he watches the men pass by. He resumes walking again. I still feel as if I am being watched, so I continue to keep my head down and try not to bring attention to myself.

I follow Anders out into a clearing where no one can see us. When he stops walking, he indicates with his hand for me to stand next to him, so I do. Then he sits on the ground and waits patiently as I sit down next to him and cross my legs. He places both of his hands on his knees and closes his eyes.

"Close your eyes, keep your mind blank, and focus on your breathing." Then he stops talking.

I watch him for a while, just sitting there, breathing slowly with his eyes closed. Facing back to the front, I look around at my surroundings first, then do exactly as he does. I'm not sure how long we sit there; I lose track of time and awareness of my surroundings. Something starts to happen. Wind starts to surround me, caressing my face, and rustling my oversized hoodie. It starts to get stronger, but I don't open my eyes, and I continue to sit there focusing on my breathing. Rain starts to fall, but it doesn't rain on us or me. With my eyes still closed, I listen in on the sounds the rain and wind make. The rain sounds heavier; the wind grows stronger, whistling and moaning as it whips around. Thunder claps and shakes the ground beneath me, and behind the lids of my eyes, I can see the flash of lightning.

"Don't lose focus. Keep focusing on your breathing." It's Anders's voice inside of my head. Through all the chaos surrounding me, I continue sitting there and focusing on breathing. Without any hint of the storm slowing, the rain and thunder stop. No more flashes of lightning and the wind dies down. Silence, there is nothing more but silence.

When I start to hear the birds chirping, I slowly open my eyes. The sky is clear; the ground is dry. There is no sign of the short storm. Turning my head, I find Anders staring at me. Not sure how to respond to him, I smile and shrug. He just gives a short grunt and proceeds to stand up. I follow his lead. He doesn't go anywhere.

Facing in the same direction, he dips his chin and slightly bends at the waist. When he's back in an upright position, he slides a foot forward and moves his arms. His body starts to sway or rock in a slow, even rhythm. He doesn't give me instructions or any indication to follow, so I just watch him in curious fascination. His movements are slow and fluid, moving his arms out then back in, moving on the balls of his feet so his body sways in tune with his arm movements. Slowly, he switches sides. His movements remind me of water languidly rolling over smooth river rocks. I want to move like that, but I'm not sure how or where to start. So, I just watch and try to commit each movement to memory. When he is finished, he holds the last position, then brings his legs and arms back to center and bows.

He places his hands in his pocket and glances at me. "I do this every morning if you would like to join me."

*"I would like that, thank you."* He turns on the balls of his feet and slowly walks back the way we came.

"I would like to talk about what happened while you were meditating."

*"Did you see it? The storm?"*

"No, I didn't see anything, but I could hear it in your mind, the rain, the thunder, the whistling of the wind."

*"No flashes of lightning?"*

"You saw flashes of lightning?"

I nod. *"Then I heard your voice, telling me to focus."*

"I didn't say anything out loud. You heard my voice?"

*"Yes, it was in my head."*

"Have you ever experienced anything like this before?"

I start to shake my head; then I remember my fall from the rock wall. *"Well, actually, last night or early this morning. Don't get mad please and don't get mad at Liam."* I wait until he gives me his full attention. He doesn't make any promises. I show him what happened on the wall. Shock, rather than anger, registers on his face.

"You pulled Liam up with your magic?"

I nod.

"Did Liam show you or tell you what he can do?"

I look down. It's a secret; I try to clear my mind.

"Jessica, I know. It's okay. He's not in trouble."

I turn my face away, unsure if I want to reveal Liam's secret, but I trust Anders. *"He showed me."*

"Okay, do you think you can keep your magic under control?"

*"I don't know. I didn't know I had any."*

He nods. "Fair point, do you still have the journal I gave to you?"

*"Yes, I've been writing in it."*

"Good, keep track of any more things that occur. We can work on control and building on it. It's important that we keep this to ourselves except for Nathan and Shakti of course. I want you to always be honest with them. Is it okay if I tell them?" I hesitate at first. What if they don't want me once they find out?

"Trust me, that will not happen."

Anders reaches for me to guide me back to the mansion. Instead of entering through the front door, we enter through the back. Tater greets us. She fusses over me and gets me to sit. She places a drink that looks like a smoothie and my supplements in front of me. She tells me that she is in charge of giving me my injections. Great, I was hoping that I forgot them at the clinic. She places a small bowl of scrambled eggs in front of me. I smile. I haven't had the chance to eat real food. I am looking forward to it. The smoothie she makes has real fruit in it. I can taste a hint of the supplement shake I was given in the clinic.

"I think you'll like my special diet a whole lot better than what they were giving you in the clinic. I'll try to think up different things we can try until the doctor gives the okay to introduce you back to regular foods again."

"Thank you," I rasp out. My voice is stronger today. I wonder if it has to do with the meditation.

"Oh, and Alpha Agnus insisted that I cook all your meals with water from her territory. Don't tell her, but I'm only going to use it in your smoothie." She places a glass of water in front of me. "Of course, I'll also make you drink it as plain water."

I laugh. I think I am really going to love this woman. Joe walks into the kitchen. "Good morning," I rasp out.

"Good morning, Princess. The Alpha King will be joining you shortly. The Luna Queen took the boys into the city for some school event. They're looking forward to seeing you later this afternoon."

I smile at him. *"Were they worried that I wasn't here this morning?"* I ask through my mind-link, not sure how much I could rasp out with my voice.

"Anders notified them that you were with him. All is well, Princess." My tension and anxiety over disappointing them ease. I can focus on eating my breakfast.

Anders and Nathan enter the kitchen, and after bidding Anders farewell, Tater places a plate of breakfast in front of Nathan. He sits at the breakfast nook with me.

"So today is my favorite day of the week. It's the one day where I get to go out and follow up on business with the pack. I am hoping that you are interested in joining me."

I nod enthusiastically.

"Great, Duck will be joining us, and he can tell you all about the pack's history and how we came to be in the dairy business."

We spend the entire day together. I fall in love with the territory, the pack members, the dairy, and the farms. I love listening to the two men share their beloved history of how the pack business came to be and how it expanded into sustainable agriculture. By the end of the day, I also fall in love with two more men who accept me and love me back as if I were truly one of their own.

# CHAPTER 28

## ANDERS'S PAST

### JESSICA

#### March 31, 2025: Present Day

My father, who is now sitting next to me, reaches over and squeezes my hand. "I remember that day as if it were yesterday," he says, eyes shiny with unshed tears. He looks back to the camera as he continues to speak. "I must admit, I wasn't sure what it would be like adopting a child, especially an older one. Both the twins and my mate were so adamant that I would love her like she was my own. Even though I agreed to it, especially since she won the hearts of the three toughest men I have ever met in my life, I was still a little apprehensive. Maybe some of it was my ego, and I worried that she and I wouldn't get along or bond as well as she had with the others." He looks down at our intertwined hands and smiles. "At the end of that day, when my mate and I saw you off for the night, all my reservations and fears evaporated, and my heart swelled with so many emotions. The same emotions I felt when I laid eyes upon my boys for the first time. There are no words to describe what a father feels when his child is placed into his arms for the first time. It's an overwhelming feeling of love, fear, excitement, and protectiveness all rolled into one big ball. When you hugged me good night, it hit me right here." He brings his hand, still holding on to mine, and places it over his heart. "That's when I knew—even though I didn't create you, you were mine."

I let go of my father's hand, lean over, and give him a big hug. When I settle back down, I wipe the tears from my eyes.

Carmen is holding up her hands, forming a *T* for time out. "I have a few questions…" She looks back down at her notes, then looks back up at Anders, who is sitting to my right. "…For you." She points a ballpoint pen in Anders's direction. He frowns at her. Somehow, Carmen convinced him to join us for this portion of the interview. She wanted both of my parents, including Anders, to be present. He protested at first, insisting that he didn't need to be involved. My mother wouldn't hear of it and insisted, along with my father, that he be present. I agreed with them. I hadn't known all these years what he really was to me, but he has always been there, just like a father, legal papers or no papers, blood or no blood. I had always thought of him as being like a father to me. I want him sitting at my side, secrets and all, because that is where he belongs.

Carmen brings her pen to her lips and hums. "I think giving the viewers a more in-depth look into your position as a head guard and how is it that she is your biological daughter is a more intimate approach. We already covered the relationship and the bond she has made with the Luna Queen and Alpha King. I want to learn more about you, Anders." Anders is sitting stiffly next to me, and I can see his hesitation. He's staring at Christian. Christian is watching Anders. Do they know each other? I reach down and place my hand into his large one, and I squeeze.

He finally takes his eyes from Christian and looks at me. "You don't have to, I know that you like to keep your personal life private." He squeezes my hand back. "Carmen, I don't want..."

Before I can continue, Christian starts, "I think Jessica should hear your side of the story. You didn't really give her much of an explanation from the sound of it. You can't just drop a bomb, a big one in fact, and then sit there expecting her to fill in the blanks on her own."

Anders doesn't answer; he just remains silent. Finally, my father says, "Anders, it's time. I have been telling you for years that your secrets will eat you from the inside and will catch up to you on the outside."

Anders squeezes his eyes shut and lets out a long breath. "Fine, what do you want to know?"

Carmen smiles triumphantly like she won a prize. "How did you become the head guard? It's obvious from the history books that a Black Obsidian guard was the original head guard, but now he's second lead. How did you earn your position?" Anders turns his head and looks at my father. He nods at Anders as if giving him permission to tell his story. Anders looks down at our still-joined hands.

"In order to tell you that, I have to start with the beginning." He looks up at Christian, who is watching both of us. "After the great war, many of the white wolf shifters fled the LS territory in search of refuge. Some stayed under the protection of some of the packs, and some became rogues. My grandmother Alpha Agnus was a baby at the time. She lost her mother in the war. It was her father who fled the LS territory, raising her in secret.

"The resistance had formed a white witch hunt after the great war, looking for any survivors and killing them. Then it turned into more. They killed anyone who showed any signs of either magic or white wolf characteristics. Even though the history books indicate that this period had passed, it hadn't. The Resistance just became more secretive with their dealings. Especially after the new monarch had become established. When my grandmother was a young adult, she met her true mate, another white wolf shifter, and they had a daughter. The white hunt caught up to them, her mate was killed, and my grandmother, protecting her only child, fled and found a pack that took her in and protected her.

"The risk was too great to keep her child and stay hidden and alive. She met a family in the Asian territory when she was younger and sent her daughter to be raised by them to keep her safe. My grandmother set out to find the white wolves in hiding to figure out a way to return home.

"Her daughter grew up and met her true mate, another white wolf shifter who was raised in the Northern A territory. They had a daughter, and a couple of years later, they had me. I was two, maybe, at the time, too young to remember any of it. Our home was broken into, and my parents were murdered. My sister, who just turned five at the time, was killed in her sleep. I was taken and spared. I'm not sure why. My grandmother tracked me down and found the group of men who killed my family and saved me. Instead of bringing me to her new pack, she sent me to live with the family who raised my mother."

He stops and pauses for a bit. He looks at me, then at Christian, then continues when my father squeezes his shoulder.

Anders emits a breathy laugh. "I was an angry kid. I felt abandoned and hurt that my own grandmother wouldn't take me in, so I started to act out. I started fights and even joined an underground fighting ring. My adopted family didn't know what the hell to do with me. My grandmother sent for me to return home. By then, she had mated with an Alpha who had children from a previous mating, and together they had returned to the LS territory. I was still so angry with my grandmother, even more so because she mated a man who had children. She raised them as if they were her own, yet she didn't raise me or my mother."

My heart breaks for him. I picture a young boy with anger and hurt from feeling abandoned. I squeeze his hand again, encouraging him to continue.

He rubs his face. "I didn't make it easy for her. I was angry with her for putting on a façade of being an older woman who mated a younger man, for being weak. I wanted revenge on the ones who killed my family, killed her mate. She tried to talk me out of it and said that things would fall into place, but I refused to listen. I would leave our territory. Not caring if I put myself at risk, I went in search of the

Resistance. Instead of finding them, I found a group of rogues who had the same goals as I did. To take down the Resistance and take down the monarchy so that the white wolves could take back what was taken from them.

"I was sixteen, almost seventeen at the time. On one of our runs, we came across a fight. From my standpoint, I immediately recognized the guards; they were outnumbered and losing. I didn't know who they were fighting against. The one thing I knew for sure was that it wasn't the rogues, even though we were blamed for every fight and every random killing that occurred. I was tired of it, tired of being labeled as the bad guys, when we were the ones out there searching to take down the Resistance. In my mind, I had made the decision that we would assist the guards, to prove everyone wrong about us. I motioned to my group to run in and help.

"As we were approaching, I saw three shifters in wolf form surrounding a woman who was still in human form, huddled on the ground, using her body to protect a little boy. I ran in, zeroing in on the three shifters. I attacked them, using my magic to build a wall of ice in front of the woman to protect her and the boy. I killed them, ripping out their throats with my teeth, and more shifters started to attack me and the other rogues. When the guards started to realize that we were there to help them, they changed their tactics and focused on the ones they were there to protect. The group of rogues and I killed many shifters that night. When the others started to understand that they weren't going to win, they retreated. I brought my wall of ice down, the one I erected to protect the mother and the boy. When I had gotten close enough..."

Anders closes his eyes and squeezes his free hand into a fist. When he opens his eyes, he looks over at my father, and I can see grief and sadness in his eyes.

"I was too late. The woman had died protecting her son. We were also too late in saving the Head Guard. He was killed in the attack. We helped the guards collect the party that they were protecting, and without a word, we disappeared into the night.

"For days, I couldn't get the image of the mother huddled around her son, bleeding to her death, out of my head. I kept replaying my actions, my decisions over and over in my mind. If I had gotten there sooner, if only I hadn't taken too long in my decision to join the fight, I could have saved the woman, and her son would still have a mother. That boy was now like me, without a mother, all because of the Resistance. I met with my group of rogues after that, and I pushed them harder and trained harder. I was determined even more to take down the Resistance."

I cleared my throat. "How did you know it was the Resistance?"

"I had one of the rogues investigate. He learned it was an attack from the Resistance. They were planning on taking down the Alpha King and his family."

I gasp and clap my hand over my mouth. "That little boy you saved was..."

"It was me," my father answers for Anders. "That night, he saved my life. His group saved my father, as well as Duck. My father sustained many injuries that night. He didn't quite recover back to his normal state, but he was alive, and my uncle was alive. I may have lost my mother, and I grieved over her loss, but I still had my family. I will be forever grateful for what Anders and his group did for us that night. We did lose our head guard, Elias's father, that night, but he was killed before Anders's group had gotten to us. The Resistance was smart. They took out our strongest guards first, weakening our defenses to get to my family."

Carmen has a look of confusion on her face. "Okay, so you saved the Alpha King and his father with your group of rogues, but that still doesn't explain how you came to be the head guard."

My father smiles. "Anders wasn't the only one who knew how to get information. When things settled down, Duck tracked down the rogues. He knew someone he trusted in the group. He learned that a teenage boy had led the group of rogues to aid us, and he and my father went to Whitemore plantation, known as Parker territory at the time, and spoke to Alpha Agnus. When my father learned of Anders's situation, he made the decision right then and there that he wanted to bring Anders into our home. Offer him guidance, be a role model to him, and fill in as a father figure, a role which he felt Anders needed. Anders is a natural Alpha; it was obvious that he needed another Alpha to help him understand himself.

"Anders came to live with us a few days later. At the time, the head guard and Duck's family also lived in the mansion. He was close to Elias and Chris's age. Over time, he had grown close to the pair. I was ten at the time, maybe a little bratty, before life circumstances changed me. Chris and Elias usually just ignored me even though I looked up to them. But Anders was my hero, still is." My father squeezes his shoulder and then slaps Anders on the back before he continues. "I was a pain in the ass back then, following him everywhere, copying everything he did. I wanted to be just like him. He didn't make me feel like I was bothering him, and he never told me to leave him alone. He talked to me all the time and taught me how to fight to protect myself. So, I became his shadow. In my eyes, he was very much my big brother."

Anders grunts. "You're still a pain in my ass."

My father laughs. "I love you too. Anyway, Duck took over as interim head guard. He and my father decided to recruit the rogues, who fought alongside the guards."

"Rogues?" I ask. Both Anders and my father nod at the same time.

"You have met them. In fact, two of them worked as part of the household staff," Anders clarifies.

"Joe? Joe's a rogue?"

Anders laughs, "He's a guard, but yes, he once was a rogue. When he learned that I would stay at the mansion, he got a job as a household staff. He was the first friend I made when I moved to the LS territory. He was protective of me and knew that I didn't make the best decisions because of where my head was at, at the time. He wanted to keep an eye on me. He also became very protective of Nathan. When his training was over, he decided to remain as a staff in the household. He served as both guard and butler. Xavier took the chauffeur position."

I smile, thinking of my two favorite staff members. "They're older than you. You just jumped into their group and bossed them around?" I ask Anders.

He grimaces. "I didn't just jump in and boss anyone around. They had a goal, one I shared, so I used my training from the Asian territory, even though I wasn't done yet, and taught them."

My father chuckles. "Even at a young age, Anders was quite skilled at what he did. Both my father and Duck were pleasantly surprised to see how well the rogues did in combat training and even more so because, in a short time, they learned how to fight, strategize, and work together as a group. All their training came from a young teenage boy. Seeing this, they allowed Anders to take over some of the training, under their guidance, of course. It was pretty evident at the time what Anders was meant to do."

Carmen interrupts, "Yes, but wasn't that a role meant for Elias?"

Anders nods. "I didn't want the role. I wasn't born into the family, and I wasn't officially adopted. So what they did was create a hierarchy of some sorts, a head guard position, and a second and third lead role. They decided that each role would be determined later when we came of age. I was perfectly fine with the second or third lead position. You have to understand, for the first time in my life, I had friends and a family. I didn't want to disrupt anything that was meant to be theirs. I was open about how I felt, and I wouldn't begrudge Chris or Elias anything. In fact, I decided to join the military. Chris and Elias wanted to come with me, but they had other obligations that needed them home, so I went alone, hoping that when I returned, the head guard position would be filled by Elias or Chris." He stops talking and looks up at Christian.

"I was nineteen before I had left for basic training. I met my true mate a couple of weeks before I was due to leave. I tried to fight the bond. It wasn't safe for her to be with me. It haunted me knowing that her fate would be like my parents and my grandfather. I tried so hard to stay away until I couldn't anymore." He keeps looking at Christian. Anders clears his throat. "I kept my relationship a secret. I didn't want anyone to know. I wrote to her every chance I had under a fake name. She wrote back. After basic training was over, I came home for a short vacation, and I snuck off to meet with her every chance I could. I loved her. I wanted to keep her safe and protected, even if it meant protecting her from me. So I didn't hesitate when I got the call to go back for a job. I finally confided in Joe and Xavier, and I asked them to keep an eye on her, to make sure she was safe. A short while later, after I returned to the military, I had gotten word from Joe that she was pregnant. Between Joe, Xavier and I, we had gotten her to the Northern A territory under the ruse that she was going to college. She did go to college; I made sure of it after. When my twin boys were born, I did the same thing that was done to my mother and me. I took them to the Asian territories to be raised by the same family that raised me. By then, my mate hated me. I wouldn't tell her where they were. She lost her children, and at the same time, she lost me. I paid for her education and kept tabs on her until she returned home back to her family. I stayed in the military, and between deployments, I visited the boys and checked in on them from time to time. I know that it wasn't enough. I needed to protect them. I... I... would rather see them alive, safe, even if it meant that I couldn't be in their lives completely.

"I wanted things to be different, especially when Chris and Elias met their mates. It killed me to see how happy they were. It bothered me so much that when I returned home five years later, I had a crazy idea that maybe we could make it work. I lived with the Alpha King and was part of the guard. I found her again and pleaded with her to forgive me. When she sent word that she wanted to see me and talk, I had hope. As we were leaving our secret meeting place, I had gotten word that I was being deployed again. I made promises that when I returned, I would find a way to become a family again. I had no idea that my deployment would extend for a few years. I couldn't write to anyone; I couldn't call anyone. When it was over and I returned to base, I had received word from Joe that the Alpha King wasn't doing well and that I needed to return home as soon as possible. I made it in time to sit at his bedside and say our final goodbyes. It was the worst day of my life, and it seemed like it was getting worse by the minute. I found a letter from my mate stating that she didn't want to see me anymore. When I returned, she didn't want me to find her.

"It was dated two years earlier. I had planned to find her anyway to explain to her why I was gone for so long. The doctor wanted a family meeting. They explained that traces of poison had been found in the Alpha's blood. Everything was happening all at once; I lost a man whom I looked up to like a father, and I lost my mate. I was enraged that the guards let someone get past them. I lost sight of everything else and made it my personal mission to find the asshole who killed the Alpha King. When I found him, I made sure he knew exactly why he was dying. My grief, anger and regrets consumed me after that, and I went back and forth to my original idea that I couldn't risk being involved with my mate or my sons. I finally convinced myself that being who I am, even being with the royal family, it wasn't safe. It was then that I decided to dedicate my entire life to protecting what I did have right in front of me, my brother. Because every time I looked at him, I saw the ten-year-old boy who lost both of his parents, like me, to the Resistance. I promised his father—"

"Our father," my father says in a hushed tone.

"Our father," Anders corrects, then continues, "that I would protect him with my life. Between the four of us, we built the guard recruit program so that nothing like that would ever happen again."

My father clears his throat. "I named Anders head guard after my father died. Elias and Chris agreed to it."

I want to be angry that Anders gave up so easily on his mate and his sons, but I understand. I understand more than he might think. I guess history has a way of repeating itself.

"When I learned you were mine, I wanted to find my mate and ask her what the hell happened. I had no idea you existed. At the time I couldn't trust myself to not hurt her, for hurting you." He looks at both my parents, then swallows hard. "After enough time passed, I realized that your mother would never allow such a thing to happen to you. I know her better than that. I know in my heart she never told me about you because she wanted to keep you, because I couldn't be the man she needed or wanted. She would at least have you." He leans forward in his seat, resting his elbows on his knees, then covers his face with his hands.

"Anders," my father whispers.

"Don't, Nathan," he says in his hands.

I lean forward and rub his back. I have never seen Anders like this, and it breaks my heart. I look to Christian and wonder if there is some way, through this stupid show thing, I could find her, get some answers.

Anders drops his hands and rotates his head back to me. "I hadn't seen your mother for twenty-five years. Every time I look at my boys, they look just like her and you. You might have my eyes and my hair, but they are so many things about you that remind me of her."

"Anders," my mother whispers from her end on the couch. Clearly, he has never opened up like this to anyone, not even my parents. "Maybe it's not too late," she finishes.

"She will never forgive me for what I had done to her. It's been twenty-five years. She probably moved on by now. If she has, I don't blame her, and if that is what she chose and she's happy, that's all that matters to me."

Making small circles on his back to comfort him, I can't help but feel his pain behind his words. "You love her," I say quietly to him.

He drops his head, hiding the pained look I glimpse on his face. "I never stopped."

We take a much-needed break after Anders's confession. He needs a breather, and my parents need to consult with each other in private. I need to catch up and answer some emails and answer text messages. We all return to the room at the allocated time.

Carmen breezes into the room just as I take my seat. "We are missing one of your family members," she says without looking up.

I glance over at my mother on my left, my father on the far end of the couch, and Anders still seated on my right. "I don't understand, I'm pretty sure I covered everyone."

"You haven't really spoken up about Luke."

I clear my throat. Luke is a sensitive subject, and I don't really want to talk about him. "Well, that's easy. He was away at school, and I didn't really know him all that well."

She narrows her eyes at me. "I don't believe you. I think it's important that you talk about him, so the viewers get to know you and your family."

"Uh, isn't the whole point to all of this is that the viewers just see a bunch of men fight over me to win a contest?" My mother pokes me in the side with her finger. Her smile doesn't falter, but I catch that side-eye, the one she usually reserves for the twins. I roll my eyes. Fine.

Carmen grimaces.

"Let's see. I can't remember where I left off." I'm trying to be evasive, but Carmen is too perceptive. She looks over notes.

"You left off with spending the day with your father. Anders explained his position in the royal family. You were going to start talking about the incident that led you here, but

I cut you off. Why don't we start with how you met Luke?"

I pinch the bridge of my nose. I really don't want to, especially with my parents here.

My mother grabs my hand and gently pulls it down. She's looking at me with concern in her eyes. "Did something happen between you and Luke that you don't want to talk about?"

There are a lot of things that happened that I don't want to talk about. I shake my head. How much do I say? It's complicated, and I don't want to paint a bad picture of Luke on national TV.

Sighing, I shake my head. When I peek over at my father, he too has a look of concern. I lick my lips before I begin. "It took me a few weeks to acclimate to my new home. I had gotten along well with everyone, but it was hard to accept the things I was given because for some unknown reason, I couldn't help but continue to feel like I didn't deserve them. So, my parents decided to give me chores. I worked with Duck at the dairy, and Tater gave me some things to do around the house. I also went with Mom when she made her pack rounds, and I pretended to be my father's secretary when he worked in the office, and on occasion I dusted and cleaned Anders's office."

My parents laugh.

"It was the only way to get her to accept her allowance and things we gave her." My father said, with a smile, "I don't think I ever met a young child who was so unwilling to accept free money. Even then when she was given an allowance, she gave me half to invest in stocks and used the rest to pay off her medical debt."

Carmen frowns. "You had medical debt?"

My mother shakes her head. "No, she didn't, but she insisted that she pay for her services in the clinic."

I blush. "I just felt it was the right thing to do." I shrug.

# Chapter 29

## ACCLIMATING

### JESSICA

September 18, 2014: 10:20 p.m.

After the first few weeks, I am finally settling into my new home. Having chores makes me feel like I earned it and that I deserve to be in my luxurious room. Everything feels right, and I am starting to feel like I belong here, among the pack, with my new family. My parents decide that I am fourteen years of age and use the date when I was found as my date of birth.

Professor Hocson, the recruits' professor, has me take tests to determine what level of education I have. He frowns when I passed all of them and accuses me of cheating. Liam has been sitting in the room with me. He knows of my link with the twins and thinks I have been linked to Liam to find the answers. He's wrong. Liam could hear my thoughts, but I could never hear his.

Anders has to intervene on my part, but Professor Hocson isn't easily dissuaded and makes me retest with Ean in the room. Afterwards, he feels better about my test scores. So, everyone agrees that I can test out with the recruits on their testing day to receive my high school diploma. Professor Hocson agrees to get me started on core college courses, starting in the next term.

I still have a habit of wanting to leave my room some nights, and I fall back into insomnia due to the nightmares. I never had nightmares when Liam sat next to my clinic bed. Even though the twins try piling into bed with me to get me to sleep, I still have them. So, I just don't sleep.

I start to feel comfortable enough around Shakti and Nathan that I refer to them as mom and dad. The first time I call them that, they look so happy, so I continue to do it.

Some nights I find my father awake at his desk, so I pop my head in and talk to him for hours. We talk about everything, the history of the LS, how some of the laws were created, and why. We have debates on some of the issues facing the LS territory. I enjoy nights like those. When we tire each other out with debates and talk, then we both retire to our rooms.

One night in particular, I feel a little anxious. The recruits are counting down the time they have left in the program, which means that I won't see Liam or Sodie anymore. It makes me sad. Ean and Charlie are two of the trainers, so I would see them, especially if I can get into the next recruit class. Both Liam and Sodie plan to move on after graduation. Sodie will be continuing guard training somewhere else, and Liam, well, Liam never tells me where he is going. In fact, it's Sodie who tells me he is leaving after graduation.

I try to push down the feeling of hurt that builds behind my heart. Liam doesn't owe me an explanation. I might have a crush on him, but it doesn't mean he feels the same way. Every evening, Sodie will come by after their training first. Liam will relieve him for the night shift. Anders explains that even though I no longer need it, he wants them to finish their assignment before graduation. I'm not going to argue; I would actually miss them if I didn't see them.

Liam is... how do I put it... hot and cold. Some days he behaves like he had when he first came to my room—silent, distant—wearing that pinched expression on his face. Other days he's friendlier, sweet, talking. I could swear on these days when he walks me back to the manor at night from guitar/band practice with Duck, he bumps into me, and I swear sometimes he grazes his hand against mine and will hold on to my pinky for the briefest of moments before he lets it go and tucks his hands into his hoodie's front pocket.

But no matter what mood he is in, he always makes me flip the light switch three times when I'm in my room. My heart sinks when I think about him leaving, but I don't have a choice. Besides, he's practically a man. Why would he want someone like me? Too young, too ugly, and no future.

Roaming the halls that night, I find myself standing in front of my father's office door. The office door is slightly ajar, and I can hear him talking. There's another voice, but it sounds distant almost. White static noise surrounds the voice. It's so faint you can barely hear it. If I had to guess, it's someone talking to him on the speaker phone.

"What the hell do you mean you're adopting her?" the voice shouts. "What the hell happened to having equality in the family and everyone having a say! I didn't have a say. You didn't even give me a chance to voice my concerns. What the hell are you two thinking?"

My father responds slowly, "I'm sorry you feel that way, Luke, but I have to admit I am a little surprised with the tone you're taking with me at the moment."

"We know nothing about her. What if she's pretending to have amnesia? What if she's working for the Resistance? How do you know we can trust her? What if the Resistance placed her into our home to kill all of us in our sleep? What if she—"

"That's enough!" My father's voice is loud, commanding, and dangerously low. "Where the hell are these conspiracy theories coming from all of a sudden?" he asks. "You were on board when we talked about bringing her into our home. You were on board when your mother wanted to make over the room for her."

"That was different. There's a difference between letting her stay with us and adopting her," the voice growls.

"I want to know right now where the hell this is coming from!" my father replies. "Luke, if I were you, you better think long and hard about how you answer me."

"I don't want her to be my sister. I will never accept her as a sister..."

I've heard enough. I pull away from the door and run out the back door. I have no idea where to go. I want to run and find Anders, but I don't want to put anyone in a position over a conversation I shouldn't have heard in the first place. I look around, and I decide to go to my next favorite place, the barn. I find the stall where Queenie is, my favorite horse. I slip into her stall, wrap my arms around her neck, and bury my face to sob. Queenie tries to reach around and nuzzle me with her nose. I would never hurt anyone. Why would he think that I would?

"Hey, little one, what's with all of this?" A large warm hand strokes my back.

I turn and bury my face in Duck's button-up Western shirt. There are too many words to use, so I show him through my mind-link the conversation I just overheard.

"Oh, I see," he says. Queenie starts to nibble at my back. She starts to nibble at my ear when I don't pay her any mind. I pull away from Duck and give her attention.

"Luke's a good boy. I'm sure once he gets to know you he will feel bad about his reaction. This family doesn't have a good history with some things that happened in the past. I'm sure he's just looking out for his family; it's hard to do that when you're so far away. You'll see."

I shake my head. *"He sounded so angry."*

"Okay, let me tell you a story then, about Charlie and Sixes. When Charlie was born, he was the only boy in the entire house. Luke hadn't been born yet, and the four eldest girls were running the house. When Charlie came along, the girls loved him. Everyone doted on him; it was like he was the prince." Duck chuckles, "He charmed all the girls to do his bidding, got away with the devilish things, I tell you. When Tater announced that another baby was going to be on the way, it seemed like Charlie was on board. He nuzzled against his mama's belly every chance he got. Would talk into her belly and tell the baby he couldn't wait to meet her. But, when the baby came, things changed for Charlie. Everyone's attention was on Sixes instead of him. He had gotten scoldings when he acted up and disturbed the baby. He got jealous. He once stole Sixes right out of the crib and buried her in a stack of hay. Another time he took her outside and gave her to one of the dairy workers and told him to take the baby home." I giggle. I can so picture a toddler Charlie doing that to Sixes. "Eventually, he got over it and accepted his new baby sister, when she had gotten older, he became an overly protective big brother, and the two have been thick as thieves ever since. My point is that once Luke gets to know you, he'll get over whatever insecurities he has, and I can see him becoming another overly protective brother. Just wait and see."

I smile up at Duck. "Feeling a little better?" I nod again, and I lean in to give Duck another hug. "Good, now let's get you back inside. A growing girl like you needs to get some sleep."

## November 7, 2024: Luke's Homecoming

Shoot, I can't remember if he likes strawberries, or is it blueberries? I have both. Maybe I can make both. Luke is due to come home this evening. I'm so nervous. I already know that he doesn't like me. I want to make a good impression. So,

I decide to make him dinner—well, everyone dinner. This week makes six months since I was rescued. So, I'm using both Luke's homecoming and my six months as being a part of the family as a way of saying thank-you. I'm also hoping Luke will see that I love his family and that I would never deliberately do anything to hurt them.

I start gnawing at my lip. I'll ask Dad. I turn off the stove so I don't burn anything while I'm gone and head toward Dad's office. I'm looking down at my notes. He likes roast beef, roasted potatoes, not mashed. Soup is okay, doesn't really have a preference. I crash into a hard wall and fall back onto my butt. Ouch, wincing, I look up. Charlie is standing in the hall. He's glaring at me and doesn't help me up. Okay then, I've never seen that expression on Charlie's face before. He folds his arms in front of his chest.

I pick myself up off the floor, rubbing my tailbone. "Sorry, Charlie, I wasn't paying attention to where I was going." I fix my glasses that had gone askew on my face, tap the bill of my hat, so it sits back in its original place.

"I guess we have a thief in the house," he spits with anger and loathing. His voice sends shivers up my spine. I squint, taking a better look. The arms folded over his chest are even. Charlie's right arm is slightly bigger than his left. He has a grim set to his lips, and dimples indent his right cheek. This isn't Charlie, but holy shit, it could be his twin minus the slight differences.

I take a step back and swallow. This is Luke.

He snatches the hat from my head. "This is mine," he says. I blink up at him in dismay; I hadn't expected this hostility. "This is also mine," he says, pulling on the strings of my hoodie. I'm wearing the hoodie I found the night I ran from the clinic. I've deemed it my lucky hoodie since then and thought I could use some luck to pull off a perfect dinner. For, well, this asshole standing right in front of me.

I lift my chin. I'm not going to let him intimidate me. I didn't do anything wrong. He takes another step closer, then another one, but I won't back down. I return his glare, not that he can see it through the glasses.

"What else have you been stealing while I was gone? Should I be worried and start locking things up, put an alarm system on the valuables?"

What the fuck is his problem? Fine, if he wants his hoodie back, he can have it. I shove the piece of paper into the front pocket of my hoodie. Removing my glasses, I glare at him for a few seconds, so he gets how much I really don't like him right now. I pull my arms through the sleeve and take off the hoodie. He's standing so close that I shove it right into his chest. He catches it as I let it go. I'm only wearing a sports bra, so I need to go upstairs and get a shirt.

"Thanks, I'll have to have this laundered. It stinks."

Anger shoots up my spine. No one has ever made me feel so humiliated, so, so depreciated than he did just now. A clap of thunder erupts right over our heads, shaking the entire mansion. I jump. Shit, I didn't mean to do that. With fear, I spin around and race up the stairs up to my room.

Placing my glasses on my desk. I start to pace back and forth, shaking out my hands and taking in slow deep breaths. Deep breath, deep breath, I say to myself. Just like the way Anders taught me. Calm down, I scold myself. Anders told me that my magic is connected to my emotions. I take another calming breath and try to think of things that make me happy. Luke's angry face pops up in my vision. Thunder rumbles from a distance; heavy rain is starting. No, no, no, calm down, calm down.

My bedroom door crashes open. "What the hell was that?" he sneers as a flash of lightning streaks right outside of my window. Trembling now, I continue to face him as I slowly back away toward the French doors. He needs to get away from me.

My hands are trembling; I can feel the buzz of electricity in my fingers and palm. I keep backing up until I feel the cool glass of the doors on my back. I grab the handle and slip outside. Standing on my balcony, I swing around away from the door. I start rubbing my thighs. *Calm down, calm down. You can do this.* I take several deep breaths. The flash of lightning and the thunder sounds farther away. I'm getting soaked from the rain, but I don't care.

"Are you doing this?"

Why can't he take a frickin' hint and stay away? I'm not bothering him. I'm trying to get away.

He grabs my shoulder and forces me to turn around. "Are you doing this?" he snaps.

Before I can stop myself, I lift up my arms, palms facing him to protect myself, and a force of wind pushes him back, slamming him into the wall next to the French doors. Lightning and thunder explode around me.

Instead of running away, he gets up, and he heads straight back in front of me. "Get it under control before you hurt someone," he mumbles through clenched teeth.

"Then get away from me," I squeak. Backing up to get

away from him, my back hits the railing of the balcony.

He prowls closer.

"Stay away from me!" I try to shout, but my voice fails me as it sounds like a rush of air. Not that it would have mattered. His menacing, haunting look sends tingles of fear down my spine.

Standing in front of me now, he places both hands on either side of me, resting them on the railing, trapping me in his space. "I swear if you don't get this under control and you hurt my family…" The wind starts circling around me, howling loudly, reflecting my hurt and anger.

"I would never hurt your family!" I whisper. The wind is whipping around us; the balcony starts to shake, not from the wind but an earthquake. I'm not doing that. My eyes widen, but he still doesn't move, his eyes narrowed, lips curled in anger.

I push against him hard, making him lose his grip on the railing, but it is only hard enough to make him back up a step. The balcony shakes even harder, knocking me back into the railing hard. I wince in pain; the railing breaks with my weight against it.

I'm falling, turning my body just in time to see the ground rushing up to meet me. I place my arms in front of my face, anticipating hitting the ground. The wind and something else catch me just in time, holding me a few feet above the ground. I feel pain in my abdomen. When I look down, part of the railing has stabbed me. Using the wind, I push myself up just a few inches. Then I right myself away from the pieces of railing sticking up. I place my hand over the stab wound, and I fall to the ground. Something slides from my waist and slithers away. What the hell is that? But I can't see clearly enough to figure out what it is.

Luke stands over me, eyes wide with fear and concern. What the fuck is his problem? One minute he's trying to kill me; in the next he's as white as a sheet worried that he actually hurt me.

"Are you okay?"

*No, I'm not. I'm angry, you piece of shit for brains.* A bolt of lightning hits the ground, close enough that it sends Luke flying back toward the house. I get to my feet. I look down at my hand. There's blood, not a lot of it. When I pull my hand away to look at the wound, thankfully, it's not very deep. Fucking asshole! Thunder booms so close that Luke jumps as he brings himself to a sitting position. Mimicking his earlier threatening movement, I prowl toward him with as much menace and threat I can muster. When he looks me up and down, his eyes widen. Since I can't talk loud enough to make my fucking point, I push my voice into his head, so he can hear me loud and clear.

*"I would never hurt your family!"* I can feel my chest heaving with anger. I squeeze my free hand at my side, digging my nails into my palms so I don't lose control of my magic. *"But if you ever come at me and hurt me again, I promise that I will hurt. You!"* To make my point strike home, another bolt of lightning strikes the ground near him, forcing him to roll out of the way, followed by another boom of thunder, so loud he has to cover his ears.

I use the wind to push me up and back onto my balcony. The cute little table and chairs have fallen over from the earthquake. Other than the missing railing, the balcony looks fine. I go back into my room, close the doors, lock them, and draw in the heavy drapes. For good measure, I run to the front of my room and lock my bedroom doors.

I don't understand. Why would he attack me that way?

If dinner was solely for Luke alone, I would dump everything I bought in the middle of his bedroom. Partially cooked and raw. I'm so mad at myself. I wanted to make a good impression, prove to him that I wasn't that monster he thinks I am. My heart hurts at the thought that he won't appreciate any of this anyway, but it's not just for him. All of my family is coming for dinner tonight, and I want to thank them for accepting me into their family as well. So, I'm going to finish what I started.

I don't bother to look for the list of Luke's likes and dislikes. He can kiss my ass. I hope the dinner turns out so well that he chokes on it when he finds out I made it. I hope it turns his guts into knots and makes him ill for at least a week. Maybe not the last part, as he will no doubt accuse me of trying to poison him and try to get me kicked out.

I put the finishing touches to the dining room table. I step back to take one final look at it.

"It's perfect." I turn to see Joe standing at the dining room door. I walk up to him and give him a hug. "I think the family will be impressed. It's nothing like Tater or I have ever done before."

I give him a tight smile. He's just being nice. We make our way back to the kitchen, and I focus on finishing up the last-minute details.

Joe is standing across from me in the kitchen, bringing down some of the serving trays I can't reach. "Jessica, what happened to you?" Hmm, I look around me and shrug. "You're bleeding. What happened?" he asks again with a stern expression on his face. I look down at my shirt, and it's covered in blood. All the moving around made the wound reopen.

"It's just a scratch," I whisper.

"Show it to me."

"It's nothing, Joe, just a scratch," I rasp out.

"Then show it to me."

Stepping away from the food, I lift my shirt. The bandage I placed earlier is soaked through.

Joe peels the bandage back and frowns. "This is not a scratch, Jessica. This looks like you were stabbed."

Sidestepping away from him, I replace the blood-soaked dressing and pull down my shirt. "It's nothing, really. I'm fine." I look down, avoiding his eyes and desperately try to think of anything else but what happened earlier. I'm surprised no one thought to look for us with all the noises and earthquake.

He walks over to a cupboard and pulls out a box. "Go upstairs and change. There's some dressings you can use in this box." I look around and vow to clean up my mess before Tater and the rest of the staff show up.

"I got it, go," Joe says firmly

I take the box from his hands, *"Thank you, Joe. I'll make it up to you."* Without looking at him, I turn to leave.

"Jessica." I stop, but I don't turn back around. "I don't care who he is. If he hurt you..."

*"No, Joe, it was an accident. All good, like I said just a scratch. I had worse."* I walk out of the kitchen before he says

anything else. I don't like lying to him, but I can't tell him what happened. I don't need Luke accusing me of being a snitch on top of everything else.

I run up the stairs, hurrying before everyone shows up. Justin and Jeremy are standing in the hallway talking to Luke, smiling, laughing, patting each other on the back.

I hold the box from Joe over my stomach to hide the blood. I think about the different ingredients I used in the meal preparation and run through a list of everything I need to do, making sure I did them. Just so the twins don't pick up on my thoughts.

"Hey, Jess, did you get a chance to meet Luke?" Justin asks.

I lift my head and quickly glance at Luke. He has a fake smile plastered on his face. When the twins turn to look at me, he drops it, shattering what little hope I had to start over. I close my eyes and take a deep breath. Ouch, that burns. Something must have rubbed against my abdomen. Returning the tight-lipped fake smile right back, I shake my head.

Jeremy places an arm around his shoulders. "This is the best big brother you will ever meet, besides us, of course."

I give a curt nod and wave. Another burning sensation rubs over my wound, ouch.

Justin frowns. "What's burning?"

"Hmm?"

Still frowning, he takes a step toward me, "Why do I smell blood?"

"Oh, I was helping in the kitchen and spilled blood on my shirt. I'm going to get changed. No big deal. I'll meet you downstairs." I push past all three of them to get to my room.

Jeremy grabs my arm and pulls me back. "I know you're trying to hide something," he says.

Justin grabs the box out of my hands. "Why do you need the first aid kit?"

Pulling my arm out of Jeremy's hand, I grab the box back from Justin. "I'm fine, just a scratch," I rasp out.

Jeremy is looking down at me and narrows his eyes. "That's not from a scratch!"

Justin pulls me toward him and lifts the hem of my shirt. "What the fuck happened? And don't try to hide it."

I shake my head, trying to inch my way back to my room. *"I'm fine, really. Go spend time with Luke, and I will meet you downstairs."* I back up into my bedroom doors, but the twins are hovering in front of me. Luke is leaning against the door frame to his room, smirking. Bastard. The twins frown at me; then they turn to look back at Luke.

"Did you see the blood on the front of her shirt?"

Luke actually moves his head to take a better look at me. For a brief moment, concern crosses his features. He stalks up to me and reaches forward, pulls my shirt up, and pulls the dressing back. His eyes widen. "Why didn't you say something?"

"What would you have me say?" I grind out. He's looking at me with those emerald green eyes. I stare right back into them, refusing to back down from challenging him. Does he want to tell them what happened? Because I'm not.

"Tell us what, Jessica?" Justin asks. "What are you hiding?"

"Jessica, you're working really hard trying not to think

about how you got injured. Why?" Jeremy asks.

I lower my eyes. "I'll meet you downstairs," I whisper. I don't lie to the twins—I don't lie to anyone. It hurts that I have to keep this from them. They're so happy to see Luke. I'm not going to be the cause of some family rift just because he has it stuck in his insane brain that I am out to hurt everyone.

Justin places his hand on my shoulder. "Let me help you clean it up." I shake my head, and he looks over at Jeremy.

I push my door open enough to slide into my room. I move behind it to close the door.

Jeremy blocks it, pushing it wide open. "I'm not letting this go. Tell me right now! After everything you been through, you got hurt again, and I want to know how."

Sighing in resignation, I walk to my windows and open the drapes. "It was an accident. I fell over the balcony." The twins look through the window.

"Shit, we're three stories up," Jeremy exclaims.

"It's embarrassing. Can you please let it drop now?"

Jeremy frowns. "Are you okay?"

I nod. "You never lied to us before or hid anything from us. It just made me worried that someone hurt you." He grabs me and pulls me into an embrace. "Don't make me worried like that." I nod against his chest. He releases me so I can finish getting cleaned up.

Justin slips into the bathroom. "Let me see." I show him. He shakes his head. "You need stitches. It's not that deep but deep enough to need it stitched, or it won't stop bleeding. How long ago did this happen?"

I shrug. "A few hours. I needed to finish making dinner."

"So stubborn," he grumbles as he places butterfly

bandages over it to keep it closed. "I'll take you to the clinic."

I shake my head. *"Go have dinner with Luke. I'll go after dinner is served. You missed him, and I can tell he missed you guys too."* I push at his shoulder so he stops fussing over me. *"Go. I'll finish cleaning up and meet you downstairs."*

I come out of the closet, wearing a dark blouse and dark jeans. I've come to the conclusion that staying here may not work out. He never once spoke up and admitted how I fell over the balcony, just let me stand there and lie to my brothers. I hate him for that. Heading downstairs, I have to pass Luke's room.

"Why didn't you tell them the whole truth?" I stop and turn toward his voice. He's leaning against the open door.

"What's there to tell?" I glare at him, letting him know that if I don't need to, I don't exactly want to talk to him.

"It was my fault you got hurt. The first person you should have run to was my father."

I take a step closer to him. *"It's not like you jumped in and admitted your part in it. Goddess forbid you show your true colors to your brothers!"* I snap. I grind my teeth and take a steadying breath before I lose control again, *"Look, I don't know why you think I'm this horrible person, but I am not here to steal from or hurt your family. I love them. I didn't run to him, and I didn't tell the twins because they love you. They missed you. I don't want to be the cause of ruining your reunion all because you're an immature asshole who thinks bullying me will chase me away. You don't want me here, fine, I'll leave. I didn't ask your family to take me in. I appreciate everything they have done for me."* I look down. *"If my being here will ruin your life and your relationship with your family, then I'll leave. No one will need to know that we even had this conversation."*

I leave him standing there before he can say anything else.

# Chapter 30

## A NOT SO SWEET HOMECOMING

### LUKE

#### November 07, 2014: 6:45 p.m.

Aunt Tater has outdone herself. The aroma of roast beef fills the air downstairs. It smells amazing. The dining room looks like something out of one of those fancy living magazines. I can't believe it. I don't think I have ever seen the room look so professionally and elegantly done. Hell, it doesn't ever look like this when we have a special guest over. I hug and greet everyone. Being with my family has taken me out of my foul mood. Despite the little feud going on between Jessica and me, I think I can manage to ignore her for the rest of the night. Or well, I'm trying to.

My mind keeps replaying that little speech in the hall with her raspy voice that had magically gotten clearer. Yeah, right, she'll leave. She has too much to lose. Who the hell would give up being a princess, not to mention free money, a luxury home, and an elite education? I know she won't leave. I know it, and she knows it, so that brave talk was just that, talk. I'm on to her; she isn't the first girl to use me to become the future Luna Queen or, in her case, a princess. The hell if I'm going to let that happen, especially not after what Sherise did to me.

A sharp pain in the back of my arm brings me back to my surroundings. Spinning around to face my attacker, I come face-to-face with Emily. All five foot nine, long, glossy black hair, and dark piercing eyes that gleam with the promise of murder in them.

"Ouch! What the hell was that for?" I bite out, rubbing the back of my arm for emphasis.

"For being a douchecanoe! I hope you can live with yourself after what you've done."

Great, Jessica must have told her or Sixes what happened earlier today. I was told by the twins that Emily and Sixes have taken up with her. This little girl trio has been inseparable since she moved in. Why am I surprised that she'd sic Emily on me? Emily's like a bulldog, overly protective, loyal to a fault. Fuck with her or those she cares about, she'll attack first, ask questions later. Now she's using Emily to fight her battles. I grab Emily by the elbow and pull her off to the side so no one can overhear our conversation.

"It was an accident. I didn't mean for her to fall off the balcony. She just made me so angry I lost control of my magic." Emily's face changes from a murderous glare to... shock?

She holds up a hand. "Wait, who the hell did you push off a balcony? Was it Elaine? Damn, I wish I was there to see that." What the...? I frown at her. She's not mad at me because of Jessica?

"Wait, what the hell are you mad at me for then?"

"You've ignored my phone calls and texts for the past few weeks. I hope your insides rot from guilt and ... Wait, don't change the subject. Who the hell did you push off a balcony?"

I glance around the room, mostly to avoid looking straight at Emily. She grabs my face, forcing me to look her straight in the eyes.

"Who did you push off the balcony?" She says it so slowly, like I'm a child who can't follow directions.

I swallow. In my peripheral vision, I see spiky platinum blond hair flitting around the dining room, mingling with my family. I shift my gaze for just a millisecond before focusing back on Emily, but it is enough for her to figure it out.

She releases my face. Her mouth drops in a mixture of surprise and horror. She hisses, "You didn't."

"It was an accident," I hiss back.

"Lucretius Jacob Langhlan, I am so going to kick your fucking ass, and then when I am done with you, I am going to tell Liam, and he is going to finish you off, cut you up in pieces, and feed your body parts to the pigs!" I look around the room. Everyone is so busy talking to each other that they don't mind Emily's outburst.

"Keep it down! Like I said, it was an accident!" I whisper harshly.

"You! You of all people should know better than that.

After everything she's been through, how could you?" Her words hit me like a knife in the back. Why is she taking her side without even hearing me out?

"You're not even going to listen to my side? Am I the only one who thinks her being here is a bit suspicious?"

"You know what, Luke? Not everyone is Sherise or Elaine." She folds her arms in front of her. "I'm so mad at you right now—I can't even look at your face!" She spins around, whipping me with her long hair as she stalks off. I want to go after her to plead my case, make her listen to my side.

Before I can do either of those things, Joe lets out a whistle to get everyone's attention.

He announces that everyone is here and asks everyone to take their seats. Usually, family dinner get-togethers are held in the music room, and food is just lined up against a wall in warmers, and when everyone is present, we all line up to make our plates. I wonder why tonight is so different, so formal. It can't be just because I've returned home.

The staff who are not direct family come in and start us off with a soup. Jessica is sitting next to Anders. Nothing is placed in front of her yet. She gets up and walks over to Joe. She inclines her head for him to go to the table.

Justin, who is sitting on the other side of her, stands. "Come on, Joe, join us for dinner." He blushes and shakes his head. Anders then stands and motions for Joe to have a seat in the chair that Jessica vacated.

She pulls him by the hand, and he finally concedes and sits down.

Jessica pats his shoulder and kisses his cheek, making him blush even more.

"You will always be family, Joe." I raise my glass to him, and everyone follows suit. I glance in Jessica's direction. I wanted her to hear that, so she knows I would accept staff as family over her any day. Her back is facing me as she makes her way out the doors. I quickly glance toward Emily and see the immediate disapproval on her face. A weird feeling sits heavy in my chest. I told myself I would ignore her.

My father clears his throat and stands from his seat. "I know we are used to having a more casual family get-together because there are so many of us. Tonight, Jessica asked if she could make a special dinner. She worked hard these past weeks, doing chores to earn money to pay for all the food and decorations. She kicked Tater and Joe out of the kitchen to prepare the meal all on her own. It was important to her to welcome you home, Luke. She wanted to make a good impression upon you since you hadn't had a chance to officially get to know her. And at the same time, she wanted to thank everyone for accepting, loving, and welcoming her into our family."

I look around at the table. Everyone is smiling, eyes shiny with emotions. Could I have been wrong to assume that she was some gold-digging manipulative person? No, no, this is part of the scam—I know it! How can every single person sitting at this table not see what she's trying to do?

My father's eyes are shiny and full of pride. He looks at my mother, who is wiping at her tears. He places a hand on her shoulder and gives her a gentle squeeze. "Before the soup gets cold, how about we get started?" he says with a nod, and everyone starts. I almost make a snarky comment, warning everyone that we might get poisoned, then think better of it. It seems that everyone except me genuinely loves her. She must be a very good actress. Acting shy and pretending to hate being in the center of attention. No one makes a comment about that, or the fact that she hasn't returned to join the rest of us.

I can't hold back my curiosity, so I finally ask, "Why is Jessica not eating with the rest of us? Especially since she went to all the trouble of making all this food."

Justin looks up at me from across the table. Jeremy answers instead, "She doesn't eat in front of anyone. She's a little self-conscious of her teeth. The same reason why she doesn't talk much."

I frown; she spoke to me. I hadn't really paid attention to her teeth. That's a bit vain. Figures.

Emily elbows Jeremy. "That's not why she doesn't talk. Her voice is still raspy and hoarse from the tracheostomy. The initial cut damaged her vocal cords. She's been working with a speech therapist to make her voice stronger." Guilt starts to rise up in my throat. The hole in her throat makes her unable to speak?

Jeremy adamantly shakes his head. "She won't eat in front of others or talk because of her teeth."

I snort at Jeremy. "A little vain, don't you think?"

Justin shakes his head. "It's more than that. You weren't here when she finally saw what she looked like after she woke up from being in a coma. That beating she took damaged her teeth. She doesn't see that, despite the scars and broken teeth, she is still very pretty. When she looks in the mirror, she thinks... she thinks she's ugly," he says with a blush. I have to admit that when I first saw her with the large glasses and the baseball cap, low, hiding her face, I didn't see it at first. When she removed her glasses and glared at me with those pale blue eyes, striking dark brows, and thick dark lashes, I barely noticed the scars on her face. I nearly forgot why I was standing there, which made me angrier. I assumed that she deliberately used her looks to manipulate me in such a way.

The staff starts to bring in the main course, removing our soup bowls. Jessica is among them. For the first time since I got home, I really look at her. She doesn't fully smile, careful not to show teeth. She makes a lot of gestures with her head or hands like she's mute. Covers her mouth when she laughs. I catch a bit of silver over her teeth. She has braces, not sure why it's a big deal. Her hair is styled in a long spiky way. If I look carefully, I can see some of the bald spots where the hair hasn't grown in yet.

She's comfortable with everyone here, but there is a hint of shyness still. Charlie is flirting with her. I roll my eyes; he flirts with everyone. She doesn't blush or drop the plate she's holding as some women do around Charlie when he turns up the charm. She murmurs something that makes Ean roar with laughter and Liam chuckle. Then she just walks away from Charlie and doesn't even look back.

Emily grabs her arm before she completely walks away and whispers into her ear. Jessica pinches her lips together, stopping herself from smiling fully. Emily wraps her arms around Jessica's waist and gives her a hug before releasing her. Jessica plants a kiss on top of Emily's head before leaving the room.

Elias leans forward to speak to my parents. "Those two are inseparable. I hope Emily's not being a pest since she never comes home anymore."

My mother snorts. "Elias, you know your kids are more than welcome here any time."

"Yeah, except Emily's a bit of a... Well for a girl... she's not the tidiest person."

"Hey, I heard that!" Emily grumbles. Ean, Elijah, and Liam start to laugh from their end of the table. Emily throws a roll at Liam, but he catches it before it hits him.

My parents crack up, not exactly at Emily's expense, but the twins are equally messy.

"Yeah, well, after Jessica cleaned the twins' rooms, I'm pretty sure she can survive anything," Aunt Tater chimes in.

"I had to pay her double and give her a bonus after she was done," my father adds with laughter.

I personally wouldn't clean the twins' rooms even if they paid me a million bucks. That doesn't mean anything. It just means she's hard up for money.

Jessica returns to place the main course in front of me. She gives me a tight-lipped smile and murmurs, "I heard this was your favorite, I hope you like it." She moves away before I can respond.

Emily raises a brow at me. "Go on. Try it. She worked her ass off, putting together this five-course meal with all of your favorites. She's even paying the staff tonight with her own money, so everyone can enjoy dinner and spend time with you. Just thought you should know." Emily stares at me while I cut into my meal and watches me place the first bite into my mouth.

This is the best roast beef that I have ever tasted, better than some five-star restaurants I have been to. Emily isn't done with me, not yet anyway.

Hearing all the little things that Jessica has been experiencing, how everyone around me knows her so well, makes me feel worse for assuming the worst of someone. She should have struck me down with lightning earlier today. I would have deserved it. As dinner continues, enjoying my meal is getting harder and harder. Guilt starts to sit heavy in my chest; before I know it, it nearly chokes me. By the time dessert comes, I notice that Jessica isn't with the staff. I want her to be at this table, to be with her family. I am just about to get up, to apologize for being such an asshole, and ask her to join us.

Emily comes through the dining room doors, "Hey!" she says loudly to the twins. "Where's Jessica? I can't find her anywhere."

Justin and Jeremy both frown when they look at each other with worried looks.

"She's not in the house. I can't hear her thoughts," Jeremy says. He can't hear her what?

Justin looks at our dad. "Before dinner started, I told Jessica she should have her wound looked at. She might have needed stitches it was bleeding so badly. I totally forgot about it and meant to check in with her."

Anders stands from his chair, takes his cell out of his pocket, and walks out. Liam does the same, walking to the farthest end of the room. Anders returns but does not look happy. "She hasn't been to the clinic. The doctor will call if she shows up."

Liam gets off the phone. "Sodie reports that he's been keeping an eye on Dustin and Marcus. They're currently in the rec room. He assumed Boris was in his room when he last checked on him a little over an hour ago. He's checking on him now and will text " His phone buzzes, cutting him off. "He's not there."

Anders starts shouting directions to Ean, Charlie, and Liam. Duck is calling all guard pack members within the territory to start a search. I run out the door, following them.

Liam turns his head. "Sodie is gathering the rest of the recruits to secure Dustin and Marcus, and then they'll join us to look for Boris."

"You don't think we're kind of jumping the gun, just a little?" I ask Liam. Liam sighs, considering a reply. As we make our way to join the other recruits, he fills me in on why this is a big deal. He explains that after his fight with Marcus, Dustin and Boris, Marcus threatened Jessica to get back at him. One of the recruits overheard the three of them talking, making plans to kidnap the VIP. The leads were made aware of what had been overheard.

Unfortunately, Anders just couldn't dismiss them because of Alpha Greystone's political pull. He increased security, but he didn't want to make it plainly obvious. He used the recruits, claiming it was part of their training. Joe, Duck and Xavier are also on high alert. Even some of the dairy hands who are also guards watched over Jessica. Unbeknownst to her, Jessica was never really left without a guard…until now.

If Liam had told this story to anyone outside of the guard, it would probably seem a little farfetched and maybe even a little overprotective. Among the three, Boris is the most evil. You can feel it oozing around him. When I first met him, something about him made my skin crawl. I did some digging around. Like Dustin, he is also from the Northern A territory, same pack. There have been several reports from the school he attended before coming to the recruit program. Reports of bullying, fights. He put two other teenage kids in the hospital. The one report that made me sick to my stomach was the one of the girl. This girl not only went to the school administration to file a complaint against him, but she also went to the authorities. He stalked her, harassed her, then raped her. I have a copy of the report. In her own handwriting, she wrote in detail how she suffered by his hand for months. After she reported the rape, she mysteriously disappeared. Not long after he arrived here in the LS territory, her body was found. She was raped, mutilated, and decapitated. I showed the reports to my father and to Anders. They both tried to get him out of the guard program, but the Sixth Territory Alpha put up a fuss and pulled some political bullshit. Since there was no proof that Boris murdered the girl and official charges were not made against him, he got to stay.

What if Jessica left the mansion to run away like she told me she was going to, and I sent her straight into the arms of a psychotic rapist and murderer?

# Chapter 31

## ONE SET OF TRACKS

### LIAM

#### November 09, 2014: 4:00 p.m.

We have searched the entire area. She's gone. We tracked her as far as the forest, leaving a faint trace of fresh blood behind. I squeeze my hands into fists. Where the fuck is she? Some of the pack men found Boris naked, beaten, and bound with zip ties. He was coming to and healing by the time we got back. He admitted that he followed her and that he had planned to coerce her back to his room. Of course, Ean and Charlie had to beat the shit out of him to get that bit of information. He said he didn't get very close to her when he was attacked.

"Boris said there were five men that attacked him," Charlie says, pulling my attention back to the debriefing. We are all sitting in the conference room at the training center.

Anders is pacing back and forth. I take in the room. Everyone looks exhausted and subdued. Justin's eyes are red-rimmed. Luke looks the worst. Well, along with Emily, she's sniffing and wiping her face next to me.

She refuses to leave like the twins. I rub her back, trying to comfort her. She murmurs, "I shouldn't have left her alone. I should have eaten with her in the kitchen."

"Beating ourselves up over what-ifs isn't going to change what happened," I tell her.

"She's my best friend, and I left her alone. She did all that work, and no one bothered to keep her company. I'm a horrible friend." She starts to cry; I keep rubbing her back. If anyone is a horrible friend, it's me. I haven't been the greatest friend to her either, and I know that it's made her confused.

There are two reasons why I've been trying to keep distant. One is to keep Marcus and the other two assholes away from her, especially if they are after her in retaliation. Two, I'm leaving after the graduation ceremony. I haven't been handling it well. I don't want to leave my family or her. The more time I spend with her makes it harder to leave.

Charlie slams the table with his fist, cracking the table up the center, snapping all of us back to attention. He has a murderous look on his face. "Did anyone hear what I had just said?" He roars, "Look, I get it. She's my little buddy too. Sitting here feeling guilty and beating ourselves up isn't going to bring her back. We need to keep our heads clear and focus on getting her back. Now, Pops was the best tracker back in his day. He thinks Boris is full of shit. He found one set of wolf tracks near where Boris was found and one set of shoe prints in the forest. He thinks this is a one-man job. Whoever took her is clever; he left just enough of a scent to let everyone know she was there. He carried her out, so there was only one set of tracks."

"Why take Boris's PT uniform?" Jeremy asked.

Charlie shrugs. "I'm guessing it could be because he was hiding his own scent to throw off the trackers."

"How does all of this information get us closer to figuring out where to look for her?" Emily asks. "We still don't have any leads. Has anyone gotten a hold of Shadow?"

Anders swings around and stops in front of the table. "He's been searching and has come up with nothing. He doesn't think she's in the LS territory."

Emily starts to drum her fingers on the table. "Has anyone checked the airport security system? The cruise ships? What about the shipping docks?" Everyone turns their heads. "What? You already did that. Okay, just a suggestion since we were all beating our heads up against a wall."

I stand up. "No, we hadn't thought of that. We were stuck on focusing within the LS territory. Elijah, come with me."

Anders frowns. "Wait a minute, what are you doing?"

"No offense, Anders, but the guards seem to lack basic technology skills. However, we have a few recruits who are very capable of finding things, maybe even hacking into system databases."

Emily squeals, "Can I help?! I know my way around cracking some codes!"

"Because I taught you," Elijah grumbles.

Elias looks up at his children. "Should I be worried?"

Emily starts pushing us out the door. "Not if it helps to get Jessica back!"

# Chapter 32

## Hard Truths

### LUKE

#### November 11, 2014: 8:30 p.m.

We search every pier, every airport. For hours on end, we search every security system we can hack into. Shadow, wherever he is, has been searching everywhere. If something happens to her, I will never be able to forgive myself.

My parents are beside themselves with worry, and my brothers... my brothers blame themselves. I head over to my dad's office. I need to tell them about my fight with her. That maybe she isn't missing after all because she ran away. Because I chased her away. They should know the truth. The door to the office is cracked open; I lift my hand to knock.

Anders's loud voice travels into the hallway. "Don't tell me to calm down, Nathan! She's my daughter!"

"I understand, Anders. She might not be of my blood, but I think of her as my daughter too."

"I made a mistake. I should have sent her to Ryuku as soon as I found out. This is my fault!"

"It's not your fault. We don't know anything—we can't jump to conclusions."

"What if it's the same ones who tried to kill her when we found her?"

"It could be, but we don't know for sure."

"Nathan! Stop trying to sound reasonable!"

"What would you have me say, Anders? Go ahead, gather all your men, take down a territory without any proof. Start a war on guesses and possibilities. I want to find her just as much as you do. I want everyone responsible to be punished. My hands are tied unless I have actual proof."

Something crashes in the office. "She's a good girl, Nathan. She never asks for anything. She works harder than any man I know. She's smart. Beautiful. I'm supposed to be worried about horny teenage boys chasing after her to get into her pants. Not worried about who's going to try and kill her next," Anders says in a low whisper now. "She's mine. She doesn't deserve to live a life like this all because she carries my blood."

"We will find her, Anders, and we will take better precautions when she returns. Isn't that the whole reason why we agreed to adopt her? So, we can protect her better?"

I close my eyes and lean my forehead against the wall. I want to throw up. I had it all wrong, so wrong. I might be too late to make things right.

# Chapter 33

## WITHOUT A TRACE

### SHADOW

November 12, 2014: 3:33 a.m.

The guards, the recruits, even the Emerald Pack members who are not guards have been searching nonstop for any traces of her. There are no leads. I have been looking everywhere I can think of, but nothing.

My phone buzzes in my pocket. "Emily, I don't have anything new to tell you."

"Nothing on our end either." I hate to be the one to say it—it hurts my heart to even think it—but I don't think we will ever find her. She could be anywhere. The only thing I am absolutely sure of is that she is not dead. "Shadow, are you still there?"

"Yeah, I'm still here."

"Do you think, is she... Did she..." I already know what she's trying to ask.

"No, she's not dead."

"Okay," she whispers. Then she's silent. I hear sniffling on the end. "I have to find her. She's my best friend," she croaks.

"I thought I was your best friend," I tell her in a monotone voice.

"You are, but she has a personality."

I let out a breathy laugh, "True."

"Did you just laugh at me?"

I smile, a genuine smile. I have been doing that a lot more lately, along with laughing, since I met Jessica.

"I did." I can hear a smile.

"She changed you too, didn't she?"

She has. I have seen the changes in Charlie and Ean before they even knew what they could do. Liam's magic has also gotten stronger, and so has Sodie's. I'm not sure how she did it or when she did it, and I am not even sure she knows she did it. Because Charlie and Ean's magic was always there, just dormant. So was Emily's and Elijah's. Somehow, she awakened them all.

As for me, she realigned my soul and gave me a piece of myself back. There is so much more to Jessica than even I can understand, which is why I have been going crazy looking for her. Fear has been lacing my very being since she has gone missing. If anyone knows half of what she could do, they will kill her, or worse, keep her prisoner and use her as their own personal weapon.

My phone beeps, indicating another call. "She did, Em,

which is why I am trying everything in my power to find her. I have to go. Someone is calling."

"Okay, you'll call me if you find anything?"

"You will be the second one I call, after Anders."

"Okay, I love you."

"I love you too, and Em, get some rest. Okay?"

"Okay." She disconnects the call, and I look down at my phone. I never said those words to Emily before. I thought them, but I never felt them, so I never said them. Emily is my best friend and has been since we were kids. Even when I lost who I was, she never stopped being my friend. She's younger than I am, more like a kid sister.

"Strap?" I say into the phone.

"Shadow, you still looking for that girl?"

My heart speeds up. "Yes, you found something?"

"Not sure if it's who you're looking for, but a young girl washed up on shore near Pier 22. Almost fits your description, except she has long hair, not short."

Long hair? "Did you notify anyone?"

"No, I told the boys to hold off until after I spoke to you first."

"Continue to hold off. I should be there shortly." I end the call, type out a text to Anders, then slip into the shadows. It must be her; I can feel it. A pulsing feeling in my chest, like a second heartbeat.

I approach Strap from behind. "Where's the girl?" He jumps when he hears my voice.

"Holy fuck! Where the hell did you come from?"

I smile. "Exactly," I tell him.

He shakes his head, "She's right over here. She washed up on shore about five minutes or so ago. I called you as soon as my boys described her. She's uh, naked. We covered her up as best as we could."

I clench my teeth, quickly agitated by Strap's report. It feels like it's taking forever to get down to shore next to the pier. I should have just gone straight down there, but I try to limit my exposure of what I can do.

I know Strap. I don't necessarily trust him, but I scare the crap out of him enough to know that he won't fuck with me. We finally reach the area. A bunch of men are standing around.

White-blond hair floats in the waves. Her tiny bare feet poke through a covering. The men part, letting me pass through, and I look down. Her lips are pale and cracked. Mouth slightly open, she's breathing; thick long eyelashes shadow her cheeks. I see the rise and fall of her chest. I bend down and touch her cheek. She's cold.

Despite some confusing changes, I know without a doubt it's her. I turn to look at Strap. I reach into my pocket and hand Strap a large wad of cash. "Pay your men and keep your mouths shut."

I scoop her up and walk back to where I came from. When I'm sure there is no one around, I slip back into the shadows and take Jessica home.

# Chapter 34

## SO MANY CHANGES

### JESSICA

November 12, 2014; 7:16 a.m.

I wake up to the bright light of the morning rays streaking in through the window. I have to blink a few times to realize this isn't my bedroom but the clinic. Slightly confused at how I got here, I start to look around the room. I'm alone. There are no machines beeping, and as I feel my body, there are no tubes or needles sticking out anywhere near or in my body. I instinctively reach for my throat. There is no hole, but I can feel the puckering of a scar there where it used to be.

My mouth is dry, and it feels like I swallowed sand. I pull myself up into a sitting position. My hand accidentally bumps into something next to me. With a start, I pull my hand back, only to realize that I bumped a head with long black hair. Emily. Was she there this whole time? Smiling, I place my hand back on her hair and gently massage her scalp with the tips of my fingers. She groans; I roll my eyes. This girl can sleep like the dead, heavier than the twins. If we were ever under attack, the attackers would think that they were dead and leave them alone. I gently apply more pressure and massage her scalp again.

She groans again, lifts her head to look around, then places her head back into her arms. I shake my head and look around again. My mouth is so dry it feels like my tongue is stuck to the roof of my mouth. My stomach starts to make noise. I guess I'm hungry too. I find the call button and press it and continue to massage Emily's scalp while I wait.

My door opens, and Ean barks, "Emily! This isn't room service. We don't—" He stops when he sees me sitting there, playing with Emily's long hair. "Jessica," he whispers.

I start to laugh, but everything is so dry it comes out in a wheeze, then a cough. He turns and closes the door, leaving me practically coughing and choking to death while Emily continues to sleep. Ean finally returns with my nurse Mimi. She tells me that my parents will be in shortly.

Ean finally wakes Emily up. When she realizes what was going on through her sleepy haze, she grabs me into a strong embrace and starts to cry. "I'm so sorry, so sorry! I shouldn't have left you alone."

I rub her back. "I'm fine," I whisper. When she pulls back, I wipe the tears from her face.

"What happened to you? You look so different." As she says that, she gently tugs on my hair. I look at the strands of blond hair she's holding in her hand, and I reach up and touch my head. That's mine. I pull some hair forward and run my hand down its long strand and tug. It's definitely mine, and it's attached to my scalp. I pull the strand up in front of my face, so I can examine it closely. Emily is watching me. I look back at her and I shrug.

Dr. York walks into the room. "Jessica, you're awake."

I'm still holding my hair up in front of my face when I turn to him and ask, "Can hair grow like this overnight?"

He places his forefinger over his lips. "No, not usually. The length of your hair is usually about a year to two years of growth." I reach behind my back and find that my hair is down to my waist. "As shifters, our hair does grow rather fast. In the past six months you have been here, if I had to guess, your hair grew about four inches. Of course, if you slept regularly, it probably would have grown just a little more."

My hair isn't the only thing that's changed. There are other changes. The wounds on my body are closed; the scars don't look fresh anymore. They look older. I no longer have a straight boyish figure. My breast have grown a whole cup size. I am slightly taller, now hitting the five feet marker (big deal, I feel cheated in the height department), and my feet are also a size bigger. My body is toned and muscular, like I work out or train. I can see without glasses, and my voice, once I have drunk enough water, is no longer raspy like a teenage boy's voice changing due to hormones. There is some rasp to it, don't get me wrong; it isn't perfect, even though I can't remember what I sounded like before I came here. But it is clear. When I speak, I no longer struggle to be heard.

The best part of all the bodily changes is my teeth. The braces are gone, I have a mouth full of teeth, no longer missing, no longer crooked, white perfect teeth. If I had to trade something in order to have a mouth full of teeth, I would have traded my height in a heartbeat. Short stature be damned, a mouth of full of teeth is so worth it.

Mentally, I feel different too. I don't feel like I am fourteen years old anymore. I don't know why I feel that way, but it has nothing to do with the physical changes.

My parents, Anders, and Dr. York sit there, bewildered at the changes. When Anders tells me I was missing for five days, I can't believe it.

Chris comes in to question me. Over and over, he asks if I was hurt or if I saw the man who took me, assuming it was a man. Was there more than one man? Did they touch me? How did I escape? Where did they take me? The questions go on and on.

But, I have nothing to tell him. The last thing I remember is I left the dinner party because I didn't want to bother anyone. I knew that Dr. York stayed at the clinic late on Fridays to finish up on charting. I figured I would catch him before he left to get the wound on my stomach stitched up. Even though it was dark, I'd walked the distance to and from the mansion and training grounds to meet Anders every morning, and I memorized the path. I wasn't worried that I couldn't see well at night.

"Jessica." Anders calls my name. "Talk to us. Tell us what's going on in that head of yours."

I frown at him. "You don't believe me? Why? You can hear my thoughts. You would know if I was hiding something."

I look at my parents, and my mother shakes her head. "We haven't been able to hear your thoughts." Chris nods in agreement.

I look to Anders. "I kind of miss knowing what you're thinking." He too gives me a sad smile.

"I'm just so confused right now. I keep replaying everything that happened yesterday in my head. None of this makes sense." I huff out a breath. "Now I'm broken." I start to rub my forehead.

"Not broken. Maybe you need time to process everything," Dr. York says gently. I nod; then a thought starts to tug in my mind, like I forget something I am supposed to do.

"Can I go to Alpha Agnus's place?" I ask. "I just... I just have this feeling like I need to see her. Maybe a few cracks with her cane will put things into better perspective," I say with a breathy laugh. The adults in the room chuckle too.

## November 14, 2024: 8:15 a.m.

Visiting with Alpha Agnus actually helps me sort through my feelings and hone some of the magic I thought I no longer had. She says that my mind has matured during my absence and that I have better control of it. This is why no one can hear my thoughts anymore unless I allow it. I also learned a few new tricks that I can do in the short time I spent with her.

By the time Xavier picks me up early Friday morning, I

feel better and look forward to returning home.

"I was told that you were scheduled to take the academy exam with the rest of the recruits this morning."

"Right, I guess I forgot." I wince. Will memory loss be a new thing? Great, now I have holes in my head. That doesn't sit well with me.

"Don't worry about your bags. I will take care of them when I return to the mansion," he says as he opens the door for me.

"Thank you, Xavier." I give him a hug before I head into the building.

"My pleasure. It's good to have you back, little one." He squeezes my arms before he lets me go.

Ean is waiting for me by the doors. He smiles when he sees me. "You ready?" he asks.

I wrinkle my nose. "I forgot and didn't study."

He pats my back. "I'm sure you will do just fine." He knocks on the classroom door and playfully pushes me inside.

"If you're looking for the head guard's office, it's further down the hall," Professor Hocson says with an English accent, peering at me with his dark beady eyes. He's an eagle shifter. I remember that.

"I'm here to take the exam, professor."

"You what?" he asks sharply.

I pull down the hood from my head. "I'm Jessica Langhlan. We agreed I would take the exam with the rest of the recruits."

He stands up quickly from his seat behind his desk. "Oh goodness, Princess, my apologies, I didn't recognize you." He motions to an empty seat. I cross the room without looking at anyone. "You will need to remove your hat and jacket."

I start to remove the zip-up hoodie I'm wearing. Then I hesitate for a moment when I remember what I'm wearing underneath. Crap, I'm wearing a borrowed bra which is a little too snug, a pink tank top from Sixes, and yoga pants. My long hair is hiding beneath the jacket because I don't know how to braid my hair. Maybe it's enough to cover my backside.

"Hat and jacket," Professor Hocson repeats.

I remove the hat and place it on the table. Taking a deep breath, I remove my jacket, place it on the back of the chair, and quickly get into my seat. Someone whistles from in the back of the room, and I can feel my face heating up. I keep my eyes on Professor Hocson. He comes around his desk to stand in front of me, placing a pencil and the exam in front of me.

"You sure you want to take the exam today? It's not too much, considering everything you've been through?" he asks in a lowered tone.

"Thank you for your concern, but I'm feeling better and would like to take the exam today."

"Okay, well, the exam started fifteen minutes ago. If you need extra time, I'll make an exception since you came in a little late." I give him a small smile and start the exam. I'm not there very long when I heard the rustling of papers and the scraping of a chair on the floor.

"Thank you, Mr. Fitzpatrick. You may leave. Grades will be posted in two hours." I glance up as Liam passes. He smiles and winks at me. I frown in confusion. I didn't expect that from him. I was expecting him to avoid me or carry that normal pinched look he likes to sport.

Then someone else stands up—Luke.

He gives me a big smile, showing those damn dimples. I frown at him the same way I frowned at Liam and look back down at my exam. What the hell is up with them? Sodie is the next one to turn in his exam. When he passes me, I give him a huge smile complete with teeth. His friendship never wavered, which is why I am going to miss him so much when he leaves.

It doesn't take long for me to finish. I turn my papers in to Professor Hocson. "Done so soon? You sure you don't want to take some extra time?"

"No, I'm confident with my answers."

"Alright, I'll let Anders know how you did. Have you thought about what you would like to major in before we start your core college courses?"

"No, I haven't made up my mind yet."

"Well, that's alright. We have about a month before you need to decide." I nod and turn to leave. Marcus and Dustin watch me from the back of the room with disdain. I hurriedly grabbed my hat and head out the door. When I reach the end of the hall, Sodie, Luke and Liam are standing there talking amongst themselves. As I continue to walk out of the building, they all follow me out. What is with them? The last time I had seen Luke, he was horrible to me and Liam—don't even get me started on Liam. His hot and cold demeanor always left me with my head spinning. Now he's being attentive and nice. I ignore them both and give Sodie my undivided attention.

"How do you think you did?" he asks.

"Not too terrible, I think. How about you?"

He shrugs. "I think I did as well as I could." Guilt spread across my chest. Did my being missing mess up his studying time? I hope not. Sodie deserves to graduate. As if he could read my mind, he playfully bumps into my arm.

"I'm not a good test taker, but I had good study partners." He points his head toward Liam and Luke. I feel a warm tingling feeling on my bare arm. When I look down, Liam's hand moves back to his side.

I realize I am not wearing my jacket. I stop walking. "I forgot my jacket. I'll be right back." They all start to follow me back in. "I don't need an escort." They just stand there and looked at me unbudging. I turn specifically to Liam and raise my eyebrow, daring him to reply. He doesn't, simply inclining his head.

I hurry inside to the classroom. When I get there, the classroom is empty. My jacket is gone.

"Forget something, Princess?" Marcus asks as Dustin holds up my jacket and waves it at me. They walk into the room, and Marcus sits on the desk closest to the door. Dustin remains by the doorway, leaning against the frame and crossing his arms over his chest.

"Now tell me, Princess, did Liam set up my cousin to take the fall for your little escape plan? Hmmm?"

What the hell is he talking about? I fold my arms in front of my chest, and I stare back at Marcus, unwavering in my stance.

"Did you two have a falling out and you planned to run away? I saw that look he gave you, but I also noticed how you ignored him. Is that why you showed up looking all sexy instead of like a little boy for a change? Trying to show him what he's missing?"

This guy is crazy—what the hell is wrong with him? I glance over at Dustin and he's grinning at me. Then he licks his lips like I'm some special treat he's going to devour soon.

"My cousin took the fall for your little game." He bolts off the desk and hovers over me. "He was kicked out of the guard, beaten up, humiliated. Because of you!"

With pure instinct, I intercept his hand before he grabs my throat. His other hand comes up to hit. I block it and step back.

Marcus chuckles. "Oh, my beautiful princess has some fight! Is that how you like it? Fight first, is that your turn-on, Princess? I can do that. When I win and have you pinned under me, you're going to enjoy what I give you." He takes another step closer; I back up two more steps. "Don't run, Princess. It's obvious that you and I were meant for each other, and I can give you so much more than that worthless bastard."

I laugh, catching Marcus off guard. "You seem to be quite obsessed with Liam's sex life." I look down his body. He's aroused. When I trail my gaze back up to his face, I smile. "Is he the one who does it for you?" I wink at him.

He scowls and starts for me. Instead of backing away, I run for him, jump up, twist and wrap my legs around his neck, and pull him down. I leap back up onto my feet and lift my leg up and land it back down into his face. My vision turns red as rage sings through my blood.

Dustin moves from his position by the door. I take two steps forward and kick him in the chest once, twice. I spin then kick him for a third time with all my might, sending him crashing into the wall. Marcus gets back up, so I turn my attention back to him. I kick him in the stomach, forcing him back into a desk. He recovers, coming back for me. Alternating legs, I kick him in the chest, then in the stomach again with my other leg. When I get in close enough, I kick him in the groin.

He falls to his knees, and I lean forward so that I am level with his face. I fist his dark brown hair and pull back. I get so close my lips is just a whisper above his. In a low voice, almost a breathy whisper, I taunt him, "Is this how you like it? Rough enough for you, handsome?" He growls. "No? I guess I'm just not your girl." I pull my arm back and punch him in the temple, knocking him out.

A hand grabs my shoulder, and I turn, using my elbow to hit something solid. I lift my other arm to strike a punch, but my arm is blocked. I lift my leg to kick, but he grabs my leg and pulls me into him.

"Fuck, Jessica. It's me." Liam releases my leg, arms wrap around me, embracing me, crushing my face into a muscular chest. The scent of a crisp, clean cologne with an underlying hint of campfire smoke fills my nostrils. Liam. "Shhhh, I got you. It's okay."

My heartbeat starts to slow down; my vision starts to return to normal.

"Shit, I thought I was running in to save you. Didn't think I would need to save these assholes from you," he says with a chuckle.

I don't answer him; I just cling on to him as if he's my air, my calm in the storm.

"Bring her to my office," Anders commands. "Get these fucking pricks out of here. I had enough of their crap to last me a lifetime."

# Chapter 35

## SUBMISSIVE

### JESSICA

#### March 31, 2025: Present Day

Carmen holds up her hand. "Did you ever figure out what happened to you during the time you were missing?"

"No, I honestly can't remember. Like I said, one minute I was walking in the dark to the clinic. Then I woke up in the clinic bed."

She nods. "Did you and Luke make amends?"

"That's just the beginning of our very long and complicated relationship. It kind of needs to start here to make sense. I know I barely scratched the surface. If you like, I can just pick back up from two weeks ago to answer your original question."

She shakes her head. "I'm quite intrigued actually. Did

Luke intentionally try to hurt you?"

I look down at my hands. "No, I don't think it was intentional. He was angry for whatever reason he had, and I was angry and scared too. We were young and didn't have control over our emotions. The balcony incident was an accident. I don't really think he would have known that the balcony railing would have broken that way. Now, I know that he did try to save me. At the time, I didn't." I swallow, pausing to choose my next words carefully. "My conflict with Luke is our own. It doesn't paint the picture of what he really is or what kind of an Alpha King he will be in the future. I just want to make that very clear. Luke is a good man. He's hardworking, generous, and kind. Unfortunately for him, his title and the responsibilities he's been born into put a lot of pressure on him. He sometimes has to think about those things first, before he can think about himself." I stop talking, unsure of how much more I really need to say. "I just don't want anyone to judge him for what I say about him. Because those are my feelings, my views. I wish things were different, but it is what it is."

Carmen clears her throat, "That's very kind of you to say. Can you tell me—because I am just dying to know—were you and Liam a couple? You talk a lot about him. Did something develop between the two of you?"

I smile sadly. "I think it's pretty obvious that I had a crush on Liam from the very beginning." I look down at my hands again. Please don't cry; don't cry, "I... It...We weren't meant to be." I look up at Christian instead of Carmen. "I wouldn't be here right now if we were."

Christian holds my gaze. "I guess we need to find your

true mate, then."

Grateful for Christian's reply, I steer away from that topic. I nod and gaze directly into the camera, "Hard to fill the role, especially when I have two amazing fathers that I have placed on a pedestal. Not to mention some really awesome uncles." My parents, who are still sitting beside me, chuckle softly. I pat Anders's knee and glance over at my father. "They raised the bar tenfold, and they expect me to find a mate who could compare." I smile as I glance between Anders and my father.

Carmen hums. "Well, your parents had selected a good variety of men whom they felt were compatible for you. We have also selected some men that might be just as compatible. I'm confident you will find someone by the end of the show."

My mother's head snaps up. "What do you mean that you have chosen compatible men?"

Carmen coughs into her sleeve. "The producers insisted that even though the time frame is much shorter than anything we have ever done, we stick to our number of contestants. Twenty..." She swallows, her eye contact unwavering. "We selected additional men that came up as a possible match in the algorithm."

"Algorithm?" My mother raises an eyebrow.

Carmen nods. "Jessica took a compatibility test when we first started. We had applications when word got around, and we also had other men who wanted to be on the show in previous seasons but were not selected to be the main star. We chose men who had high percentages that matched Jessica's from our database." She pauses, watching my mother, and then continues, "It wasn't something I had control over."

My mother's eyes narrow. "Perhaps, but it was something that you could have brought to our attention sooner."

Anders swears under his breath. "Were any of these men vetted?"

Carmen looks to my father, avoiding Anders's deadly stare. "They were vetted by our standard protocol."

Anders and my father both stand. "Not good enough. I want their names."

"I... we... can't. It's too late. Actual filming starts tomorrow evening."

My father looks down at Carmen. "This is our daughter's life, her safety. Who do I need to call?"

Carmen pales. "It's out of our hands. The men are already here, currently being interviewed and—"

My mother holds up her hand. "If anything happens to our daughter's safety, I am warning you right now, not only will I take your company to court for breach of contract and personal harm inflicted on my daughter for the company's own personal gain, I will rip it apart and sell it off piece by piece, and everyone, including your producers, will never recover from what I will do to all of you."

Carmen slides off her chair and stands. "I can show you our protocol, how we vet all of the contestants. I can call the producers." She straightens her shoulders. "You do realize that if you stop production now, you also breach contract, and the company can sue Jessica. She signed and agreed to be here, and we agreed to your terms of bringing on the men you have chosen, but the producers have a right to make changes on what they seem fitting for the show."

My mother hums. "I will need to look it over then. My

understanding is that the changes are only to be made in how the direction of the actual filming will take place, not the men chosen to be in the competition."

Carmen shrugs. "You can take it up with our production's lawyers."

My parents argue with Carmen as they all leave the room. They aren't going to leave the changes alone. I look to Christian, and we both start to laugh. He shakes his head.

"So do we continue, or do we wait for Carmen to return?" I ask him.

He checks the camera. "I'm still filming. We can continue if you want. Who knows when they will be back? Doesn't sound like your parents are going to back down."

I laugh; Carmen doesn't know what she's up against. He smiles. Then he just studies me for a few seconds.

"I don't get it," he finally says.

"You care to elaborate?"

"You, sitting here. You seem so... so... I don't know, for lack of a better term, submissive."

My eyebrows raise. "Submissive? I'm anything but submissive. Trust me."

He cocks his head to the side and narrows his eyes. "When you talk about what happened to you in the classroom, you took down two trained recruits. It seems you were starting to have more confidence. Now, you're sitting here, letting your parents fight with the producers. You always appear so nervous—you even looked like you were ready to have a panic attack when we started."

I sigh, "I did have more confidence for a period of time. Losing my best friend Emily brought back the panic attacks, feeling insecure, hiding. She wasn't supposed to have died. It should have been me."

He looks at me thoughtfully and exhales audibly. "How about we pick up from what happened two weeks ago? You were getting ready for the unannounced guest who showed up to your home."

# Chapter 36

## STAYING THE COURSE

### LUKE

March 14, 2025: 12:30 p.m.

"No matter what Jessica's reaction is, I need you to stay the course." I nod as my father and I walk down the hall toward the conference room.

Three gentlemen at the table stand as we approach. I immediately recognize Alpha Rhineheart, a tall man with dull chestnut brown hair and a rectangular face. I haven't seen him for several years. I remember him as a strapping man, but now he looks beaten down, far too old for his age. I can't help but notice the blankness in his eyes.

To his left is Beta DuPont, a short man with thinning dull brown hair, a round face set in a pale pallor, crooked yellowing teeth, round body, and a gut that sits over his belt line. To the Alpha's right is a young man, the spitting image of what I remembered the Alpha to once look like; he's young, maybe around my age. The only difference in comparison to his father is his eyes; they are much lighter in color, more of a golden honey brown than that dull, lifeless brown his father is sporting now.

"Gentlemen," my father acknowledges as we step closer to the table. We exchange handshakes with these men. Alpha Rhineheart shakes our hands with less vigor than I expected of an Alpha, almost as if he is on autopilot. However, the Beta's handshake is vigorous and firm. I glance over to my father, and he nods to everyone as he takes his seat. We all follow suit.

"Thank you for agreeing to meet with us, your majesty," the Beta says as he positions himself in his seat.

"Yes, well, it appears that I wasn't given a choice in the matter since you have refused to leave," my father replies bluntly with a stern look on his face.

"I apologize for the intrusion, but it is of the utmost importance that we meet with you. I have been trying to get your attention for several months. My pack is in a state of crisis, and it's all due to your daughter."

My father raises an eyebrow. "My daughter is the sole reason for your pack's critical state?"

"Yes, your majesty, she has been attacking us for years. Both financially and physically. It's almost as if she has a personal vendetta against us."

What the fuck is this bullshit! The Beta wastes no time getting to his allegations.

"Your majesty, wine sales have gone considerably down

over the past five years, putting our pack in a financial situation. I have a reliable source who has told me that your daughter's affair with the world-renowned chef Jacques Gattefosse has persuaded him to stop purchasing our wines. Because he is popular and sought after, many restaurants follow his trend."

My father catches my eye, then asks the Beta, "Who is your credible resource linked to the famous chef?"

"Well, uh, your majesty, I cannot divulge that information, but I can assure you my source is a close friend of the chef and has worked alongside him for many years."

My father starts to chuckle, and I can't help but laugh.

Young Alpha Dimitri snorts, adding, "I didn't realize that Jacques Gattefosse had any friends. He's known for being a bit of a loner. The last I heard, the longest employee to work with him lasted six months."

Beta DuPont's face reddens. He starts to gnash his yellow crooked teeth together. "Whose side are you on, boy?"

He laughs, not all intimidated by the Beta. "Just stating a well-known fact to those that work within the restaurant business."

Beta DuPont leans forward. "Your majesty, our territory has been attacked repeatedly by rogues. We have been asking for aid. When the guards come to the territory, they refuse to train our young pack members. Most recently, one of your guards attacked our pack members, leaving them no choice but to defend themselves against him. Your daughter crossed our territory lines, attacked innocent pack members, and killed two of them! We came here to tell you our side. I'm sure your daughter has made up lies to gain your favor, but...."

I lean forward in my seat. "I hope you have concrete proof and substantial documentation to support these allegations, Beta." I sneer at DuPont.

"I, I, well, yes, I...."

My father looks over at the Alpha. "Well, do you?" he says in a commanding voice. The Alpha doesn't flinch, just stares straight ahead; his gaze slowly shifts toward my father. My father leans forward. "Alpha! I asked you a question. Do you or don't you have substantial proof to back up these allegations?"

Alpha Rhineheart starts to open his mouth but falters.

"Your majesty, I have several witnesses that can attest to these attacks...." the Beta starts.

"I am asking your Alpha. You better have a damn good reason for wasting my time," my father growls. "You come into my home unannounced, refuse to leave, start throwing allegations at my daughter without proof…"

Beta Dupont stands. "Your majesty, please if you will just listen!"

"Is there a reason why your Beta is taking a stance like he's the one in charge of your territory?" my father asks the Alpha, but Alpha Rhineheart doesn't answer, nor does he look at my father. The Young Alpha is looking at his father, concern etched on his features.

"Your majesty, I am speaking for both the Alpha and Young Alpha because I have been the one in charge of these affairs. The Alpha has not been doing well, and the Young Alpha has been away between school and business over the years."

"I wasn't made aware of Alpha Rhineheart's health

condition, Beta DuPont," my father says, eyeing Alpha Rhineheart as he speaks.

The Young Alpha leans forward to look at Beta DuPont. "Neither was I," he states pointedly.

Beta DuPont continues to protest and pleads to be heard, but I stop listening. He and his son are to be fully blamed for the destruction of their winery and pack business. Everyone knows this, and all of the LS territory has refused to do business with the Ruby Falls Pack. There have been no known formal reports of rogue attacks on any other territory, just theirs, but as usual, there have been no witnesses. I can safely assume that those are lies as well. But why the hell are they targeting Jessica?

"Alright! Enough!" My father barks out, "This is all hearsay, Beta. There is no proof to support your accusation without a paper trail, written statements, or an actual witness stating my daughter's direct involvement with sabotaging your sales."

"But your majesty, what about the attacks? Our territory has been attacked repeatedly by rogues. Just a few weeks ago, your daughter refused to send aid."

"Where is your report?" my father roared. "My head guard has been asking for your territory report on that incident for the past few months, and he did not receive one to date."

"But your majesty, I did send one, not once but twice. I'm sure your daughter must have intervened in our email communication and destroyed the copy."

My father turns back to the Alpha. "Where is the report?" Alpha Rhineheart turns his head to look at Beta

DuPont.

Beta DuPont continues, "Your majesty, sir, I have told you, I sent one in."

"Alpha Rhineheart, your Beta is crossing a very fine line with me. I have personally sent you an email and a handwritten letter asking for your pack's account of what took place. I asked for a detailed report along with accounts from firsthand witnesses. You have not responded. Then you come here accusing my guards and my daughter of personally attacking your pack. How do you answer for this?"

Again, Alpha Rhineheart turns his head to his Beta.

"I am not asking your Beta, Alpha! I am asking you!"

Clearing his throat, Alpha Rhineheart responds, "Your majesty, all of the accounts my Beta is relaying are true."

Growling, my father stands and slams his fist on the table.

Young Alpha Dimitri immediately stands. "Your majesty, I apologize for their behavior. I didn't come here to accuse your daughter of anything, and I am quite familiar with how Beta DuPont and his son operate." He glances between his father and the Beta. "While it is true I have been away from the territory for some time, finishing my degree and looking for other business opportunities to sustain our pack financially, I came here for answers, as I am sure there is a reasonable explanation for the princess's actions behind these allegations."

The door to the dining room opens, cutting off Young Alpha Dimitri. Joe clears his throat and announces Luna Queen Shakti and Princess Jessica.

Alpha Rhineheart and I rise with the announcement, seeing as we are the only two not on our feet. My father's face is red. He looks over at my mother as she approaches the table. She smiles at my father and gently pats his arm.

She looks at our uninvited guests. "Gentlemen." The three men bow their heads to her in respect. Then she glances down at the table. "Why don't I see to the kitchen staff and bring in some refreshments?"

My father glares at Beta DuPont. "Not necessary. They will not be staying much longer." The Beta's face reddens, and he glares at the Young Alpha.

"Well, in that case, I will leave you all to it then." My mother places a gentle kiss on my father's cheek and turns to leave.

Taking her cue, Jessica steps out from behind my mother, places herself between my father and me, and with a smile, says, "Gentlemen." She dips her chin in acknowledgement. Taking my eyes off Jessica, I look around to check the men's expressions. Alpha Rhineheart continues to sport his blank expression, Beta DuPont is frowning, but the look on the Young Alpha's face is full of disbelief, eyes wide like he has seen a ghost. Mouth slightly agape, he turns pale.

He stammers, "Grit?"

"This is Alpha Princess Jessica Langhlan," I interject. She returns her attention to the Young Alpha. Frowning now, he starts to shake his head.

"I guess the allegations are true then?"

Schooling her features, Jessica glances over at the other two men. Then, when she turns her full attention back to the young alpha, she asks, "Allegations?"

# Chapter 37

## ALLEGATIONS

### JESSICA
#### March 14, 2025: 12:45 p.m.

The second territory leaders are notoriously known for their disdain toward successful women. The second territory or the Ruby Falls Pack is a traditional pack and feels women are beneath men. According to their traditions, women belong in two categories: in their bed and in low subservient positions such as housekeepers or servants. Despite how the world around their territory has evolved, they strongly keep to their beliefs. It's obvious how Beta DuPont feels about my position when he tries to shame me through his correspondence.

  Even though my intention behind the responses was to show him that I wanted peace, he would attack me by saying that women like myself only bring downfall to those around me when we try to stick ourselves in a leadership role. Of course, the stubborn part of me isn't going to let him make me feel inferior to his status. Alpha Agnus taught me better than that.

Mother has turned to leave the room. I step out from behind her to give the gentleman my attention. It's evident that a confrontation is going to take place. I just wish it wasn't today of all days.

The young man standing to the right of Alpha Rhineheart looks like he is in shock. He stammers out, "Grit?"

"This is Alpha Princess Jessica Langhlan," Luke interjects. I glance over at Luke; then I return my attention to the young man. Frowning now, he starts to shake his head.

"I guess the allegations are true then?"

My brow furrows in confusion. "Allegations?"

Beta DuPont starts to laugh, and Alpha Rhineheart joins in. "This all makes sense now, the attacks on my pack's winery, the drop in sales for the past five years, the personal attack a few months ago from one of your guards and you, might I add." Beta DuPont points a finger at me. "Tell me, has this been your plan of revenge all along?"

"I have no idea what you're talking about, Beta DuPont."

Beta DuPont looks to Alpha Rhineheart. "After all this time." Alpha Rhineheart nods. Turning to look at my father, the Beta continues, "Your majesty, I am not sure what she has told you over the years, but I can assure you it is all lies."

What the hell is he talking about? My father places a hand over mine and gives me a meaningful look. "You better start making some sense, or I'm going—" my father starts to say, but Luke cuts him off before he can finish.

"Actually, I want to hear all about these lies." I look at Luke. "I always had my suspicions, the way you ran into our territory begging the guards for help, manipulating your way into my family, into my pack all those years ago. Not to mention how you ruined my relationship with my mate." Sharp pain pierces my heart from his words. "I think it's time for the truth to come out finally. Don't you think, Jessica?"

He gives me a cold smile. My eyes widen, and I can feel the threat of tears starting. I look down at my hands before I raise my chin and stare straight at Beta DuPont. "I never lied or personally attacked the second territory—I have no reason to!" I'm still standing, but Luke grabs my shoulder and pulls me down onto a chair.

"Sit," he says sharply. "Let the Beta talk."

Beta DuPont smiles like the cat who got the cream. He leans forward. "I didn't recognize you at first. You've grown into quite a young woman. But the hair and those eyes." He has the nerve to look heartbroken right now. "We thought you were dead all this time, what you put your mother and brother through. Our family has never been the same—the pack has never been the same."

The young man who called me 'Grit' scoffs and runs his fingers through his hair. Before he can say anything, Alpha Rhineheart growls and turns. "One word, boy, and I will strip you of your title and banish you from our pack!"

"No, Alpha, it's really not his fault. The poor boy is part of all of this tangled web of lies and manipulation woven together by this horrible monster." I try to stand again. I am not going to let this asshole make up lies about me, but Luke continues to hold me down and tightly squeezes my shoulder.

"I can't believe you. Whatever happened to you having my back too?" I hiss at Luke, but he doesn't respond, doesn't show any kind of emotion, just continues to look on at the Beta as if he is invested in hearing what he had to say.

"Your majesty, I'm so ashamed to involve you in this. This really should have been pack business. I have tried my best to raise my daughter to be an upstanding member of my pack."

Daughter? What the fuck?!

"She was always such a difficult child. The lies she would tell, manipulating young men to do her bidding, cause fights amongst the pack members. We would punish her to correct this behavior, but she would run around the pack and tell anyone who would listen that we were starving her, beating her, and locking her out of her home. Making us look like monsters when it was she who was abusing us."

I squirm trying to get out of Luke's hold, but he just squeezes my shoulder even harder.

"She manipulated the Young Alpha into taking her side, pitted him against his own father against his best friend, my son Bart. She used the betrothal contract between the Young Alpha and herself to manipulate him, knowing the contract was binding."

"Betrothed?!" my father and I say in unison.

"No fucking way, you're lying! There is no way that I am betrothed to anyone!" I scream.

I look to the Young Alpha. His eyes are averted, and he shakes his head. "The contract is real, Grit," he replies softly.

"What the fuck did you just call me!" I shout.

"Grit, your name. Oh, come now, I know you never liked

it, but don't be so dramatic." Beta DuPont has the audacity to look sincere. I want to scratch his eyeballs out with my fingernails. He chuckles again, seeing the angst on my face.

"Your majesty, I can supply you with the contract if you like. It was made a few months after she was born. It's very legal and very binding. Of course, it's written in her original name, Grit DuPont."

My father stares at the Beta. "Yes I want a copy of that contract in my office by the end of the day."

I turn to my father. "No! I am not that horrible monster they're claiming me to be! I will never mate with anyone who thinks so little of the opposite sex!"

"Grit, I—"

"That is not my name!" I yell at the Young Alpha. Luke squeezes my shoulder.

"Let go of me, or I will make you regret it!"

He ignores me and addresses Beta DuPont. "How is it that you thought she was dead?"

"Oh, well, you see, she had made so many problems among the pack that even her peers were starting to hate her. She would start fights and then cry that she was being bullied. My poor son tried everything to save her from herself. I believe what we were told was that she had started a fight with one of her best friends, uh, Kat, I think. Anyway, she had been messing around with Kat's boyfriend behind her back. A group of friends and peers had gotten together to confront her about it, she started a fight, and according to my son, it was a bad fight. When the fight was over, she had gone home. Bart, my son, said he found her in the bathroom indulging in wine she stole from my cellar, mutilating herself.

She told Bart she was going to kill herself, and she was going to make it look like she was murdered.

"Bart tried to stop her and called his friends for help. She's a strong girl, even though she's quite tiny. They chased her all the way to the falls, but then he lost track of her. She was missing for, what, a week? Almost two weeks? The entire pack kept looking for her. Then my son found her body in a ravine, near the falls. Her body was so unrecognizable by then, all we had to go on to recognize her was the color of her hair. My son has never recovered. He was so devastated that he couldn't help his sister. My mate has never forgiven herself for not trying to do more, for her daughter, and well as for me. How are you supposed to recover from losing a child?"

"You are not my father, you horrible piece of shit!" I struggle against Luke's restraining grasp. His grip on my shoulder tightens and with enough force pushes me back down. I swear I am going to break his fucking hand!

"If she is here," my father asks, "then whose body did you find?"

Beta DuPont shrugs. "Your majesty, we had no reason to believe that it wasn't her." Then he hesitates for a second. "She's a very smart girl. She was taking junior year courses when she should have been a freshman. She's a musical prodigy. We had wanted to place her in a special school for gifted children, but we were so afraid of the trouble she would cause outside of the territory. I can only imagine that she must have found another child similar in height and weight to make it appear to look like her."

I glare at Beta DuPont.

"You murdered a child, Jessica?" Slowly, I turn my head

to look at Luke. My body trembling, I clench my teeth; I ball my hands into fists. "You accused my mate of setting up the murder of your best friend Emily. This makes me wonder if..."

"Don't go there," I hiss through clenched teeth. I swing my right arm up and around, gripping Luke's arm and twisting, tearing out of Luke's grip. Still holding onto his arm, I stand and smash my left fist into his face, not giving anyone else a chance to get a hold of me.

I jump on the table and grab Beta DuPont by the throat and squeeze. He grabs my wrist with both hands, digging into my flesh with his filthy nails, but I don't flinch, or release my grip; I just squeeze harder. Kneeling onto both knees, I get in closer to Beta DuPont. I can smell the stench of his rotting breath.

"Listen you miserable, fat, power-starving, Alpha wannabe. Listen well because I am only going to say this once. Seven years ago, when your territory suffered from a drought, reducing your crops and slowing down your wine production, even though I was advised against it, I bought 30 percent of your business shares. I even convinced my brothers to invest in 8 percent, and my parents to invest in at least 3. When you and your horrible son pissed everyone off within the LS territory with your assholery and unprofessionalism, I still bought and stocked your wine in my hotel. Even when my restaurant manager and concierge threatened to quit if they had to deal with both of you one more time. Five years ago, when I discovered that your winery had started to expand outside of the LS territory, I started to import your wines from Rome even when it cost me more money, just so everyone working under me could avoid dealing with you. I jumped in as a silent investor in your whiskey distillery. Not only did I front thousands of dollars to your startup, I sent other investors, and marketers. If that is not enough for you, I buy and stock your whiskey in all of my hotels, restaurants, and clubs. It is my clubs that exclusively use only your whiskeys and wines in our signature drinks. When your son pissed off my friend and business partner Jacques Gattefosse, he wanted to burn your business to the ground. I'm the one who worked my ass off to convince him to let it go. I have copies of all of my investments, purchase orders, and more if you want to challenge me on this."

Beta DuPont's face starts to turn purple. I ever so slightly loosen my grip so he can get just enough air in so he doesn't pass out. He swallows, and when I see color return to his cheeks, I lean in again and squeeze.

"I sent investigators to your territory to look into all the attacks you claim are being done by the rogues. Do you know what we found instead? There are no rogue attacks. Each attack you filed a claim on came from within your own territory. In fact, the incident between your son, his fellow pack members, and my guard is the result of my guard catching them in the act of vandalizing your warehouses. Your pack attacked and nearly killed my guard, and if that wasn't enough, they chained and collared him to a wall in one of the storage closets near your facility and tortured him for three straight days." I squeeze his fat neck even harder.

"Jessica…" my father warns.

"The only thing you have on me is that I crossed your territory line to save my guard! When I find that coward son of yours, I'm going to make sure he endures every form of torture that he imparted on my guard."

He starts to squirm and dig his fingers even harder into my wrist, but I have one more thing left to say.

"You need to think long and hard about how you want this to go. Unlike you, I have the power to continue to be your salvation, or I can be your destruction." I squeeze his throat one last time before I shove him back away from me.

Landing in his chair, he instantly grabs his throat, wheezing and gasping for air. Large hands grab me and pulled me off the table. When my feet touch the ground, arms wrap around me to keep me in place.

"Enough, little one, let us take care of the rest," my father whispers into my ear. "Guards!" my father yells. The conference room door crashes open. Anders leads in with three guards, and the twins. I look over the three men on the opposite side of the table. Luke is standing off to the side, wiping blood from his nose with the back of his shirt sleeve. He sends me a murderous glare. Fuck him, traitorous ass. *Glare at me all you want. You deserved that punch.* Despite all the commotion, Alpha Rhineheart is still seated, staring vacantly straight ahead, not even showing concern for his Beta.

Young Alpha Dimitri looks down at his father, concern registering on his face. "Aren't you going to do something about this?" he asks his father. Alpha Rhineheart starts to laugh.

Beta DuPont, still wheezing and coughing, chokes out, "I want her arrested for murdering an innocent child to fake her own death, murdering two of our pack members, threatening my son's life, and threatening my own."

Luke, still dabbing at his nose nonchalantly, turns toward Beta DuPont and nods. "I agree an arrest should be made today." Beta DuPont's eyes light up with triumph. I twist and turn, trying to get out of my father's arms.

Young Alpha Dimitri stands from his seated position. "You can't arrest her. I can testify that everything he has said is a lie!"

"She murdered two of our pack members!" Beta DuPont rasps in a wheezy voice.

"Enough!" My father's booming voice echoes within the room.

"Guards, arrest this man for the abuse of a minor living in his household and arrest these two for conspiring in the attempted murder of a minor living in the protection of their pack," Luke says.

I stand still in shocked silence and confusion. Wasn't he on their side, several minutes ago?

Luke leans forward, his hulking form hovering over both the Alpha and the Beta. "I know that you lied about everything! You want to test me and ask me how I know?" His lips curl in a snarl.

"She set it all up to make it look that way! She mutilated herself, cutting her arms, stabbing herself in the leg, and cut off her eyelashes and her hair. Please, you can't believe her lies!"

Luke slams his fist into the Beta's face. Jeremy is standing behind the Beta and catches him before he falls to the floor. Luke replies, "You wouldn't have known any of that unless you were involved. She didn't run to the falls, because I found her hanging from a tree just over our territory boundary."

Still insistent and refusing to back down, the Beta starts

to stammer, "She—she—she planned it, I'm sure of it!"

Luke grabbed the Beta by his shirt. "She was dead when I found her. She wasn't just mutilated—she was beaten until her face was unrecognizable, her back torn to shreds by wolves! I had to cut a hole in her throat so she could breathe, just to perform CPR. When her heart started to beat again and she was getting some air, we still weren't sure she would survive because she nearly bled dry! I carried her barely living body to the clinic. I stood there as I watched a team of medical professionals continue to work on her lifeless body, doing everything they could to bring her back to life! Through all of that, her survival was not guaranteed because her little body was malnourished and wasn't able to heal on its own. I sat next to her bedside, while tubes, wires, and machines kept her alive. For two weeks while she was in a coma, I prayed for a miracle to bring her back to life, healthy and fully functioning. Do you want to know the best part of all? When she finally woke up, she had no idea who she was, no memory of who attacked her, and no memory of her life before she came into ours."

The Beta's face pales, and his eyes widen.

"You set yourself up with all your lies! As much as I want to kill you right now, I want the motherfucker who put his hands on her!" He pulls his arm back and punches the Beta again. This time, Jeremy steps aside, letting him fly backward, slamming into the wall behind him.

With a menacing glare, Luke sets his eyes on the Young Alpha, who stutters, "I wasn't there! I wasn't there that night it happened. I have proof—I can bring it to you," he shouts. One of the guards is wrestling with him, trying to restrain him. "I wasn't there! I would never have let them hurt her like that!" He looks to me, "I would never have let them hurt you! You have to believe me!" Tears start to drip down my face.

I don't know what to think. I don't know what to believe. I only know what I looked like and what I went through when I woke up in the clinic.

He shoves into Alexis, knocking him to the side. He makes an attempt to get around the table, but Justin comes around, crashing into him and taking him down.

"Get them the fuck out of here!" Luke roars.

The Alpha starts laughing like an insane madman as Anders and another guard have him in their hold. "All this trouble over an unwanted child." He continues to laugh hysterically. I glance at Luke, and we share a look of worry over the Alpha's mental wellbeing. I link my mind with his, but I can't make sense of any of his thoughts. A sharp dagger slices through my link, throwing it back at me like a dart. Shit, I slap my hand over my temple and lean forward.

An unfamiliar voice shouts in my head, and an image of an angry teenage boy forms in my mind. "They should have left you near the falls, where they found you! They should have thrown you into the waters and let you drown!"

The room starts to spin, and the Alpha's maniacal laughter gets louder. Then, he shouts, "I should have left you out on the cliff when you were a baby to die!"

# Chapter 38

## MURDEROUS ALPHA

### LUKE

### March 14, 2025: 1:24 p.m.

I should have been closer to her. My stupid Alpha ego got in the way. I want to tear apart the Young Alpha and show him that she's mine. That he is in my territory and whatever part he had in hurting her, I am going to hurt him. I should never have moved away. When I turn to look at her, something happens. She is holding her head with one hand and holding herself up on the table with the other. My father is shouting orders, and the Beta is putting up a fight to get free. It is a loud chaotic mess, with shouting and crazy laughter coming from the Alpha. Before I can reach Jessica to check on her, the Alpha breaks out of his restrained hold and transitions into a large chestnut brown wolf. He bounds over the table in one swift move, attacking Jessica and knocking down my father at the same time.

"No!" Dimitri and I yell at the same time. Justin and Alexis have him pinned on the ground now, and he is frantically fighting them to get free. The Alpha is on top of Jessica, arms held out in front of her, pushing and punching at his head, his jaws snapping at her. Teeth tearing into one arm. She's in human form, fragile, breakable. She manages to roll out from under him, army crawling away. He grabs her from behind with his teeth and flings her body across the room as if she is nothing more than a rag doll. Her scream fills the room. Wolves jump onto the Alpha's back, attacking him and preventing him from continuing to stalk forward toward Jessica. One of the golden wolves, larger than the Alpha, knocks him over—my father.

No, no, no! I run toward the two Alphas fighting, growling. I transition in midair as I pounce onto Alpha Rhineheart's back. He's too strong. His large jaw clamps down on my father's leg, and I can hear the cracking of bone and the growl of pain. The Alpha throws off another wolf, but I'm still in this fight. I grab on to his haunches, pulling him back, tearing at flesh. He turns his attention to me. In a flurry of teeth and claws and vicious snarls, we fight each other, aiming for the jugular. He's too damn strong; it's like he's on steroids.

What the hell is this? In human form he's an empty shell; in wolf form he's like a killing machine. He throws more wolves off him, and then he grabs me by the shoulder and whips me across the room. He's not interested in killing any one of us. His focus is on Jessica. Free, he returns to stalk toward Jessica, who is lying unconscious on the ground. Another wolf joins him, a smaller chestnut brown wolf with a hint of gray mixed into its fur. I pull myself back up onto all fours. I hear cursing and shouting. Dimitri is still in human form, fighting Alexis who is trying to hold him down. A black wolf and another golden wolf, Chris and Elias, run into the room, immediately attacking the Alpha and the other wolf who I can only assume is the Beta. Shortly, a gray wolf runs in next, all teeth snarling, immediately putting himself before my father. Joe?

Running back in, I join the fray. Together, we work to pull down the Beta and the Alpha. A large white wolf jumps into the array. Steel jaws clamp down on my hind leg. I feel the crunch of bone, immediately followed by searing pain. The Alpha hovers over me. Just before he gets a grip on my neck, Chris slams into him, knocking him over. With my shoulder injured and my hind leg broken, I can barely move.

*"Get her out of here!"* Anders's voice snarls through our mind-link. Crawling through the violent fight taking place, I make my way to Jessica. She's unconscious, and her breathing is shallow, but she's still alive. Blood drips down from a wound on her scalp, and her arm is bent under her at an unnatural angle. I nuzzle her face, but she doesn't move. I can't carry her or drag her out due to my injuries. I lay down, practically on top of her, protecting her the only way I can for now. The smaller chestnut-colored wolf approaches me, snarling, warning me to get out of his way. I refuse to move and try to stand, but sharp pain forces me to fall back down. He steps forward threateningly, and I calculate how I can grab him when he lunges forward so I can rip out his throat.

I want to use my magic. I'm sure we all do, but should this asshole survive, it puts all of our lives in danger. I growl in warning.

*I'm going to kill you, motherfucker, just try.*

My body tenses in anticipation. A smaller golden wolf with longer fluffier fur rushes through the door and lands on his back, gripping the scruff of his neck. Anders pulls away from the chaos going on with the Alpha and joins in. The smaller wolf is my mom, relentless, tearing into the Beta, all teeth and claws. Anders is just as ferocious, merciless. They've been waiting for this moment for a long time. The two of them together kill the Beta. Dark red mats Anders's perfectly white fur, and blood covers my mom's muzzle. She rears up, prepared to jump into the frenzied fight taking place not far from where we currently are, but Ander blocks her way. She tries to get past him, but he blocks her again.

"*No!*" Anders says through our link.

The Beta has transitioned back into human form. There is a gaping hole in his throat and abdomen. My mother turns back toward the Beta, bends down over him, and rips his head off, flinging it across the room. She leaves no room for that motherfucker to survive. In a huff, she leaves the room.

Anders returns to the fight with the Alpha. Alexis is still fighting with Dimitri, who shouts, "Let me go! I can help. He's my father!"

I lick Jessica's wound on her scalp and nuzzle her head. She groans slightly. I need to get her out of here. I hear growling, whimpers, and yelps of pain. The Alpha is not giving up; he's not even tiring. He throws Anders and Elias off him. A low deep growl emanates from his chest as he stalks toward us. As other wolves continue to jump on him, and grab at his hindquarters, he merely brushes them off like pesky flies.

My heart races as he gets closer. Shit! With my injuries, I'm not a match for him. I'm fully prepared to put my life before hers. I shift my weight, preparing myself for another fight as he stalks closer.

Through my peripheral vision, Dimitri has thrown Alexis down and slams a fist into Justin's face. He transitions into a large chestnut-colored wolf, equally as big as the Alpha. I force myself to stand and roar through the pain. Instead of charging for me, the Young Alpha collides into his father, just before he reaches me, catching him off guard.

It's a blur of sharp canines, fur flying, and murderous snarls. Claws dig into flesh. Both are strong and unyielding in their fight. I hear the Alpha yelp out in pain. Then there is nothing but silence. The Alpha falls on to his side. Dimitri transitions back into human form and falls to his knees.

No one moves, anticipating the Alpha getting back on his feet for another attack, but it doesn't come. Dimitri is covered in blood, scratches, and open bites. He reaches forward and places his hand on his father's large wolf head.

Slowly, everyone starts to transition back into their human forms. Alexis, whose face is a bloody mess, and Justin, who looks just as bad as Alexis, finally restrain Dimitri's hands behind his back. He doesn't fight or resist, still looking down at his father's lifeless form. As the Alpha starts to transition back into human form, Dimitri winces when he sees the front of his father's throat torn out.

Dimitri scans the room. He tells Anders, "You need to

call Shadow. He's my commanding officer and lawyer. He can vouch for me." Anders frowns. Dimitri continues, "I didn't train here. He sent me straight to Ryuku Island, but I'm still a guard."

Chris steps forward. "You're the shield?"

He faces Chris. "Yes, my identity was kept a secret, and I have been working undercover for you for the past eight years now." Anders just stares at him. "Call him and I will tell you everything I know. Everything I have been working on."

Anders directs Elias, "Get him some clothes and place him in containment until we hear back from Shadow."

I transition back into my human form while he is talking, and as Alexis and Justin lead Dimitri out of the room, he asks, "Is she okay?"

"She's alive." He looks her over, caressing her with his eyes. I pull her closer into the cradle of my arms and growl. Mine. He smirks as if he's thinking the same thing.

# Chapter 39

## WE SHOULDN'T

### JESSICA

March 14, 2025: 4:15 p.m.

My head is throbbing; my shoulder aches. I blink open my eyes and take in my surroundings. It's dark in my bedroom. I slowly bring myself to a sitting position and slide to the edge of the bed. I rub the back of my neck, then my shoulder.

"Jessica." Luke walks toward me from my little sitting area, kneels in front of me, and caresses my face. "Are you okay?"

"Yeah, I'm fine, you know, nine lives and all that." I say it with a breathy laugh.

"Not funny." He scowls.

"It kind of is," I retort. I start to look him over; he's not wearing a shirt. Goddess, why is he not wearing a shirt?

As much as I should just look the other way, I don't. My eyes caress his defined muscles of his arms, chest... He has a bite mark on his shoulder. I reach up and touch it; it's already starting to fade away. My hand slides down his shoulder, over his pecs, then down to his abdomen, faintly brushing over a thick, ragged scar he had gotten just over seven years ago. Guilt squeezes my heart, reminding me again why he and I can't be together.

I tear my eyes away and look at his face. "Are you okay? Is Dad okay?"

"I'm fine. Dad is fine, all the guards, the twins. We're all fine." He searches my eyes.

"That was a lot of information today—how are you handling it?"

I scoff. "I just woke up, remember? I haven't had time to process it all yet."

He rests his forehead against mine. "I'm here, babe. I'm right here. I'll be here for you while you work through this. You don't need to do this alone." I drop my eyes, and of course, it lands on his scar again. Gently, he pulls me closer to him and he kisses me. Slow and sensually, his tongue traces my lower lip first before he slides in to caress his tongue with mine.

I should stop this—no, I need to stop this.

He slides one hand down to my back and slides me closer, forcing my knees to part. He's now resting between my legs. I can feel the heat of his body against my inner thighs. His kiss becomes urgent. His other hand slides down my neck, gently over my collarbone, down to my breast. I moan as his touch sends a pulsing electrical sensation up my spine, tingling my skin. Moisture pools between my legs. He pulls back, sucking my lower lip and tugging it gently between his teeth. When he releases it, he starts kissing my jaw, making his way down my neck, licking, and sucking my skin.

"I've been so fucking hard for you since this morning." He grabs my hand and places it over his hardened cock, pressing my palm and rubbing it against his thick length. He moans as I curl my fingers around him through the barrier of the fabric of his pants. His fingers curl around my... I just realized I'm barely wearing any clothing. Someone must've removed and changed my clothes. Gently, he pushes me back.

Releasing him, I place my hand behind me to hold myself up. I have to stop this. I can't... He pulls down my camisole. "Luke," I whisper, "I... need to..." I let out a moan as he rolls his tongue over my nipple. "I have to leave. The clock on my nightstand says it's four thirty." He sucks on my nipple and pushes his hip forward against my core.

"Stay," he whispers against my skin. "Stay with me... make love to me... talk to me," he murmurs as he makes his way down my body, lifting my camisole as he licks, bites, and sucks on my skin over my abdomen. I lean back even further. My free hand reaches for his hair.

I shouldn't be encouraging him. I need to stop. I have to stop this; this is so wrong.

He grips my knees with both hands and spreads them wider apart. He slides one hand up my thigh, slipping a finger under my panties, pushing it to the side, then sliding his finger down my slit.

He hisses, "So fucking wet for me, babe. It's been too

long, too long since I tasted you, been inside of you. Stay." He runs his tongue up the entrance of my pussy and uses the flat of his tongue to massage my clit.

"You taste so fucking good." He does it again, and I fight the urge to press his face harder into my center, to grind my hips up against his tongue and lips. "Don't fight it—let me love you," he whispers against my clit, gently blowing over it, making it pulse.

I throw my head back. Gods, I want more, and I almost give in.

"Stay with me, babe..." He licks and sucks, pushing a finger inside. "I want to make love all night long." He pushes a second finger into me and curls it just so it hits the right spot. I let a breathy moan escape. "I want to talk and get past all the crap between us so we can start over." He rolls his tongue over my clit and sucks harder, thrusting his finger in and out of me. "When we're done making love and talking, I want you to be mine. I need you to be mine."

My body freezes, and I close my eyes briefly. I pull his head back by his hair, and I push myself back. No, this is a mistake. I let things get too far. I should have stopped him when he was kissing me.

Luke looks up at me and grips my legs. "Don't—don't run from me." I shake my head and try to push myself back even further. "If you don't want to go any further, then we won't. I need to talk. We need to talk." He grips me harder and drags me back to him. He wraps his arms around me. "I'm in love with you, Jessica. You were meant to be mine. It started before I brought you down from the tree. I fucked up—I know I fucked up in the beginning. I've been trying to make up for it for years. Please, don't run. We can get past everything if you will just give me a chance to explain."

He's not making sense, or my brain can't process what he's talking about. This is too much. "I need to go. I can't do this right now." I push at his shoulder to release me.

"Please, stay with me, so we can talk."

I push against him harder. This time, he slowly releases me. I back up and push myself as far away from him as I can without falling off the other end of the bed. The pained look in his eyes makes me feel guilty for allowing things to go as far as it did. "I'm sorry, but I can't be with you, Luke."

He glares at me. "Can't or won't?"

"Both," I whisper.

"If you would just talk to me—you've been avoiding me for three years!" he yells.

"It's too late, Luke. I'm with someone else."

His eyes narrow. "Then call him and end it. I don't share what is mine." He growls. "Tomorrow, we'll have our talk—we'll talk for however long it takes. I'm not giving up on you, on us." He stands and turns to stalk out of my room.

"I'm not yours, Luke. You lost me a long time ago." I don't shout it; I don't say it in anger. I just say it in a low, toneless voice void of any emotion.

He stops. I see his hands tighten into fists at his side. He doesn't turn around. Standing still in the doorway, he replies, "Tomorrow, Jessica, you promised me tomorrow."

# Chapter 40
## It Doesn't Change Anything

### JESSICA
### March 14, 2025: 7 p.m.

My thoughts are all over the place while riding in the back of the car to the city. Thoughts of earlier today after Alpha Agnus's funeral, Anders being my biological father, thoughts about that dickhead Beta, everything he said. Young Alpha Dimitri calling me Grit, telling me that we were betrothed by a contract made years ago. As much as I have always disliked Territory Two's leaders, there was something about that place that I held a soft spot for. I don't recall ever being there, nor did I ever meet anyone from there. When they were in financial hardship, I wanted to help. Not for the leaders, for those in the pack. I never understood why I felt the way I did. Now, well, I guess that could be why. I apparently grew up there.

Then there are thoughts of Luke—why does he always have to come at me this way? If he's not after me for some stupid made-up bullshit in his head, he comes at me hard with declarations of love. I'm not going to fall down that rabbit hole again. I gave him my heart once; he took it, ripped it out, and stomped on it hard. I could still feel his lips against mine, feel his touch. He's always been able to do that to me, even when I am so angry with him and want to dig his eyeballs out. He always has a way of making me melt, and I want to give him anything he wants, even if it leaves me hurt and broken when he's done.

"What's the deal with you and Luke?" Odyssey asks.

"Stay out of my head, Odyssey."

He laughs. "Stop thinking about him then."

"I'm not."

"Sure, you're not."

Why does he always do this to me? I glare at Odyssey sitting next to me.

"He loves you, Jessica. He really does love you. You should have seen the way he was behaving when we got there. He wouldn't let anyone touch you. He was hurt so badly, but he insisted on taking care of you first."

Guilt curls its way into my gut. "I don't want to talk about him right now."

"Jessica, you need to talk to him. What you think happened, that's not how it went down. He's been hurting over it for the past few years."

I fold my arms over my front. "Why are you taking his side?"

He shrugs. "I'm not taking anyone's side. Theres the truth and there's what you think happened. You need to hear the truth. You deserve to know that truth."

"It doesn't change anything. Can we talk about something else?"

"Fine, then let's talk about why you're doing this tonight. I can't believe you're going through with this, especially after the day you had." I narrow my eyes at him. He scoffs. "I'm serious, you've been through a shitstorm of a day. You don't have to do this. You should be at home with your family working through everything that came up today."

"Stay out of my head, Odie."

He growls. He hates my nickname for him. "Whatever it is that you're planning, you don't have to do it. This isn't going to bring her back."

I don't answer him. I just continue to look out the window. After a while, I finally speak. "Who says I'm doing this only for her?" I ask quietly.

"I'm not. I'm just saying that your whole plan, it's putting your life at risk. It's suicide. You know it, and I know it." The hairs at the back of my neck bristle at his insinuation. Electricity starts to crackle in my palms. He ignores the anger rising inside of me and continues, "You and I have been friends for years. I'm not one to pull punches. I'm saying this because I care about what happens to you. What you're planning tonight, it's dangerous. You need to reconsider what you're doing."

I clench my jaw and turn my head away from him.

"What would that be? Continue to hide, like I have been my entire life?"

"You're home now. You have the entire guard at your disposal and then some. There's a better way to do this."

"I'm not talking about this anymore." I continue to look out the window lost in thought, ignoring Odyssey for the rest of the trip. When we are close to the venue, I start to put on my mask.

Odyssey places his hand over mine. "It's not too late. We can turn around and take you back home." I move my hand out from his larger ones and continue to fix my mask into its place. He persists, "If we return home, I'm sure Luke will be a very happy guy. Maybe you can finish what he tried to start."

I stop and glare at him. "Stay out of my head!"

He scrunches his nose. "Well, you could have at least let him get you off." I show him the finger, just before we pull up to the curb. He laughs as he gets out of the car.

The backstage of the runway is a catastrophe. Akiyo meets me near the doorway. "Just as I predicted." She motions for me to follow her through the chaos. I'm late, not just a little late, really late. I missed the stage rehearsal and sound check.

Odyssey's and Elijah's eyes bulge and zoom around the room. Half-naked tall, beautiful men and women all over the place. Odyssey's cheeks are red.

I laugh, "You look as if you have never seen naked people before, Odie."

He glares at me, making me laugh even more. Elijah recovers from his initial shock, then just keeps walking, back in bodyguard mode.

I'm standing behind the entrance of the stage. I peek through the silk and gauzy fabric, adorned with fake diamonds and pearls. I sneak a look over at the VIP section. The guards are escorting my parents, twin brothers, and Luke to their seats.

Anders stays behind to get answers. When I left, I was told that they kept the Young Alpha Dimitri in containment. I should have stayed behind, but the truth is I really don't want to learn anymore about my past today. I can barely process everything so far. All of this—tonight, this runway show—I planned this before I learned about my past. I probably should have taken today's events as a sign and stayed home. Of course, the stubborn part of myself wouldn't or couldn't let this go. I am committed, and I'm not going back on what I aim to do.

The house is full tonight; cameras are everywhere. Tonight's runway show is being streamed around the world. I take one last look over at my family. I didn't think Luke would be here. I watch him for a few seconds. He looks sad, unfocused, like the weight of the world is resting on his shoulders. Why, why do I have to feel so guilty every time I put my foot down with him? He has done way worse shit to me then I have ever done to him.

I let the material fall back into its place. Taking a step back, I roll my shoulders, take a deep breath, and slowly let it out. I look over to Odyssey, and he nods. I look over to Elijah, and he nods too. The host starts his opening, the music starts, and the band Raw slowly starts to rise in the center of the stage. Their lead singer Ray is playing his Stratocaster.

Charlie walks out from the opposite side of the runway with his guitar, singing the opening lines, and when I hear the chorus to "Let Me Love You" come up, I make my way onto the stage.

I forget everything that I have been through today.

I forget that I am the newly named successor of the Whitemore pack, the CEO of W&P Corp, Princess Jessica Langhlan. The person formally known as Grit. I'm not even G the rock singer. I'm me, all of me, heart and soul all laid out for everyone to see, to hear. My words, my voice singing to anyone who will listen to my joys, my sadness, my heartache, my anger.

# CHAPTER 41

## NOT HERE

### LUKE
#### March 14, 2025: 8 p.m.

I take my seat in the VIP section. I was hoping to see Jessica sitting here. I showed up tonight even after she rejected me in hopes that I can talk to her. I know she promised me tomorrow, but I know her—she'll come up with some excuse to avoid me. She's been avoiding me for three years. Fuck, we're business partners, and somehow, she avoids direct in-person meetings with me. When we do have meetings, she's available through video chats, and we are never alone. If I call, she doesn't answer. Her only response to me is either in text or email. But she's home now, and I'm not giving up. I need her to see how much I love her, care about her. I need her to see that I am not that spoiled, vindictive person she believes that I am.

I get an elbow to my ribs, and I let out a breathy oomph. "Why are you here if you're going to mope?" Jeremy hisses into my ear.

"I'm not moping. I'm just thinking about the shit that happened earlier today."

He chuckles. "You worried that the betrothal contract still holds water?"

No, I'm not fucking thinking of that. Leave it to Jeremy to bring shit up that most people would rather forget about. "Now I am. Thanks for that," I mutter under my breath.

"You saw the way he looked at her when they were taking him out of the room?" He glances sideways at me, but I refuse to acknowledge his question. Just to piss me off even further, he lets out a low whistle. "C'mon, man, I mean, he killed his own father to protect her." I am so ready to throttle Jeremy if he keeps this up. I don't care if there are thousands of people in this venue watching us; I will hit him.

"Can you not talk for the rest of the show? Or here's an idea—switch seats with Justin." Jeremy ignores me and hands me a pamphlet. I don't take it from him.

"She's not sitting here because she's part of the main attraction." I look down at the paper he tosses into my lap and ignore most of what is written, but the bottom catches my attention: Special guest model featuring petite line: Princess Jessica Langhlan. Musical guest featuring Raw, Charlie Langhlan, and 'G.'

Why is she doing this? Princess Jessica has never made any kind of public appearance, ever. She has been seen here and there in photos, but none of the pictures were clear enough to capture her facial features. It is kind of a standing joke with all of us that she's a ghost. Once a reporter had the nerve to ask Jeremy if she was ugly, thus the reason for her staying out of the limelight. Jeremy broke the reporter's nose, and our PR guy had a field day trying to calm the media down.

Before I can think any more about it, the lights flash, getting everyone's attention to quiet down and sit. The host rambles off an opening that I don't quite catch, because I'm still thinking about Jessica.

The music starts. Models walk out onto the runway. Charlie descends onto the runway, playing his guitar, and starts to sing. Then I hear her; my girl makes her way onto the stage. She's wearing a spectacular faux-leather outfit with a flowing cape. Fake tattoo mesh sleeves cover the scars on her arms. Her long hair is made up in a fancy braid that almost looks like a faux hawk, and her signature choker necklace covers the scar at the base of her throat. That very scar I made to save her life. She starts to sing the chorus along with Charlie.

I become mesmerized. It's as if everything else around me disappears. I don't see or hear the crowd screaming for her, cheering for her. I don't see the band; it's just her. Singing, dancing, happy, free. It's like everything she is or isn't melts away when she sings. I hate that she sings with a mask on. I always did. I have told her many times before—it's a grave injustice to her fans to hide her face. Her face when she sings shows everything she feels. Her music, the lyrics that she writes, is like her diary. It's everything she feels, poetically written and composed into a song. It's why her fans love her—they can relate to her.

I feel it too but maybe a little different compared to her fans, because some of her songs are written about me. She hasn't come out and said it, but I know and it hurts how I have angered her, betrayed her, broken her heart. My heart bleeds just thinking about it. She's written a thousand songs for other artists, but she's kept and sang the ones that she identified with the most.

She's standing between Raw's lead singer Ray and Charlie now. She has one arm on Charlie's shoulder as he does a solo riff. Jealousy runs up my spine. He's my doppelganger in every way, yet their friendship is so much more than I have ever had with her. She loves him, trusts him, believes in him. It pains me to know that I may never have that with her. She's smiling up at him. Her mask covers most of her face, exposing only the right side of her face and her mouth. I want to see her face.

A piece of paper flutters from above and lands near my foot. I look around, but I don't see anyone standing or moving to pick it up.

Jessica moves forward facing the crowd, belting out the lines to another song. "You're supposed to protect me, love me, take care of me. Instead, you shattered my soul." Pain grips my heart.

Jeremy is side-eyeing me. I try to hide my pain by bending forward to pick up the paper. When I turn it over, it's the picture of a tarot card "Death." Fear seizes my heart, transporting me back to memories ten years earlier.

# CHAPTER 42

## DEATH CARD

### LUKE

November 14, 2014: 11:55 p.m.

The recruits and I arrive in town. My mother, Jessica, and the other girls are shopping. We try not to make it obvious as we approach the little restaurant where I know my mother likes to eat.

"Luke! Hey, baby, I have missed you so much!" Shit, I forgot Wills, Elaine, and the rest of their crew are in town. Elaine crashes into me and turns up her head to catch me in a kiss. I turn my head just in time and push her back by the arms to avoid further contact. I don't acknowledge her. This is one girl who just cannot take a hint. Any kind word, sometimes even a smile, gets taken out of context.

Ignoring her, I turn to Wills and shake his hand. "Hey,

man, what are you doing here?" I ask him, pretending I didn't know that he was already here.

He gives me a look. "I texted you earlier. We all came in a day early for the ball. Haven't seen you for quite some time, wanted to hang out, catch up."

"Ah, yeah, sorry, man, been busy. Must have missed your text."

"No worries, you're here now. We can hang and catch up later tonight at your place. It will be just like old times." Oh hell no! How the hell do I always get sucked into their bullshit? The worst part is I never know how to say no, so they always get to me.

Darwin clears his throat. "Sorry, man, we're here to get some lunch, pick up some supplies, and then we're heading back to the training center. We recruits have some things planned. Last hoorah before the ceremony and ball. You're gonna have to catch up later."

Wills narrows his eyes at Darwin. Before he can question him, I jump in, "Yeah, sorry, man, got plans. I didn't know you guys were coming."

His face instantly changes from irritation and suspicion to indifference. "No worries, we already ate, but we can hang with you until you get what you came into town for. Then we can catch up tomorrow night." I nod; Elaine is pouting, arms crossed over her chest. Wills goes to her and whispers something in her ear. Cassie, one of the girls in their group, is staring up at Liam as if he hung the moon and stars himself. I huff out a breathy laugh. Liam has a pinched expression on his face and is trying his best to ignore the girl. The other two girls have their hooks into Sodie and Stan. I leave them to their own devices. If they know what's good for them, they'll stay far away from this bunch.

The recruits and I have gotten closer with the disappearance of Jessica. We weren't enemies before I had left, but we all weren't exactly close friends. When I had first started with the recruits, there were those who kissed my ass and those who didn't like me right off the bat. They had assumed that because I was the Young Alpha Prince, I would get away with pretty much anything. They were all wrong. I got picked on the most, and expectations of me were much higher than those of the rest of the group. Slowly over time, many of them dropped out, fed up with Marcus, Boris, and Dustin's antics and bullying. The ones that remained just kept to themselves. I look around the group of recruits intermingled with the preppy fake kids from my former private school. True friends stand out among the group, and I feel lucky to have had the opportunity to have been among them in the program.

When Wills and Elaine are farther away, I slap Darwin on the shoulder. "Thanks, man, I appreciate the interception."

"Just doing my job." I raise an eyebrow at him.

He smirks. "It's our job to protect not only the princess but all of the royal family. My gut instincts tell me that this group of friends of yours, especially your girlfriend, are nothing but trouble."

I grimace at his reference to Elaine as my girlfriend. "She's not my girlfriend, and yeah, those two are always up to something."

He laughs. "I think someone missed the memo 'cause that girl thinks she owns you."

I shudder at the thought. "Then I guess it's a good thing I roped Emily in to be my recon, mission keep the Powers twins away," I say with a laugh.

Darwin brightens up at the mention of Emily's name. "Emily?"

"Yeah, for some reason, Elaine is scared of her."

"Yeah, I can see that. She's pretty fierce." Oh man, poor dude, I can see the hearts in his eyes. She's going to break his heart. Darwin and Emily worked together on hacking into some of the government's security systems when they were searching for Jessica. Darwin might not be the best of the recruits when it comes to combat training, but he is wicked smart when it comes to computers. That's how Shadow found him. Darwin had gotten expelled from school in his territory. He was caught hacking into the school's system, changing fellow classmates' grades for a nominal fee. Shadow felt that with the rise of technology, it would be good to have more recruits that were familiar with technical operations.

The leads didn't agree, until it came time when we needed him. Darwin was the first person Liam thought of when Emily asked if we had already searched through the airports and ports systems. He not only hacked into the LS territory systems; he hacked into the Northern A systems and then some. He proved himself this week, and although we are not best of friends, I couldn't be any prouder of him that he stuck it out these past two years and finished.

"So, how close are you and Emily?" Darwin finally builds up the courage to ask.

"I didn't sleep with her if that's what you're getting at."

He huffs. "I wasn't, but thanks for the info. I mean, are

you close enough to know if she's dating anyone, met her true mate, that kind of thing?" I internally groan at his remark. Emily is going to owe me big time. I constantly have to fend off guys who are interested in her, so much so that sometimes they think it's because I'm in love with her.

"No, man, she's single, as far as I know. But, uh, I wouldn't get your hopes up. She's um... picky, and she never gets involved for the long term." I can see the wheels turning in that big brain of his.

"I can live with that. Not sure where I'll be heading off to after graduation. A short-term relationship would be fine."

I shake my head. "Please don't."

Darwin's eyes narrow. "Why? thought you two were like family." I sigh, look around me, and see that the rest of the recruits are caught up with the girls. Elaine tries her best to flirt relentlessly with the recruits in hopes to gain my attention.

"Look, Emily doesn't get involved in relationships because she's betrothed. I'm not supposed to say anything, so keep it to yourself." His eyes widen. "She's been betrothed to the Obsidian Alpha's son before she was even born. She knows it, she's fine with it, she's accepted it."

Darwin frowns. "What about what she wants?"

"Sometimes we don't always get what we want. I know she's an awesome girl, and you can probably see yourself with her short-term or long term. She won't go there. There's no room for what-ifs."

His shoulder sags. "Alright, thanks for the heads-up." I nod. I feel bad for the guy; he really does like her, but this isn't my first rodeo, and until Emily becomes mated, I'm afraid it won't be my last. Maybe I should start telling everyone we're dating. It's getting harder to fend them off.

This time, I didn't lie to Darwin. The original Blackguard Alpha of the Obsidian Pack did truly make a binding contract to the Obsidian Alpha who migrated to LS territory after the great war and established the Obsidian Pack territory. Not sure how the Obsidian Alpha has come to be here, how the two know each other. The contract states that the first female born of the true Blackguard family line, or the Obsidian Alpha family, will be mated with the Alpha child of the same blood origin. For generations, neither of the families had a female child. All were male. When Emily was born, her fate was sealed. Because of that, she was given the best education, sent to the elite private school in the city. Her college education is paid for. She was also trained in martial arts and weaponry. She is everything the Obsidian Alpha could ever hope for in a mate for his Alpha son.

Except for one thing. She doesn't like men and doesn't want children. I love Emily, and I am proud of her for accepting things the way they are. She never complains and doesn't fight with anyone about it. I can't say that I would be that compliant. I am grateful for my parents. As the Alpha King, my father could have set up a betrothal contract to ensure our family's bloodline. He didn't. He and my mother are true mates. We, my brothers and myself, are the products of true love. Both of my parents want that for us, the freedom to find our true mates or at least a mate that we love.

Elaine's flirting with Stan, talking loudly. I continue to ignore her. Sometimes I think Emily has a good deal. At least she can always use the betrothal card to fend off unwanted male callers. I, on the other hand, have to deal with manipulative, gold-digging women who only want me for one thing, my title.

We finally get close enough to my mom's favorite restaurant. I can see them having lunch at one of the outdoor tables. I look around the town and don't see anything amiss. I look over to Stan. He's doing the same thing. When he catches me looking at him, he nods, confirming what I already concluded. The group of girls are squealing and making a ruckus in front of an old woman who has set up a table outside of one of the stores. I take the opportunity to look over at the table, since no one is paying attention to me. Jessica is sitting there with her baseball cap on, so low it hides her features. Emily and Sixes are talking animatedly. My mother and Jessica laugh at whatever it is they are saying. She looks so tiny compared to the other women she's sitting with. If onlookers didn't know better, they would just pass her off as a little kid, until they look at her body.

She's definitely older than a little kid. She takes a bite out of food, and I can see the pleasure she takes in whatever it is she just popped into her mouth. I'm quite far away, but I swear I can see the goosebumps along her arms, the way her body sags in pleasure. She closes her eyes as if relishing the taste of the food she's rolling around in her mouth. Damnit, I tear my eyes off her. I'm reading too much into it. She's eating lunch for crying out loud. I look around the town again, but my vision lands right back on her. She's smiling and throws a balled-up napkin at Emily. Emily laughs when she catches it. Why didn't I talk to Emily first before I jumped to conclusions?

I wouldn't be standing here right now pining over a girl who hates my guts, not that I could blame her. When I was finally able to tell Emily what happened when I came home, she gave me a black eye. I deserved it. I was already feeling like shit over what Emily had said at the dinner table, with Jessica's disappearance, and learning about Marcus and his asshole followers. The guilt has never really left.

I don't know how to fix it. Most girls would have fallen for my charm by now. She won't give me the time of day. My charm doesn't affect her. I was so wrong about her. Had I given her a better chance of getting to know me, the real me, we could have at least been friends.

Laughter erupts from the group. I finally turn my attention to them. Elaine is watching me with narrowed eyes. Crap, how long has she been watching me stare at Jessica? Maybe she'll think I'm looking at Emily. Fuck I hope so. I take a step closer to see what everyone is so excited about. It's an elderly woman sitting at a table, holding a deck of cards toward Liam.

"Come on, give it a try. Maybe it will tell you that we are destined to be together," Cassie purrs in Liam's ear. Liam grimaces, not holding back that he doesn't like her one bit. Cassie is pretty, light brown hair, long and wavy. She's curvy, dressed in the latest fashion. She's taken to social media and is hoping to become discovered for acting or modeling. Cassie may be pretty, but she's average. There is nothing special about her looks or her personality.

Sodie slaps Liam on the back. "Just do it. The faster you get it done, the faster she will realize she's not your destiny." Sodie chuckles. Liam takes what he says into consideration and silently motions with his finger to the elderly woman to hand him a card. She shuffles the deck, fans it out, and tells Liam to pick one.

He pulls a card, then flips it over. He frowns at it; everyone starts to laugh and whoop. Cassie looks smug and bats her fake eyelashes at Liam. Liam shows the elderly woman the card. She smiles.

"Ah, The Lovers card. Destined to be together, joined by fate. True mates." Then she frowns. "You're fighting it, I wonder why?" Then she shuffles the cards again and pulls one from the top of the deck. "The King of Cups, reversed," she says. "If you don't let love in, you will still have everything you're destined for, but you will live a very lonely and miserable life. The monster within will be unleashed and leave you a very feared man. A man you have been fighting so hard to refrain from being." She takes The Lovers card and places it over the King of Cups. "Let love in, and you will have everything your heart desires. The choice is yours."

Cassie smiles and intertwines her hand with Liam's. He looks down at their hands and then at Cassie. She doesn't acknowledge the fact that he's looking at her like she's a bug that he wants to swat away. "I told you we were destined to be together," she announces.

The old woman starts to cackle. "Oh sweetheart, it's not you. He knows exactly who it is." I see a slight reprieve cross Liam's features right before he schools it into his normal pinched expression.

Cassie huffs, "We'll see about that!" She turns to leave, stomping away and looking back at Liam. He doesn't follow.

"Take it. You'll need the reminder," the old woman says

to Liam, handing him the cards.

Elaine slides her hand into mine. "Your turn, baby," she sings. I remove my hand from hers and move in front of the table, taking Liam's place. I smile at the woman, flashing her with my dimples, and she blushes.

"You're a horrible flirt," she says. At least I know it still works. I wink at her; she blushes again and starts to shake her head. "You know, that charm will not work on everyone. Sometimes you need to work a little harder to gain a certain someone's attention," she says to me and turns the tables on me and winks.

I laugh, "I hear you, old woman, loud and clear." She cackles, showing her brown and yellow teeth. I don't flinch at the sight. I continue to hold her gaze and my smile. She fans the cards in front of me, and I pull one, but another falls from the deck onto the table. She places her hand over it and slides it closer to her, but she doesn't place it back into the deck. Just keeps it there. She gestures to the card in my hand. I flip it over, the King of Pentacles.

"Ah, you will be a great king when it becomes your turn. But we already knew that, didn't we?" I look at the woman. "That's not what you want to know, is it?" She smiles widely and has a look on her face like she knows a secret. I don't answer her. She takes the card that fell on the table and flips it over, the Queen of Wands reversed. She tsks. "You have let the influences of others drive you to make a very wrong and hurtful decision." I feel all the blood drain from my face. How could she possibly know that? Am I too late? "But fear not. There is hope. You cannot rely on charm and that pretty face. You have to dig deep and work very hard to make things right. It will not happen overnight. Be mindful of those around you. The influences can create more damage than your prepared for." She turns the card upright and flips a card on top of it. The World. She smiles. "Big changes are coming, some bad, some good. If you handle it well, it can be all yours. Just remember one important thing. It will look nothing like how you think it will. Once you can accept that, she can be yours too." I frown. I don't really understand what she means by that last part. She doesn't explain, hands me the cards, and tells me the same thing she told Liam.

Elaine huffs and pushes me to the side, standing in front of the table. "Who's she?" she asks with arms crossed in front of her. The woman cackles. She shuffles the deck of cards; one falls out facing up. The High Priestess. "Someone very important." She looks to all of us when she says that, then picks up the card and places it back into the deck.

"It's my turn," Elaine whines. I'm not sure why I stay there to listen, but my feet seem rooted in place. I stand there, waiting for Elaine's cards to show. I notice I'm not the only one who stays. Everyone else does too.

Elaine looks smug, knowing she is now the center of attention. She thrives off of it and would steal the spotlight from anyone taking full credit even if she didn't put in the work. Elaine has a cute face, tan-colored hair she perfectly styles. Like Cassie she is dressed in the latest fashion. She doesn't have the curves Cassie does. Underneath all of the carefully placed makeup and clothing, she is the ugliest girl I have ever met in my entire short life. Elaine is shallow, petty and manipulative, but everyone knows it. Unlike the girl who used me, who hid and lied, Elaine wears her colors. It's probably the only reason why I tolerate her as much as I do.

Elaine growls, "What the fuck is this!" In her hand she holds the Devil card. Snickers came from the girls. Wills, her own brother, starts to cough, and uses his hand to cover a smile. "This is not funny, Wills," she screeches.

The old woman looks amused. "I don't have to explain this card to you. I think it's obvious you know what this means. But the divine is giving you a chance, a chance to choose a different path. Jealousy is your one true enemy."

"And where the fuck did you get that from? One of your tacky quotes you put in those ugly handmade cards in your store!"

"Elaine," I say in a low warning tone.

She turns on me with eyes shiny, ready to spill tears, "This isn't fair." Here come the theatrics. "I want another card!"

The woman obliges by shuffling the deck. She pauses before she fans them out. "You may not want the other card. Greed doesn't make you a better person."

Elaine's features turn menacing. "I want the other card."

The woman starts to fan out the cards, then pulls back, "I will give you the other card only if you let me tell you what you need to hear." She raises an eyebrow in anticipation of Elaine's answer.

"Fine," she snaps. The woman leans forward and fans the cards out in front of her. Elaine pulls a card, and another one falls out of the deck and lands on the table. She palms it and pulls it toward her, the same way she did to me. When Elaine flips the card over, it's the Death card. Elaine starts to breathe hard, her face turning red. She looks like she's seconds from flipping the table over. I side-eye Sodie, who looks like he's getting ready to grab her if he needs to.

"What the fuck," she breathes out. The woman sits back and eyes Elaine, studying her and contemplating what she's to say next.

"I was going to tell you that you have an opportunity to change, that jealousy will only eat you alive and ruin your life. It's not going to ruin just your life; your jealousy will ruin others." The old woman searches Elaine's face. "I'm afraid you have already made up your mind, and as a result, someone will die because of you. In fact, many will die because of your jealousy and your greed." The woman frowns. "But maybe, just maybe, you can change."

Elaine growls, "I've never been jealous of anyone in my entire life! I think you have it wrong. People are jealous of me!"

The woman sadly shakes her head. "Then you have made your choice. I see." She lifts the card only enough so she can peek under it, then places it back down. She looks hesitant, like she doesn't want to show Elaine. "You will meet a great adversary." The woman quickly takes the card and places it in the deck.

"Give me back the card!" Elaine screams at her. The woman looks down, slides the card back out of the deck, and flips it over. The Fool.

"You won't win," she whispers to Elaine.

Elaine screeches and throws the cards at the woman. "You changed it on purpose. You're trying to make me look like a fool. Well I have news for you! I don't believe in any of this crap. I make my own destiny! I. Always. Get. What. I.

Want!" Elaine turns, hesitates, then turns back, taking the money from the old woman's tip jar, and stomps off. I roll my eyes after Elaine. The girls start to follow Elaine.

Stan snorts, "She's a piece of work."

Darwin lets out a low whistle. "That's the definition of crazy. I think we need to tighten security on you," he says, looking at me. My blood is running cold.

"I'm not going to lie—she fucking scares the shit out of me," I say, halfheartedly trying to lighten up the mood. I take my wallet out and place a fifty in the jar.

"Sorry about that. I hope this makes up for what she took." The other guys start to do the same, placing bills in her jar.

The old woman smiles. Then she crooks her finger, stopping us in our tracks. "I need to show you something." She takes a card and places it on the table. The High Priestess.

"This is the card I didn't want to show her. Her greatest adversary. You need to protect her. If that girl gets what she wants…" She bends down and picks up the cards Elaine threw at her. Without looking at the cards, she covers the High Priestess with the Death card and covers the Death card with the Devil. "Let her win, it will destroy the entire LS territory." The woman looks sad, moves the cards she just placed on top of the High Priestess, and taps it. "Protect her. Protect yourselves. Take care of one another."

# CHAPTER 43

## IS THAT SUPPOSED TO BE COOL?

### LIAM

#### November 14, 2014: 4:45 p.m.

It has been a long day; it feels like we've been in town for hours. No, we've been in town for hours, keeping an eye on Jessica. I swear if this girl touches me one more time, I really just might hit her. We're sitting outside at the restaurant Jessica had been to earlier. It's the perfect spot, center of the town. I can keep an eye on both ends of the town. Jessica has gone into one of the shops at the end. They need to make their way back this way to get to the car.

A car passes by, slowly, at the speed limit. As it gets closer to the end of town, it stops, then backs up.

A young guy sticks his head out of the back window. "Hey, baby, you need a ride?" The girl he's shouting at doesn't turn around. "C'mon, baby, don't do this to me. I just want to take you for a ride." The girl starts to look up and down the sidewalk. "Yeah, baby, you, I'm talking to you, beautiful." The girl turns around to face the guy. "Holy fuck! Are you mated? No? Good because I am never letting you out of my sight." He gets out of the car, climbing though the window. Does he think that makes him look cool? Or does the passenger door of the car not open?

Sodie stands up from his chair and whistles. The girl looks over at him. "Jessica!" he calls out. She takes a step forward. No fucking way, Jessica? She looks, she looks...wow. I have to blink a few times to make sure that it is really her standing there. Her long white-blond hair is a darker shade of blond with streaks of purple. She's wearing ripped jeans that barely cover her muscular thighs and a long-sleeved crop top that fits snugly over ample breasts. She raises her hand to move a stand of hair off her face, showing a little skin over her smooth abdomen that tapers down to a narrow waist. I already knew that somehow her physical features changed when she was brought back to the territory after she had been found. But this transformation...I feel like I can't breathe, and my limbs feel heavy and weak. Shaking myself out of my dismay, I start to get up. Cassie grabs my arm and pulls me back down.

I pry her grip off me. "Sorry, girl, I'm already taken." I push off my seat and follow the rest of the recruits across the street.

"Hey, what the hell, man! I saw her first!" the guy protests. Luke and Sodie are hovering over him, and Darwin and Stan stand in front of Jessica. She looks confused, like she doesn't understand what's happening right now. I push my way between the group and crack my knuckles, intimidating the hell out of the guy who is slowly backing up to the car.

Sodie growls, "Get in the car, my friend." The guy looks at Sodie, then to me, then back up at Jessica, then to Luke.

"Luke, holy crap, tell them you know me. What the hell? I just want to talk to the pretty girl."

Luke smiles at the guy. "She's off-limits. Get back in the car, before the guards break your jaw."

His face turns red. "What? Why? She's not even from here."

Sodie growls again, taking a step closer. "She's the princess. Now get in the car." His eyes widen, and to push things further along, I crack my neck and stare him down. He turns, runs back to the car, and jumps through the window.

"Go, go, go," he shouts. The driver peels rubber and speeds out of town. We all start to crack up and high five each other. That's actually fun. Jessica does not look amused. She rolls her eyes at Luke and shakes her head at me.

Sodie's still laughing. "Aww, come on, little one, you know that was funny. The guy practically pissed himself before he jumped through the window."

She's trying hard not to smile. "Please don't tell me this is what I'm to expect, when I start bringing dates to the house." She looks at Stan and Darwin.

Darwin shrugs. "Depends. Is that how you're going to dress when you go on a date?"

She shrugs. "Maybe, since my mother bought my clothes. I assumed this was perfectly acceptable attire." Darwin and Stan start to laugh. Dates? Over my fucking dead body. Dates...

Luke's idiot friends make their way across the street, just as the Luna Queen, Emily, and Sixes come out of one of the shops.

The Luna Queen addresses the group. "Well, I think we'll call it a day," she announces. We offer to take their packages and walk them back to the car. Jessica refuses to let me take her packages. Why is she being so difficult? She won't even look at me. Wills tries to make his way, next to Jessica, but Emily maneuvers herself so she's blocking him. Darwin places himself on the other side of Jessica, and I walk behind them, leaving no room for anyone to get to her. Luke is walking with his mother in the front, Sixes on the other side of the Luna Queen.

We get to the car, and Elaine tries to invite herself back to the mansion. "I'm sorry, sweetheart. Our rooms are quite full, and we have some things we need to take care of for the ball tomorrow, perhaps another time." Elaine is clearly upset with this response, but she smiles and graciously accepts the rejection.

Cassie bumps into me and whispers, "Text me and I will sneak over later tonight."

"Not interested," I respond.

Wills finally gets to Jessica. "Hi, I'm Wills, Luke's best friend." He holds out his hand to shake Jessica's. She looks down at it but doesn't move to shake it. Yes, good girl.

She looks back up to Wills. "Never heard of you, Luke's best friend." He laughs, ignoring her dry intone, and continues to speak to her.

"So are you friends with one of Luke's cousins?"

"Sure," she deadpans.

"I mentioned that I am Luke's best friend, right?"

She fully turns to him now and narrows her eyes. "Is that supposed to earn you brownie points?" she asks sarcastically.

He laughs again, rubs the back of his neck. "I was hoping it would."

She's still holding onto her package and tries to get into the car, but Wills blocks her way. She looks up at him, irritation clear on her face. "Some words of advice, dropping names doesn't impress anyone." She looks over and notices Luke standing on the other side of the car. "Especially when someone's not quite impressed with your best friend."

She pushes him out of the way and gets into the car. Wills gives her a triumphant smile. "Noted," he says and closes the door.

Luke taps the top of the car. "Hey, I'm gonna jump in with them. I'll meet you back at the dorms."

I feel arms start to snake around my waist; my skin starts to crawl. I run up to the driver's side of the car. "Hey, Xavier, got room for one more up front?" He nods at me. I reach into my pocket and toss the keys to the shuttle to Sodie, run around to the front, and jump in. I hear laughter coming from the guys. I stick my hand out the window and show them the finger.

# Chapter 44

## I WAS A FOOL

### LUKE

#### November 15, 2014: 12:14 a.m.

It's after midnight when I finally make my way back to the house from the dorms. I decide at the last minute that I want to see Queenie. I haven't spent nearly as much time with her as I had wanted to with the way the week turned out. That's when I see them. Charlie and Jessica. Charlie has his arm around her shoulders. They haven't seen me standing in the dark. What the hell, Charlie? She's fourteen; Charlie could have anyone. I mean literally anyone. Why her—why Jessica? He's much older than her. He's, what, almost twenty-one, or is he twenty-one? Anyway that doesn't matter. He's older, and he has been with so many other women and can have as many women as he wants, older women, experienced women.

I should turn away and go back home. But I am angry and want to know exactly what the hell is happening. Quietly, I follow them into the barn. I catch Jessica's purple-streaked ponytail entering Queenie's stall.

"Words can't describe how I feel right now," I hear Charlie say in a low voice. "It was perfect, so fucking amazingly perfect for our first time." What the fuck! I kick something in my path, causing it to scatter across the walkway. I duck into one of the stalls and plaster my body against the wall in a crouching position.

I hear boots coming toward me. "You hear something, little bird?" Charlie calls out to Jessica.

"No," she answers.

"Huh?" I hear his boots walk away from me back to where he had come from.

"So, when are we going to share our little secret, or do you still want to keep it as a surprise?" he asks her.

I hear her light laugh. "I think the whole point was to keep it as a surprise." Silence, are they kissing? Images of Jessica kissing Charlie form in my head. Charlie who virtually has the exact same face as mine. Images of Jessica straddling Charlie in the corner of the stall, his hands touching her, caressing those perfectly sized breasts and that curvaceous ass.

"How do you think everyone will react?" Charlie asks her.

"I don't know. This is all still very new to me too," she says in a quiet voice. Queenie decides to join in on the conversation.

I hear her sweet laughter. "Aww, you want to be

included," Jessica says to Queenie.

"Nah, I think she wants you to know that everyone will be stunned, at first. I think Aunt Shakti will cry. My mother will definitely cry. Emily is going to be pissed you're holding out on her."

"What makes you think I am holding out on Emily?"

"Wait, she knows?"

"Not all of it. Who do you think came up with the idea?" I just can't right now. Emily, fucking Emily, she just has to be involved with their little hookup. But why tell anyone? Did he mate her? He couldn't have, could he? I think I've had enough. I need to think things through before I confront them. I can't believe Charlie would do this. Just when I thought that I was wrong about Jessica, I was a fool.

Lying in bed, staring at the ceiling, I keep replaying the conversation I overhead over and over in my mind. Charlie is twenty-one; we are not barbarians. While it's not uncommon for some shifters to mate early, it's just not us. It's not who we are, unless it's our true mate. Well that's a different story. Still, maybe I have it all wrong. Instead of blaming Jessica, I should be blaming Charlie. Everyone knows that Charlie is a fuckboy; maybe he's using her. No, as much as I want to think badly about Charlie, that's just not him. He knows better; he knows when he shouldn't cross the line. It has to be Jessica.

I hear footsteps just outside my door. Is she only getting in now? I look at the clock on my nightstand. It's almost four in the morning. Thanks to her, I just realize I haven't slept at all. I want answers. Fuck this lying in bed, trying to pull answers from my bedroom ceiling. Before I can think it through, I'm crashing into Jessica's room.

She looked shocked to see me at first; then she recovers quickly, looking pissed. I don't give her a chance to attack me or speak. I'm on her, grabbing her by the front of her neck and pushing her against the door to her bathroom. She was closing the drapes when I forced my way into her room.

"What the fuck do you think you're doing?" I growl.

"What the hell are you accusing me of this time?" she spits out.

"Everyone said you suffer from insomnia, so you use your time to hook up?" She lifts her hand in an attempt to hit me. I catch it and pin it against the door. I push my weight into her so she can't kick me. Her other tiny hand is gripping my wrist, digging her nails into my skin, but I don't release my grip, even if it stings.

"Answer me! Are you running around fucking the men in my home, in the guard?" Before she can answer me, I lean down and rub my nose against her jaw, down her neck, inhaling. Her nails dig even deeper. I waver for a moment because I don't smell Charlie on her skin. I smell a mixture of different male scents, but there is one that is most fresh on her...Liam.

A burning sensation creeps up the back of my neck. I lean in, tightening my grip on her neck. "You gave Charlie your V-card. Then you ran to others and ended with Liam. Did you lie to Charlie, convincing him that you were a virgin when the truth is you're not one at all?" I pull her forward just a fraction before I slam her back into the door. Tears are streaming down her face. I'm right; she's just like everyone else. Instead of playing me, she's playing my best friend, my cousin, and whoever else she has been with tonight.

I bring my face closer to hers. She winces. I smile. She should be afraid of me. I'm going to teach her a lesson that she will never forget, one that will make her think twice before she ever plays games with anyone else. She might have fooled me twice now, never again. I pull back so I can get a good look at her face, when I catch the sight of a bruise forming on her jaw. The bruise isn't from me. I pull back even further. A bruise is forming under my hand down her neck. Some of them look like bite marks. What the fuck?

An explosion forces my body off Jessica and into the wall. I'm staring up at the ceiling of Jessica's bedroom as a fist comes flying toward my face. I block it; another fist comes at me. I'm not fast enough. It catches me in the eye. I flip over, so I can get to my feet, and a kick lands in my ribs. Ignoring it, I bring myself to my knees. Another explosion crashes into me and I'm flat on my back. Blinding fury consumes me. I push to my feet and fight back, blocking punches, landing punches, throwing out magic. Someone crashes into my middle, and I land on something soft. A cracking noise echoes in the air, and whatever I land on collapses beneath me. Things start to fall around me; I don't let that deter me. I continue to fight back. Two hard bodies fall on top of me, restraining me.

"Enough! What the fuck has gotten into you!" Jeremy's voice pulls me from my rage, just enough for me to comprehend that I'm fighting with my brothers and not Jessica. Hands tighten around my wrists, holding me down, and another hand tightens around my throat.

"I want her out of my house! She's a fucking whore!"

"What the hell are you talking about?" Justin shouts out.

"Ask her! Ask her who she's fucking! She's fucking playing them!"

"Where the hell did you get that idea from?" I start to fight their restraint. I don't want to answer any more of their questions—I need to find her. I need answers.

"Jeeze, calm the fuck down!" Jeremy snarls. When it's clear that I won't be able to get free, I stop fighting against their hold. I swallow a few times and take a couple of deep breaths, trying to get the rage under control.

"Explain to us what the hell you're talking about," Justin barks out in a command.

The twins think I'm insane. They insist that they've been with Jessica for the entire evening and until late at night. But they couldn't confirm nor deny my suspicions of what I overheard.

As far as Liam goes, I'm not sure how to justify when he and Jessica hooked up, only the fact that she smells like him. His scent is all over her, which they just passed off as my being unaware of their friendship. Nothing they said or what I said made any difference, just left the three of us pissed and stomping to our rooms.

# Chapter 45

## MISUNDERSTANDING

### LIAM

November 15, 2014: 3:39 a.m.

I see the lightning in the sky, but I don't get there in time. She is walking back to the house by the time I get to her. Her shirt has been ripped open. Bruises are forming along her jaw line. She has bite marks on her neck, one on her chest, but the marks don't penetrate through her skin. Not that it makes me feel better. I want to kill whoever did this to her. I study her face. There is no emotion there. No tears, no anger, no fear. She refuses to make eye contact with me, keeping her eyes trained on the ground. She smells like Queenie to mask the scent of her attacker. I give her my hoodie to cover her up. She won't talk to me. She won't tell me what happened. I want to shake her. I want to... I want to kiss her. I just hold her in my arms instead and kiss the top of her head. Even then, she doesn't respond to my touch or my murmurs that she is safe, that I have her now. She won't answer me when I ask her who did this to her. The only thing she says is that she wants to get inside. Reluctantly, I let her go.

I watch her go into the house through the back entrance and run around to the back so I can see her window and wait until she flips the light switch three times. Our signal, that she is in the room safe. My signal to her, "I love you," even though she doesn't know what it means. I stay and watch her drapes close, but I can't bring myself to leave the immediate area just yet. So, I send a quick text to the group that I found her. To keep an eye on the road to make sure that the Powers twins' group don't make their way back onto the property. Sixes replies quickly after that they found Wills and Elaine and are escorting them to the main road.

Fuck, did they attack Jessica? Why am I questioning it? It had to be them. I'm going to fucking kill them. Where the hell is Luke? He still hasn't responded to any of the text messages. I check the vicinity twice, taking my time to ensure that there is no one else lingering. I make it around to the kitchen entrance of the mansion when she comes bolting out of the door, breathing hard, crying.

She crashes into me holding on to me, like I'm her lifeline. What the fuck!

She grabs onto my shirt and starts to shake her head. "It's fine, it's fine, just a misunderstanding."

I frown, a misunderstanding? A misunderstanding wouldn't leave her shaking like this. She's scared; I can smell the fear on her. I can smell Luke on her. I push her to the side so I can go into the house. Did he attack her again? He confessed to me what happened on the day he met Jessica for the first time. How they fought, how he took things too far because he was under the misconception of what she was really after. I didn't say anything at the time, only because the twins were there and they reamed his ass, so I just stood there and had their backs. He looked remorseful, and after talking to him about it, I thought it had gotten into his head that she was genuinely looking for a family, a place to belong and nothing more.

I pinch the bridge of my nose. "Jessica, let me go in there."

"No, please, Liam, the twins are with him. It's fine." I raise an eyebrow at her. She's covering for him, the same way she covered for him the first time.

"Then tell me what the hell happened." Her face ashen, the bruises on her face and on her neck darken. At least she's responding to something, but I hate the wild look of fear in her eyes.

"He thinks I gave Charlie my V-card and then met you after."

What the hell is wrong with him? Luke usually seems like a pretty levelheaded guy. Why the hell does he fly off the handle when it comes to Jessica? But after what she has been through, this shit isn't going to sit well with me. This whole time he has been home, ignoring our calls and texts. Was he with Elaine? None of this is making sense. I glance at the door; I should go in there and slap some sense into his head.

Jessica tugs on my shirt, vehemently shaking her head. I need to get her out of here. I need to get her to talk to me, to tell me what the hell happened.

I take Jessica by the hand, and lead her away from the house. I take her to the cliff where I like to sit and overlook the seventh territory. The sun should be rising soon, and it's quite pretty as it touches the territory. There's a large rock that I like to sit on to think. Taking her by the hand, I place her on the rock, and I sit behind her so I can hold her. She doesn't protest.

I won't see her after this, unless I return to visit my family, which I'm still not sure I could. The thought of not seeing my family and friends, not seeing Jessica, finally sinks in. I haven't let myself think about leaving.

What would that look like? If I can return home to visit my family and see Jessica on those occasions. What if she has a boyfriend? I bring her in closer to me. A burning sensation snakes its way into my chest. I don't want her to be with anyone else but me. But she isn't mine.

Hell, I've been trying to keep my distance from her, except the few times when I just couldn't not touch her. I wanted to hold her hand, kiss the top of her head. Hold her in my arms. But I had to constantly remind myself that I couldn't get attached. I also needed to remind myself that Marcus, Dustin, and Boris were sneaking around watching her. Watching me.

Pressing my nose against her hair, I take her in, smell her hair, and kiss her head. I've been longing to do that since she returned, since she was found. I give myself this one last moment before I leave. She stiffens and leans forward. Crap, too much, but I don't pull back. I place my arms on my knees instead of keeping them wrapped around her. If this is my last moment with her, I'll take however much she will let me.

I'm watching her, no longer looking at the sunrise. She's lost in her thoughts. I wish she would tell me who hurt her. I wish she would tell me what's on her mind. I can no longer hear her thoughts, and I hate it. I never needed to talk or ask her questions. She never stopped thinking; she's observant. She would study me all the time, when I sat in the corner of the room. I liked it. I liked that she looked at me more than the others. I liked that even though I rarely spoke to her, she felt the most secure with me. She turns her face; I lift my hand so I can trace her scars. They are lighter now, not as raised as they had been. She winces when she feels my thumb on her skin. I lean forward, and I kiss the scars.

"You're still very beautiful," I whisper against her temple and press my lips there. She turns away, facing back to the front.

"You shouldn't be kissing me or holding me." It feels like she stabs me in the heart, shit.

"Sorry, I didn't mean to—I just..." Crap, I don't know what to say. I pushed too much. She was just attacked. Here I am touching her, holding her, kissing her head.

She shakes her head. "I don't need your girlfriend coming at me too. That's all."

Girlfriend? "I don't have a girlfriend." Leaning forward, I angle my head so I can see her face. She doesn't move to face me.

"She was all over you in town. I saw the lingerie she bought when she was going to come over to meet you tonight." She squeezes her eyes shut. "Oh, gods, and I've been letting you kiss me, and you were with her." She inches forward, but

I wrap my arms around her so she can't move.

"Are you talking about Cassie?" She nods, keeping her eyes closed. I laugh. "She's not my girlfriend. Did you not see me run from her and get into the car as fast as I could to get away? Hell, I haven't been able to live that shit down since it happened."

She shakes her head but still doesn't open her eyes.

"Look at me," I tell her softly, but she doesn't. I lift my hand, placing two fingers under her chin, bringing her face closer to mine. "Look at me, baby, open your eyes." She slowly opens them. I search her eyes. "I want you. I wanted to kiss you every night I sat in your room. I stayed in the corner every night because I couldn't trust myself to not do something stupid to chase you away. I wanted to kiss you that first night when they moved you to the main house, but I didn't because I was afraid."

She blushes. "You don't have to lie to make me feel better," she says and casts her eyes down.

"Make you feel better?"

"I'm ugly, Liam. I was even uglier then, practically bald and broken teeth, face full of scars. I was blind, but I could still see what I looked like."

I growl, "Kiss me right now." She looks up at me, lips slightly parted in shock. Before she can protest any more, I grip her chin between my fingers and thumb and pull her face toward me, crashing my lips into hers. Electricity brushes against my lips. Her tiny hand touches my face, sending sparks and flames up my spine and into my chest. I deepen the kiss, taking advantage of her slightly parted lips.

Fuck, I finally do what I have wanted to do for a long

time. I wish I had done this sooner. I hate that I have to leave tonight. I pull her in closer, not wanting this to end. I can't push it; she's already been through so much. I gently release my hold on her and pull away slowly, so slowly, so I can forever commit this moment to memory.

Her face is flushed, eyes still closed. The tip of her tongue brushes against her lower lips. When she finally opens her eyes, I search them. Gauging her feelings, I don't see fear; I only see sadness and something else I didn't expect to see—love.

My own emotions reflect back at me, through the windows to her soul. She doesn't speak; she just faces forward and leans back into me. I kiss her head, taking another deep breath, so I can commit her smell to memory. I want to tell her I love her, but if I do, it will only make leaving harder for both of us. I can't do that to her. We sit there in silence for several heartbeats. I hold her and cherish her for as long as she lets me.

I lean in closer as if we weren't close enough, but I want to feel every part of her, soak her in as much as I can for what little time I have left. This strange feeling takes over, nostalgia. I want to share it with her.

I point to a large hill on the seventh territory. "See that hill over there?" She nods. "Before my mother died, she would tell me stories about kings and princesses in some foreign place as a bedtime story. The first time, she brought me to a place where we could overlook the seventh territory. She told me to close my eyes and imagine the seventh territory to be a beautiful place full of shifters, a happy place where there was no crime, and Alphas who actually cared about their packs. She made me promise that whenever I found myself in an unhappy or sad situation that I would think about my happy place.

"As life got shittier, I couldn't picture that happy place anymore. Instead, I would pretend that the hill was a large castle surrounded by dragons and ogres who ate shifters." I clear my throat nervously, starting to feel uncomfortable that I'm revealing a silly, vulnerable, part of myself.

She reaches up, places her hand against my face, rubs her thumb along my jawline, and presses her temple against my other cheek, giving me the confidence to continue.

"I would daydream that a princess was locked away in the castle, held against her will as a prisoner. I would show up one day to slay all the dragons and kill the ogres. Once inside, I would fight the evil witch who held the princess captive and use my magic to burn her to a crisp. I would search the entire castle and break the princess free from her prison."

She turns her head slightly to look up at me. "Did you fall in love and live happily ever after?"

I shake my head and smile sadly. "No. You see, in my fantasy the princess had magical powers beyond any one's imagination. I just wanted her to bring my parents back from the dead so we could be a happy family and live in the world my mother imagined. I would repay her by serving as her guard for the rest of my life in gratitude for saving us back."

She drops her hand and twists her body to face me. Her other hand cups my cheek as she searches my face with those clear blue eyes. I shift my gaze away. I don't want to see her sadness or her pity. She slides her hand to the back of my neck and pulls me down, gently placing her lips over mine. Her kiss is sweet and gentle compared to my crushing one earlier. I wrap my arms around her to hold her close.

I break our kiss, and I whisper against her lips, "In all my life, I never once thought I would serve as a guard to an actual princess. I will slay all the dragons and ogres and kill the evil witch with my magic for you. I would protect you and keep you safe for the rest of my life."

She rests her forehead against mine. "I know," she whispers. She pulls back and looks down at my chest. "I wish you weren't leaving." She turns back to face the front and angles her head so I can't see her face. I pull her body flush against mine and wrap my arms around her.

I whisper into her ear, "I don't want to. Leaving you is the last thing I want to do." She doesn't answer, just nods. "Baby, you asked me if I fell in love with the princess and lived happily ever after. I never imagined it would be because guys like me don't know how to fall in love or have a happily ever after. Or I thought that until I met you. I've fallen in love with you, but a happily ever after just isn't in my cards. That's why I need to leave." She wipes her face with the sleeve of my hoodie, and I know she's crying. I want to make promises, to tell her that somehow, I'll figure it out. But those promises would just be lies. I don't make promises I can't keep. I tighten my hold on her, not wanting to let her go.

We just sit there in silence, wishing there was something I could say or do to take away the sadness that envelops us. I can't think of anything that will make it better, and I don't want to make things worse.

Her soft raspy voice breaks through the melancholy. "Can I kiss you one last time before we need to go? Before you leave and I never see you again." I press my face to the side of her head and squeeze my eyes shut. Something inside of me breaks. Emotions I have never allowed myself to feel, couldn't allow myself to feel, flood to the surface. As this wave of suppressed emotion takes over, I can feel the threat of tears build behind my lids, taste them in the back of my throat. I haven't cried for nearly thirteen years, not since that horrible night my mother died. How? How could I have fallen so hard for this tiny, resilient being, full of magic and unwavering love in such a short amount of time? How could I have found her and lose her at the same time?

"Anything you want." My voice is hoarse, raw with emotion, I want to tell her that I love her, tell her that I'll figure out my shit life and come back to her. Instead, I lean back so I can look down at her beautiful face, look into those fucking amazing eyes. I feel my lips tremble. Fear of losing her paralyzes me.

She tilts her chin up, reaches back, curling her tiny hand behind my neck, and pulls me down and presses her lips up to mine. Pushing back all the angst, regret and sadness that filters through my mind, I show her how much I love her by deepening the kiss. I lose myself in her sweet soft lips.

Our spell is finally broken when we have to head back. I hold her hand, loving the way it feels in my own. Gently, I rub the back of her hand with my thumb. Looking down at our entwined fingers, I remember the first time I held her hand in mine the night we brought her back home from Whitemore plantation. That was the moment, that first touch, when I had given her my heart.

# Chapter 46

## CHAOS AND QUESTIONS

### LUKE

#### November 15, 2014: 10 a.m.

My growling stomach forces me out of my room and down to the kitchen. The kitchen is bustling with staff and Aunt Tater ordering them about. They are prepping for tonight's ball. My mother is amongst the many bodies busy working on putting together trays of hors d'oeuvres. I kiss her cheek as I pass her. She smiles at me and pushes away from what she was doing and grabs a plate for me, piling it with food. "Have a good time celebrating your accomplishments," she says as she places the plate of food in front of me. I did until Jessica ruined my mood.

"Yeah, we had a good time hanging out."

"Good." She gives me another small smile. There's a

wistfulness in her eyes. She reaches over and pats my hand.

"Time flew by so fast; I'm going to be sad when you leave to go back to school tomorrow."

"I'll miss you too, Mom." I sit there stiffly, waiting for her to question me about what happened this morning. The questions never come.

"Uh, did you see the twins this morning?"

"Yeah, they left with Jessica a couple of hours ago." She holds up a hand. "Before you start, Charlie went with them, along with Sixes and Emily. She's fine. They will be back before the ceremony." I wasn't going to ask, but good to know. I really don't care what happens to Jessica anymore. I just want her to stay away from my family, from my friend. I lose my appetite, but I force myself to eat it while my mother sits in front of me and I engage in small talk with her. I should be enjoying the moments I have with my mother before I leave. Instead, I'm brooding over Jessica. My mother leaves the table, allowing me to sit there alone with my thoughts. Aunt Tater brings me samples of things to try, like she always did when I was a little boy.

"Joe! I think you need to get Anders. Jessica's room is destroyed. It looks like she was attacked."

Everyone in the kitchen stops what they are doing and turns to my mother. "I would get Nathan to do it, but he's busy right now."

Joe doesn't move from where he's standing. He starts to laugh. "I'm sorry, your majesty. With all the prep work that needed doing this morning, I forgot to inform you that Jessica told me before she left that the twins had discovered some new... abilities sometime early this morning. It was quite catastrophic, but she will clean up her room when returns."

"Clean up her room? Joe, it's destroyed. It really looks like she was under some kind of attack or in a bad fight. There are scorch marks on the carpet and walls.... What exactly can the twins do?"

Joe cracks a smile. "They make things explode."

My mother grimaces. "Of course they can. If it's not one thing, it's another." She huffs and starts to drum her fingers on the kitchen counter. Everyone resumes what they are doing as if this isn't surprising. This staff has been with my family for years; they're loyal and can be trusted. They know my brothers well. "I let them leave the house. I should have them return right away."

Joe holds up his hand. "They were fine when they left. They didn't leave a path of destruction in their wake. I'm sure they'll be fine. I also sent a message to Anders before my attention went elsewhere." My mother lets out a heavy sigh.

"I can straighten out the room, Mom."

She shakes her head. "It's fine. I'll take care of it tomorrow."

"No, really, I can straighten out what I can before I head over to the graduation ceremony."

"Thank you, sweetheart, it really should be your brothers cleaning up that mess." No, it's Jessica who should clean it up. But I don't want my mother to suffer for it.

I haven't seen the twins, Emily, Sixes, or Charlie. The ceremony will be starting shortly. I'm still in a mood, but it has lessened somewhat over the course of the day. Sodie places his hand on my shoulder.

"Can you and I talk in private?" I look at him, and

he doesn't look happy. I wonder if Jessica told him what happened.

"Sure." We move to a more secluded area.

"Hey, what's the deal? You haven't answered your phone or responded to your text after you left the dorms," he says. I start patting myself down, looking for my phone. I'm sure I grabbed it before I left. Then I remembered that I didn't grab it or look at it all.

I give Sodie a look. "Shit, I must have left it at the dorms."

He gives me a dubious look. "No, I don't think so. Stan and I had cleanup duty this morning. Didn't come across it." Where the hell is my phone?

"I guess that explains why you went MIA after you left. Anyways, did you see Jessica at all today?"

"No, I haven't seen her or the twins all day." Not exactly a lie. He nods.

"Your girlfriend and Cassie showed up not too long after you left. They gave us a hell of a time to round them up. Your girlfriend went missing after we tossed her friend off the property. We searched for her but couldn't find her."

I raise an eyebrow at Sodie. "So what, you thought I went MIA because I was with her?"

Sodie shrugs. "I'm not that desperate for pussy," I retort.

He shakes his head. "Nah, that's not it. Liam found Jessica with fucking bruises on her face, neck, and arms. She wouldn't tell him what the hell happened. Charlie insists she didn't look like that when he left her early this morning. He said he left her sometime after midnight, not quite one in the morning." That was around the time I got back into house, but Jessica came in a few hours later. She was probably with

Liam then. "So, when did Liam find her with bruises?"

Sodie frowns. "Close to four a.m." I stare at Sodi. His eyes are narrow, head slightly turned. His breathing is even, heartbeat steady. He's not lying or covering for Liam; he's studying me.

"You think I was the one who attacked Jessica?" He doesn't deny it, and his eye contact doesn't waver, nor does he look guilty.

"We think if Elaine saw Jessica with Charlie and thought it was you, she could have attacked Jessica." Heat starts to rise in my face. "And what exactly were Charlie and Jessica doing to stir up crazy notions in Elaine's head?"

"Look, I may not know your friend or her brother, but something isn't right about those two. I'm sure if she just saw the two of you standing next to each other, she would attack Jessica first and ask questions later." He's not wrong; Elaine is crazy. We all witnessed firsthand how she can fly off the handle. Did Sodie just confirm what I had seen and overheard between Charlie and Jessica? That burning sensation starts to creep up my neck again.

"So, everyone knows about Jessica and Charlie except for me?"

Sodie makes a face. "Don't say it like that, man. It was supposed to be a surprise. Anyway, I healed Jessica, so the bruises are gone. I think it's a good idea we keep a close eye on her tonight. She won't tell us who attacked her. We can't point the finger at Marcus or Dustin. They were locked in their rooms until this morning. Boris is back home. Darwin confirmed it. I haven't spoken to the twins yet. I'm hoping they picked up on something since they can hear Jessica's thoughts."

"If I hear anything, I will let you guys know." Satisfied with my answer, he places his hand on my shoulder and squeezes. He hasn't answered my question if he thought I was the one that attacked Jessica. I did attack her, but I wasn't the one who left all of those bruises.

---

Everyone shows up moments before the ceremony begins. Jessica presents each of us with our guard rings and pin. When she reaches me, I see a glimmer of fear in her eyes, and her hand starts to tremble. Who the hell attacked her? Why won't she tell anyone? Did she really get attacked? When the ceremony is over, we move to the ballroom.

"Luke! You look so handsome!" Elaine yells out, waving me down frantically. She's surrounded by her minions and Wills. I smile at them and allow them to hug me. Elaine tries to go in for a kiss, but I turn my head in time, and her lips land on my cheek.

"Hey, man, you didn't tell us yesterday that beauty is your sister." Wills elbows me in my ribs, which are still tender.

"Nothing to tell. She's not my sister. She's adopted," I say with very little emotion.

Elaine whirls around. "Adopted? Isn't she too old to be adopted? I thought people adopt babies."

I give Elaine a bored look. "Children can be adopted at different ages." What an idiot. She is so self-absorbed, probably worried about what color to paint her nails to match her damn dress.

She places her hands on her hips. "So what the hell does that mean?"

Wills grabs her by the elbow. "Relax, Father is here. Don't make a scene." Wills grimaces and gives me a fake apologetic look. "She's just feeling a little threatened. She's convinced she saw you flirting with her last night." Last night? I think back to my conversation with Sodie.

"No, I said she was flirting with him."

Cassie crosses her arms over her chest. "I thought you said you found Luke and were with him after I got kicked off the property?" Cassie questions Elaine.

Elaine smirks. "Jealous?"

I roll my eyes and turn to leave. I've had enough of their bullshit; I'm not in the mood to correct her. "Oh, baby, you left your phone behind." I turn back to see Elaine holding up my phone. She walks up to me and places it in my hand.

I grab her wrist. "Where the hell did you find my phone?"

She gives me a look that send shivers up my spine, not the good kind. Then she smiles. "Don't worry. I won't tell anyone about our secret spot." She leans in closer. "I left you some pictures to remember me by." I release her wrist and take my phone back. I turn in time to see Jessica and Emily passing us. Emily gives me a disgusted look.

I take an opportunity to turn away, greeting one of the guests. I'm confused as hell, but I don't have time to inquire about Jessica's whereabouts for those missing hours. I'm too busy making small talk and answering questions from our guests. I have to admit as the night wears on, guilt starts to eat away at me. At some point, I let Sodie know that Elaine gave me my phone back, insinuating I left it behind after a secret hookup. He gives my phone to Darwin to check it out and make sure it doesn't have spyware or a tracking device on it. I stay away from Wills and Elaine as much as I can. Cassie still guns for Liam, but he does a good job avoiding her.

I find my father out on the balcony, talking to someone. I've been avoiding him all day, and I hate it. I'm leaving tomorrow, and other than phone calls to check in, I won't be here with him. I'm going to miss him. He sees me approaching and inclines his head, acknowledging me. "If you will excuse me, I would like to take this opportunity to bond with my son," he says to one of our guests. They leave, addressing me and congratulating me on their way out.

My father reaches for me and gives me a big bear hug.

"So proud of you, son, you'll make a great Alpha King one day." I wish he hadn't said that. Guilt and self-loathing consume me. Why does Jessica bring out the worst in me?

My father was always good at reading me. "Want to tell me what's on your mind?" I move to lean on the balcony. I don't know what to tell him. Should I just come clean and tell him what I know about Jessica? I already tried that; he just won't listen. My temper gets the best of me.

"Why did you have to introduce her as your daughter, as my sister?"

"Luke, I thought we were past this. Can you..."

"Nathan." I hear my mother's soft voice behind us. We both turn; Jessica is with her. Great, that is just great. She looks like she is ready to cry.

"Is everything okay?" my father asks them.

"Yes, Jessica is going to play the piano. Alpha Agnus

insisted on it. C'mon, we get front-row seats." My mother turns her head toward me.

"You too, Luke."

Taking a seat next to Liam, I look around for my brothers. "Where are my brothers?" I ask Liam. He doesn't look at me; his eyes are glued to Jessica who is standing next to the piano looking nervous and like she's ready to run at any minute.

"I haven't seen them for a bit," he answers me but doesn't look my way. Sodie leans in from the other side of Liam and whispers something to him that I can't quite catch.

My father takes the stage and introduces Jessica again. She takes the seat at the piano. Her hands are shaking. Everyone is quiet in the ballroom, waiting for her to begin. I hear rude and loud snickering coming from the back. In a quick glance over my shoulder, I see that it's Elaine, and her friends. Liam puts his fingers up to his lips and lets out a whistle. Sodie shouts out and starts clapping. The entire room starts to follow, encouraging her to go on. She's looking at Liam, or is it Sodie? From where I'm sitting, I can't tell.

She closes her eyes and lets out a slow breath. Her fingers begin to move over the keys, smoothly like she's done this a million times before. I have never heard this particular piece that she's playing. There are no music notes in front of her, and her eyes are still closed. My mouth falls open in awe. She's astounding, and I'm transfixed as she moves with the music, and her facial features no longer look taut or scared. Her entire being lights up from within and burns around her so brightly that an ethereal beauty starts to shine.

As her piece comes to an end, she doesn't stop. She goes straight into another song. She stops my heartbeat in its tracks when she opens her mouth and starts to sing. A strong voice, with a slight rasp, it's sexy. If I thought she was transfixing just a few moments ago, I'm enthralled now by everything she gives. I don't move a muscle. I don't think I even breathe.

I'm shocked that something so substantial could come out of that tiny body. I am not the only one she captivated. When I am finally able to take my eyes off her to look around, the entire room stands enraptured by her amazing talent. I want to bottle it up and never let it out of my possession.

She immediately goes into the next song. A guitar sounds from the far end of the stage. Charlie emerges, playing and singing along with her. It is like they are meant for each other the way they blend their different voices together. I hear collective sighs behind me, witnesses of a love story unfolding. They sing one more song together. When it ends, Charlie waves her over. She gets out of her seat, and they hug. The entire ballroom erupts with whistles and cheers. For the first time in my life, I want to be Charlie. I want that perfectly beautiful, tiny girl to look at me in that way. All smiles and blushes, eyes shining with admiration. When the ballroom calms down, Charlie speaks into the microphone.

"I told you our mothers were going to cry." He points at our mothers, who are dabbing their eyes. I immediately think back to the conversation they had in the barn. Sharp pain stabs through my heart. The burn at the back of my neck intensifies. "Last night, Jessica and I sang together for the first time. I was amazed at how well we did, how perfect we sounded even though it was our first time singing together." It's like someone poured a bucket of ice water over my head. I close my eyes.

"We have a little surprise for all of you. This is an original song, that Jessica and I wrote together." Charlie starts to strum his guitar. "Ready, little bird?" I want someone to make me disappear. I did it again. The fear I saw in her eyes at the ceremony when she looked at me now haunts me. The words from the elderly woman in town yesterday ring through my ears.

"*Don't let the influence of others affect you.*" That is exactly what I have done, not once but twice.

My night continues to get worse. After she and Charlie sing their original songs, Jessica announces that she wrote a special song for the guards as a thank-you for everything they have done for her. She uses the words *protect* and *care*. I start to rub my jaw and my face, feeling more uncomfortable than I have ever felt. She motions her arms, shooing Charlie off the stage.

"This song is called 'Armor.' Ready, boys? One, two, three." Music from behind her starts to play. As she sings, the curtains behind her open. Jeremy is playing the drums, and Justin is playing bass. A mixture of Justin and Jeremy's friends and young men from our pack who work on the dairy are in her makeshift band. She sings two verses. A female voice joins her. Someone else has taken over, not once missing a beat, continuing right along.

Jessica says into the mic, "Sammy Cane." Just then Sammy Cane, the winner of the song contest that hit the mainstream a month or two ago, walks over from the end of the stage to the center and sings Jessica's song. Jessica points at our table with a big smile and clasps her hands together in a thank-you. She repeats the same gesture to Charlie and Ean. Another song starts to play. Jessica speaks into the mic.

"I didn't forget about all the badass women in my life too. This one is called 'Unstoppable Women.'" Sammy insists that they sing it together, since it is a song written by Jessica. Jessica sings backup to Sammy Cane. As the song comes to an end, a different beat blends into the end of the song. Sammy Cane introduces The Kittens, a popular girl group.

The lead singer of the group announces in the intro, "The next few songs we're here to sing tonight are originals written by the very beautiful, very talented, your very own Princess Jessica Langhlan." I look over at my mother and Aunt Tater who are jumping up and down. I can't help but laugh at the excitement and huge smiles on their faces. My mother is a huge fan. I look around, and everyone is standing from their seats, clapping, dancing, and smiling. Everyone is happy and enjoying themselves. I feel like absolute shit. I watch Jessica from afar, dancing with Emily and Sixes and a slew of men who now want her attention.

That burning sensation starts up the back of my neck again. "That's called jealousy, Young Alpha Prince." I turn to see Alpha Agnus standing behind me.

"Alpha Agnus, enjoying the ball?" I bow my head in respect to her. Her eyes narrow, and I swear a growl tumbles forth deep from within her chest. I try not to cringe, as guilt roils in the pit of my stomach. Did Jessica tell her about me? How awfully I have treated her. She lifts her cane and whacks me in the abdomen, hard, causing me to pitch slightly forward.

I clear my throat and stand up straight. Beads of sweat start to form over my forehead. If she had hit any lower, she would have would have gotten me in the balls. "Get your shit together, young man. Stop behaving like them." She points her cane to Wills and Elaine. She's right; I'm behaving just like them. Alpha Agnus steps closer.

"Continue to act like them and you will suffer for it." She walks away, leaving me to stare at her retreating back.

I look around the ballroom. I've waited for this day for so long. From the first moment I was allowed to attend a guard ceremony, I couldn't wait to be among the graduating guards. I remembered feeling enamored by the men dressed in their formal wear, taking their oath, vowing to protect my family and me. When Elias and Charlie had their graduating ceremony, I was so proud of them and I couldn't wait for it to be my turn. The moment I have an opportunity to prove that I am worthy to wear the crest of a guard, I let shit from the past influence my feelings and actions toward someone who is very much innocent in everything that has happened to her. I don't deserve to be here.

I should probably leave. I take one last look at the dance floor. Emily and Sixes are dancing with the recruits. Jessica is probably mixed in there, but she's so short I can't see her clearly.

"Hey, man, can we talk?" Wills approaches me from the side. He has a guilty expression on his face. Normally, I would brush him off, but something tells me that this isn't good.

# Chapter 47

## UNFINISHED BUSINESS

### LIAM

#### November 15, 2014: Night of the Ball

I leave the dance floor in search of Luke. I need to talk to him before I leave. I need to make sure that he has his shit straight and doesn't fight with Jessica anymore. I search everywhere for him, even outside of the ballroom, but I can't seem to find him. I find the rest of the recruits and Ean lingering by the balcony entrance.

"You were going to let them threaten you, hold your life over your head?" Emily is loud; her hands are balled into fists at her side. She's standing just a few feet before Jessica. Jessica meets Emily's angry glare and doesn't waver.

I glance at Ean. "What the hell did I miss?"

He has a bored look on his face. "Not exactly sure, but I

think the Greystones had a word with Jessica. Elaine Powers got involved. Emily broke her nose and the other one who had her hooks in you earlier." My spine stiffens, and my palms tingle.

"Are you fucking kidding me?" I can feel the rage building—if Marcus laid a hand on her...

Ean shakes his head and places a hand on my shoulder. "Calm down. This is why we didn't look for you. Uncle Nathan and the leads are handling it. You need to focus on you right now." Focus on me? How the fuck am I supposed to do that when nothing is resolved?

"Yes! If it means protecting all of you, then yes!" Jessica takes a few steps forward, closing the distance between her and Emily. "If it means that I would have to die so that you can live, then yes! You each mean something to someone, your family, to me. My life, my protection, is not worth losing any one of you. I'm just a stray, some poor little girl who was supposed to have died anyway. No one misses me from where I came from. No one cares that I'm not home. There's no missing child reported. No one on the news crying that their little girl has gone missing. I am not worth putting your lives at stake."

I wince at her words. After everything that passed between us this morning, how can she possibly still feel that way?

"You're wrong!" Tears streak down Emily's face. I take a step in closer to Emily. She takes a step closer to Jessica, but before she can say more, Jessica cuts her off.

"I love all of you. If I have to sacrifice my own happiness or my life for all of you, then that's what I am going to do."

"You're an idiot!" Emily bites out.

Jessica makes a face, a cross between irritated and hurt. "I never said I wasn't one."

I have to press my lips together to prevent myself from laughing out loud. I just hadn't expected that to come out of her mouth. Now if that came from Emily, that would be entirely a different story.

Emily doesn't find it amusing and continues on her rant. "No, you're an idiot because you think no one would hurt if something happened to you! How the hell do you think we all felt when you went missing! We didn't just sit around and wait for you to show up. We worried, we cried, we searched, we banded together. We fucking lost sleep. Your mother was devastated—your father was ready to start a war! Anders was going to kill anyone who hurt you. My father, my brothers, Charlie, Uncle Chris, all the guards would have been right there with him. You have no idea how much it affected all of us! Especially me!" She grabs Jessica by the arm and pulls her into a ferocious hug. "You are our fucking family too!"

Jessica buries her face into Emily's shoulder and wraps her arms around her. The emotions resting on everyone's face, the tears welling up in their eyes, say a lot about this girl. This girl that showed up one stormy night and tornadoed her way deep into our hearts. I shake my head, these two girls, so different and yet so similar.

My sister and my girl. She will always be my girl, will always be my family.

Ean rests a large hand on my shoulder, bringing my attention from Jessica. "We got this. Xavier is ready when you are, no rush. All of your belongings are packed in the car."

"Thank you."

"I'm not one for sentiment, but should you change your mind, you will always be welcomed back home. You're our family too."

I crack a thin smile and hold out my hand to him. He looks down at it and frowns. He grips my forearm and pulls me into a manly hug.

"Brother, safe travels, and keep in touch. Don't forget family always has each other's back."

I slap him on the back and nod. Pulling back, I guess it's my time to go. I turn to take one last look at my girl who is still in Emily's arms crying. She lifts her head as if she can sense me looking at her, and I mouth to her, "I love you."

I quickly turn away not waiting for a response, for fear of rejection, fear of tears, fear that I will tear her out of Emily's arms and kiss her senseless until I convince myself that I shouldn't leave.

I still need to find Luke.

I walk down the hall leading to some private quarters or offices away from the ballroom. I hear loud voices.

"Luke, calm down!" It's the Alpha King's commanding tone.

"Calm down?! They threatened her. We can't just let this go!"

"We aren't. However, we must proceed cautiously with the Alpha from Territory Six. Now he has Territory Three involved. Our hands are tied right now."

"This is bullshit. We can't let them get away with this kind of crap, not just because of Jessica, but for everyone else they have hurt. We have to stop them!"

"I can't agree more, but just because I'm the Alpha King,

I can't just execute every asshole that exists. What they do on their own territory is out of my hands."

"This was done on our territory! You're going to stand behind political bullshit!"

Good for Luke. I give him credit for his stance. I'm not sure what I would have done if I were in his shoes. I know what I *want* to do.

I turn to leave knowing that Luke won't exit that room until he gets a satisfactory outcome. I know he will do what's right by Jessica—well, I hope he does. My mind wanders back to when Jessica ran out of the mansion. She looked scared, frantic, even though she tried to reassure me it was something small. I still want to talk to Luke about it, but for now, I'll have to leave it alone.

Maybe I should talk to Sodie before I go. He wasn't on the balcony when I left, so I go in search of him. I find Sodie outside on the phone; he doesn't see me standing in the shadows.

"No! You fucked up not just once but twice! You were supposed to keep her there. How the hell did you let her escape!"

What the hell? Is he referring to Jessica?

"All I know is that when you get into the recruit program, you do your job. There's been a change in plans, and I won't be here like I planned to, which is why you were supposed to take her—"

Take her? Was he part of Jessica's kidnapping? We still didn't figure out what happened or who took her. Hell, there is so much shit unfinished. How can I leave her now? How am I going to keep her safe if I am not here to protect her?

"She's not going to remember you if you see her. She doesn't even remember me."

Remember him? Remember him from her past, before she came here?

"Stop your sniveling. I can't help you—I'm already in enough shit! Well, figure it out. You're on your own. I'm done talking." He pockets his phone.

I retreat further back into the shadows, and I watch him leave. I debate for a few seconds if I should follow him and call him out on his shit. A hand on my shoulder stops me before I can take a step further. I turn, taking a defensive stance.

"Whoa, I didn't mean to startle you." It's Shadow. His hands are out in front of him in a nonthreatening manner.

I relax my stance, just a little, not completely letting my guard down.

He turns his head in the direction Sodie left in. "I think you and I need to have a little talk."

I cock my head to the side, looking in the same direction with just my eyes, not taking my attention completely off him. When he turns back to face me, I wait for him to talk.

"Relax, I heard what you just heard. We should go somewhere a little more private to have our talk. You're going to have to trust me, especially if you want to help me to keep her safe."

# Chapter 48

## I'm Going to Kill Her

### LUKE

March 14, 2025: 9:45 p.m.

Silence takes me out of my trip down memory lane. I look up from the piece of paper in my hand. The models are still on the runway, carrying on. Murmurs are starting to grow louder from the onlookers. Then I hear it, Jessica's voice. She steps out onto the stage. I hear gasps all around me. She's not wearing her mask. She reaches the front of the stage, and it's evident that it's her own voice. There's no music playing in the background, no gimmicks, just her voice. There is no mistaking that she's G. What the hell is she doing? As much as I wanted to see her face when she sang, today, of all days, this isn't the right time. I crush the paper in my hand. I take another look around the venue; guards are posted everywhere. Is this enough? I turn to look at my brothers, and their faces mimic my own thoughts, worry, and anger.

My father's face is turning red, and my mother's eyebrows are arched so high, I swear they could disappear into her hairline. I want to jump onto the stage and throttle her. Why would she take this risk? Dammit! The music starts, she starts to move again, and a male model starts to dance with her, slowly taking off her trench coat. Just before the song comes to an end, her covering is removed, and she isn't wearing anything except for barely there lingerie. Through my peripheral vision, I catch Justin slapping his hands over his eyes. Jeremy claps the sides of his head and squeezes his eyes shut and moans, "Please tell me when this is fucking over!"

I place my hands over my mouth as I snarl, "I'm going to kill her!"

# Chapter 49

## NO TURNING BACK

### JESSICA
### March 14, 2025: 11:11 p.m.

I need some fresh air. Rampant thoughts are running through my head. I feel my throat closing, and it's getting harder to breathe. Doubt starts to settle in my chest, although it's too late for that now. I set everything in motion. There is no turning back. A growl behind me breaks through the silence I sought. A tingling sensation creeps up my neck, a warning sign that I am not quite safe here alone. Shit. I thought I was hidden deep enough in the alleyway that no one could see me. I strain my ears to listen for footsteps; there are none. Either he's flying or he knows how to sneak up on his victim. He isn't exactly trying to sneak up on me. I just can't see too well in the dark. Night blindness thanks to the trauma I endured almost eleven years ago.

I can feel their presence. Soon they'll be on me. I hold my breath and still myself, waiting for the right moment. The soft whisper of rubber brushing against concrete prompts me to move. I swing around with an open palm, intending to strike out and hopefully catch him in the carotid artery, but my arm is blocked. I strike out with my other hand, but that one is blocked too. Large arms extend out to wrap around me. I spin clockwise to get away from my attacker. These stupid heels cause my ankle to wobble.

That's all it takes, a fraction of a second too long. An arm snakes around my waist. I use my elbow to strike up. He grunts as my elbow connects into his hard muscular chest, and his grip slightly loosens. Twisting the opposite way with an open hand, I strike down toward his arm. He releases his hold around my waist to block my strike, catching me by surprise. He's a trained fighter.

Taking advantage of my surprise, his large hand grips me around the throat and slams me into the wall of the building. He presses his large body against mine, so I can't kick or knee him in the junk. He snakes his free arm around my waist, lifting me off the ground so I'm almost level to his height. He brings his face close to mine, so close I can feel his warm breath on my face.

"What the hell are you thinking? Do you have any idea of the potential dangers you're going to face?" His masculine scent surrounds me, clean fresh cologne with an underlying hint of campfire smoke. Liam. He doesn't wait for an answer; his lips crash into mine. His tongue coaxes my lips apart, so he can slide his tongue in against mine.

He deepens the kiss, pressing his hard muscular body further into mine. I lift my arm, opposite to his grip around my neck. Just as quickly, he slides his hand out and grabs my wrist, pinning it above my head. Letting go of my neck, he runs his hand down to my arm on the opposite side and brings it up in the same position, using his body to keep me pinned against the wall. He doesn't stop kissing me and I don't want him to. So I don't slide down the wall; I wrap my legs around his waist, my dress tearing in the process.

He softly moans and grinds his hips into me. He positions both of my wrists into one hand and slides his free hand down the length of my body. My body tingles with electricity and heat. I want more. As if sensing what I want, he breaks our kiss and leans his forehead against mine.

"Baby, you fucking drive me crazy. I don't know if I want to strangle you or fuck you right now."

I reach out with my tongue and sensually lick his bottom lip. "Fuck me," I whisper as I bring my lips closer to his, "Right here, right now." I need it; I need him. He groans and kisses me again, deeper, harder. With his free hand, he pulls my dress up higher and pulls his hips back just enough to slide his hand between my legs.

"I can smell your arousal." Sliding his hand further down, his fingers slipping under my panties, he places one finger between my already slick folds. I tip my head back and moan. "Already so fucking wet." He lets my wrists go. I place my arms around his neck. He grinds his hardened cock into my center. I groan in response. He licks and nips at my neck, slipping another finger into me. "Are these the same panties that every man in the venue has seen you in?"

I push my hips forward, and I bite at his lip. "Yes."

His lip curls into a sneer. He pulls his fingers out, grips my panties in his fist, and tears them off me. My hips jerk forward with the force, and I whimper in response. "Then I don't feel bad about ruining these." He tosses them over his shoulder, igniting them in a burst of flames, and pulls me against him, the material of his pants grinding against my clit.

I want them off; I want him inside of me. I reach down to undo his belt.

He chuckles. "My greedy girl, always my girl," he murmurs against the sensitive spot against my neck.

"Please," I whisper. He slides his hand down my chest, cups my breast, and gently squeezes. I finally manage to open his pants, sliding my hand down to find what I need. Curling my fingers around his thick, hard cock, I slide my hand down, then back up.

"Fuck," he groans and bites down on my hardened nipple through my dress. He readjusts our position, holding me firmly against the wall. I pull my dress up higher to give him more access. He slides the head of his cock against the slit of my opening, torturing me, playing with me, until I'm panting and pleading with him to enter me.

He finally slides himself in, in slow tortuous increments. He pulls back out almost completely; then he slams his hips forward, burying himself deep inside of me. He captures my whimper with an openmouthed kiss. He grinds into me, pushing me further into the wall.

"Do you know how many men must be fucking their mates right now, pretending that they're you?" He pulls back and slams into me again. "How many men are fisting their cocks, wishing it was your pussy wrapped around them?" I moan as he starts to slide in and out of me, slow and deep.

"Please, just fuck me. I can't..." He's torturing me, punishing me, holding back.

He nips at my lip, and he gives a slight laugh. "Oh, baby, I'll give you what you want, but I'm going to punish you first for showing the whole fucking world what is mine." He slowly cants his hips. I try to push forward with my own, but he holds me firmly against the wall.

Nibbling and teasing my lips, he won't even give me his mouth, pulling away every time I try to go in deeper. I dig the heels of my shoes into his ass. He still doesn't give me what I want, what I need.

"Say it, baby, and I will give you what you want." He grinds into me slowly, rolling his hips tortuously slow. I'm gasping at the delicious friction he's creating.

"Please," I whimper. He pulls my strapless dress down, releasing my breast. He slowly licks my nipple. I grip his hair. He teases and licks, giving me just a taste, but not giving in completely.

I growl in frustration. I want him to ravish me, take me hard. He doesn't give me what I want. He licks his way back up my neck, and when he reaches my lips, he smiles, continuing to roll his hips in slow circles. I bite his lip, but he doesn't give in.

"Say it." His jaw is clenched, his chest heaving with desire, with need. His muscles tremble beneath my touch. He's torturing himself too.

I can play this game. Biting down on my bottom lip,

trying to hold back my smile, I rotate my own hips, thrusting against his when he circles back around. His breath hitches; his lips slightly part. I capture his lower lip, sucking it in between my teeth, sliding my hand from his hair down to his neck, to his chest and his abs. I love the way his muscles twitch from my touch through his dress shirt. Reaching down, I pull my dress up higher. I watch for a moment as he slowly glides his hard cock in and out of my pussy.

Inching my hands down lower, I reach my clit. I look up at him through my thickened lashes and massage my clit with my fingers. Leaning my head back against the wall, my eyes roll back, humming as I relish in the pleasure of both his cock and my fingers.

"Fuck," he whispers. I grin up at him because I know I won. He crashes his lips back into mine, thrusting his tongue against my own in time with his thrashing hips. My back slams into the wall with his every move. His large hand cups and squeezes at my breast; his other holds me up.

He breaks our kiss, to suck at the sensitive spot at my neck. He groans as his pace quickens, slamming into me, filling the silence of the alleyway with the sounds of our bodies slamming into each other and our breathy moans.

"Say it, baby." He releases my breast, slides his hand down my arm, and removes my hand over my clit, licking and sucking my fingers before he replaces my arm back around his neck. "Say that you're mine."

Tightening my hold around his neck and his waist, I writhe under him, loving the feel of him, the friction, the pleasure. He hovers his mouth over mine; I finally give him what he wants, whispering against his lips, "Forever."

He slams into me harder, giving me what I want, what I need. My head falls back as I let out a long, gravelly moan. His fingers dig into the back of my thigh. Canting my hips forward, I meet him, thrust for thrust. My clit is throbbing, aching. I need more. I want more. As if knowing just what I need without stopping, he repositions his arms and slides one hand between us and starts to massage my clit with his thumb.

"That's it, baby. I know exactly what you need." He increases his hard penetrating thrusts. I start to tremble. "Fuck, yes, right there. Come for me, baby." He slams into me, again and again, taking my mouth into his.

Lightning flashes behind my eyelids, my body thrums in pleasure, and my pussy starts to throb around his thick length. Dropping my head on to his shoulder, I cry out as a strong wave of ecstasy rips through my core. He follows right behind me, burying his face into the nape of my neck, and lets out his own cry of release. His hips start to lose their rhythm; his merciless pounding slows to short jerky thrusts. He brings his face back up to mine, pressing his lips tenderly against my own.

"I missed you," he murmurs.

# Chapter 50

## SO MANY EMOTIONS

### LIAM

#### March 14, 2025: 10:33 p.m.

I stand there watching the show from afar with a slew of emotions running through me: pride, awe, admiration, and love. Watching Jessica sing as her alter ego 'G,' then watching her as herself walking the runway in her designer clothing. With everything that she has been through these past almost four years, I am so damn proud that she took this leap—that is until she comes out singing without her mask on. Another rush of emotions hits me: fear, anticipation, and jealousy, especially when that male model dances with her and slowly removes her trench coat while she's singing. I want to jump up on the stage and kill him.

What makes it worse are the men I am standing in

between. The one on my left starts to grope his mate, and the one on my right keeps adjusting his pants and starts to breathe hard. I am so close to reaching over to grab him by the throat and telling him that his hard-on is for my girl. If he wants to keep it, he needs to get his shit under control. Sure, there are other models in less clothing than my girl, but I only had eyes for her. I'm a cocky bastard, and my ego is pretty big. I always think everyone is after my girl. Instead of losing my misdirected shit, I continue to stand there with my hands clenched to my sides. Keeping my flurry of emotions under control. That isn't the worse part of the evening. It is the ending, the closing song of the night. Jessica steps out surrounded by other models dressed similarly to what she's wearing, all faux-leather dresses in different styles similar to what a submissive or a dominant would wear. Akiyo steps out alongside her, harmonizing and singing with her. Her song is seductive, powerful, and dangerous, all about women being looked at as submissive, but they have power, they are in control, and fearless. When the backdrop shows a picture of Emily with the words dedicated to Emily Blackguard Larson and the year of her birth and death on the bottom, I know exactly what my girl is doing. She was sending a big fuck-you message to the Resistance. She is done hiding, and if they want her, they need to come get her. Fear and fury grip my gut. I leave my position just as the song ends, intending to seek her out before anyone else finds her.

It has been a long time since I have last seen her. I miss her so fucking much. Just the sight of her alone drives me over the edge. Once she starts to strike out, and I catch her scent, I am done. I can't even finish what I had intended to do, which is get her the fuck out of here and tear her ass apart for what she's just done. Instead, I let my jealousy from earlier and my need for her take over. When she tells me to fuck her, how the hell can I say no? The irrational part of my brain still wants to punish her for putting her life at risk, for torturing me the only way she can when we stay apart for too long. I have her pleading and panting, struggling to get more of what I can only give her. Be damned that we are fucking up against a wall in the middle of an alleyway; I've taken her in worse places when she drives me absolutely crazy. Jessica, being who she is, knows exactly how to turn the tables on me, and I cave, giving her exactly what she wants. But I want it too. We stay there in the alleyway in our postcoital bliss, pressed up against the wall, unmoving, catching our breaths, breathing in each other's scents. I miss her so much. It kills me that I have to stay away from her as long as I do.

She finally breaks the silence between us. "How long are you staying for this time?" I wince at her words. There is no undertone of irritation or sadness. No, Jessica has accepted the way things are between us. She never questions it, never fights it, although sometimes I wish she would. More specifically, my ego needs reassurance that she still wants me as much as I still want her.

I gently kiss her lips. "A couple of days." She nods. I slide out of her, even though I'd rather stay there, but this isn't the time or place. I guide her back down onto her feet. Once she's steady, I cup her face in both of my hands and lean in to kiss her again. When I gaze into her face, there's a hint of sadness and worry that wasn't there just a few seconds ago.

She steps back to adjust her clothing. She won't look at

me now. I start to do the same, except I don't take my eyes from her.

"Talk to me, baby. Tell me what's going on." I step closer to her.

"A lot has happened since I have last seen you, and it's been one hell of a day."

"Okay, so come back with me to the hotel, and I promise we can talk first before I bury myself inside of you for the next forty hours." I'm trying to lighten the mood. I hate seeing her this way, fighting some internal turmoil.

She shakes her head and gently pushes me away. "I'm staying, Liam."

I frown. What? She never turns me away. What the hell is going on? There is no point in trying to fight with her or cajole her into coming with me. I know my girl, but I also know that there is something I can do that might work. I step forward closer this time, and I grab the front of her dress. When I look down at my hands, part of her red bodice is peeking out beneath the fabric of her dress.

"Then I change my mind. I'm going to take you to the hotel, rip this off you, burn it as I did with those panties you were wearing, then bury myself inside of you for the next two days." I pull on the front of her dress, bringing her in closer to me, and grab the nape of her neck, pulling back her head to expose her neck. I lick slowly from the base up to her ear. "You can tell me everything that's been going on as I ravish your body and pump my hard cock in and out of that sweet pussy of yours." I press my body against hers, so she can feel how ready I am to make good on my promise.

Before I can capture her lips between my teeth, she

surprises me by grabbing both of my wrists and tugging them down. I immediately let go. "No, Liam, I'm staying." She says it softly; there is no fight behind her words. I take a step back to allow her some space. I frown down at her. What the hell is going on?

"Okay, then we'll stay." Moving in closer, I reach for her. Before I can wrap my arm around her waist, she steps out of my reach. She avoids looking at me and pretends to be worried about fixing her dress and hair. Slow tendrils of irrational fear start to weave their way up my spine.

We've been here before. She behaved this way when she chose to be with someone else. Not just anyone else, my former best friend. I squeeze my eyes shut, forcing the thought away. My fear of losing her is making me paranoid. Her behavior could have everything to do with what she did tonight.

"Baby, talk to me. Don't push me away. We can stay, or we can go. I don't care. I just want to be with you. I'm here for you." I crane my neck, forcing her to look me in the eyes.

She covers her forehead with a hand. "Liam." She breathes out my name; her face crumples. "Alpha Agnus passed. She has named me as her successor, but that's not the worst part. The seventh territory comes with the title."

I inhale sharply. As a female successor, it's mandatory that they mate to keep their position as Alpha. It's a common tradition but rarely implemented due to the fact there are so few female Alphas named. A young female Alpha like Jessica, especially here in the LS territory, will be forced to mate, or she will be challenged to the death for her position. The Whitemore pack is small; no one will make a big deal if their

Alpha is unmated. No one would really care, but adding the seventh territory into the mix—shifters have fought and died over that territory.

There's a reason why it remains vacant, why it's been protected for years by the Alpha King. Her life is in danger more now than it ever has been.

Thinking back on what she has just done, she did that on purpose. Fear coupled with panic for her starts to grip my chest like a vise. A flurry of different possibilities start to race through my mind. I involuntarily take a step back, feeling like someone punched me in the gut. A flicker of hurt crosses her features. Instantly, I recognize that she thinks I'm rejecting her.

She turns away from me. "I'm staying here."

I take the few steps now separating us, and I grab her arm. "Wait, you didn't give me a chance to…"

"What the hell were you thinking? Exposing yourself like that!" We both turn toward the booming voice coming from the entrance of the alleyway.

Stepping in front of Jessica, I place her behind me. Luke angrily stomps toward us. As he gets closer, his nostrils flare, smelling our recent coupling still lingering in the air. Jessica is trying to come around from behind me, but I reach behind me, gripping her arm to hold her back.

"Is he the one you're with?" he snarls, eyes flaring wide, his face reddening. He's glaring at me now, but I refuse to move from my position.

I look over my shoulder to peer down at Jessica; she's not looking at him. Her cheeks are heated, and she almost looks guilty.

"You selfish bastard, still stringing her along, after all this time?" he spits out. My head jerks back to face him.

This is long overdue. We might have had a small truce between us for Emily, but I'll never forgive him for what he did. He took her from me, and now he's trying to get her back after he screwed things up.

"Stringing her along? We would still be together if it weren't for you!" I grind out.

"Together!" he shouts in more of a statement than a question. "I had nothing to do with what happened. You had an obligation, a responsibility to your pack that you were trying to run from."

I cut off his bullshit. "There are no rules that forbid us from being together. If you want to talk about rules, how about we take a look at the legal documentation that states you're her older adoptive brother, but that hasn't stopped you! As soon as you got rid of me, you slid your way in to make your move."

He closes the space between us, getting in my face. "You had your chance to come back for her, to write to her, call her, text her. You're the one that chose to ghost her. I stood by and watched her fall apart, while she waited for you to return. I'm the one who—"

"Enough!" Jessica shouts, fighting out of my grip and forcing her way between the two of us, pushing us apart.

"Did you tell her why you never came back?" Luke sneers. I give him a low warning growl; he barks out a sharp laugh. "You never told her, didn't you?"

I look down at Jessica. Her hand is on my chest. I can feel the crackling of electricity from her palms, but it's nothing compared to the pain wrapping around my heart.

In a low whispered tone, she asks, "Tell me what?" I don't answer her right away. "Tell me what? Liam!" She's louder now, and I can feel her hand trembling. I just can't bring myself to say it. She turns to look at Luke. Motherfucker, he actually has the balls to look remorseful. "Tell me!" she shouts, sending small electrical shocks onto my chest.

"He's betrothed, Jessica. The invitation," more shocks of electricity shoot from her hands, and he clears his throat, "the invitation to his ceremony is dated for one week from today." She drops her head and both of her hands from our chests.

I don't know what to say. I don't know what to say to fix this. I squeeze my eyes shut as if waiting for the execution to take place.

I hear the clicking of her heels on the pavement. Luke's voice is soft now when he addresses Jessica. "Let me take you home." Of course, he's going to step in and act as her savior. I can't see this. I can't see her leave with him.

"Luke!" she shouts at him. "Stop it, just stop! You're not any better than he is!"

I open my eyes and look at Jessica. She's shoving him away.

"You're mated, or did you forget? You're mated to the most horrible piece-of-shit woman on the planet. Elaine has made my life miserable for years. Now you expect me to—what? Choose you? Choose you after you had chosen her over me?" I look at Luke, who is frozen in what looks like grief and regret.

She whirls around to face me. "I already knew that you

were betrothed, but for some stupid idiotic reason, I still let you in." She takes a step closer, tears now streaking down her face. "So what was this visit for this time, huh? One last goodbye fuck, or a proposal to continue on as your side piece? No, wait!" She snaps her fingers as if she had a great idea. "You weren't planning on saying anything. Just disappear like you always do without a word, leaving me wondering if I will ever see you again. Then maybe show up, just when I finally feel like moving on again."

I grind my teeth and clench my fists at my sides. I can't seem to make the words I need to say come out of my mouth. The pain around my heart intensifies, and yet I can't seem to say a fucking word.

She raises an eyebrow. "I have loved you for ten years, and you have nothing to say?" She looks down at her hands. "That's fine because I have one last thing to say to both of you. I'm done. I'm done playing these games." She lifts her head back up and raises her chin, letting the tears streak down her chin. "I don't choose either one of you. So please, just leave me the fuck alone!" She turns to leave, but I won't let her, not like this.

I can explain; I can and will fix this. I ignore Luke and rush forward to catch her. I hear his footsteps fall behind me, but I don't care at the moment. I need to stop her. She needs to hear what I have to say. I catch up to her, grabbing her by the arm and turning her to face me.

"Please just listen to what I have to say, Jessica. Don't leave. Not like this." Desperate, I grab her face, bring her close to mine, resting my forehead against hers. I can see how much she's hurting, and I want to take it away. She pushes me away, but I won't let her go; she starts to fight me.

Luke grabs me, pulling me from her. I turn on him. Everything, all of this, losing her, started because of him. I land a punch to his face, knocking him back. He comes right back at me with a punch to my ribs and one to my jaw.

A boom sounds over our heads. We both stop mid-fight, covering our ears, which are now ringing.

She walks up to Luke and grabs him by his shirt. "Go home, Luke! I don't want to see you. I don't want you in my life!" He wipes blood from his lips and sneers at her.

"That's a bit hard given the circumstances, don't you think?"

Through gritted teeth, she grinds out, "I've managed to make it work for three years. I'm pretty sure I can make it work for the rest of my life!" She pushes him away.

The anger in his eyes turns to despair as she walks toward me. I move to wrap my arm around her waist.

She steps away and holds up her hand. "Liam, go home. I'm pretty sure your fiancée must be wondering where you are." She glares at me, ice blue eyes that I once likened to the warm sky, now hard and cold. With a warning rumble, she turns with finality and walks out of my life, taking my heart with her again.

# Chapter 51

## Tired of Hiding

### JESSICA

March 31, 2025: Present Day

I start to cry so hard after telling Christian what happened that night after the fashion show. He hands me a box of tissues and sits next to me to console me. I can't stop crying. It has gotten late. Carmen hasn't returned, so he decides to call it a night. After he escorts me back to my room, he reassures me that we can resume the rest of the interview tomorrow morning. I refused to let myself think about Liam after I walked away. It's probably why it hit me so hard talking about it again. I assume by now he's mated. Chris and Elias, with the rest of their family, left for his mating ceremony.

Liam is like a son to Elias, and I can't begrudge him that. The same way I won't let my family choose me over

Luke. I flop myself on my bed, after glaring at the ceiling, angrier at myself than anyone else. I turn over to bury my face in my pillow and start to cry again.

I guess a small part of me hoped that he would have at least called, sent me an email or text, but in typical Liam fashion, it has been radio silence on his end. I let more tears fall. I was so stupid to love him, to foolishly believe that he would have chosen me, fought for me, for us. Help me when I needed him the most.

I feel my bed dip, and a hand pats my head. I turn to my side. Sixes. "That was a rough one."

I wipe my face and nod.

"Why are you doing this?" she asks.

I avoid looking at her by rolling over onto my back. "Time to move on, and since I make crappy choices in men, might as well go through the process like I'm choosing a business partner."

She snorts. "If you're looking for a business partner, then why not choose Jacques? You two have a bunch of businesses together and not to mention you're probably the only person in his life that has stayed by his side as long as you have."

"He's the wrong species," I grumble.

"Well, now you're just being a speciest."

I chuckle, "Is that even a word?"

"Yes, I'm pretty sure it is," she retorts.

"Besides, he doesn't have a pack. I need a mate that will merge packs with mine."

She lets out a raspberry. "Stupid political bullshit."

I turn to my side to face her and rest my head on my hand. "I need to protect my pack. It doesn't matter what I want anymore. The other option is I don't mate, and I get challenged until I die. Or start an all-out war." I blink up at her, waiting for a response, but she doesn't respond. "You think about it and let me know which option is better," I say sarcastically. She lies down beside me, placing an arm behind her head, and continues to stare up at the ceiling deep in thought.

"What about that Henry guy you chat with online?"

I frown at her. "Henry? I don't know Henry that well, and we don't chat online."

She hums. "I see the way your face lights up when he sends a text or an email, and when your computer dings when an instant message comes through."

"He's not real. He's some fantasy that I mostly built up in my head. Besides, I think he's an old guy who's just a little lonely, which is why he spends so much time sending emails and text messages."

She turns her head to look at me and rolls her eyes. "I read some of those texts, remember? And I saw the pictures of his abs and his..." Her face turns red. "Anyway... He did not look nor sound like an old guy."

I roll my eyes. "Can we not talk about Henry?" I ask dryly.

"Let me guess—you went on a destructive warpath and ended things with Henry after everything happened with Liam and Luke."

"No."

"I'm pretty sure that is exactly what happened. You went down the 'I don't deserve anything good or things that make me happy' spiral."

I cross my arms over my chest and pout. "I did not."

She shakes her head. "What am I going to do with you? I thought we worked past all of that."

I let out a sigh. "I still have my moments." I rub my face. I know she's right, but I just don't want to hear it right now. "Can we just not bring this up right now?"

We both continue to stare up at the ceiling as if it will give us an answer to all my problems.

My bedroom door opens. Carmen walks in. When she stands at the foot of my bed, she crosses her arms. "Your parents are adamant that they have the day tomorrow to do their own background checks. I would prefer that things get started tomorrow to keep to the schedule."

I move to stand from the bed. "Well, let's go talk to my parents then." She eyes me suspiciously, as if she thinks I have no sway when it comes to my parents. Smiling, I push past her and head out of the room.

My parents are absolutely livid. The producers threw another five men into the lineup in addition to the eight I was already aware of. I just didn't tell my parents that I knew. Carmen didn't know about the changes that the producers had made, which I think is quite odd, seeing as she is the one in charge and making all the arrangements. The producers said it was last minute and felt it would make for good ratings and were planning on letting Carmen know of the changes tonight.

I insist that even with the changes, we move forward with the meet-and-greet tomorrow evening. The sooner we can get started, the sooner I can just move on with my life and focus on my duties as the Alpha and whatever other disasters will ensue. I assure my parents that all will be fine, and that Anders can do his checks starting tonight and all day tomorrow until the meeting.

Carmen is flipping through her clipboard pages. She returns it to her lap, then places her forearms over it, clasping her hands together before she starts to address me. "I'm sorry we need to continue at this late hour. Thank you for being such a trooper. Life in front of the camera is not always easy. I appreciate you being amenable and a team player. I understand that you have been through quite a lot these past two weeks. Especially with all the unwanted attention from the reporters and paparazzi. I just wanted to check in and see how you're doing with all of that."

Since I revealed myself as both princess and 'G,' the media took off with it. I became an overnight sensation. An anonymous source leaked to the media that I was originally from Territory Two, that I came to live and become adopted by the royal family, and, hours following, that I am the successor for not only the Whitemore territory but the seventh territory. They even had pictures of what I looked like when I was in a coma, proof of how I have been a victim of abuse. The media portrayed my life as if I was a living, breathing, fairytale princess.

As the week passed, the media turned on me, and I went from a real-life Cinderella to a sneaky manipulative evil witch. Past news clips resurfaced, and entertainment series brought up the rumors of my affair with Luke as 'G' and rumors of an affair with Jacques. Questions were raised.

Is she manipulating the royal family for her title? Did she con the old woman Alpha Agnus to name her as the successor? Why did she always wear a mask when she performed as 'G?' Did Young Alpha Prince Luke Langhlan know he was having an affair with his own sister? Was Jessica Langhlan responsible for the terrible breakup between the Young Alpha Prince Luke and Elaine Powers?

Then the accusations started. Princess Jessica Langhlan conned the royal family to adopt her. Sources from Territory Two state that she was a horrible child, a monster. Quotes from artists who wish to remain anonymous states 'G' is difficult to work with. 'G' is almost banned from the music industry for being eccentric. Princess Jessica Langhlan used the royal family's money to buy businesses, businesses where money is not returned to the pack.

Reporters and news channels run with this information, and more rumors and speculations of how I came to be with the royal family are discussed. News channels, magazines, social media, bloggers, you name it, had a field day. Of course, most of it is fake news. No one does a good job at really digging into a story and finding out the truth anymore. Opinions and gossip are misconstrued as fact. People who don't know any better believe it. If it's on the news, it has to be real, right?

When the announcement was made that I'm going to be the star of *A Game of Heart's Desire*, the media went crazy. It has been quite the experience. Gary, my PR guy, handled everything. As much as I dislike him and he dislikes me, I have to hand it to him. He is actually very good at his job. I also have to give props to my lawyer Reggie. He too had a hand in some of this craziness. I need to remember to give them both a raise before this is all over.

"Yes, I have learned over the years that people can be cruel. The media has its own form of bullying. Sometimes I don't really know what is worse—taking a beating or dealing with the aftermath of cruel words and false accusations. I knew when I signed up for the show this is what I would be facing. I just hope that those who really know who I am believe the truth, believe me. That and I hope there are some good journalists out there who know how to do their job and find real information."

Carmen frowns and then narrows her eyes at me. I shake my head and softly laugh at her expression. I have to say—she's pretty good at reading people.

"What? Did that sound too scripted? You can thank my PR guy. He wrote it himself. I've been spewing that shit for the past week. Figured I'd get it in there and you can use the clip somewhere when you edit."

"Can you just be real with me about this whole thing? Your true feelings on all of this. It's a lot, and it can weigh on a person's emotions and mental wellness."

How real does she want me to be? I glance at the camera. Christian was told to take the rest of the night off. My parents are busy with the background checks. It's just Carmen and me.

I let out a long breath. "You want to know what I really think about all of this media crap? The truth is I don't think much about it. It really doesn't bother me, not in the way you think it should."

Her brows raise. "What does that mean?"

I cross my legs, fold my arms in front of me, and grin. "It doesn't bother me because I'm the one who started the media frenzy."

Her eyes widen; then she leans back in her chair. "Can you elaborate on that?"

"Sure. Revealing myself as G wasn't accidental. It was planned. I gave Stancy Danton, the famous gossip journalist, front-row seats to the fashion show. I also gave her the exclusive backstory on Princess Jessica Langhlan. Where or how she got those pictures I'm not sure. I don't even have a copy of those."

Carmen blinks at me as if she's seeing the real me for the first time. "You're the anonymous source?" she asks in disbelief.

I grin. "Yes, Stancy and I discussed at length how we were going to take control of the story before someone else spun it out of control. To get ahead of the gossip and bad press, we brought up old articles, gossip blogs, news clips, and reports. You can thank Beta DuPont for inspiring me to paint that horrible picture of myself. I gave Stancy permission to spread some of the lies Beta DuPont had been spewing. It took off from there. Everyone loves a good story. Everyone loves gossip."

She shakes her head. "You're doing this all for the attention?"

"Yes and no. Yes I'm doing this for the attention, but not in the way you think. I don't need money or fame. I don't need to paint myself as the victim, and I am sure as shit not at all evil or manipulative, well, in most aspects of my life. But I do want the attention."

"Why?"

I think for a moment before I answer. "I want the bastards that have been hunting me for most of my life. The ones who have been hunting magic wielders, using them for sex trafficking, medical experiments, and killing them for no other reason than just being able to wield magic. The ones who forced the white wolf species to become nearly extinct and the survivors to go into hiding." My voice cracks. I swallow down my rage.

"Jessica, what you're doing is putting a target on your back. You can't do this alone. What you're trying to do is start a war—you're just one person. This is not only dangerous. This is committing suicide."

I clench my fist in my lap. "They started this war out of selfishness and greed. And they've been getting away with it for centuries." The threat of tears burns in my eyes. "They could have won if they just focused on killing me. But they didn't—they killed my best friend! They came at my family! I am not going to stop until I take down their leader, even if it means killing myself in the process."

I hold Carmen's gaze, unwilling to back down. If she decides to pack up and abandon ship, then so be it. I will find another way. I've already planted the seeds outside of this show, and I'm not afraid of finding another avenue. She has no idea what I've been doing for the past three years, no idea of what I am truly capable of. No one knows, and I much prefer to keep that part to myself.

Recognizing the determination in my eyes, Carmen nods. "Okay. Okay." She lets out a long breath and looks down at her clipboard. "I think we should take five and probably resume your interview from where you left off with Christian."

I wipe the tears from my face. I hear a click. Turning toward the noise, I see Carmen's hand pull back from the camera.

"I had you figured all wrong, didn't I?"

I don't answer her. She's either on my side or she's with them. I did my research on her, didn't find anything significant, no glaring warnings.

She rests her elbows on the arms of the chair and steeples her hands in front of her mouth. "You're either going to make or break my career, you know that?"

"Figured as much, it's why I asked for you. What I still don't understand is why you chose a career in reality TV when you've won so many awards as an investigative journalist."

She drops her hands away from her face. "I really did underestimate you."

I grin at her. "I told you from the very beginning I'm good at hiding out in the open. You have to when you're one of the last of your kind and you spend your entire life simply trying to stay alive."

# Chapter 52

## THE AFTERBURN

### LUKE

#### March 17, 2025: 9:22 a.m.

After Jessica leaves us in the alley, she disappears for two days. She won't answer her phone. No one knows where she has gone. The media goes crazy; she is the highlight on every news channel. The paparazzi and reporters camp out in front of our home, the Whitemore plantation, and our hotel in the city. My parents, including Anders, are practically climbing the walls with worry. Has she been captured or hurt physically?

I'm sure she harbors some emotional damage after the day she's had. The twins keep trying to reach her. She won't respond to their calls or those of the guards she is especially close to. It is Sixes who finally admits that she knows where she has gone off to and reassures everyone that she is fine.

On the morning of the third day, she finally responds to Jeremy's text and tells him she is on her way home. When she returns, we are all waiting for her in the conference room. Before she can even sit at the table, both my parents, Anders, and the twins lay into her. I sit there quietly. She never once brings up what happened between her and me, and I'm not going to bring it up. Sometimes there are just some things our parents and family don't need to know. If she would just talk to me, I hope I can clarify some things and start over. I want to start over. But for now, there are some other things that need attention first.

Anders slams his fist on the table, grabbing my attention back to the argument. Jessica doesn't back down. I have never seen her like this. She won't back down, even with sound reason. Some part of me feels that she has every right to be upset. There are so many secrets that have been kept from her. These secrets were meant to protect her. Even her becoming mated is designed to protect her. She is so damned stubborn. She honestly believes that she doesn't need a mate. Maybe she doesn't.

She's successful in her own right, independent, and able to protect herself to some extent. But she doesn't understand that she needs a mate and the backing of his pack to not only protect herself but to protect her pack.

I look over to my brothers, who are red-faced. My mother looks like she wants to cry. My father's jaw is tense from grinding his teeth. With palms planted on the table, Jessica is standing and leaning forward, mirroring Anders's stance. Ice crystals are forming around his hands. He looks like he is ready to murder her.

I pinch the bridge of my nose with my index finger and thumb and let out an audible sigh. "Jessica! Knock it off!" I yell. Somehow in the heat of this argument, I think they all forgot I was even sitting here. Jessica is the last one to turn those clear, icy blue eyes on me.

A growl escapes her lips. Fuck it, so much for sweet and soft talks. She always seems to respond better to me when we are fighting anyway.

"Sit your fucking ass down and just listen," I bark out.

Her eyes narrow, and she sneers, "Fuck you! What makes you think that I will listen to anything that you have to say!"

I narrow my eyes right back and lean in over the table. "Stop acting like a brat and sit down!" Thunder rumbles from a distance.

"A brat? You think I'm acting like a brat!"

"As a matter of a fact, I do." I set my jaw in defiance.

"This is my life, Luke. I don't need a man to help me lead a pack!"

"No one said you couldn't. This is about laws and rules. This is about protecting you *and* your pack."

"*I* can protect my pack. I can teach them how to protect themselves if that's what I need to do!"

"Yeah, right. You're going to teach a bunch of geriatrics and pediatrics how to fight in a war, if that's what your stubborn ass brings to them. You out of all of us sitting here know this pack. Haven't you taken a good look at them? There are no young adults, no warriors among them. If an Alpha shows up with his pack and decides to take you out, what about them? What about their lives and their families?

You would rather leave them vulnerable for your own selfish reasons?"

Her spine softens a little; she drops her glare. She knows I'm right. This pack that she acquired are all made up of elderly men and women, too old to learn how to fight, and the younger ones are just too young. I never really understood why there were no teenagers or young adults present in the pack. I just assumed that they all left for school or jobs, but none of them ever returned. I don't even know where the young children have come from. She flops herself back onto her chair with a huff.

"He's right, Jessica," my mother says softly.

"We would never ask you to consider Alpha Agnus's decree if it wasn't for your safety and the safety of your pack," my father adds, rubbing his temples.

"I don't want to be mated," Jessica whispers.

Anders slowly takes his seat. "We know that, but your pack is too small. There are about a couple of hundred shifters in total. Not enough to build a small army, not enough to protect you from what's coming." Jessica leans her forehead on her clasped hands. She closes her eyes, finally listening to what our parents have to say.

I lean back in my seat and place one hand back on the table. Maybe I can turn things around to make it appear like a business transaction, something she may consider. "There is one solution," I say softly. Everyone sitting at the table turns their heads toward me. My eyes are still on Jessica; her eyes remain closed. "If you mate me, we can combine our packs. The Emerald Pack will include the Emerald Guards. This will solve—"

"Are you out of your fucking mind!" she roars. Her eyes fly open just as she rips herself out of her seat. A torrent of wind whips around her hair, and a clap of thunder erupts just above our heads. The twins duck slightly as their heads whip up to look at the ceiling. "I would rather mate with that sexist asshole from Territory Two than mate with you!"

My father stands to his feet and plants his hands on the table. "Enough!" His face is red, his breathing is a little labored, and the veins at his temples are popping out. "There isn't another option, Jessica!"

"There is always another option!" she growls.

"You are already a part of this pack. You are already a part of the guards. This makes good sense! Whatever your reasons are, you have to put them aside and—"

"No! I will not mate with Luke! Not. Now. Not. Ever!"

My heart deflates. Does she hate me so much that she would be willing to mate with a man she has no memory of? A man that could still be possibly involved in what happened to her all those years ago? Anger and jealousy burn in the back of my neck. I stand to argue with her, but my father holds up his hand, stopping me from what I am about to say.

"Jessica, if you will not accept this proposal, then you will mate with the Territory Two Alpha. I have the contract on my desk. He couriered it over just yesterday."

Her face screws up as if she is in pain, and her eyes shine with unshed tears. "No!"

"Then you will accept Luke's proposal."

"No, I will not be his second mate!"

I close my eyes briefly. She still doesn't know the truth. Has she not read my letters?

"You don't have a choice!"

She glares at my father defiantly, tipping her chin up slightly. "I have choices. Everyone has a choice." She turns her icy blue eyes toward me, piercing right through to my heart. I didn't have a choice. I wish she knew that.

"I'm giving you two choices, Jessica. Now choose!" My father's roar should scare anyone, but Jessica shifts her glare back to my father.

"No!"

He stands up, straightening his spine, his Alpha energy building, forcing everyone around him to get out of their seats and take a step back, including myself. Jessica doesn't move; she holds her stance firm, chin still tilted up.

"No!" she answers in a low tone, balling her fists at her side.

"Choose!" The command in his tone is harsh. He pushes out his power even more. I have never seen my father do that before. I have heard of it, but I have never seen it in person, nor have I ever borne the brunt of such power.

Her face cringes, and a tear falls down her cheek. I want to stop him, but an invisible force keeps me planted in my place. The twins take another step back. My mother starts to object, and he holds a hand up to stop her. She drops her chin and bows slightly, taking another step back.

"Choose!" This time, his roar shakes our surroundings.

Jessica lifts her chin higher, and beads of perspiration starts to form on her lip and her hairline. "No!"

My father clenches his hands on his side. "Jessica! You will be mated, and you will choose either Luke or the Territory Two Alpha!" He pushes more of his energy out. My body starts to tremble; it makes me want to fall to my knees. This isn't how I want things to go. I hate that she's being forced to decide. At the same time I'm hoping she chooses me. I close my eyes waiting for her answer.

The air shifts. I open my eyes. I look up at her through my lashes, not able to lift my head from the pressure of my father's influence. I notice a shift in Jessica's eyes and in her posture. I can't really describe it. I have never seen anything like it before.

Her hands start to relax at her side. Her face relaxes. A touch of red flashes deep within her irises, and power starts to emanate from her body until it swirls all around her, pushing my father's own Alpha powers back. My father's eyes widen in surprise. A touch of wind starts to sway her long white-blond locks around her gently. Her body starts to lift off the ground.

"No." Her voice echoes in the room. Her body lifts just a little more, her power pushing harder against my father's. We all fall to our knees, bowing our heads. The air thickens with so much power that it nearly crackles.

My father tips back, falling into his chair.

"If I am going to choose a mate, it will be on my terms. My. Choice." The last word echoes between the walls, giving her voice added layers.

My father's head is bent down, but he doesn't submit easily. "But you will mate." It isn't a question but more of a subdued statement.

"Yes," she concedes.

He nods, and at the same time, their powers retract, giving those of us around them air to breathe. Taking a deep breath, I bring myself back onto my feet, helping one of my brothers to stand.

Jessica's feet are back on the ground. The wind swirling around her ceases. A look of regret crosses her features as she takes in the room, realizing for the first time what she has done. She steps back, shaking her head. Tears start to spill, and before anyone can stop her, she runs out the door.

I start for the door, intending to go after her. With every new situation Jessica has ever been in, a new magic power emerges, and with each new power, she always comes close to freaking out, worried that she will accidentally hurt someone.

"Luke, stop." I brace myself on the frame of the door. "Let her be. She needs time to get her bearings," my father calls out to me.

I turn back as Anders approaches my father. "Are you okay?"

My father waves him off and they both start to laugh. I look around the room. Did I miss something? My brothers look at each other, confusion lining their faces. Glad to know that I'm not the only one missing the joke.

Jeremy elbows Justin. "I think she broke them," he mutters. Justin nods, eyes still wide as Anders and my father continue to laugh.

My mother has her arms crossed over her chest. "Did you have to push her so hard?" she asks pointedly, looking between Anders and my father.

My father sighs. "I know you didn't like it, sweetheart. It was hard for me too." She moves to sit in his lap.

Anders picks up a chair that fell over and sighs as he takes a seat. Running his hand through his hair, he finally speaks. "She knocked you on your ass. I don't know if I am proud as hell or terrified."

Before I could grouch out a question, Jeremy takes his seat and grumbles, "I hate it when you three talk in codes, and we don't know what the hell is going on."

Justin takes the seat next to Jeremy. "What the hell was so funny?"

Warily, I take the seat opposite of everyone. My parents watch Anders, as if waiting for him to answer the twins' questions.

"I needed to test her," my father finally answers. "We knew that she was always a natural Alpha, but your mother felt there was something more to Jessica than just inherited Alpha powers and white wolf magic. In order to test that theory, I took advantage of her heightened emotional state." He starts to shake his head and chuckles a little. "I wasn't expecting that." He looks at my mother, who copies his smile.

I clear my throat. "I don't understand. What the hell did she do? What the hell was that?"

"I told you. A mother knows her child," my mother replies.

Anders finally states, "I'm her fucking biological father, and I didn't see that coming."

"Can you three please just get to the damn point!" Justin bellows.

"Yeah, I'm not getting any younger here," Jeremy chimes in.

"Only a true royal-blooded Alpha can challenge another royal-blooded Alpha, and a young one barely of age just knocked the Alpha King on his ass," my mother answers proudly.

My head snaps up, and I make eye contact with my father. He smiles and nods his head.

"That doesn't make sense. Jessica is adopted," Jeremy grumbles.

"Think about it!" I snap. I watch him intently and wait for the realization to sink in. The twins look at each other, and in unison, they exclaim.

"She's the prophecy!"

"Alpha Agnus, Jessica's biological great-grandmother, is of the original white wolf bloodline. This whole time I thought she acquired her title from her mate who passed away. This entire time she was the true owner of Territory Seven. She was never just any white wolf species. She would have been the queen if she wasn't hiding who she truly was," I explain to the twins.

"If Alpha Agnus was supposed to be the true queen, doesn't that make Anders the rightful king?" Justin asks. I shift my attention to Anders for the answer.

Anders shakes his head, "The history books omitted the fact that the original White Wolf Alpha was a female. Only the women in my family line hold the title of queen and are born with that kind of powerful magic. But not every female…" He trails off and starts to rub his forehead. "Not every female is known to have that kind of power. We were not the line of the direct queen."

Jeremy frowns. "I'm not following."

My father steps in. "Alpha Agnus's mother wasn't the trueborn Alpha Queen. It was supposed to have been her older sister. She was murdered or executed, depending on who tells the story."

"So you mean to tell me that your family line of three, maybe four generations of women never possessed the true Alpha Queen's powers until now?" I ask in disbelief.

Anders looks out the window. "Yes," he answers on a sigh.

"The original queen's declarations are coming to fruition," my father says softly.

Anders nods in response, still looking off in the distance.

"Declarations?" Justin asks

"On the day of her death, she declared she was going to return to take her rightful place as queen and seek revenge for being wronged. For her kind from being wronged. A few decades later, the great war happened. Some say the Resistance had gotten scared and was determined to kill every female in the royal bloodline. Then the prophecy came to be known, and that's when the white hunt actually started," my mother explains.

That means someone knows Ander's secret and knows he has a female child. Silence falls upon us as we ponder over this new revelation.

"Holy crap, Luke, looks like you're out of a job," Jeremy snickers.

Actually, it couldn't be further from the truth. Our bloodline is only meant to hold this space as Royals temporarily. I'm not sure how or when that agreement was made, but it's why the secret of the true ruler of Territory Seven was kept in our family.

My Jessica is the rightful queen, a true Alpha Princess. One would think I should be jealous, considering I have been groomed and prepared for the position of king my entire life. I push my tongue up against the roof of my mouth as if tasting this new reality. I smile because it is not bitter at all. I never really wanted the title, and for some reason, being free of it makes me happy.

"Jessica is the rightful ruler of the entire Luna Solar territory. The true Alpha Queen," I announce to the group.

Anders nods his head slowly as if he is still in disbelief. In a whisper, he says, "That is if history doesn't repeat itself."

# Chapter 53

## I'm Not Giving Up

### LUKE

#### March 17, 2025: 1:32 p.m.

It's been a couple of hours. Jessica hasn't returned to the manor, even though my brothers try to convince me to let her be. I ignore them and set out to look for her anyway. I follow her scent and her tracks and find her sitting on a large boulder just at the cliff's edge overlooking the seventh territory.

She's in a sitting position, legs crossed in front of her with her eyes closed, chin tilted up toward the sun. I take a few steps closer, quietly, so I don't disturb her. I enjoy seeing her like this. Calm, at peace.

Trails of dried tears streak down her face. Is she crying over what had happened a couple of hours ago, or is she crying over him? This was their meeting spot, and I only know that because I saw them coming here together once. I remember the looks on their faces, how happy she seemed, how in love she looked. She never looked at me in that way.

I want to punch something. No, I want to run up to her and shake her and ask, why? Why him and not me? Why can't she love me in the same way that I love her? But I already know the answer to all those questions. Because she did once, even though some part of her held back a little. She loved me. Then fucking Elaine, that manipulative bitch, happened.

My hands tighten in front of me. If she wasn't already rotting in jail for the rest of her life, I would hunt her down myself and kill her. As I look at Jessica one last time, sadness takes over the anger as I lower my fist.

I can't force her to take me back. I can't force her to love me again. Feeling defeated, I turn to leave. A twig snaps under my foot. Shit. Birds fly off the branches from a low-lying tree branch just above me, and bird shit lands on my shoulder. I close my eyes in disgust. Just fucking great! Laughter comes from behind me.

"You think that's funny?" I ask, turning to face her. She covers her mouth, trying to hide her laughter, but it doesn't work. I look down at my shoulder, and I wrinkle my nose. She laughs even harder. I let out a snorting sound. In a few quick strides, I reach her as she stands on the boulder. "You didn't answer my question." She clears her throat, trying hard to stop smiling. I miss that smile.

"Well, I was planning on attacking you for spying on me, but I think the birds did me a solid." She lets out another laugh.

I can't help but smile at her. Then an idea hits me,

narrowing my eyes at her. I lunge forward and grab her by the legs, swinging her upper body over my shoulder, right where the bird shit landed.

"Oh, ewww," she screeches. I chuckle. I think the birds did me a solid too. She pounds my back. "Put me down! Luke!" I slap her ass hard. "Dammit, Luke! Put me down!"

I ignore her and run into the forest. Trees and brush part, making a clear pathway, and I keep running, her tiny fist pummeling my back. Her legs try to kick free from my grasp, but I hold firm.

"Luke, this isn't funny. Put me down!"

When I reach my destination, I set her down on her feet. Roots and vines from the ground surface, encasing themselves around her legs and arms to hold her in place. She tries to fight the bindings, but the hold is too strong for her. I finally have her right where I had always wanted to bring her. This time, she can't run, and she will listen to me.

"Luke, let me go!" I see the fear flash in her eyes. I run my hand down her cheek, and I grip her neck, bringing her forehead to mine. Her breathing quickens, and she struggles just a little more.

"I just want you to listen. I'm not going to hurt you." Her eyes dart back and forth between my own as if she needs confirmation. The roots and vines turn her in the same direction as I turn. I point up to a low-lying tree branch. She looks up with her eyes first. Then her chin tilts up, following her line of vision. She gasps. There is a bit of rope still hanging from the branch, evidence of where we found her.

I pull her into me, and I kiss the top of her head. "It was Queenie who led me here. Something spooked her, and she ran. Every time we got near her, she would run again. She's never behaved that way before. It was almost as if she were leading us directly to you. When she reached this very spot, she started whining, snorting, and stamping on the ground. The rain was getting heavier, and it was starting to storm. A bolt of lightning struck through the sky right above where we were standing right now. When the second flash hit, Queenie reared up, waving her legs around. That's when I saw you hanging from the tree. At first, we didn't know what the hell we were looking at. I brought you down using my magic. I didn't care that I was keeping my magic a secret and that I wasn't alone. The rope was barely hanging on by a few threads. It was easy to break. We couldn't administer CPR because your throat and face were so swollen. I found a knife on the ground, and I used it to make a hole in your throat. Well, you heard the rest of it the other day."

Waving my hand in the air, I let the vines release their hold on her. "Something deep inside of me told me that there was still some spark of life inside of you. Everyone thought I was crazy, but I wasn't going to let you die."

# Chapter 54

## I HATE YOU

### JESSICA

#### March 17, 2025

I search his deep emerald eyes. As bad as things have been between us, I actually still miss looking in them. What am I doing? I break eye contact and push him slightly away. Without looking at him, I ask, "When you say us, you mean the twins and Duck?"

He doesn't answer me right away. There's a brief hesitation when he nods his head. "Anders and Liam were also among us. Queenie nearly ran him down when she ran through the training facility. Liam was with me when Queenie took off." I picture a stern-faced Anders being nearly mowed down by a 1000-pound animal. I smile at the image in my head. When I look back at Luke, he looks sad.

"I'm the reason they sent you to the academy. I took you away from your family." No wonder he was so mad at me when he returned home. In his eyes, I really was a thief. Pushing him out so I can take his place.

He shrugs. "It didn't go down like how you think. When it was brought up, I didn't mind. I wanted to go. I had little control over my magic. I didn't want to accidentally hurt you or anyone else." I frown at his admission. So, if being angry with me had nothing to do with his leaving, why was he so mad at me? I eye him curiously. What the hell happened to him to lose his trust in others? In me, before even meeting me when I was awake. My heart tugs, and an ache for him fills my chest. I want to ask him what happened, and a part of me wants to reach out and soothe his heart. I drop my hand that is reaching out to touch him.

"I need to go. This doesn't change my decision, Luke."

Luke grabs me before I turn around. "Jessica, just wait, please. I—"

I twist around and instantly shift into my wolf form and run through the forest as fast as my four legs will take me. He does this all the time. He gets under my skin and pushes me until I can't stand him. Then he acts all sweet and sincere, like a little lost puppy, making me fall for him. I have to keep reminding myself it's a tactic. Nothing more than manipulation for him to get what he wants.

I'm almost out of the forest when a large, heavy wolf's body rams into me and rolls me to the ground. I instantly get back to my feet. Luke charges after me again. I growl, standing my ground. I take his hit. His body is so much bigger than mine. He rolls me to the ground again; I unleash my canines, and I bite into his shoulder. He lets out a sharp whine. I scratch at him with my claws. He lunges for me again, rolling me onto my back. He lands on me, snarling. I snap my jaws and try to bite anywhere I can sink my teeth into. He places an enormous paw over my head, pinning it to the ground. He uses all of his weight to keep me under him.

"*Damn it, Jessica, stop fighting me!*" His loud booming voice echoes through our mind-link.

"*Get off of me!*" I roar back.

"*Shift!*" he commands. I try to wiggle free, but I can't escape from under him. "*Jessica! Shift, or I will drag you by your nape and tie you to a tree until you come to your senses!*"

Even though I know it's pointless, I continue to wiggle underneath him. I growl out, "*Get off of me!*"

"*Jessica!*" he growls, "*There are fucking paparazzi everywhere. If they see you in your wolf form, it will be all over the damn news!*"

Shit, I forgot about them. I still my body. "*Get off me! If I shift, you're going to crush me!*"

"*Stop fucking with me and just shift! Dammit, Jessica! Now!*" I cringe at the harsh tone ringing in my head. I close my eyes and transition back into my human self. When I slowly open my eyes again, I'm expecting to be face-to-face with Luke's wolf. Instead, his human face and very naked body is hovering above mine.

He's breathing hard, and so am I. Before I can push him off, his lips crash into mine. I want to protest—I should protest. When I open my mouth, his tongue invades the open space. Caressing my tongue with his. His hand leaves my head and starts to skim down my body, leaving tiny electrical pricks ghosting across my skin. I feel his erection pressing against my thigh. He pulls back slightly, nipping at my lips.

"Tell me you don't feel this," he whispers against my lips as he glides his hand back up to my breast. "Tell me you don't want me as much as I want you." He doesn't give me a chance to respond as his lips press back into my mine. His hand roams back down, bringing my leg up to hook around his waist. "You can't lie to me; I can smell your arousal. I can feel that there is still something between us in your kisses." He lifts his body just a little from mine, leaving enough space for the cool breeze to ghost against my skin.

Although the movement was brief, my body instantly misses his warmth. I miss him, his scent, his kisses, his touch. I curl my hands around his biceps. In my head, I am going to push him from me, but my traitorous body pulls him back down to me instead. I start to kiss him back, allowing his tongue to dip into my mouth deeper. I feel his smile form against my lips. He moans as my hips roll up, pressing into his erection.

He pulls back again, searching my eyes. "Don't fuck with me, Jessica. I don't think my heart can take you leaving me again."

I turn my head away. "I can't be with you." A look of hurt crosses his face, and he slams his fist into the ground near my head. Jolted by his sudden violent reaction, I push against him and try to roll myself out from under him. He grabs me back and pins me down with his weight.

"Damn it, Jessica, I am trying to tell you that you're my true mate. I didn't understand it back then. I was too mad at the world and untrusting. I know that I fucked up, and I know that the things that happened between the two of us hurt. They hurt me too. I was just as much a victim of what happened. This isn't some manipulation tactic; this isn't me trying to get revenge or hurt you. I really am trying to just tell you—"

"Please don't say it, just don't." I struggle under him, trying to get free. I don't want to cry anymore, but tears start to fall.

He leans his face in close. "I'm in love with you, and I have been trying for years to get you to see that." I squeeze my eyes shut. "Look at me—please just look at me," he whispers against my ear.

"You can't be my true mate. What you felt, what you think you feel isn't that."

He lifts his body. "Open your fucking eyes and look at me!"

I force myself to open my eyes. "You can't be my true mate…because I don't feel it." I lift my eyes to meet his.

"Stop lying to me!" he spits out and moves off me. "You still want him, don't you?" He swings his arm, punching the air. "How can you fucking still want him? How can you forgive him for leaving you, for lying to you? But you can't forgive me!"

I sit up from the ground, and I cross my arms to cover myself. I start to shake my head, tears falling freely now. "This isn't about Liam. This has everything to do with me!" I shout at him. I move to stand. I need to leave.

He reaches down, grabs me, and starts to shake me. "I am just as much a victim in all of this," he repeats.

"A victim?! You want to call yourself a victim?" I twist and turn, freeing myself of his grip. Once free, I push him, anger getting the best of me. I start to laugh cruelly. "You were in her bed, naked!" I push him again, but he regains his stance. "She answered the door naked with your mate mark, fresh and dripping with blood!" I scream, and I punch him so hard he falls back, not before he reaches out and grabs my arm, taking me down with him. "You didn't just fuck her! You mated her! I hate you!"

Luke wraps his arm around my waist and flips me on my back. He grabs my hands as I try to land another punch and holds both of them above my head. But he doesn't say anything. He has me pinned under him. Years of hurt and anger that I have been holding back for so long have taken over, and I want to hurt him the same way he hurt me.

"I hate you for making me love you! I hate you for breaking my heart! I hate you because you mated her! I hate her for taking my best friend away from me, and I hate you for letting her!" I narrow my eyes, hating the tears that freely fall from my eyes. "I. Hate. You." He presses his face in the crook of my neck, and drops of moisture trickle down my skin. We both stay that way, no longer fighting, breathing hard, crying.

In a gravelly tone, he whispers against my ear, "I lost her too, Jessica, and I hate myself every day knowing that I lost both of you, and there was nothing I could do to stop it from happening." He pulls me over so that I am on top of him now. I take advantage of his movements, and I push off him and run back to the manor.

Once inside my room, I lean up against the door, catching my breath, and force the sobs escaping my throat to stop. I immediately start packing my things. I need to leave. I know Luke, and even after everything I just said, he's not going to stop. We're going to just fight more or end up fucking, then fight again.

My door crashes open. Luke stalks over to me. He has sweatpants on, bastard. "We aren't done talking!"

"I have nothing more to say, so get out of my room!" He grabs my arm, pulling me against him. "Just stop!" I yell at him, yanking my arm out of his grip.

He runs his hands through his hair, face full of rage. "I can't keep doing this!" he shouts.

"Good! Now get out!" I shout back. His jaw tenses; his hands fists at his sides. I reach into my bag and pull out a manila envelope. I had planned to leave this for him when I left. I guess it's now or never.

"Here," I tell him and shove the envelope into his chest. He catches it before it falls to the floor. I continue to pack my things and start looking for some clothing.

"What the hell is this?" he asks, taking the documents out and looking them over. In the two days that I had been gone, I had collected documents of our businesses and signed everything over to him. "What the fuck is this!" he roars, rage evident in his tone.

Without looking at him, I answer him quietly, "I meant what I said."

He looks up from the document to me. "I did this for you!"

"I know, and that is why I am giving it to you."

"I don't want this without you!" His voice cracks, heavy with emotion.

"I want you to take it," I say so softly that it is barely

audible. I can't look at him. If I do, I might change my mind, and I can't afford to do that.

He shakes the document in his hands. "You hate me so much that you're willing to just give all of this away?" I don't answer him. He throws the documents onto my bed. "Sell it! Sell all of it!" I shake my head. He turns to leave my room.

He stops just before the door, just as he had done a few days ago. "I'm done, Jessica. It's obvious there's no in between for us. I tried, I really have tried, but you won't hear me out." I can feel the heartbreak in his words. My mouth opens, but I can't seem to form the words I need to say. I close it. There is no point in twisting the metaphorical knife any further.

His energy shifts. I can feel the push of his Alpha magic against my skin. "You leave me no choice. After that shit you pulled earlier today, disrespecting my. Family. My. Father! And now. Me!" He roars, clenching his jaw, his lip slightly curling in a sneer. "I don't want you anywhere near my family."

I taste the tears burning in the back of my throat, threatening to fall again. I lower my head in submission. I have to take it. If I continue to fight him, it won't fix anything. It will only lead to more fighting. I look up at him through my damp lashes, his face contorting even further with rage as he takes in my stance.

"I want you out of my house, I want you off of my territory, and I never want to see you again!" His last word holds such force that the windows shake, and he punches the door off its hinges.

I crumble to my knees and start to sob.

# Chapter 55

## It Had to Be Done

### LUKE

#### March 17, 2025: 3:45 p.m.

I watch from my bedroom window as Jessica gets into her new SUV, taking the pieces of my broken heart with her. I grip the windowsill to prevent myself from running after her as I watch the SUV drive through the gate. I commit to my decision, and as much as it pains me, I must stick with it. What other choice do I have? She hates me. She fucking hates me. I hear footsteps approaching from down the hall. I don't need to turn around and see who it is.

"It's done," I tell them, just as I hear them walk into my room.

"I know. We all heard." My father sighs. "I told you I would take care of it."

I shake my head. "She needs you and Mom. It's better this way." To extricate her from the pack and remove the ones she loves in her life would destroy her. I don't want that. I also can't see my mom going through it. My mother cried when my father and Anders made the decision to remove her from the pack. It wasn't to hurt either one of them but to force Jessica to understand her situation. She also needs to be on her own, to lead her pack and rebuild it.

Gentle hands rest on my shoulders. "You were protecting me, weren't you?" my mother asks.

I shake my head. "I can assure you it was purely selfish."

She scoffs. "I know a liar when I see one." She leans in closer. "It's my superpower, remember?"

My hands tremble, so I grip the windowsill tighter. "I finally told her the truth, that she's my true mate. She..." I pause, trying to hold back the emotion. "She gave me the businesses that we built together." I sniff; her handing me those papers ripped my beating heart out. It was a piece of finality, one I wasn't prepared for. She ended everything about us. She submitted to my hurt and rage and didn't even fight back. She was truly done with me.

"She signed over the hotel business to you?" I nod, and my mother releases my shoulder. "Nathan?"

"Just the hotel business?" he asks.

"No, all of them—the clubs and restaurants. She signed over everything to me."

"Where are the documents?" my mother asks. I shrug. I threw them on her bed, hoping she would take them back. She could have taken them with her, destroyed them, I hope.

"I told her to sell them."

My mother leaves my room and returns with the envelope. "Nathan! She left everything to Luke and the twins."

"What?" we ask in unison. I turn to face my parents.

"It's all right here. All her businesses with the boys. She gave it all to them!" My father grabs the papers and looks them over.

"Luke, this is more than your joint business. She even left you and the twins her personal businesses." What the hell is she doing?

My mother cried, "Nathan, she's going after the Resistance."

# Chapter 56

## AWAKENING THE ALPHA QUEEN

### JESSICA

March 17, 2025: 5:45 p.m.

When Joe and Xavier get out of the car, I see them pulling several bags out from the back of the SUV. "What's all of this?" I ask Joe.

"Sixes will make arrangements to have the rest of your things delivered." I look around at the bags. Those are not mine.

"Who do these bags belong to?"

Xavier nonchalantly continues to unload the car. "Us," he answers. I look between Joe and Xavier.

"Your bags?"

Xavier nods.

"I don't understand."

"We no longer work for the royal family," Joe fills in, not bothering to elaborate further.

"No, you can't do that. They need you. You've been there for years."

Joe shakes his head. "Our loyalties lie with Anders. You are Anders's daughter, so our loyalties lie with you."

"Joe, I can't ask that of you."

Xavier shakes his head. Before he can protest, a voice speaks up from behind me.

"You didn't have to," Anders says. "They came here on their own. Why don't the two of you go find a place to take your belongings and I'll meet you in front of the pack hall?" he says to the two men.

"What are you doing here?" I ask Anders. I didn't even know he wasn't in the manor.

He shrugs. "I moved back home." His eyes look down. "I wanted to live near you. I hope that's okay."

I tsk. "This place is more yours than mine. You shouldn't feel like you need to ask."

"It's not mine. It's yours. It was left to you. And thank you for letting me live here. I needed a place to stay now that I no longer work for the Emerald guard."

My eyes widen with shock. "What the hell are you talking about! Anders, you cannot leave the guard! They need you!"

"My daughter needs me more, and besides that, I hoped that the Alpha Princess would hire me as her new lead guard." Now I'm floored. Did I just enter a crazy town?

"Have you lost your mind? Anders, there are no guards to lead! Were you not involved in that argument we just had several hours ago!"

He chuckles. "Okay, maybe I was getting ahead of myself just a little. Why don't you come with me?" He motions with his finger for me to follow him. Narrowing my eyes, I reluctantly do.

As we get near the pack hall, I see the entire Whitemore pack and at least twenty-five guards standing among them, including Sixes. I look at her. *"What's happening?"* I ask her through our link.

She smiles, *"You'll see,"* but doesn't offer me more information.

Miller walks away from the pack and approaches me. He places his hand behind my back and hurries me along until I'm standing directly in front of everyone. He raises his hand, getting everyone's attention. Everyone quiets down. Some of the pack members are hushing the young children.

"Princess Jessica G. Langhlan," Miller boasts to the group, "you have been named as successor by our Alpha Agnus Whitemore, the sixth-generation Alpha of the original Quartz Pack, ruler of the seventh territory. Do you accept this position?"

I scan the crowd before me. I look like a hot mess. I'm wearing an oversized hoodie and yoga pants, not to mention I just spent the last two hours bawling my eyes out. Who in their right mind would want an Alpha who looks like they can't keep their shit together? We're doing this, now? Couldn't Anders have just let me use the bathroom first?

*"Can you stop overthinking everything and just say yes?"* Odyssey practically shouts in my head. I look among the guards and find him standing with the pack.

*"What are you doing here?"*

"*Answer the question.*"

"*Fine!*" I clear my throat and look at Miller. "Yes." He smiles at me and nods his head in approval.

"Is there anyone here who disagrees with this decision made by our former Alpha? State your concerns now and rise up to a challenge."

I swallow. A challenge? I look at Anders, but he just stares ahead. After a few moments of silence, no one speaks up, and no one issues a challenge.

Miller continues. "Very well, if there will be no challenges, for those of you who do not want to live under the leadership of the Alpha Princess Jessica Langhlan, you may choose to leave and live out the remainder of your existence without a pack. Do so now."

No one moves; not even the children make a peep. I continue to look around me.

"Very good, now swear your allegiance to your new Alpha Princess Jessica G. Langhlan." Everyone, from the entire pack to the guards, including Anders, Sixes and Miller, fall to one knee and place their right hand over their hearts. In unison, they all recite:

"We swear to you our loyalty, faith, and allegiance for as long as you shall live." They bow their heads in submission. My heart swells with unwavering loyalty and love. A pulsing and hum of electricity starts to take place from my solar plexus. With the next pulse, a white light vertically shoots up through my core, lifting me slightly off the ground. I take a deep breath and close my eyes, allowing the light to consume me.

Alpha Agnus's voice, inside my head, starts to speak,

"Welcome home, Alpha Queen of the Lunar Solar Realm, Alpha to the white wolf shifters. Make us proud."

Behind my eyelids, I can sense the white light bursting out through my hands, and my feet, continuing up and out through my crown. A beacon of light shoots up to the sky.

A clap of thunder erupts, and I can see flashes of lightning behind my eyelids. Raindrops splash on my face as more flashes of lightning set off, and the loud booming claps of thunder continue. The wind starts to whip around my body, pushing me up higher until I hover above the pack and slowly turn into a small circle.

A wave of varying emotions fill my soul. Memories of generations past fill my head. Love, trust, faith, betrayal, heartache, pain and death. So much death, so much loss, so much pain. I make a silent promise that I will take down the leader of the Resistance. The suffering will end with me. A rumbling from the distance sounds, and the ground starts to shake. The raindrops increase, hardening as they pelt against my skin and ground.

The wind picks up its speed, spinning me faster. The thunder lets go its muffled whispers and intensifies in booming depth. Lightning creeps in closer, streaking across the sky. Then everything comes to a full halt.

My feet return to the ground. The sun shines intensely bright, blessing everything under its warm rays. The harsh winds return to a gentle breeze, caressing my skin and filling the air with a sweet floral scent. Birds start to sing as if in approval. I drop my arms back to my side and slowly open my eyes.

Wide eyes stare back at me from the onlookers.

I look at Odyssey. *"Did that just really happen?"*

He looks bewildered and unsure of how to answer me. *"That shit really fucking happened."* I look around again; everyone is still in a kneeling position.

I clear my throat. "Is everyone okay?" I wince, waiting for them to stand to their feet and run for the hills. I see heads start to turn, back and forth, checking on their neighbors and the children within their clutches. No one stands up.

Miller clears his throat getting my attention. "Princess, uh, Alpha Princess, you need to tell us to stand."

"Oh, uh." I think back to the Alpha King, how he commands the room when everyone is around him at conferences and meetings. Okay, I can do this. I square my shoulders, lift my chin slightly, not too much, and say, "You may rise." I wince at the shakiness in my voice. Everyone stands. Miller announces that dinner will take place in the pack hall tonight.

Anders places a hand on my shoulder. "Don't worry. You will get used to it. Think of it like you're bossing around a board member in a meeting room."

"I don't boss anyone around," I reply.

"No, but when it comes to business, you have command. I've seen it. You're a natural. This too will come to you naturally." I shrug. "Speaking of business." He walks toward the twenty-five guards, twenty-seven if you include Xavier and Joe. "Your new pack members." He waves toward them. I raise my eyebrows. "Alpha Princess, these men and women have voluntarily joined your pack, sworn their allegiance to you, and would like a position among the pack as your guards."

"Didn't you swear your allegiance to the Emerald Pack as guards?"

Odyssey and Alexis step forward. "We resigned," Alexis offers.

"I can't let you do that."

Anders puts up a hand to stop me. "There are over 300 guards in the Emerald Pack and then some, some training now as we speak. This was their choice. These are the ladies and gentlemen that could be here today. As time goes on, I am sure there will be more." Sixes is among them. I frown and slowly nod my head as if I need to think things over. I place my hand on Anders's arm.

"As a former lead guard, who among here do you think will qualify as the next lead guard?" I ask him. He quirks an eyebrow at me.

Alexis chokes in shock, startled by my question.

*"What are you doing?"* Odyssey exclaims in my head.

*"Relax, I'm just messing with him."*

*"Please don't. He's still my boss, and I've seen him pissed."*

"Oh, I thought you were retiring, no?" I chuckle. Wrapping my arm around Anders's arm, we shift back to face the former guards of the Emerald Pack together. "This, ladies and gentlemen, is the Quartz Pack lead guard, Anders Knight. He will oversee your positions within the guard." He lifts his chin, and the guards, with a fisted right hand placed over their hearts, dip their heads in respect, "Shall I leave you to it then?" He nods. Before I fully turn away, I think of something. "Oh, I have one request. I need one of your guards to be my assistant."

Anders smiles. "Sixes will be your assistant, Joe will be your head of the household, Xavier will be your driver. Odyssey will be the second in command. Alexis the third in command. Does that meet with your approval?"

I smile. "It does." I look over the group. "Thank you. You have no idea how much this means to me."

After the festivities, I return home. The house looks exactly the same as it had when I left it a few days ago. Except now it's mine. I don't know how much money is in the pack account or if there is enough money to accommodate all the new pack members. So, I go to the office to look over the business accounts and anything else I need to learn about my new pack.

I've been at this for hours; pages and numbers start to blur. A knock at the door startles me. The door slowly opens.

It's Sixes. She winces. "Don't tell me you were up all night working on pack business."

I look back down at the papers in front of me. "Then I won't."

She wrinkles her nose. "Are you going over the financials?"

"Yeah, I honestly thought I was walking into a stable but moderately low financial situation. But..." She comes around the desk to look at my numbers, which I transferred to a software program that Justin designed.

She lets out a whistle. "I did not see that coming."

"Me either." She cocks her head to the side and starts to tap her thumb against her leg. I can see the wheels turning in her head.

"Have you broken down the numbers? What you can use

for housing, repairs, pack allowances, the school." I click a button and show it to her.

She lets out a low short laugh. "Damn."

"What do you think?" I ask her.

She lets out a breath. "I think we should upgrade the place. There is more than enough money for it. I think the pack will appreciate it. Build new homes for the existing pack members with larger families and fix the current ones for the new single members. Build a training facility for the guards. Maybe even upgrade the tea plantation, work on marketing. With that kind of money, the opportunities are endless."

"I was thinking the same thing. I also have the entire seventh territory. We can expand into that area if I need to, even look at other business opportunities for the pack."

She bobs her head up and down as if listening to a beat that only she can hear.

"It's like a blank canvas. I even put money aside for investments, and I..." I was going to say that I would talk to Justin to start a stock market portfolio, but then I remember I'm not supposed to talk to him anymore. "I also have my own money that I can use to expand into other business ventures if I need to."

Sixes studies me for a bit. "Yeah, we can sit down and work on a plan. I think we should start with upgrading the place and finding you a mate."

I don't want to fight about the mate thing anymore, so I just agree with her.

"Oh shoot! I forgot. The whole reason I came in here was to let you know that you have a guest. He's waiting in the dining room."

"He?"

"Yeah, so go get ready, and please wear something presentable."

I wrinkle my nose at her. "Seriously, this is my home."

She rolls her eyes. "Yes, but you are an Alpha now. You know what? Forget it. I'm just going to lay out some clothes for you to wear. I planned to send your things down, so they should arrive today." She's out the door before I can say anything.

When I finally make my way to the dining room, freshly showered and dressed like an Alpha, according to Sixes, Gary, my parents' public relations guy, sits at the table. I had to get dressed up for him, really? He's frowning down at his cup.

"Good morning, Gary. Is there something wrong with your coffee?"

He doesn't even bother to look up at me and grumbles into his cup, "I'm just sitting here wondering why I'm drinking coffee out of a teacup."

I sigh and plop down in a chair opposite him. "I just got here, Gary. The previous Alpha didn't drink coffee."

"She could have at least had a cup for the coffee drinkers that stopped by."

"Except she never offered it. Why are you here, Gary?"

"I'm here at the request of your parents. I was told to meet them here. I guess I got here early. You should try it sometimes." Begrudgingly, he takes a sip of his coffee.

"Gary, if you continue to talk down to me like I'm some prepubescent, lazy-ass teenager, I'm going to hand you a paper cup with your coffee in it and shove—"

"Sweetheart!" My mother's voice rings through the dining room. "How was your first night in your territory?"

I narrow my eyes at Gary and stand from my chair to greet my mother. She brings me in for a hug.

"Good, everything has gone well. I didn't expect to see you," I tell her.

She kisses my cheek. "Don't worry about Luke."

"Gary, you're early as usual. Thank you for coming," my father says as he walks in. I glance behind my father. There are no guards. "I told them to take a break," he explains. Then he hugs me. "Plenty of guards to go around."

"The paparazzi weren't a problem?"

"Nah, I'm a recluse Alpha King, too boring for them to waste their time on."

Gary clears his throat. "I'm happy for this little reunion, but time is of the essence here, and I need to have some things in order to get the media under control."

---

"Wait, you want me to do what?" I shout in surprise mostly.

"Well, you agreed to move forward with finding a mate, so we thought this would be a suitable alternative," my mother says while she sips her tea.

"So, the three of you or four of you, if you're including Gary, get to choose random men that I go on dates with, and I pick one and mate them before midnight on my birthday?"

"It's not random men," Anders grits out.

"We know them and approve of them," my father adds.

Gary shrugs. "You have had two proposals and have

shut both of them down, so I think your parents' alternative is good."

"First of all, Gary, the betrothal contract is null and void according to my lawyer because, for one, there is no birth certificate of a Grit DuPont. Grit DuPont was never born or existed on the LS or anywhere else in the world, and two, they were dumb enough to fake a death certificate. So in either case, Grit DuPont does not exist. I am not obligated to fulfill that contract. As far as Luke goes, that's personal and none of your business."

"Sorry to burst your pink twinkling bubble, princess. There is a shitshow of crap going on just outside the territory boundary. Your life is my business, especially if you need me to clean up the shit that you started," he sneers.

Fuck him, pink princess bubble. I'll give him a pink princess bubble! "You know what, Gary, since you hate your job so much, why don't we just save you some time and paste my crappy life on some reality TV show for a tell-all? While we're at it, just throw in the men I need to meet so the entire world can see just how incapable I am of choosing a mate for myself! At least that way, you don't have to lift a finger and do what you are actually getting paid to do."

This time, Gary frowns and then leans back in his chair. "Actually, that might work. I can make the arrangements."

"No, Gary! I was sarcastically suggesting that I want to get rid of your ass!"

But he isn't listening. Then he laughs, snapping his fingers and wagging his index finger at me. "I'll be right back. Let me make some phone calls." He leaps out of his chair and exits out through the back door.

"You're fired!" I yell at him, even though I'm pretty sure he can't hear me.

My parents laugh. "I know he has an attitude, little one, but he's actually great at his job, or I wouldn't have kept him around for as long as I have," my father says.

"An attitude? More like a personality disorder," I scoff.

Gary doesn't take long to return from the phone calls he made. He crashes through the back door with a bag hitched over his shoulder and a huge smile from ear to ear.

"What the hell is that?" I ask, gesturing with my hand to his bag.

"You, Alpha Princess, are going to be the star attraction on the popular reality TV's dating show, *A Game of Heart's Desire*!" he exclaims, clapping his hands together.

"The hell I am!" I shout at him, standing from my chair.

He laughs at me, "Oh yes you are. This was, after all, your suggestion." He waggles his eyebrows. "And whether you like it or not, you and I will be spending quite a bit of time together. Filming starts in less than two weeks."

# ACKNOWLEDGEMENTS

To Aunty Cindy Lei and Uncle Reed: Thank you for reading the very rough drafts. Providing constructive criticism and honest feedback. For pushing me to continue to write because I left you hanging on the last chapter. For talking me back down when I had it up to Uncle Reed and felt like giving up. (Aunty Cindy understands what this means.)

To my mama: For introducing me to the supernatural and spiritual side of life. For allowing me to read books from a young age that ignited that crazy and wild imagination inside of my brain.

To the Paper Raven Books Team: Thank you for putting on a retreat. It was the stepping stone I needed to make my dream come alive. For coaching me along the way, helping me to get out of my head. Answering all my ridiculous questions. Every single one of you is amazing.

To my son: For helping me to imagine up different magical powers my characters needed to wield. Making sure one of the villains in my story has a badass scar on their face and giving me ideas for plot twists along the way. One day, when you're an adult and you read and understand what your mother actually wrote, I hope you will find it humorous that you had a part in it.

Last but not least, to my hubby: For having my back. For standing by my side in silent support with every dream, goal, or journey I set out on. For letting me do my thing no matter how crazy or time-consuming it is. For taking the kids out of the house when I needed to focus on writing. For listening to me go on and on about the fictitious characters in my head, the crazy plots I dreamed up, and most of all for reading the book even though it's not your thing. Thank you for being the inspiration to many of the MMCs in my book. I love you more than you think I do.

# ABOUT THE AUTHOR

Meet Lilinoe K. Russell, a true island soul hailing from the beautiful Hawaii Island. Growing up in the charming town of Honokaʻa, where the population barely tipped 2,000, Lilinoe was immersed in a captivating blend of cultures and traditions, thanks to the town's proximity to the Sugar plantation and the Paniolo (Cowboy) lifestyle.

In the heart of this tight-knit community, she found herself spellbound by the rich narratives shared by the kupuna (elders). Their tales, woven with the threads of history, myths, and legends of Hawaii, along with stories from diverse cultures, formed the tapestry of her upbringing.

Lilinoe has always had a soft spot for stories that flirt with the supernatural, brimming with magic and mystery. And who could forget the spine-tingling obake (ghost) stories—her second-favorite indulgence! These tales, passed down through the generations, have become an integral part of her very being.

Fueled by the inspiration drawn from these enchanting stories, Lilinoe harbored a lifelong dream of becoming a writer. Now, the time has come for her to unfurl her own tales, continuing the legacy of storytelling ingrained deep within her bones. Get ready to embark on a journey through Lilinoe's imagination, where magic, mystery, and the echoes of ancient stories come to life.

Made in the USA
Columbia, SC
19 October 2024

8a8c1a4a-c051-4c4f-8a92-0d54f6ad899cR01